Life Turns On Its Head

Helen Bowles

Copyright © 2015 by Helen Bowles

All rights reserved.

No part of this book may be reproduced in any form or by any electronic or mechanical means including information storage and retrieval systems, without permission in writing from the author. The only exception is by a reviewer, who may quote short excerpts in a review.

This book is a work of fiction. Names, characters, places, and incidents either are products of the author's imagination or are used fictitiously. Any resemblance to actual persons, living or dead, events, or locales is entirely coincidental.

Dedicated to Humphrey my rock

With much thanks for their encouragement and help. I would like to thank Chris, Anne, and to Tom for his invaluable technical input on flying.

Contents

1	The Crash	9
2	The Children	15
3	The Police Station	17
4	Jean Brown	34
5	Elizabeth's Clients	42
6	The Hospital	49
7	Hilda comes to tea	54
8	Domestic Bliss	60
9	Enter Jack Big	73
10	Christine	87
11	The Cave	95
12	Barbara	99
13	Aftermath of Barbara	108
14	Poor Carol	113
15	Jeans Flat	119
16	The Docks	123
17	Trip for Provisions	129
18	Robin Hood's Bay	138
19	The Fight	142
20	Bad News	151
21	Elizabeth Perplexed	158
22	David in trouble	164
23	Jean goes to the Police	175
24	The Arrest	183
25	Heart Attack	192
26	Jack meets his Solicitor	197
27	Michael's Hunch Pays Off	202
28	Barbara Stirs Up Trouble	207

29	London	217
30	Christopher	226
31	Jack meets Martin Forbes	233
32	Andrew Visits	246
33	Jack's Fortunes Change	249
34	Dinner Party	255
35	Elizabeth in Court	262
36	Jacks Schemes	267
37	The Eclipse	285
38	Christopher Goes Home	294
39	A Frisson with Barbara	296
40	Tulham Manor	305
41	The Inquest	313
42	David weakens	321
43	Christmas	324
44	David Explains	335
45	Custody Hearing	341
46	Update	355
47	The Web Tightens	365
48	Patricia in Trouble	369
49	The Devil puts out his hand	376
50	The Law Society	381
51	An unexpected visit from Trevor	388
52	Elizabeth Falters	401
53	Jonas has Fish Stolen	406
54	Michael and Elizabeth in Danger	410
55	The Effect on the Children	422
56	Tulham Manor	425
57	Christopher Succumbs	434
58	Confrontation Time	439

MARCH 1970

A woman in a man's world had to fight much harder to be taken seriously. Her blonde hair blew in the wind. Glancing in the mirror she felt a little smug that she had managed to retain her figure even after the birth of her two children.

CHAPTER ONE

The Crash

Why are men such pigs? Elizabeth thought as she remembered the three minute lecture David had given her that morning on how to drive her new red Porsche. Why do they always think they know what's best? She was still mulling on this as she left the Hull Magistrates Court by the rear entrance. Her Porsche was parked in the judge's car park and it did look splendid, her first sports car which gave her such a thrill. Throwing her briefcase and law books onto the back seat, she settled herself into the car. She looked in the rear mirror and saw her client emerging by the same door. Sighing, she got out of the car and called to him. "Mr Parsons may I have a word, please?"

Parsons shambled over, dark unwashed tousled hair resting on his shoulders, hands in his pockets. Leaning over on one leg, he replied, "yeh?"

"Mr Parsons, as the duty solicitor of the day I do have to represent you properly. But after speaking with the prosecution solicitor it appears that you have been stringing me along, in other words telling me a pack of lies. If you want me to continue to represent you, there must be trust and truth between us. If not, I cannot act for you. Your choice, make an appointment as soon as possible or go elsewhere!"

By reply Parsons simply shrugged his shoulders and shambled off. Getting back into her car, Elizabeth reverses a bit too quickly and nearly hits the judge's Mercedes. Looking at her watch she speeds off, anxious to get back to the office as soon as possible, taking her normal route from Hull to Scarborough.

She knew one thing, if the case went for trial she was not prepared to continue to act for him if he persisted in lying to her.

The road from Hull to Scarborough was a pleasant drive through open countryside. The sun was shining and she turned the radio on and relaxed.

Her reflexes changed in a split second as she saw in front of her women pushing a pram off the pavement in the direct path of her car.

The woman looked at her, lifted her hands to her face and stepped back, leaving the pram in the middle of the road. Elizabeth watched in transfixed horror as the maroon pram came nearer and nearer; she tried desperately to wrestle the car to a halt. She thought she was going to be able to stop in time, but then she heard the scrunching noise of metals connecting as her car hit the pram. It capsized on impact and was shunted along the road. Another three feet, and she would have been able to stop.

Elizabeth jumped from the car and ran towards the pram hardly daring to breath. The mother was still standing on the pavement screaming hysterically. Two women grabbed hold of Elizabeth and started shouting at her.

Mayhem broke out. From an empty road cars suddenly seemed to appear from nowhere.

Two slewed across the road and put their hazard warning lights on, she assumed in an attempt to try and stop the traffic. People came running from nearby houses. The two women still had hold of Elizabeth although she could not hear what they were saying she thought she must be in a state of shock. Two small heads could be seen in the stationary mangled pram. Elizabeth tried to move towards the pram but the women restrained her. The ambulance and police car arrived at the same time. There was so much noise, so many people shouting, Elizabeth saw blood on the road as she slid to the floor in a dead faint.

Elizabeth came round to find two policemen either side of her, helping her to her feet, they walked her gently to her car and advised her to sit inside. Elizabeth slumped on the wheel her head resting on her hands; she lifted her head just in time to see two prone little bundles were being lifted onto stretchers, with great care by the Para medics. The Mother who had now stopped screaming had come forward and followed the stretchers into the ambulance.

A policeman on a motor bike had turned up, radio blaring, he was passing and had picked up the call on his radio, and he had decided to see whether his assistance was needed. It was, because as usual when there is an accident, the general public agog to see the blood and gore, travel past as slowly as they can, or worse stop and watch the proceedings.

He set about getting the traffic going again; he could see his mates were having trouble.

"Look love, we know you mean well but if you would like to give your names and addresses to the officer standing over there, he will come and take statements from you later." This seemed to placate them and they moved off.

Her head was fuzzy as she stared numbly at the policeman. He asked her whether she was all right; she managed to nod her head. She found she could not speak, her mouth was so dry.

The pram was being taken to the side of the road, and

the traffic was now moving slowly; policeman were taking measurements presumably of her skid marks, if there were any she didn't know. For a split second she forgot the presence of the police officers. She didn't know whether she was going to cry or wet herself; her emotions seemed to be totally out of control.

This is a very fast car, what speed were you doing?"

Elizabeth exhaled slowly. "I know this is a fast car, officer, but I drive down this road regularly, and I'm aware of the restricted zones through the villages. I wasn't speeding, if that is what you are trying to infer".

"Mmm! if you say so, Madam, we will have to take you down to the police station for you to make a proper statement, but if you would like to tell me anything at this stage then please do so, but remember anything you say may be taken down and used against you".

She looked at him, still without speaking, her movements seemed to be so slow as if her mind was working at quarter speed. However, she felt she must make enormous efforts and try and pull herself together; she had to consider her position. Had she done anything wrong? She thought not. She was just driving down the road when this woman seemed to have pushed her pram directly in her path. Elizabeth of all people knew how facts could get distorted. Her voice quavered as she spoke.

"Here is my driving licence; my name is Elizabeth Markham of Markham's solicitors in the town. I feel extremely shaken. Is it possible for you to ring the station and ask them to contact my husband, David Markham?"

"Ok love, would like to go to the hospital to be checked out"?

"No thanks officer, if you would just give me a moment to try and collect myself". She leaned back in the seat and closed her eyes. Taking deep breaths she wished her heart would stop beating so fast and her body would stop trembling. After a few minutes she looked at the officer signalling she was ready to go.

"We would like your car to remain here until we have taken measurements and photographs please leave the keys in the ignition. It will be safe with us."

He held out his gloved hand for her to hold onto as she got out of the car. Grabbing hold of it she swung her legs onto the road and stood up, only to find her legs buckling under her. He caught her under her arms, and stood her up against the car saying, "now love, take nice deep breaths". Which she did. After a few minutes he said, "Come on, love, we will both help you to the car".

She was aware of people standing on the pavements either side of the road, nodding and shaking their heads. She sank into the car with relief. P.C. 140 sat beside her. His face seemed familiar to her but he obviously didn't recognise her, if he did he made no mention of it. He radioed his station to say he was taking her in for questioning.

She couldn't bear to look at the staring faces any more. Putting her head in her hands she covered her face. Thankfully the car slid into gear.

The journey went very quickly, she was numb with her own thoughts.

"Hello, Mrs Markham" said the desk sergeant, "now what's the problem?"

He was clearly embarrassed by the situation but knew he had to be non-committal. His voice took on a grave and distant tone.

Elizabeth on the other hand, for the first time since the accident saw someone she knew. It was some time since she had seen Paddy. Paddy said.

"I telephoned your office and asked your husband to

come to the station as you requested, he should be here soon. Would you like a cup of tea? I've just ordered one for myself?" She nodded weakly and sat down.

"One cup of strong tea coming up"!

David, where was David? She supposed he had difficulty in getting away from the office. She knew he had been in the County Court that day on a contested matrimonial, and the Judge may have been running late.

She and her husband were both solicitors in practice in Scarborough. It was a small office, started by David's father Christopher thirty years ago. A general practice; she did most of the conveyancing, some matrimonial and crime, but mostly these cases were handled by David.

Christopher handled the probate. Most of the commercial work he was starting to hand over to Elizabeth, big deals between corporate clients could be quite exacting and tended to put him under a great deal of pressure.

That's how she knew Paddy, and various other faces in the station seemed familiar from seeing them in the magistrate's court, or the mags as they were referred to in the profession.

Here she was on the other side of the coin, waiting for a statement to be taken. She started to go back over the events of the day. Just then the door burst open and in marched David, oh! How she loved him. He was wearing one of his dark pin stripe suits that always looked so smart. He came straight over to her, his face creased with worry. He settled his six foot three frame down beside her. Even now his close proximity made her want him; she wanted him to crush her to him, to protect her.

His deep blue penetrating eyes searched her face, his features were regular, his hair was nearly black, and she loved his generous lips and an open smile which was not present today.

CHAPTER TWO

The Children

They had only been married a short time. She had joined David in the practice shortly after they had met. Both their previous marriages had ended amicably, or as amicably as any divorce can be, the year before. David had divorced his wife Barbara, in January, 1968; two months later in the March Barbara had turned up at his flat leaving both their children Carol and Robert with him saying that she could no longer cope with them. That they got in the way of her new life. She decided she wanted to go off around the world with her boyfriend and they would simply be a burden. She had said she would contact them when she could, but she never had.

A week or two later Elizabeth had moved in with David having left her husband Andrew because of his intolerable behaviour. He was quite simply an alcoholic, after six years of his erratic behaviour her patience was exhausted and she knew the marriage was over. She had met David casually at a Law Society dinner sometime before. He was not the cause of her leaving Andrew, it was inevitable.

She really didn't know why she put up with the marriage for so long. She also had two children, Pip short for Phyllis who was six, with long blonde hair, which she nearly always wore in a pony tail. Her eyes were blue round and saucerish, giving her a surprised look. Her nose was thin and a little pointed, her skin was very fair, somewhat translucent and sensitive. She was tall for her age, and was always complaining about her skinny frame.

John was three; his fair hair had a tendency to wave. He was small for his age, stocky framed, gentle blue eyes, a snub nose, and a wicked sense of humour.

As for David's children, Carol was aged ten; her chestnut hair always seemed to shine. Her brows were rather heavy, taking after her father but were definite in shape, and the same piercing blue eyes which changed colour with her mood. Her second teeth had erupted straight, and hopefully no brace would be needed. She was well proportioned, with long slender fingers, which helped in her piano playing. Three year old Robert had a mass of mousey dark curly hair, whatever Elizabeth did the curls just bounced back. He had a little gummy smile showing his straight baby teeth.

It was a year now since Barbara had abandoned them, something Elizabeth could never understand however hard she tried.

She and David together had bought a large rambling house, overlooking the sea on the cliffs at Scarborough and had taken all the children to live there with them.

CHAPTER THREE

The Police Station

David shook her from her daze by gently squeezing her hand and holding it tightly. He said, gently, "Will you please tell me what's been going on before I go mad?" Elizabeth ignored the question. "Please go and ask Paddy about the children". Her eyes implored him. "What children, for goodness sake?"

"Please do as I say and then perhaps we can go into a private room and talk for a few minutes".

David went over to the desk and spoke with the sergeant. She could see them shaking their heads. He returned to his seat.

"Paddy has no news from the hospital. One of his men is there and as soon as they hear anything, they will let us know, if they can. He said we can use the interview room, over there, for ten minutes and then he would like to talk to you".

They went into the interview room, soulless, two basic chairs and a table, the gloss paint on the walls was starting to peel.

"Well, you had better start at the beginning", which is precisely what she did. When she had finished, David's face was grave.

"Well, it obviously depends on what happens to the

children, I understand they are both very ill but that's all they would tell me, which is quite understandable. The great question will be whether you were exceeding the speed limit".

She replied, trying to reassure him. "Although I had just come from a de-restricted road into a restricted thirty miles per hour zone, I had slowed sufficiently to be within the limit". The door opened, and the constable walked in.

"If you are ready, Mrs Markham, the sergeant would like to take your statement now". Elizabeth's head throbbed.

"Of course I am thank you". Paddy walked in.

David said. "This is a bit beneath you, isn't it?"

Paddy sat down heavily. "Seeing as it's you, we had better take special precautions to get everything right, if you know what I mean. I've come up against you far too often in Court to know that you don't miss a trick. I suppose that's what you're paid for. Mrs Markham let's start at the beginning if you don't mind, your full names please and date of birth......."

As they left the station Elizabeth clutched David's arm, he kissed her on the nose.

"Come on, it's going to be all right".

She just looked at him with her big doleful eyes, his heart went out to her as he bundled her into the passenger seat of his car.

"We'll pick up your car on the way, and I'll take some measurements of any skid marks, if there are any. I'll also take some photos; you never know they may come in useful. It's lucky I put the camera in the car this morning."

As they approached the scene of the accident she saw her red Porsche exactly where she had left it. The Police were stowing their equipment away, they were about to drive off when they saw David's car slowing down. He beckoned them from his window; the junior officer came over to his car. The Policeman explained that he was from the crime reconstruction unit, but said that he was not prepared to discuss anything.

After they had gone, David walked up and down the pavement. "What a mess!" he muttered to himself as he ran his hand through his hair. What on earth was his father going to say?

Although the Markham's family business was small, it had been going for thirty years. Started by his father after the war when he left the Navy, it had, he thought, a very good reputation locally. However, they certainly didn't need the sort of publicity the accident was likely to bring. He had always got on very well with his father. They not only liked each other but had a very good working relationship, based on mutual respect.

Since David's mother died of cancer two years before, his father had thrown himself even more into his work. David missed his mother very much. She had been a local G.P. and insisted on working as long as she could. She was a women of intellect yet she had an element of a no-nonsense Yorkshire woman about her which he always found endearing. She really wore herself out for others. His father had begged her to take it easy but she wouldn't listen. She suffered terribly towards the end. The Macmillan nurses helped her through the last few ghastly nightmarish weeks.

David expected his father would be very supportive over the accident, he knew he must tell him before he found out from someone else.

Christopher had welcomed Elizabeth into the family and the practice, although he had told David in the first few weeks that he had one or two misgivings about working with a woman.

Elizabeth was still sitting motionless in the car watching David as if in a trance. She really had had the stuffing knocked out of her today, normally she was so resilient. David slid into the seat beside her, "Which car do you want to drive, darling?"

"Neither truthfully", she said, "but I know I must pull myself together I'll drive yours, if that's O.K. with you".

"Sure, by the way the police asked us not to wash the car as they may want to take further samples".

She smiled weakly. "That's the last thing I would think of doing at this moment. It's going to take about ten minutes to get home. Did you ring Mrs. Fraser, and are the children all right?"

"Yes, and yes they're fine".

She waited whilst he took the photographs and measurements in case he wanted to ask her anything. Then, when he waved to say he'd finished, she slowly drove home. She looked at her watch, five o'clock; the children would have finished their tea. She had luckily bought some pork chops that morning with some vegetables; blast, she'd left them in her car. Oh, never mind, David would be home shortly, she knew he would pop back to the office before coming home, to make sure the girls sent off all the post and that there were no outstanding urgent messages which needed attending to.

David had a thing about being up to date with his work, unlike most solicitors, who happily sat behind piles of files, seemingly drawing some strange umbilical comfort by having the files around them.

She decided she must ring her parents as soon as she got in.

Her father Jonas would probably not be home yet, anyway. She expected he would go mad, he always made such a fuss of her, as opposed to her brother Michael, and he'd always been much harder on him. Her father had his own wholesale fish business called "Prince" which he inherited from his father before him. It was just a fish stall in those days. He had built it up and now owned four retail shops in the town and surrounding areas. Michael worked with his father, but sometimes they did not see eye to eye. Too alike, her mother used to say monosyllabic and stubborn.

One of them always had to be down at the docks, especially first thing in the morning when the fleet returned with its load. It was then auctioned on the side of the quay. The expansion of the firm meant they now employed twenty five men. They owned two "cobles", and were able to sell off spare fish on the quay. A "coble" boat was classified as a fair weather boat. Originally a sailing vessel, they now operated with a two stroke engine. They varied in size between twenty-five and thirty-six feet long. Two women were employed working from a small office in the docks, responsible for despatching orders received from all over the country.

There had been a decline in the sale of wet fish recently so Jonas had turned two of the more successful shops into fish and chip shops as well as the sale of wet fish. Jonas and Michael worked a rota system, so they both new exactly what the takings were from each shop. Jonas and Hilda, Elizabeth's mother, lived in a small hamlet outside Scarborough.

Her mother was the local mid-wife and because the population was so spread out, she had to cover a wide area. Hilda was rather short about five feet, a little overweight, she bustled with efficiency. She was a strong as a horse and a good match for her husband.

Her parents had both had a hard life and wanted something better for their daughter. They were so proud when Elizabeth triumphantly went from her Grammar School to Durham University where she succeeded in obtaining a first class honours degree in Law. It was a bit of one in the eye for the Dons at Oxford who had not considered her good enough to give her a place in one of their sacred colleges. Her A level grades had been excellent. She was convinced her refusal had nothing to do with her academic ability, but the fact she had been educated at a grammar school and not at a public school, plus the fact she was of course a girl.

Never mind, her First had meant she had no trouble securing articles with a very good firm of solicitors in London.

She slowly turned into the gates of their drive; the noise of the pebbles crunching under the wheels of the car would alert the children to her arrival. Although they had only owned the house for a short time, she already loved it and always reacted to its warmth.

Opening the back door, she took off her coat. Kicking off her shoes at the same time, she slipped her aching feet into a comfortable pair of flat ones.

Pip came running towards her

"Mummy, Mummy, where have you been, why are you late? I was worried about you. John has been naughty and poked Robert in the eye at the tea table because he had the last chocolate biscuit." She folded her arms smugly.

"Now, now", said Mrs Fraser as she came through the kitchen carrying Robert. "Let your mother get in the door before you start".

"Mrs Fraser, is everything all right?"

"Oh, good lord, yes, there was a little skirmish at the tea table, but we soon sorted that out didn't we, young man?" she looked directly at John.

"Yes", he muttered squirming.

"Right, Mrs Markham, if that's all, I'll be off. You won't forget I have to leave early tomorrow to get to the dentist, I did tell you."

"Yes", replied Elizabeth. "I remember. See you in the morning, good night and thank you".

She turned to the expectant faces. "I must just phone Granny about a serious matter, go on into the television room, and I will be with you in a moment". They were instantly fed up, they had been waiting to see her and, now she was home. Granny was more important than them. They all turned to leave the kitchen, shoulders sagging in grim disapproval.

"Please, darlings, I'm sorry".

"You always do this", said the petulant Pip.

"Don't be rude".

She went into the study, closing the door behind her.

"Hello, Mummy, something terrible has happened today", she started to weep as she related the accident details to her mother. Her mother listened without interruption.

"Where's David?" she asked.

"Oh, he will be home very soon".

"I should jolly well hope so, fancy leaving you in this state. Now, listen, you are not to worry".

"Mummy, how can I not worry?"

"Because it won't do any good, I'll ring my friend Mavis at the hospital tomorrow and ask her to see whether she can find out any information for us, she is not on duty at the moment."

"What about Daddy?"

"Don't worry about Jo; you just leave him to me. I'll stop him from rushing round and fussing. I'll tell him you will let him know as soon as anything happens".

"OK Mum, I love you, I must go now and deal with the children. They don't know anything, and that's the way I want it at the moment. They are fed up because I was late home and then I said I had to phone you".

"Give them a big kiss and hug from Granny. If only I'd known, I could have come over and held the fort for you, and remember, no matter what happens, life has to go on, keep your pecker up,...love you".

"I'll speak to you tomorrow, bye".

She went into the children, "Now tell me what you have all been doing today. Where's Carol?"

"Oh, she went upstairs after tea, saying she couldn't stand us anymore. I don't like her, she gets on my nerves", Pip grumbled.

"None of that, you must remember to be kind to her, as she is obviously missing her mother".

"Well, it's not my fault!"

"I know that, but, hush, hush, and come to me". She cuddled her. Unless as a mother you dealt with things mentally in different compartments, you would go mad, she thought. Drained as she felt, she must find the energy to be a mother to the children and give them some of her undivided attention.

The children prattled on about their day, and she managed to make the right ooh's and ah's. Robert and John started to scuffle and roll on the floor.

"Right, you two, it's time for your bath. Let's race to the bathroom and see which one of you is going to get undressed first". Shrieks and yells came from the two little creatures as they ran to the stairs, jostling each other to try and reach the top first. "I'll get your pyjamas", she called, "and you two take your clothes off and don't forget to undo your sandals." They were far too engrossed in wrestling with their clothes to take any notice. She arrived in the bathroom to face two very red and hot faced little boys, still tugging at their unwilling socks.

"Right, I declare a tie, into the bath both of you".

They looked at each other and gave each other a shoulder push. She always wondered why boys and, for that matter, men always have to nudge and push each other? She emerged from the bathroom wetter than the boys and worn out. They did smell lovely after their baths, and, with their hair combed, looked quite angelic.

She called down the stairs for Pip to come and have her bath while she read a story to the boys. They were both sitting in their beds looking so tiny. They always wanted different stories read to them. To keep the peace she had agreed to vary the stories on alternative nights, they knew them off by heart anyway. She bent over to kiss them good night, how she loved John, sometimes she felt she could eat him, he was so much part of her. He gave her a big wet kiss saying,

"I love you Mummy".

"I love you darling".

Robert turned and hugged her; a suppressed sigh erupted from his body. She picked him up. How could anyone want to leave such an adorable and good looking child, quite the image of his father? Giving Robert a big kiss and a hug she placed him back in his bed and left the room.

Carol had taken the break-up of the marriage very badly. All children after all want to be with both their parents and don't want to be put in a position where they have to choose between them. Carol had become sullen and withdrawn over the past few months, and Elizabeth knew she spent long periods in her room crying. It made her feel so helpless but all she could really do was to be there if and when Carol wanted her. In the meantime she had the job of bringing her up and disciplining her, which was not easy with an unhappy and rebellious child. David tried, but it was very difficult for him to understand a young girl's emotions.

Walking across the landing Elizabeth stopped and listened outside Carol's room. As she knocked, she heard David's key in the door.

"I don't know why he comes in the front door making the carpet dirty, instead of coming in the back way. I must train him", she thought. However, this was not the time; she must not be deflected from dealing with Carol.

Elizabeth opened the door and went in. Carol was sitting on her bed fully dressed reading.

"Hello dear, why are you in your room instead of with the other children, and why didn't you come downstairs?" Carol carried on pretending to read. Elizabeth raised her voice.

"Carol I'm speaking to you. Please, do me the courtesy of replying!"

A great surly head looked up. "Why should I, I don't like you, I don't want to be here, and I want my MOTHER".

Elizabeth exhaled slowly. "Look, Carol, we have been over all this many times before. We don't at this moment in time know where your mother is. As soon as she contacts us, I promise, I will let her know you want to see her urgently. Now please let us try and be friends. I don't want to try and take your mother's place, I can't, but we have to make the best of things. Now, come on, how did you get on at school today?"

Carol swung her legs over the bed.

"I couldn't do my sums".

"Well, you're not going to get any better reading Enid Blyton, you should save that until you have got your sums right. Have you brought them home?"

"Yes I have".

"Show me!"

"The new maths teacher is making us show our working out in a different way, and I get in a muddle". Elizabeth picked up the book.

"You haven't got many wrong; I think you're doing very well. The trouble is the way I was taught when I was at school was different once again, and I don't want to confuse you. May I suggest you ask the teacher, is it Mrs. Matthey?"

"Yes".

"Ask her to explain it once more to you and, if you still

are having problems, I will go and see her personally after school, how is that?"

"Great, thank you very much".

"If it's OK, do I get a smile now?" Carol looked up and gave a smile with a little tear trickling from one eye.

"Poor darling" Elizabeth bent down and gave her a hug.

"Come on down and see Daddy, I just heard him come in. You can have a nice half hour with him on your own before you go to bed while I'm getting the evening meal".

Carol slipped off the bed and put her hand confidingly into Elizabeth's and they went downstairs together. They found David in the drawing room with a gin and tonic in his hand, half asleep in the chair.

"Hello, Daddy," she shouted as she ran across the room and jumped on his lap, giving him a big hug at the same time David put his arms round her and mouthed to Elizabeth, "See you in a minute".

She silently closed the door and went into the kitchen.

David had brought the shopping in from the car. She poured herself a large scotch, downed it in one and poured herself another. It had been a dreadful strain trying to pretend to the children that everything was normal. As the scotch started to take effect she went over the events of the day whilst she mechanically prepared the vegetables. David was bound to be hungry. She found some pate in the fridge from the weekend and rice pudding from yesterday; they would have to do for starters and pudding. What a day! She stood sipping her drink. Distractedly she laid the table. They usually ate in the kitchen unless they were entertaining.

Returning to the cooker, she steamed the vegetables and was in the process of making the wine sauce to go over the chops when Carol and David appeared at the door. Funny she thought whatever happens routine seems to run on automatic pilot.

"She's off to bed, now, say good night to Elizabeth, Carol" Carol did as she was bid, pecking Elizabeth on the cheek.

David said. "I'll go and get out of these togs and be with you in a minute, darling".

He put his arms round her shoulders as they mounted the stairs together. "Have you been giving Elizabeth a hard time, I detected a slight atmosphere between you?"

"Yes, I suppose so", she mumbled.

"Well that's not very nice darling she hasn't done you any harm. It's not her fault your mother is behaving in such an irresponsible way".

He found himself getting annoyed, he always did when he thought about Barbara and the way she had treated the children. She had what was generally viewed as a sympathetic attitude towards the Bohemian style of living, flower children, that sort of thing. Since they had parted, she had tried to act like one, which he considered a bit late. He classified it as dropping out, but then he was probably old fashioned. But if that meant behaving in a responsible manner, then he was happy to be stuck with that label. After the divorce she had reverted to her maiden name of Johnson-Bloice.

He turned his attention once more to Carol.

"Now listen young lady, you come and sit beside me on the bed. You know you can always come and ask me anything that is troubling you, and I will try and answer your questions honestly."

"You are never here". She countered.

"Well, that's not strictly true, you know I have to work and, if there is any sort of crisis you can always reach me at the office. If I'm not there and Granddad or Elizabeth are out, you can always leave a message with my secretary, who will usually know where to contact me in an emergency.

"Why doesn't mummy love us anymore Daddy?"

"I think she does in her own way, she is just being a bit silly at the moment. Hopefully darling she will soon return to her senses and come and see you both".

"I do hope so," Carol said, her head bowed, a tear trickled down her nose, hanging precariously on the tip, "I do miss her, I really do". David held her tight and kissed her on the head.

"Now, are you going to be a big girl for Daddy, and try and put mummy out of your mind for a while? After all, you are the eldest, and the others do look up to you.

They have all suffered, and are still suffering, as well as you, you know".

"I know Daddy I will try," she smiled, and he left the room, blowing a kiss from the door.

What a cow that woman was, he thought, as he went into his bedroom, absently and mechanically removing his clothes and hanging them up in the wardrobe. There were times when he could cheerfully strangle her for hurting the children so much. The least she could do was to ring and speak to them.

He would never understand women, he decided. Robert may be young, but it was obvious that he had been terribly disturbed for a while after she left. Thank goodness Robert had John, who now seemed to fill his life.

The trouble with their marriage was that Barbara had been spoiled to death all her life. Her father was a wealthy industrialist. She had been sent to one of the best public schools in the country and then on to a finishing school in Switzerland. On returning to London, her father had bought her a flat in Kensington and given her a generous allowance. She had no need to work and had spent her days going round art galleries and buying clothes. David had been swept off his feet by her. At the time he thought she was so sophisticated and wonderful. They were married within months of meeting, as she was pregnant with Carol.

Her father had kicked up a stink, threatening to cut her off, but had relented, of course he was delighted when the marriage failed and willingly paid all the costs of the divorce.

Funnily enough David felt she had coped quite well with Carol in the formative few years. Her mother was either in the house or on the 'phone, an ingredient they could both have done without. They had struggled on for eight years. Of course they should never have had Robert, but, after several bad patches, he thought they were getting along a little better, or so he kidded himself. What a waste of time, or was it, he at least had two beautiful children and he could not think now of life without them. Hopefully, they would get over their mother leaving them and learn to cope with it.

He came into the kitchen and put his arms around her and swayed Elizabeth gently, rocking her soothingly and gave her a long lingering kiss. She started to weep gently into his shoulder. It's all right darling, I'm here."

Interrupting him, she found her hanky and blew her nose, before he continued.

"I honestly don't know what the police's attitude is going to be, and nothing will be decided in any event until the children's condition is more stable.

The papers will have to go before the County Prosecuting Solicitor for a decision anyway".

She left the pate untouched, toyed with the chop, the sauce tasted quite good considering she had made it in a rush. She pushed her plate away unable to swallow another mouthful, lit a cigarette and took a long puff, and immediately stubbed it out. She got up and paced the kitchen. "I must know what's happened to the children, I'm going to telephone the hospital".

"You're wasting your time, you know they'll refuse to tell you anything" warned David.

"I know, but it's worth a try, someone might slip up". She went into the hall, found the number and telephoned the hospital, her voice sounding unreal, too clipped and efficient considering her inner turbulence.

"Casualty please"?

"Can I help you?"

"Two children were brought into casualty today after an accident," she paused for breath.

"Do you mean the babies called Brown?"

"Yes, can you tell me their condition please"?

"Are you a relation?"

"No!"

"Then I'm afraid I can't tell you anything".

"Please, it's most important I know how they are, you don't understand".

"What's your name? It's more than my job's worth to give you any information without authority, over the telephone".

"Can I speak to someone in authority?"

"It won't make any difference".

"I understand I'm sorry to trouble you"

"Of course, thank you, goodbye".

She telephoned the police station, Paddy McVane answered. "Hello Paddy are you still on duty?"

"Yes, madam I am."

"Could you tell me about the children"?

His reply was emphatic; "No not now but I'll pop in to see you on my way home."

As she put the 'phone down she noticed she was sweating from head to toe, her mouth was dry and she had to sit down on the stairs.

Putting her head in her hands, she rocked herself. David knelt beside her.

"I think I've killed those babies. They are coming to arrest me, I can feel it. I know I've done nothing wrong, I wasn't driving dangerously, or fast, I promise you". She was mumbling into her hands.

"Stop being hysterical, this isn't like you. You are normally so down to earth". The doorbell rang, and they both jumped. David opened the door,

"Hello Paddy, that was quick".

"Good evening, Mr. Markham, is Mrs Markham around? Oh there you are".

Elizabeth stood up, "Shall we go into the drawing room Paddy?"

"This is not an official visit, Mrs. Markham, but I knew you were worried, and I'm afraid the news is not good. There were twin boys in the pram, Geoffrey and Nicholas Brown. Geoffrey is still in a coma, and Nicholas is conscious but they are concerned over possible damage to his spine."

"Oh, my goodness, poor children, how old are they?"

"Five months, Ma'am. You have given us a statement, and once the Police Reconstruction Unit files their report, the papers will be placed before the County Prosecuting Solicitor, but, of course, you know this ma'am.

"Yes, do, please call me Elizabeth, Paddy?"

"OK, Ma'am, oh, sorry Elizabeth" They all laughed, breaking the tension.

"Can I go and see the twins mother Paddy?"

"Well, if you don't mind, I'll check at the station that they have no objection, and let you know".

David held the door open. "Goodnight to both of you".

It was only nine thirty, but Elizabeth thought she would

have a nice long bath and go to bed early. David had some work to do, so she left him to it. Wearily she climbed the stairs.

Having decided to take a sleeping pill to prevent her ruminating on the day's events all night, she removed her clothes and ran her hand over her body gently massaging the tensions of the day away. Pinning her hair up, she climbed into the hot bubbles, how good it felt! The sounds of Handel's Water Music drifted up from the drawing room, David liked music to listen to whilst he was working, conversely she found it distracting, but each to their own. She began to relax.

She was still desperately worried about the twins, at least they are alive. She made up her mind to go and see the mother at the first opportunity.

Covering herself in body lotion and slipping into a pretty nightie, she slid under the duvet. Through the dressing door she heard David come up and start gargling noisily. She picked up a glossy magazine, turned the sound up on the television to hear the news headlines, rugby and film stars, no news. David jumped in beside her. "And how's my beautiful baby now, feeling a bit better?"

"Yes", she said as she snuggled into his arms, "let's not talk any more, hold me, please hold me", she whispered.

CHAPTER FOUR

Jean Brown

Elizabeth was at her desk by nine. Thankfully David had taken Pip and Carol to school on his way to work. She was left with Robert and John whom she dropped off at their nursery school. It was agreed that Mrs Fraser would pick them up at twelve if her schedule delayed her. Elizabeth usually worked three mornings a week and two full days, depending on the work load. The afternoons spent at home enabled her to keep the running of the house under control; an internal telephone link with the office meant clients could be put through direct from the main switchboard without the caller knowing she was actually a mile away at home. She also managed to get through a fair amount of paperwork at home and would take her dictation in for Sally, her secretary, to be typed the following day. As Sally took shorthand urgent letters could be dictated over the phone.

Sally was comely, brown curly hair, with natural high colour to her cheeks; she looked years younger than thirty-one.

Elizabeth walked out of her office to find Sally intent on getting out the morning files. Sally had decided that, although she had read about the accident in last night's evening paper, she would not mention it unless Mrs Markham chose to.

Elizabeth broke into her thoughts as if reading her mind.

"It's all right, Sally, it's just that I don't want to discuss it at the moment, I'm so worried about the children. What appointments do I have this morning?"

Sally came over from the filing cabinets. "Here is your list of appointments. I typed it for you last night, Mr Morgan about a sale and purchase at 9.30a.m and a new client at 11.30 who wants a second opinion".

"I would like to try and go to see the twins, Sally, between appointments. How much of the post can you get on without me dictating it?" Sally was an experienced legal secretary of many years standing and was more than capable of carrying out simple procedures on her own. She replied at once. "There are two draft contracts for approval on new purchases. I can make the local searches and return the files for you to approve the contract and raise preliminary enquiries".

"Have you a plan for the local searches?"

"Yes".

"Do the local search but make sure you return the files to me before they go off, as I would like to check the contract first".

"There are also two contracts to be drafted; shall I prepare the copies of the deeds for you?"

"Yes, please, there is a tape in my briefcase from yesterday. That should keep you going for a while".

Sally gave a weak smile and closed the door. Elizabeth looked at the pile of files on her desk and started work.

The telephone interrupted her yet again, the fifth time in half an hour. "Your nine thirty appointment, Mr. Morgan, is in reception, Mrs. Markham", trilled Clare the receptionist.

Elizabeth grabbed his file from the side of her desk and asked Clare to show the client to her office.

"Good morning, Mr. Morgan, it's very nice to meet you". Elizabeth put out her hand.

"Good morning, Mrs. Markham, I've heard a lot about you", He took her hand and shook it warmly.

"Oh, I hope it's not all bad," she smiled, "do sit down. Now I'm afraid little progress has been made with the legal side on your sale and purchase yet. The details only arrived two days ago"........

Mr Morgan stood up. "Thank you very much. I was a little nervous as it's the first time I've sold and purchased another property. You have put my mind at rest and explained everything. I will wait to hear from you".

"Yes, that's right, thank you for coming, and I will be in touch".

Elizabeth wondered how many times she'd had the same conversation saying more or less exactly the same thing. Still, that's what she was paid for.

David put his head round the door.

"Off to court darling, wish me luck, I've got that bastard Soames against me, never know what tricks he might get up to. I'm pretty sure the husband has been deceiving us over his assets".

"Who's the client?"

"Peterson, you know, the estate agent out at Brittle, we are acting for the wife. I thought I was getting somewhere with his solicitors but there was an enormous row yesterday between them, and he is threatening to take his assets out of the country. I want to persuade the Judge to agree to an injunction there and then without him knowing about it, which will immediately freeze all his assets. This will give us some breathing space, and is bound to bring him up with a jerk. Another date can then be fixed for him to fight it out properly in Court".

"See you later".

"Oh, by the way, my father wants to see you, and I have

found out that the name of the mother is Jean Brown and she lives at 4, Tapel Street".

"Thanks darling". Elizabeth grabbed her handbag, looking at her watch. "I'm going to see her now".

"Do you think that's wise?" he called over his shoulder as he rushed out of the room laden down with files, briefcase and law books under his arm.

"I have to".

"Ok, bye". She looked at the map to find out exactly where Tapel Street was. It was going to take about twenty minutes to get there. She would have to hurry if she was to be back in the office for her eleven thirty client.

She found herself driving down a very narrow street of extremely dilapidated terraced houses, most of which had paint peeling, windows broken and boarded up.

They looked like the set for one of those bleak 50's kitchen sink dramas. Elizabeth felt as though she should be seeing them in black and white.

She stopped outside number 4. Standing on the pavement she looked up at the house. It looked very dingy. Most of the woodwork was bare to the elements, but some tatty bits of green paint still clung onto the timbers as if defying nature. The gate creaked as she tried to open. It was tenuously held by a half supported hinge, resting on the ground. She had to shove it open, scraping the bottom on the overgrown concrete path as she did so. She knocked on the door. A net curtain, grey with age and dirt, moved in an upstairs window. She waited and knocked again. The door was opened by a young woman in her early twenties who had clearly been crying.

"Mrs Brown?" Elizabeth enquired.

"Miss Brown. What do you want," she demanded.

"My name is Mrs Markham and I have come to ask you how the twins are".

Her face changed immediately from suspicion to open hostility and anger.

"How dare you show your bloody face round here you murdering cow. You tried to kill me and my babies, and you have the cheek to come round here and knock on my door. Clear off, and don't come back, before I lose my temper and bloody strangle you".

Elizabeth gulped, her heart was pounding but she went on! "I realise you're angry and upset, Can't I come in for a moment and have a few words?" there was a note of such pleading in her voice that although Jean Brown had nearly closed the door, Elizabeth looked so entreatingly at her that she relented, "Ok, ok, just for a moment, but I must be out of my bloody mind. My room is upstairs, first on the right, it's open, and dam door handle's broken anyway".

Elizabeth cringed, as treading carefully; she climbed the tacky threadbare staircase. What a dreadful place, she thought. She cautiously pushed open the door, unsure as to what she would find. The room had one double bed, a cot, and a television which was on with the sound down. Various dirty cups and saucers littered an old chest of drawers. Elizabeth noticed that the door of the rickety wardrobe had been kicked in.

"You will have to sit on the bed; I don't have the luxury of any chairs".

Elizabeth sat on the edge of the bed wondering how people could live like this today with all the different social benefits available. Surely she didn't have to live in this squalor?

Jean Brown's hostile attitude continued.

"Well what have you come for?"

Elizabeth found herself mumbling.

"I wanted to know how the twins are and whether there is anything I can do."

"Don't you think you have done enough?"

"I haven't come here to upset you, but I have been desperately worried about the twins. I honestly cannot for the life of me understand how the accident happened. I'm normally so careful".

"Come here to save your own skin. Worried are you? I bet you are, you should swing for what you have done to my babies. If either of them dies, I don't reckon much for your chances".

"If I'd been speeding or driving carelessly you would have every right to say that, but I wasn't, and I simply don't understand why you didn't see me. I obviously took a risk in coming here today, but my worry for the twin's overrides any feelings I may have for myself."

Jean Brown's tough facade seemed to crumble as she sank to the floor sobbing. Elizabeth felt wretched. It was quite obvious that this girl's life was already living hell without the accident. Jean sat slumped with her back against the wall, her head hanging on her chest. Her tight jeans revealed a slim figure. Her blouse, well worn, was coming apart at the seams. Elizabeth could see bruising to her body. Her long dark curly hair hung loosely over her face. She seemed to have regained her composure, but then started to weep again.

"I'm frightened to bloody death myself. Geoffrey has woken up and Nicholas is getting better, but supposing there is something permanently wrong with them. "There're both still in intensive care. Need help with their breathing.

 It's nothing short of a miracle there're alive." She lit a cigarette and drew on it deeply. "I don't want them taken into care. They will do that if they think I'm not fit to look after them."

She was now talking abstractedly. Elizabeth thought she had forgotten she was there.

Elizabeth leaned forward. "Why should they think that,

I would have thought they would help you to get out of these appalling living conditions not penalise you".

"You don't understand no one ever does. To be stuck in this room with no money with two small children to look after, and the other lodgers complaining about the noise. I know I'll get the blame for all this, and maybe they will prosecute me".

Elizabeth was very confused. "What do you mean?" I must say as I've already said I am more than a little concerned as to how the accident happened; you know I'm sure I was not speeding. Why didn't you see my car?"

"I was in a complete daze. My boyfriend or rather my ex-boyfriend, the boy's father came back the night before and beat me up". Elizabeth exclaimed. "Oh no"!

"It's not the first time. I was only glad he did not pick on the children. Well, I took some sleeping pills when he went, to try and forget the pain. In the morning I took a valium. The children had been woken up by one of the lodgers. They then in turn woke me up. I was still very dopey. I shouldn't have taken more drugs. I was catching the bus on my way to see the housing department when the accident happened. I had an appointment with one of the housing officers".

Elizabeth stayed silent. Jean went on hysterically. "You have to stay in this terrible accommodation until they are satisfied you have nowhere else to go, then you might get moved to a flat, but it's very hard.

You see, sometimes I really hate the children because I feel so frustrated that I can't do better for them but I really deep down love them. I think they may say that I deliberately pushed the pram in the path of your car and the trouble is, I was in such a state at the time, it's all muddled".

Elizabeth felt awful she didn't know what to say. "Is there anything I can do?"

"No, why should you bother," she said bitterly. "You are a solicitor, aren't you, so the policeman told me. What do people like you know about going without and living in rooms like this, nothing, that's right, I try and keep the room clean but I have to go downstairs for the water and what with the children's clothes, everything just seems to be always in a mess.

"Well, I have to go back to the office to see a client, but I can take you to the hospital this afternoon, if that helps, I would very much like to see the children if you would let me.

You look worn out, please try and have a sleep and I will return about two, Miss Brown".

"Oh call me Jean. The anger had now been replaced with nervous compliance. "If you mean it I will wait for you, otherwise I will make my own way back to the hospital

"No I won't let you down; I promise I will be here."

Elizabeth left the room, leaving Jean sitting slumped on the bed.

She got back into the car. She was not sure what she had expected when she decided to come and see the mother of the twins but, one thing's was for certain, the girls story was a complete surprise. She let the clutch in and drove back to the office, deep in thought. She made up her mind to have a word with someone at the housing department.

CHAPTER FIVE

Elizabeth's Clients

When Elizabeth got back to the office, her client was already waiting for her. Clare beckoned her over, "I thought you would like to know Mrs Ridsdale has been waiting for ten minutes, and Mr Christopher would like a word with you." Elizabeth nodded and went down the corridor to her father-in-laws office. She knocked on the door and went in. He was standing looking out of the window onto the garden. He turned as she entered.

"Good morning, my dear, I've been waiting to have a word with you."

"I'm sorry Christopher, I wanted to see you too, but everything has been so rushed this morning. I've kept my new client waiting for ten minutes already".

"That's all right, my dear.

"How about lunch at the club?" Elizabeth bit her lip and flushed as she remembered her promise to Jean Brown.

"I have an appointment at two, I'll tell you what; as soon as I've finished with my client I'll send out for some sandwiches, and perhaps we can have a light early lunch in the office".

"Splendid see you later". Elizabeth closed the door.

Christopher was of similar build to his son except his hair was now heavily flecked with grey. He was reasonably fit, but like most people with a heavy work load, he did not take enough regular exercise. After Elizabeth had left he resumed looking out onto the small back garden, which he always found so restful. George the gardener had planted more bulbs this year, and with the mild spell of warmer weather they were all bursting into a profusion of colour. Christopher had bought the house when he first started in practice. It was in a very good position, just a few yards away from the main High Street. He supposed it was worth a tidy sum today.

He had always kept the office comfortably furnished for his clients. He didn't hold with the shabby brown lino and cracked leather chairs some of his colleagues' clients had to put up with. After all one spent a sizable part of one's life at work, one might as well be comfortable, was his motto. There was a kitchen for the staff to use. It was all very civilised, so much nicer than the modern type of high-tech offices.

Every hour of every day he missed his wife Anne Marie. They had been married a long time, and she had always been his best friend and mentor, apart from being an excellent doctor. She had a first class brain, and it was the stimulating discussions they used to have that he missed the most.

He looked at his desk piled high with files; he thought he had better get on with some work. His work had given him something to live for since Anne Marie had died, but he was still sometimes very lonely. He had always enjoyed helping people and had never considered himself to be a particularly good businessman. Some of his clients were reasonably well off, some were not, and he occasionally found himself working for nothing. However, a few grateful clients made up for it. A great many of his clients had been with him since he first put his name plate on the door.

He rang for his secretary, Joan, who had been with him for many years. Short, forty five, she dressed in the same shapeless skirts and blouses all the time. Her hair worn close to the head was grey and frizzy from over perming. She sat down on the chair opposite him, waiting for his instructions.

"Joan, would you please engross this will and make an appointment for me to call at the nursing home this afternoon to have it witnessed. I would prefer a Doctor to be one of the witnesses if at all possible. Let's hope he doesn't die before I get there." He handed her the draft will and continued. "Have you finished the draft lease for me yet?"

"Nearly, Mr. Markham, I should have it ready after lunch".

"Don't forget to bring me all the plans; I'm not happy with the service clauses". Joan nodded as she left, closing the door quietly behind her.

Elizabeth put her head round the waiting room door. "I'm sorry to have kept you waiting, an emergency came up, and my name is Mrs. Markham". The woman got up and came across to Elizabeth, they shook hands. "How do you do, my name is Mrs. Rachael Ridsdale".

"Would you like a cup of tea or coffee?"

"Coffee please"

"Two cups of coffee, with some biscuits if you can find some, Clare. Let's go into my office. Please come this way.

After Elizabeth had settled her client down in her office she said "how can I help you?" Mrs. Ridsdale replied, "I already have a solicitor acting for me, but he is so slow, I don't feel that he is trying his hardest for me. You were highly recommended by a very good friend of mine, who said you would see me and tell me if there is anything you can do to help. I've brought some copies of correspondence with me for you to look at". She handed over a sheaf of letters. Elizabeth took them and looked at the first letter.

After half an hour with the client she picked up the telephone. "Sally, please bring in a letter of authority for Mrs. Ridsdale to sign." Whilst they were waiting, Elizabeth explained.

"As you are legally aided, I will get the certificate transferred to my firm; until then I cannot do any work for you as I would have to look to you for my fees which you cannot afford. Hopefully, it won't take too long, probably about three weeks".

Sally dutifully brought in the required authority and handed it to Elizabeth. "Now, if you sign this, I will send it to your solicitor and he will forward all the papers to me.

Elizabeth then stood up. "I think you have done very well and should be proud of yourself. As soon as I receive the papers I will contact you again for another appointment".

"Thank you very much, I feel much better now for talking to you".

"Good bye and take care of yourself. Here's my card, any more nonsense from that husband of yours, you give me a ring at home if it's urgent".

She closed the door sinking back into her chair. Poor woman, some people do seem to have very bad luck and she has had more than her fair share, she decided. Elizabeth picked up the handset, and immediately dictated a file note, she had a feeling this case could turn out to be rather difficult.

She looked at her watch, 12.30; she had better get a move on. All the girls were busy, so she popped out and bought a selection of sandwiches. Back at the office she laid a tray in the kitchen and carried it in to Christopher.

"Are you ready for me?" she asked politely.

He looked up from his papers, "yes, I must admit, I am a bit peckish. Oh! That looks good, how about a small glass of sherry?"

"I don't normally drink at lunchtime, but I think we could probably both do with a little something".

"Good girl".

One of the advantages of the old fashioned partner's desk was that they were double sided. On one side were the normal drawers, and the other side two cupboards. In one he kept the glasses, the other the drink.

"My secret supply" he said. "A drop of brandy often helps clients when they are distressed".

"Actually", Elizabeth said, "I thought I heard someone crying when I came in this morning. Was she all right?"

Christopher shook his head, "That wasn't a she, that was a he making the most awful noise, had to lend him my handkerchief and leave the room until he composed himself. I don't have to tell you, my dear, but most matrimonial cases are very upsetting for the client especially if one of the parties still loves the other one. Men are no different to women. I shall be handing this case over to David. Dry or sweet?"

"Dry, please".

"Here we are"! He handed Elizabeth her glass of sherry and took the chair opposite her. "Now, let's talk about you, shall we?"

"I'm not sure what David has told you".

Christopher looked grave. "He did speak to me, but I would rather hear it from you, if you don't mind".

Elizabeth relayed to him what had happened, being careful to leave nothing out. Christopher ate his sandwiches in complete silence and did not interrupt her once. When she had finished, he drained his glass and got up.

"I'm going to have another one, how about you?"

"No, thank you. I must keep a clear head for this afternoon, also I'm driving."

"Yes, yes of course you are going to the hospital to see

those poor little mites. My dear, there really seems very little one can do at the moment. I realise it's all a nightmare for you, but if you are sure you were not driving carelessly or too fast then, you have nothing to reproach yourself with. It would obviously have been preferable if it had not happened at all, but life's like that. Now...."

He leaned forward decisively in his chair, fingering the half hunter in his waistcoat pocket. "You say this poor woman lives in very bad conditions. Would it not be helpful if you were to write to the housing department and see whether anything can be done to re-house her?"

"Yes, I'd already thought of trying that".

Deliberately changing the subject, he asked "How is everything at home, the children? Are they all right?"

"Yes, demanding as usual, why don't you come over on Saturday for tea and stay to dinner?"

"That would be lovely. If the weather's fine I will try and have a round of golf in the morning".

"Do you mind if I creep off now, I don't want to be late? I'm not exactly Jean Brown's favourite person at the moment". As she got up to leave, Christopher put his arm round her shoulder and gave her a hug.

"By the way, I bumped into David at Court this morning. He's managed to persuade the Judge to freeze that chaps assets. There will be fireworks now. It will force him into the open. I think David was taking his client for coffee".

"No doubt I will hear all about it tonight". Elizabeth laughed. "Bye".

She dashed back into her office and telephoned home. "Mrs Fraser, is everything O.K.?"

"Yes, fine, your mother telephoned and she is coming over this afternoon for tea, the children are looking forward to it."

"I will pick up Carol and Pip from school, see you later". Elizabeth practically threw the telephone back on the receiver and dashed out of the office.

CHAPTER SIX

The Hospital

As Elizabeth pulled up outside Jean's house, she saw the curtain move, and the next minute Jean was at the door. "Get in", Elizabeth said as she held the door open from the inside. "I think I'm a little early, I hope that's not a problem?"

"Oh yes, I've been waiting for you. Blimey this is a posh car. It's the first time I've been in such a posh car". She settled down and couldn't help her fingers stroking the soft leather. They drove in silence to the hospital lost in their own thoughts. On arrival, they went straight to the intensive care unit in paediatrics. Sister's office door was closed, but as they drew level, she came out. "It's you, Miss Brown, I thought I told you to go home and have some rest. There's not much you can do here, and you need your sleep". She spoke kindly but still seemed irritated.

Why are nurses always so bossy, Elizabeth thought, poor girl, she felt bad enough without Sister shouting at her; even if she meant well in her own way. Sister had already turned her back on them and was marching off in the opposite direction.

Elizabeth felt that her dismissive attitude was completely unnecessary. She called after her. "Are we going to see the children or not?"

Sister turned round. "And who might you be?" she asked imperiously.

"A solicitor" Elizabeth countered in the same tone.

"Oh! I see," there was a distinct change in her attitude now. It was always the same, as soon as Elizabeth mentioned her profession, people tended to take more notice and be more civil, even if they didn't mean it. She wished she didn't have to pull rank so often and she decided not to offer any explanation as to why she was there. It was nothing to do with the sister anyway.

"Come this way", sister said without further comment.

Jean caught Elizabeth's arm and whispered. "Well done, it's about time someone stood up to her. She is such a dragon and frightens me to death and everyone else, I suspect. The other sister is really nice." Elizabeth gave a confiding wink.

"Would you both put gowns and masks on"? Sister pointed to a cupboard. "Over there in sealed packets".

They put the gowns on, with Sister standing waiting for them. "Are you ready, follow me, and please be quiet, we have some very sick children in here".

The thought flashed through Elizabeth's mind that Sister was the only one making a noise, but she said nothing.

The cots were side by side; two dark haired little heads. They looked so defenceless with tubes coming from their tiny frames and plaster looking awkward on their little limbs. They were both sleeping with just their nappies on, as the temperature in the unit was so high. Jean mouthed to the Sister whether she could touch them, and received a nod back.

Jean stood stroking their faces with the backs of her fingers. Geoffrey's eyes flickered towards his mother and held her gaze. He tried to move but couldn't. Elizabeth felt at this stage that she was intruding on Jean's grief, and crept outside. Sister came with her; she now seemed a little more human.

"How are they getting on?" Elizabeth asked nervously.

"Not too good, I'm afraid. One of them is not responding, and the other one is very listless and keeps running a high temperature. Its early days for us to give a definite prognosis".

Elizabeth suddenly felt very humble as she realised the high level of devotion from the Sister and her nurses towards their patients. "Yes, of course, and thank you". She went and sat in the waiting room. After about half an hour Jean joined her and sat down, her head bowed.

"Let's go and have a cup of coffee, shall we", Elizabeth said, to cheer her up.

Jean nodded, and they went to the canteen. "I'm so sorry that this should have happened. They look like such beautiful children. You should be very proud of them". Jean drew deeply on her cigarette and started to weep again. "I feel so helpless", she said

"If I stay here, I feel in the way, you heard what the Sister said, and yet I don't want to leave them. They say I can stay, but the nurses are always rushed off their feet and it just makes me feel even more in the way. I'm probably being over sensitive".

"I think you are a little, but don't worry about it. If you want to stay here, you must do that, but if you want to go home, then I will be pleased to take you. Only I have got to pick up my children from school, and they will never forgive me if I am late again". She smiled at Jean. "Would you like me to write to the housing department for you and see whether I can persuade them to help you? Mind you, I don't hold out much hope".

"Yes, please, but they are a pretty hard lot. The stupid thing is that they would give me a house straight away, if I were an illegal immigrant with ten children. She couldn't keep the bitterness from her voice.

"As its Friday I won't be in the office tomorrow, thank

goodness, but if you need to speak to me urgently about anything, here's my number, and please contact me if you want to. I would like to make sure you understand that I only came to see if the children are all right. I was desperate to know how they were. My intention is not to pervert the course of justice in any way. The police will conduct the case their way, and I will have to deal with whatever happens. You know that I'm absolutely distraught about the whole wretched business".

"I know, I understand" said Jean, "in a way it's helped me a lot to meet you. When you first came round, I really hated you and would have done anything to hurt you. I was very rude to you, and I'm sorry, but I must give you your due, you took it on the chin and did not fight back at all. It's funny, but I feel I can turn to you for help, and deep inside me I know that if you could help me you would. Life's very strange. You see, I feel wholly to blame for what happened. In a split second of madness and depression, I pushed that pram straight into your path". She grabbed Elizabeth's hand, "You won't tell anyone will you, I beg you. Please, please. I will never do anything so wicked or irresponsible again. I just pray I get another chance, and the boys get better".

Elizabeth could not believe her ears. This morning Jean had said some strange things, but she had put it down partly to hysteria. Now, this afternoon Jean had confirmed, the indications she had given that morning; that she was in fact responsible for the accident. What was she to do! If she went to the Police, Jean would be in serious trouble, but on the other hand she had to consider herself. It was no good, she was now emotionally involved with Jean and the twins. She didn't want to make their situation worse. If the twins recovered maybe the Police would not prosecute her. Jean could also deny this conversation taken place. She decided that she wouldn't take any action on Jean's confession, just at the moment. As gently as she could, she said

"Look, let's just deal with one thing at a time. The only important thing as far as I can see is the welfare of the children. Everything else is second to that. Let's just deal with them first, shall we?"

Jean nodded.

"Ok. I must go now, thank you for letting me come with you and I will call round and see you next week, if I don't hear from you in the meantime".

CHAPTER SEVEN

Hilda comes to tea

Elizabeth pulled up outside the girls' school just as they were coming out. They waved frantically when they saw her, jumping up and down and gesticulating to their friends. Pip ran to the car panting.

"Mummy, Mummy".

"Now calm down speak slowly. What is it?"

"It's my friend Shirley, her Mummy can't get here to pick her up, and I said you would take her home, Oh. Please!" she pleaded.

"Of course I will, silly".

"Oh! Goody-goody. I'll go and get her". She ran off shouting at the top of her voice. "My mummy said you can come with us, see, I told you".

Elizabeth thought, the whole road must have heard with all that noise.

"Hello," said Carol. She opened the door, and throwing her satchel in the boot, she lumped down beside Elizabeth.

Why can't children sit down without falling, and whatever has she got in that enormous satchel? Elizabeth decided it was prudent not to ask.

The other two arrived, Carol got out to let them in. "you

will have to squeeze in it's not a very big seat".

The children just nudged each other and jostled for position.

"What on earth have you been doing to your hats?" They took them off their heads, examined them and chorused "We have been playing football with them". They then jammed them back on their heads. Oh what's the point she thought as she drove off. The two girls shrugged their shoulders and fell about laughing. In sombre contrast Carol sat imperious and silent, staring out of the window.

Elizabeth turned to her. "You're not in a mood, are you?"

"No".

"Well, what's the matter; you have a face like a kite".

"It's these two; they're so noisy and silly".

Pip poked her tongue out and went cross eyed twisting her ears at the same time in an ugly way. She leant in front of Carol making sure she saw her.

"Stop that at once, you naughty girl". Elizabeth shouted. Carol went on trying to ignore the presence of the two inferior beings behind her.

She addressed herself to Elizabeth. "Pip also follows me around at school, she gets on my nerves. It's so embarrassing for me with MY friends. We are trying to talk about important things, and she just keeps on making silly remarks."

Elizabeth could hardly contain her mirth. Carol was obviously in one of her "Madam" moods again.

"And another thing" her outrage continued, determined to have her say. "You know we sometimes get to school early. Well, she keeps marching into the Headmistress's room before school starts, and proceeds to read her a story. Miss Blandford calls me in, and I have to remove her, she did it again today. It's the third time this week. Miss Blandford is very nice about it, but it's so humiliating. I never see her slip in, and she's so thick she doesn't understand that Miss Blandford is trying to work and hasn't time to listen to her burbling on".

"Oh! It's not fair, Mummy," wailed the offended Pip.

"Why do you go into her office, darling? no-one else does, or do they?"

"I just thought she would like it if I read her a story. She always has biscuits on her desk with her coffee, and she never offers me one", she said in a hurt tone.

Elizabeth couldn't contain herself any longer, and burst out laughing. "Darling, I think it is very sweet of you, but maybe you should find someone else to read to".

Pip looked non-plussed and started picking the paint off her fingers absently. Elizabeth could see poor Carol's point of view, but decided that they'd have to sort it out themselves. "I am sure Pip doesn't mean to upset you, Carol". Carol smiled at Pip, "I suppose not".

"Here we are, Shirley, home, out you jump. I'll just wait until your Mummy opens the door, and you are safely inside".

Thank you very much", she said sweetly, "Bye". She ran off, her pigtails flying behind her. Her mother opened the door and waved; Elizabeth waved back and pulled away.

"Now, children, Granny's at home, she has come round to tea".

"Whoopee!" said Pip and jumped up and down. Carol turned smiling towards Elizabeth. "I like Granny", she said. "Is it all right if I call her Granny?"

"Of course, she is your step granny anyway".

Elizabeth was glad to be home. The children scuttled inside to greet Granny. Hilda put down the cake she was taking out of the oven and gave them all a hug. She came to greet Elizabeth. "Hello, darling, how are you?"

"Lovely to see you, Mummy, whacked out". Pip ran and

jumped into her arms and proceeded to hug and kiss her granny, swinging on her neck.

"Phew! Darling! I will have to put you down, you are getting very heavy. Now how's Carol?"

"I'm alright Granny, thank you. I've got a lot of homework", she said importantly. Hilda's reply was to chuck her under the chin. "I've nearly got tea ready. I suggest you have your tea, before settling down to your homework. The brain needs food".

"Great, can we have it now?" Elizabeth, walking into the room, heard her comment. "No you can't, go and change both of you". Elizabeth cupped her hands and shouted after them.

"Don't throw your school clothes on the floor and put your dirty ones in the bin". She trailed off, knowing they couldn't hear her and would probably not do it anyway. Worth a try she thought. "If you would excuse me for a moment, Mummy, I must go into the study and buzz the office to make sure everything is all right".

"Right, I'll brew the tea".

Everything seemed in order at the office, after gently replacing the receiver she sat at her study desk for a few moments, gazing absently out of the window. Yells and screams came from the hall. She needed a drink, taking the bottle of whisky from the lower drawer, together with the hidden glass, she poured herself a large tot and downed it in one. It made her cough, a little. She found she was relying on her nips of whisky to help her get through the day a lot more since the accident. Feeling she had to show she could cope she emerged to find the boys romping on the floor. Picking them up, one under each arm, she carried them upstairs, much to their delight.

"You two can come with me and wait whilst I change, that way I know where you are". She tickled them as she dropped them on the bed. Opening the wardrobe, she grabbed a pair of jeans and blue jumper. After hanging her clothes up, she caught hold of the boys again.

"Right, you monsters, I am ready, let's go and have tea!"

"Goody, goody", John said as they both raced off down the stairs. When Elizabeth entered the kitchen, the girls were already tucking in. Hilda was pouring out the tea. "There you are darling, I forgot to mention David telephoned earlier and asked me to babysit this evening as he would like to take you out to dinner. I've agreed so it is all settled". Hilda waved her hand dismissively.

"Oh, Mummy darling, it would be a nice treat. Are you sure you're not too tired." "No problem, your Father is working late anyway", Hilda turned to the children, "and you will behave, won't you?" They all looked at each other, nodded their head vigorously and continued eating.

Tea finished, after asking politely to be excused, the children scampered into their playroom, with Carol deciding they would play mothers and fathers and Robert wailing that it was just an excuse to boss him about. Hilda laughed. "What a delight they are".

She had taken Robert and John for a walk along the promenade earlier in the afternoon. The tide was out, and they both had a lovely time splashing in the puddles on the sand. It was just as well she had remembered to put their wellington boots on.

Of course, they wanted to sit on the sand and dig, but the sand was too wet and cold so she had chased them about to keep them warm. On the way she had bumped into one of her "Mums", as she liked to call them. The baby now three months old looked bonny.

It always cheered her up to see the children whom she had delivered grow into little people.

She had resisted buying the boys sweets, and by the time she got them home they had a healthy glow in their cheeks and had run off some of their inexhaustible energy.

Hilda got up from the table. "I'll make us another pot of tea, and perhaps we can have five minutes peace for a little chat".

Elizabeth nibbled idly on a biscuit. "I went to the hospital today with Jean Brown, the Mother. I didn't stay long in the intensive care unit I felt I was in the way. The boys seemed very poorly to me."

"The news is not good". Hilda sighed. "I spoke to Mavis today, and she told me she had made enquiries. Apparently, both babies are giving cause for concern. I'm afraid darling it's very much a daily progress report at present".

CHAPTER EIGHT

Domestic Bliss

David was exhausted. It had been that kind of day. He felt the Judge this morning would have liked to refused his application, but, after he had outlined in detail the history of the case and the husband's cavalier attitude towards the law, the Judge had begrudgingly granted the injunction. Hopefully, the Solicitors acting for him would now put forward proposals for settling the financial side of the dispute. David hoped that they would offer a substantial lump sum settlement on his client, and generous maintenance, in accordance with Peterson's means and their living standards during the marriage.

With Peterson's bank account and other assets frozen, his cash flow would soon dry up......

However, this afternoon had been most productive. Two new clients had cheered him up. One was a probate matter which he would pass to his father; the other case was an accident claim. He had been given brief details of a car crash by the parents, their daughter was still dangerously ill in hospital. It sounded like a substantial claim would be made for personal injuries.

His secretary was beginning to concern him. She had only been working for him for a few months. Her qualifications were excellent and it was difficult to find fault with her work, which was of a very high standard.

It was not her ability to do the work, only her personal attitude to him. Her name was Christine, twenty six years old, with long blonde hair which she always wore loose. Her figure could only be described as voluptuous; it definitely went in and out in all the right places. When she came for her interview, she had worn a modest tailored dress which carefully concealed her physical attributes. Almost from the first day she had taken to wearing tight skirts well above the knee, and there was always one too many buttons left undone on her blouse.

This afternoon, he could not help but notice, as she leaned over his desk, that she was not wearing a bra. It was very disconcerting for a chap, with his wife and father in adjacent offices, and this girl clearly indicating she was there for the picking. He knew that he really must have a word with her, but had not the faintest idea how to approach the subject. He did not want to offend her sufficiently to cause her to hand in her notice. Elizabeth had not commented on her yet, but the whole thing made him very uneasy.

He looked at his watch, 6.30. He had better get a move on, otherwise he would be late, Elizabeth would be upset and the evening would be ruined, and he did so want to take her out for a nice meal.

Elizabeth was feeling thoroughly spoilt her mother had helped put the children to bed, and Carol had sat chatting to her in the bedroom whilst she got dressed for dinner. Elizabeth had quickly put her hair in heated rollers and slipped into the bath, whilst Carol had carried on the conversation through the open door of her en-suite bathroom. Carol asked whether she could have her hair cut in a fashionable style, without waiting for a reply, she raced off to get a magazine from her bedroom and returned with a picture she would like to emulate.

"We had better think about it, in case you change your mind" Elizabeth laughed, Carol's enthusiasm had temporarily overwhelmed her.

Elizabeth decided to wear a black velvet cocktail dress, which came just above the knee. Her wardrobe contained a few designer outfits, and this one had very classical lines. She had nice legs which she did not mind showing off. The black complemented her blonde hair, the rollers had helped give it a lift and it now curled under resting on her shoulders, it looked sleek and shiny, she undid the top button of her dress showing a little cleavage, and put her pearls on as a finishing touch.

Carol said. "You look so pretty, may I have a squirt of your perfume?"

"Here you are madam, now off you go and finish your homework, Granny will check it for you".

David having just arrived home, galloped upstairs to change.

Elizabeth turned as he walked in from his dressing room, gin and tonic in hand. "Been having a nice gossip with Carol?" he said.

"Yes", Elizabeth smiled. "She has been very sweet this evening."

He put his drink down, bent over and started kissing the back of her neck. She stood up, running her hands over her hips in a sensual way. He stood behind her and continued to kiss her neck, then placed his hands on her bottom, making pleasurable grunting noises in his throat. She turned round and exclaimed; "Shirt, underpants and socks, very vulnerable now if I placed my hand between your legs, like that, we would never go out at all, would we?"

"Oh! I do love you." He gasped.

"Get dressed then, I'm ready, otherwise I might find someone else to take me", she teased.

They went to their favourite restaurant. It had lovely views out to sea. It was a small restaurant run by a husband and wife team. She did the cooking and he the waiting. The size made it quite intimate the decor was pink and pale grey, with subdued lighting, fresh flowers on the table and comfortable chairs adding to the general ambience.

Elizabeth studied the menu, enjoying the luxurious feeling of escaping from the clutches of the kitchen for one evening. "I would like watercress soup, followed by grilled sole and fresh vegetables."

David decided to have escargot, followed by lobster thermidor and salad, with a bottle of Macon Louis Latour to complement the meal. Elizabeth picked up her brandy sour, sipping gently. "I'm hungry!"

"Me too"!

They proceeded to go over the events of the day with each other mutually exchanging views to help them to bring balance to a particular problem.

At last David sat back, feeling replete. "That was excellent, best lobster I've had in a long while, Peter!" he asked, "did you catch it yourself".

"No, Mr. Markham," Peter laughed, "but it's local, I will leave you with the pudding menu".

David put the menu on the table and looked at Elizabeth. "I had a telephone call this afternoon." His tone of voice had changed to one of apprehension, which made her uneasy "Who from?"

"Barbara!"

Immediately on her guard, she replied stiffly. "What did she want after all this time? She wrestled with herself, trying to control the feelings of annoyance this woman managed to produce. David gulped he hoped they would not have a row.

"She wants to come and see the children next weekend. Apparently she is back in the country for only a short while and has this sudden urge to see the children," he trailed off lamely.

"What did you tell her?"

"What do you think I said I would talk to you about it, which is precisely what I'm doing, I can't see how we can object Carol desperately wants to see her."

"I know, I know, it's just the thoughts of disruption to our family life," she groaned. "All right, I presume Sebastian is coming as well? They can come next Saturday and take Carol and Robert out for lunch on their own and have tea with us".

David sank deeper into his chair. "Well, I'm not sure she wants to take Robert with her, she thinks he might be too much of a handful". As soon as she spoke he wished he hadn't.

"Oh, does she indeed!" Elizabeth exploded, her hackles rising even further. "She goes off, dumping her children, not caring what happens to them, never 'phones or writes to find out whether they are alive or dead, then turns up out of the blue. Well, it won't do. What about me!" She banged her fist on the table. "I have to take the children with me when I go shopping. I have no choice." She put her head in her hands. "Now you make me feel I'm complaining and object to caring for them, which I don't, I love them, but why is she so bloody pathetic? How could you marry someone so feeble?"

Peter appeared at the table, apprehensive at the change in atmosphere between the couple. David waved him away silently.

Elizabeth felt cross, weepy and put upon. She could easily have thrown her wine against the wall.

David, trying to regain lost ground, leaned forward, taking her hand. "I didn't expect this tirade. If you don't want them to come, that's all right with me, I'll tell her and make other arrangements. I'm not having you upset like this."

"No, for goodness sake, of course she must come, the children come first, and Carol definitely wants to see her." Although she couldn't help feeling cross she knew reason must prevail.

David felt upset. "I will telephone her in the morning. Now would you like a pudding?"

"No thank you, can we go home, please?"

"Of course, wait a moment while I settle the bill?"

In the car park he opened the car door for her. She turned round, changing her mind about getting into the car, and put her arms round him. "I'm sorry". They stood kissing in the car park, until David carefully extricated her arms from round his neck. "We can't stop here, people will talk."

"I don't care," she muttered, "I want you."

"Get in the car, you hussy"

She was quite impervious and not at all contrite about her behaviour.

As they drove home, she allowed her hands to roam. In the end David was forced to stop the car on the sea front and give her a cuddle. He cupped her face in his hands. "Look this is a bit unfair, I'm supposed to be driving and you are being outrageous."

She put her head on his chest, "I'm sorry, I get upset, but I can't help it. I think I'll always be a bit jealous of her."

David expostulated, "What! You must be joking, you silly girl. Nothing to be jealous of, I assure you. Come on, let's go and rescue your mother?"

They drove off laughing.

Hilda refused David's offer to drive her home, she brushed it aside, grit came flying up from her wheels as she whizzed down the drive in her Austin 1100.

"Your mother is amazing." David smiled.

"Like mother, Like daughter"" She cheeked him and ran back into the house.....

As he eased himself towards her, she rolled over at his touch. Placing his hands on her bottom, he pulled her gently to him. Their toes touched, their mouths and tongues interlocked, moulding themselves together as if they were one. It was not always as sensuous as this, how he wished he could hold onto this moment of passion, like being in another world, forever. Actually ten minutes would be quite good he thought and nearly laughed out loud, which would have ruined the moment. It was, after all, supposed to be only women who let their minds wander!"

She laid back, exhausted and feeling complete, with her head on his chest. She gently kissed his hairs and pulled them playfully with her lips. "Phew! That was good, darling," he murmured lovingly as he ran his hands through his hair. "I do love you so".

"Me to," she said. "Let's do it again."

"Good heavens, woman, you are very depraved."

Ignoring him, she used her finger to play with him. He stroked her soft skin all the way and then buried his face in the soft folds of her body. They managed to get themselves in an extraordinary position and both collapsed laughing. How incongruous the sexual act was she thought. They started biting, tickling and slapping each other playfully. Their emotions becoming fiercely intense, and, as she sat on him, they were both lifted to exalted heights of passion. Afterwards, tender words passed between them, and they both fell into an untroubled slumber.

My God, we have overslept," David yelped, as the alarm went off for the third time. He turned towards her, "Come here my beauty, what a night, sleep well?" She grunted, smiled and rolled out of bed, landing on the floor with a bump. "It's Saturday," she wailed.

She looked round to see two little faces kneeling at the bottom of the bed, leaning on their elbows, drinking everything in. "Here, you two, how long have you been there?" David asked.

"I don't know! We're hungry", came the disgruntled reply from Robert.

Elizabeth climbed back into bed, snuggling up to David. "Come on, come and have a cuddle?" They struggled up onto the bed and crawled in beside them. "Your feet are like blocks of ice, come here and let me warm them," said Elizabeth.

"What were you two doing?" asked John wrinkling his nose.

David laughed. "We forgot it was Saturday, and we don't have to go to work today. We thought we had stayed in bed too long, and then Mummy fell out of bed, by accident.

"Mmm!" grunted John, "Mummy looked funny".

"Yes, I agree she does quite often," joked David dangerously. "For that sir, you can shut up and go and make a nice cup of tea", jeered Elizabeth as she reached under the bedclothes and gave his bottom a hard pinch.

David jumped and yelled "O.K. I know when I'm beaten. I give in, tea won't be long." The boys settled down one each side of her, looking very smug.

Carol and Pip wandered into the bedroom and sat on the end of the bed, pulling their dressing gowns round them.

"What's all the noise about, and why were you all laughing?" Pip asked yawning.

"Daddy and I thought we had overslept, and then I fell out of bed, these two were watching and thought it was funny. Granddad Markham is coming to tea today; shall we make a chocolate cake?"

"Yes please," they chorused.

"Can we have jelly and ice cream and sausages on sticks?" asked Carol.

"Why not"? You girls can make some gingerbread men, if you like."

"Yes we would." they said, clapping their hands together in glee.

"Here's Daddy with the tea."

"Can you all budge up so that I can get into the bed? Now, everyone, sit still and drink your tea, otherwise there will be an accident all over my side of the bed" David pleaded.

"Daddy, don't fuss." said Carol.

"Right I've finished, let's get up. Can you girls dress the boys today?" asked Elizabeth.

"We can dress ourselves, we can" whined John crossly.

"Yes I know darling, but let the girls help you this once. You do tend, sometimes, to put things on back to front".

Without more ado the girls grabbed them, dragging them from the bedroom saying, "come on, we've got lots to do".

David sank back on the pillows, "I feel exhausted already.". She yanked back the covers."Come on, get up you lazy toad, I'm having the first bath," she said playfully.

David groaned, "I'm having a shower then, I can't wait for you with all those bubbles."

"David", she called as she sank into the bath, "I will dash to the shops and skip breakfast. Can you feed the children please?"

"All right," his intonation was of resigned defeat.

She liked to get out early on a Saturday before most people surfaced. Keeping a pretty comprehensive store cupboard meant she usually only had to shop for perishables. She completed her shopping within the hour and returned to hear a terrible noise coming from the kitchen. The sight that greeted her as she opened the kitchen door nearly made her drop her shopping.

"What on earth is going on?" she yelled.

John nearly dropped the saucer he was manfully trying to dry up, and said "Daddy said we could wash up."

"That's very bright of Daddy, now the kitchen floor is soaked, and so are all of you by the look of it. Robert take that wet cloth off your head at once. Out of my way, all of you whilst I clear up, and go and put some dry clothes on."

They were all very happy to escape from the kitchen and the mess they had just created. Elizabeth settled down to restore order.

Once the kitchen was tidy Elizabeth felt a little calmer. Preparations for lunch were well under way. She decided she could cope with the children again.

She called through the door. "Where's your father?"

"I think he's hiding," replied Pip. "He thinks you are cross with him."

"He could be right I have made a quiche and salad for lunch. I can help the girls with their gingerbread if you like and bake a chocolate cake. You two boys can help make the jelly." She sat the boys at the table and gave them a jelly each. "Now pull the squares apart and put them in the bowl. Pip, do try and flour the board and not yourself. Roll it out, then use the cutter like this, now place the gingerbread men carefully on the baking sheet." She turned round to catch the boys munching the jelly squares, having lost complete interest in what they were supposed to be doing.

"Ok you monkeys, give it to me, Mummy will finish it."

She took the jelly away. They hurriedly stuffed the remainder in their mouths, in case she decided to remove it from their sticky fingers.

She put the cake in the oven, and then went in search of David, who was sitting in a corner in the sun room with his nose in a book. "I should think you were hiding!"

Sheepishly he lowered his book. "They told me they could wash up."

"Without supervision, "Oh really you are very naughty." She bent down and put her arms round his neck, "Coffee?"

"Yes please as she entered the kitchen, there were four figures, all armed with teaspoons, engrossed in cleaning out the chocolate bowl in which she had mixed the cake. She crept up behind them.

"Oh, yes," she stood with her hands behind her back. Four pairs of eyes looked up at once.

"Caught you if you have quite finished, you had better go and wash your hands and faces. I hope you haven't spoiled your appetite for your lunch." she added reproachfully.

After lunch when Christopher arrived, he found the table very neatly laid for tea, and great excitement amongst the children. They were all very anxious to explain what their contribution had been to the preparation of the food. They were dying to taste everything and begged him to have tea straight away. Smilingly he agreed. "It all looks jolly good", he laughed as he sat down.

"You three grownups stay in your chairs and we will serve," said Carol grandly, taking command.

John climbed down from his chair to help. "No John, you can't help, you are too small, sit at the table," she told him bossily, ignoring the hurt look on his face. He backed away, thinking plenty.

"Jolly good gingerbread men," said Granddad, "A bit misshapen but jolly good". The children looked at each other in smug delight and satisfaction, at the same time tucking in heartily.

After dinner, when the children were in bed, the three grow ups played three handed bridge. After Elizabeth and Christopher had taken the first rubber, they decided to have some coffee. "Bit of trouble up at the golf club today", Christopher remarked. "They are planning to ban ladies from the snooker room, and a few of the lady members were getting quite excited about it, threatening to chain themselves to the snooker tables in protest; seems a bit over the top to me."

"What did you say?" asked David.

"Good heavens, nothing, I kept right out of it, had a good game with a retired Registrar. He has certainly got a sense of humour, had me in fits, did old Bertie. I am going to a concert tomorrow. North Yorkshire Philharmonia, should be good, the programme is a mixture, Beethoven Fifth, and Dvorak New World Symphony. Would you like us to come? It's in the afternoon."

"Yes, we would love to, but I have got far too much gardening to get on with." David grimaced.

"The vegetable garden needs some heavy preparation and I have some seeds to start off in the greenhouse."

"Prefer to have a gardener myself, but you always loved gardening, David, just like your mother, and the best of luck to you; keeps you in nice fresh vegetables for these children anyway. Lovely children, you both should be very proud of them. It must be difficult to start out in a marriage with a readymade family, but you two seem to be coping."

"Well. Barbara has condescended to come and see the children next weekend. I haven't dared tell Carol yet, in case Barbara cancels, you know what she's like."

"I do indeed; can hardly bear to speak about the woman myself. Too scatty and self centred for my liking, but then I suppose I compare her to Anne-Marie. Magnificent woman,

I will never stop missing her, you know. It gets worse as time goes on, not better." His eyes filled with tears

"I know father, I miss her very much as well, but it doesn't help to get maudlin. Come on, I will see you to your car. Don't forget, you are welcome here anytime, just turn up if you feel like some company or want a free meal." David gave Christopher a loving embrace as he saw him to his car. Elizabeth gave him a kiss through the open window.

CHAPTER NINE

Enter Jack Big

Jean fell into her bed, utterly exhausted, having been at the hospital all day. She awoke with a start as she heard the sound of footsteps on the stairs, and a cold chill went through her. The door opened, and he was standing there, Jack Big, the man she thought she had fallen in love with a long time ago.

In those days she had been completely taken in by his roguish good looks and brusque charm. He stood six feet four inches tall with broad shoulders and a strong muscled body. He was a fisherman, as were all his family. His face was powerful, his teeth straight and white, which gleamed and sparkled when he cared to show his wide smile, his face was heavily lined for his age, ravaged by weathering at sea and too much drink. Fishermen had a reputation for being hard men and heavy drinkers. It was supposed to compensate for their suffering at the hands of the elements.

He had once owned his own "coble" boat, but had lost it when he was forced to sell it to pay off his gambling debts. He had a big chip on his shoulder.

His mother had died in childbirth, and his father had drowned at sea in a very bad storm; all his childhood he had been farmed out to relatives, who really couldn't afford to keep him and who made no attempt make him feel welcome or loved. In consequence, he became moody and withdrawn, and prone to sudden violent rages. All the other fishermen were very wary of him and tended to steer well clear of him.

None of this Jean knew in the early days of their relationship. It was only gradually, as he trusted her, that he told her more about his early life, as his unruly temperament started to manifest itself to her. It began to dawn on her that he was terrified of taking responsibility of any kind. The birth of the twins had affected him badly. He felt tied and threatened and was unable to cope. It was then she first knew that their relationship was over and she had thrown him out. Since he had left, he had found lodgings elsewhere, but was lonely, finding it hard to make new female friends, she had been told. Through his gambling he had also lost the deposit they had saved up for a house of their own. At the time they were renting a flat, from which they were evicted because of non-payment of rent.

After their parting, she had, as explained to Elizabeth, thrown herself on the mercy of the social security.

At first, the officials were deeply suspicious, because it was not unknown to them for a couple to pretend to separate in order to get re-housed by the council as a priority. Once the mother and children were ensconced in a house or flat, the boyfriend would move back in again, which was obviously unfair to other people on the waiting list.

This was not the case as far as Jean was concerned. She only felt contempt and fear for Jack now, but the council officers did not seem to, or want to, believe her, so here she was in her one squalid room.

She turned the light on, blinking as the light hit her eyes. Jack looked as if he had been in a fight. His jeans were dirty, and there was mud and blood on his sleeve. She could smell the drink on his breath from the other side of the room.

"I thought we'd finished with each other," she said.

"We finish when I say so, you bloody cow." He unbuckled his belt, and his jeans fell to the floor. "Get up, there's only one thing women are good for." He yanked her to her feet, grabbed the straps of her nightie and pulled them until the garment fell into shreds at her feet. He staggered as he yanked his shirt over his head and pulled his underpants off.

"You smell awful," she said cringing away from him.

"I've just come off the boats, you silly cow." A blow hit the side of her face, "You can take that for starters."

She yelped in pain and nearly fell backwards, putting her hands up to her face for protection. He picked her up and threw her on the bed. She lay inert, whimpering, there was no point in resisting when he was like this.

"I'll show you whether we have finished let's see how many times we can do it, shall we."

"Oh God!" the thought screamed in her head, "How will I endure it." Bitter experience had taught her that to fight him would only make it more painful for her. She heard herself say, half muffled, "I've stopped taking the pill." He plunged into her, she had to open her legs really wide, he was such a big powerful man. He was leaning on his elbows, looking down at her, leering and breathing heavily, drops of his sweat were landing on her face. He finished, and stayed where he was. "I love you," he said.

"You're a fucking liar," she replied.

She wondered why she continued to provoke him, but the end was always the same, what did it matter, she thought.

"Aren't we the brave one making remarks like that, with a fifteen stone man on top of you?"

He lashed out at the bedside lamp and sent it flying across the room. It crashed into a cupboard and lay in pieces on the floor.

"I don't want the bloody light on, this way I don't have to see your ugly face," he laughed cruelly. She tried to move.

"Oh no you don't, you're not going anywhere until I've finished with you." He suddenly let out a bellowing laugh.

"Mind the others in the house, they are trying to sleep."

"Shut up, I don't bloody care about them", he lunged in so far it made her cry out.

"That's it, now we know who's the boss around here I haven't given you a love bite for a while." He buried his head in her neck and proceeded to suck and gnaw at her skin until it felt raw. She knew she would have a large red mark for some days for all to see, although he was too drunk probably to be able to formulate that kind of thought.

"There now, girlie." He rolled on his back.

She just lay there, not daring to move, just staring at the ceiling.

"I had a fight tonight you know," he said as he lit a cigarette. She decided it was best not to reply.

He went on. "Two blokes, Billy and Taffy, accused me of not handing over their share from the last trip. They also owe me some money. Well, I weren't having that, so we went outside and I showed them what for. I am not the kind of bloke to make a fool of. I think I broke one of their bloody arms. Silly bugger, he'll know better next time." His voice was slurred and was hardly intelligible. He stubbed his cigarette out on the wall and threw the butt on the floor, as he turned over and started to snore.

After a while, she held her breath and tried to ease her way out of the bed. A big arm fell across her chest.

"No, you bloody don't, you stay right where you are, otherwise, I will kill you."

Tears of frustration started to roll down her cheeks.

What could she do? Screaming wouldn't help, no one would come, they were all as bad as one another in this house. Despite herself, she started to doze.

She was woken with fetid breath on her face. His hand went across her stomach and started to knead her bottom in a vicious way.

"Does it really hurt, let's get on with it shall we?" She could feel his penis hard against her side. She wished she had a knife to cut it off; she was so numb and sore.

"Come on, you bitch, respond." She thought, of the man she had once loved, who was now just an animal. She started to move her hips about to placate him, terrified of what he might make her do next.

This time he entered her, she started to cry into the pillow.

"Stop that!" he shouted and punched her in the hip. Feeling utterly broken her body was now too numb to feel anything.

When he had satisfied himself, he threw her to the ground. She just lay there, not daring to move. He started to pull his clothes on.

"I've had enough, but don't think you have got away with anything. I'll be back anytime I want. Where's your bag?" She pointed without speaking. He turned the contents on the floor, grabbed the purse, he emptied the contents in his hand.

"Is this all you have got? I need a drink." He stuffed the money in his pocket. "You useless cow," he chanted. As he staggered from the room he aimed a kick at her, which thankfully missed her head.

She waited, motionless, until she heard the street door close. Slowly she dragged herself up off the floor and stumbled to the bathroom, where thankfully she was sick.

She ran a bath, the water was only tepid, but she didn't

care. Sinking into the bath, she knew she would be unable to walk properly for days. While she was lying there she firmly resolved that she would never subject herself to such degradation again.

He had not even asked after the boys, or noticed they weren't there, so bent was he on his own carnal satisfaction. He was obviously unaware of the accident, and the fact that the twins were lying in hospital dangerously ill.

She sunk beneath the water, trying to hide in its protection, letting the water flow through her hair as it floated, washing, washing away every last trace and smell of that beast. The bruising was starting to come out, the cold water did little to stop the tingling and pain which was beginning to rack her body. Wrapping herself in a clean towel, she placed another round her head, and tried to climb the stairs. Her legs trembled beneath her and seemed unwilling to move, half kneeling, she dragged herself up by the handrail. Once in her room, she found some clean sheets in a bottom drawer and changed the bed. She fell into bed, draining the remnants of her emotions into the pillow. Utterly exhausted, she fell asleep.

*****

She was woken by a tapping on the door. It couldn't be him, he wouldn't knock. She sat up, blinking. "Come in", she said weakly.

She was relieved to see the smiling face of Elizabeth.

"Good gracious, what on earth happened to you?" She came over and sat on the end of the bed. Jean started to weep uncontrollably. Elizabeth moved beside her, placing her arms round her. You look as if someone has beaten you up."

Jean sobbed. "Jack came back last night."

"He did this to you?"

She nodded.

"I must take you to the hospital and call the police, this is disgraceful."

"No, please, I'll be all right."

"Nonsense, I'm not leaving you like this. Listen, could you hang on a minute. I've left David and the children in the car. I only called in to see if you were all right on our way back from Church, jolly glad I did now.

She ran to the car. David and the children were happily playing word games. They looked up as she approached.

"David, it's awful, she's been beaten up by her boyfriend last night, she is in a dreadful state, and clearly needs medical attention. I must take her to the hospital. I also feel the police should be told. It looks criminal to me."

"Let me help. If I take you and the children home, you can get lunch, and I will return and take Jean to the hospital and wait with her."

"Ok but she doesn't know you. You had better come in with me now and I will introduce you."

She leaned into the car and spoke to the children. "You are on your honour to behave for five minutes we must help this poor lady."

She heard John say as she walked away. "What's honour?"

Elizabeth knelt down beside Jean and explained gently what she proposed to do. Jean agreed, not having the strength to disagree with anyone.

"Now, let me help you into some clothes before I go."

When Jean was dressed, Elizabeth called, "You can come in now, David."

David had been waiting on the landing, feeling thoroughly uncomfortable. The smell alone was really awful. Taking a deep breath, he walked into the shabby room. "Hello Jean, I will just take my tribe home and come back for you. I will probably be about thirty minutes."

"Are you sure?" "Of course, see you soon and don't move. Just lie there and rest.

Driving home, David turned to Elizabeth, "Darling, we do seem to be getting rather involved, if you don't mind me saying so." Elizabeth already felt upset, and was now irritated by his attitude.

"Look, if you don't want to help, kindly say so now, and I will deal with it myself. There is no way I am prepared to dump this poor girl, and you either help me willingly, or I will do it all myself."

"All right, old girl, there is no need to bite my head off women and their emotions, what little chance us poor men have. Trying to understand women is a lost cause. You will only wear yourself out, and we will be the ones to suffer."

"Well, be that as it may, it's too bad. I fully intend to help this girl in any way I can."

"OK, as long as you can cope, I'm with you," he said, pecking her on the forehead. She squeezed his hand.

Elizabeth had just finished clearing away the lunch when David's car drew up. Jean was with him. She watched them through the window. David was helping Jean out of the car, her arm was in a sling, and she was walking very slowly. One side of her face was a mass of bruises, and her left eye was so swollen it had closed.

"Sorry we were so long, had to wait for the x-rays. Dr. Parker was on duty, you know, one of my clients, so he got things moving for us. They seemed very busy today."

"Come and sit down, Jean." Elizabeth helped her into the armchair by the fire.

Her face was white and she was obviously relieved to sit down. David launched forth "Do you realise, darling, that beast has broken two ribs and given her a black eye. They are also concerned about internal injuries, and she has to go and see the gynaecologist as soon as possible."

"I think the first thing to do is for you both to have the lunch I have saved for you. It was quite good even if I do say so myself," she added lightly, trying to relax the atmosphere.

Jean's face lit up when Elizabeth came in with two steaming plates of roast beef, with all the trimmings. Elizabeth proceeded to cut Jean's up; although any facial movements caused her great pain.

Jean was determined not to give in and ate with great relish. The pain defeated her in the end. Her ribs were really hurting. She reached in her bag for some of the pain killers the Doctor had given her. There was apparently no treatment for cracked ribs except rest.

"In a little while, perhaps you would like to try some of my apple pie?"

"I certainly would, that beef was delicious, I'm so sorry I couldn't finish it."

"In your own time I would like you to tell us everything that happened last night. We're not prying, only trying to help, but if you would rather not, we will respect your wishes, and we will say no more about it."

"No, I would like to tell you, it might help, it's just that it's so embarrassing and sordid. I don't think I could relate everything in front of Mr. Markham." She hung her head, her face colouring.

"That's all right, I understand, I will make myself scarce," said David.

"Please, it's not that I mind you knowing, I would just rather write it down for you if you want the details."

David left the room and went back to his gardening; Jean relived the events of the previous night. Elizabeth sat and listened in silence, and only when Jean had finished did she speak. "I honestly feel we should contact the police. To my mind, this has to be GBH and rape."

Jean sank even further into her chair. "I'm not sure I can stand it."

"Well, I for one wouldn't blame you, but in my opinion you have no choice, if only because we must try and prevent any attempt by him of a repetition of last night. I'll go and find David and have a word."

Jean felt the tears running down her cheeks. She felt utterly desolate. Robert came running into the room, oblivious of the upset. "Hello, I'm Robert, what's wrong with your face, and why is your arm like that?" he asked.

Jean explained quickly, "I walked into a door by accident, silly me."

"Would you like a sweet?" He held out a tube of sweets which he had held in his hand much too long, and they were all stuck to the paper, in a gooey mess.

"No, thank you, it's very kind of you, you eat them."

Robert sat on the floor, completely engrossed in trying to wrestle with his sweets. He gave up in the end and rammed the whole packet in his mouth, sucking vigorously and making a dreadful noise.

My father is in the fishing industry, and I am going over to see him now to try and find out where Jack Big is. On the way, I will call in at the Police Station and inform them of last night's events on your behalf. They will then want to see you. We both insist you stay here in the spare bedroom, for tonight, at least."

"I couldn't do that."

"Why not, unless you have a relative or friends you would rather go to. One thing's for sure, you should not be on your own at the moment. Where are your parents?"

"My parents live down south in Surrey. They disowned

me after I met Jack. They were right about him, of course, I now wish I had listened to them, but my pride got in the way. In any event I can't leave because of the twins. Mr Markham very kindly popped down to see Sister for me whilst I was in casualty. She told him they were responding to treatment at last. I'm dying to see them."

"Right, well that's settled then."

David poked his head round the door, and Elizabeth beckoned him in. "It's all agreed, darling.

I'll go and see my father and the Police, and you hold the fort here. Tea is prepared in the fridge." She grabbed her coat and handbag and slammed the door. By the time she was halfway down the drive, Jean had fallen asleep.

Her parents lived on the outskirts of Harwood Dale, set in a valley skirted by a forest, in a pretty village about six miles from Scarborough.

They had moved there when she was about fourteen, and she remembered at first not liking the gloomy house, which was in much need of decoration. Her mother soon stamped her own identity on it. It had become home to Elizabeth, and she had grown to love it.

It only had four bedrooms, whereas her present house had seven; a small Victorian stone house, fairly typical of the area, with an acre of land, which was mostly laid to formal garden. To the side of the house was a hard tennis court. The lawn was carefully manicured; each flower bed was planted with the same varieties of plants each year. Behind the shrubbery were the vegetable garden and a heated greenhouse, much needed in this part of the country. The house nestled in the dale, which afforded it some protection from the cold winter winds which swept unchecked across the moors. The pine forest made the scenery very picturesque. Yorkshire, with its wide open spaces, was not to everyone's taste, but she loved it and couldn't imagine living anywhere else. The drive gates were open as she pulled in.

No-one was about, yet her mother always closed the gates, if she went out.

Elizabeth let herself in with her key. The house was silent, smells of lunch still hung in the air. Dad would most probably be asleep having gone down to the local before lunch as usual on his way back from church. With any luck, he would have slept it off by now, she thought.

She found them, having their Sunday afternoon snooze in the sitting room. There was a welcoming log fire blazing in the fireplace. Boozy the old Labrador got up from his place in front of the fire and came towards her, tail wagging. Hilda looked up as she came in.

"Elizabeth, my dear, twice in one day, whatever is the matter; what are you doing here?" her mother asked.

Elizabeth sat down on the stool, trying not to disturb her father, and in a whisper related the latest events to her shocked mother.

Her father's head popped out from under his newspaper.

"Elizabeth this is a pleasure. Come and give your old Dad a kiss. What's this, did I hear the name of Jack Big?"

"Yes, that's right, father."

"They were discussing him down the pub, at lunchtime. He was involved in a fight last night, and both of the men are badly injured in hospital. One of them had knife wounds and is very poorly. The police are looking for Big, I do know that. He got into debt apparently.

He will gamble, and he also had a couple of bad trips where the catch did not cover the cost of the fuel and provisions which the office had loaned him. If he does not pay his debts next time, he will not be able to get another trip, and that would be the finish of him. Well, he won some money from this chap on a bet, and he couldn't pay, so they had a fight. He always did drink too much, did Jack Big. You know most of the fishermen drink heavily, but he could certainly put it away. It didn't agree with him either, always made him quarrelsome and aggressive. I knew him when he was a boy. He was a nice young lad."

"I'd like to go down to the harbour to see if he's there or if anyone knows anything." Elizabeth suggested.

"Now, you listen, my girl, you'll do no such thing; any road the place is dead today, the boats won't start coming back until tomorrow at the earliest, depending on when the freezer boys are due in. You leave it to us men, love, Michael and I will find out what we can."

"Where is Michael, by the way?" she asked.

"He's gone flying, one of his new fangled ideas; don't know how long it will last. Any road, he's having lessons, costing him a packet too."

Hilda got up and went into the kitchen. She yawned as she filled the kettle with water. Always something, she thought, your kids never really leave home. Sometimes the pressures got to her, a wearing down process.

One day your opinions were sought by your children, and the next day your comments were classified as interfering and unwelcome. Elizabeth had certainly had a basinful of problems recently. She didn't feel they would be over quickly, either. She poured the boiling water into the pot and placed it with the sandwiches and cake on the trolley.

"That looks good, mother, I could do with a nice cup of tea and a piece of your Dundee cake before I go.

I promised to call in at the Police Station on my way home, to report Jack's attack on Jean. He's already in trouble with them, they are sure to be very interested. Has Jack been inside before?"

"I don't know, love, but I certainly know he travels close

to the wind and always seems to be in one fracas or another."

On the way home Elizabeth called in to the local Police Station. Her reception was much more cordial this time, thankfully. She secured a promise that they would be round to interview Jean as soon as possible that evening.

She found that David had managed very well. The boys were ready for bed, and the girls were in the bath. Jean looked a little better and handed her the statement she had written out. Elizabeth poured herself a gin and tonic and settled down to tell Jean what her father had said about Jack Big.

During the evening, just after they had finished a light supper a Policeman arrived to talk to Jean. He made notes, and obviously didn't want to have to make any personal comments about Jack Big's other misdemeanours. After fifteen minutes he left taking Jeans statement with him. Before going, he said. "I would ask you not to make any direct contact with this man he's known to us and is very violent. If you hear from him, phone us immediately, don't try and handle it yourself." He smiled. "Goodnight".

Jean was grateful for the Markham's hospitality. She did not want to return to her grim room, ever, but knew she would have to in the end. Elizabeth showed her to the comfortable guest room with its own private shower room. Jean sank into an untroubled sleep, her first for ages.

CHAPTER TEN

Christine

David had made his mind up to have a word with Christine about her dress. He had discussed it with Elizabeth, who agreed that he should do so but left it to him. Even before he started he knew he was going to make a mess of it; dealing with women was so tricky, you never knew which way they would jump. Christine had looked really stunning this morning when she had brought in his coffee. It was enough to make a man forget himself and leap across the desk.

He left it as long as possible, then, summoning up all his resolve, he picked up the internal 'phone and asked her to come in.

"Christine, please sit down, there is something I want to say to you."

She smiled and sat down demurely, all expectant. Oh God, this is awful, he thought. Desperately he shuffled the papers on his desk and cleared his throat.

"I would first like to tell you your work is very good, I have no complaints in that department." She continued to look at him steadily.

"It's your clothes," he burst out, and gabbled on. "You see, whilst your clothes are very nice, they are a bit revealing for a solicitors' office. Is it possible for you to wear longer skirts and dresses which are not so tight fitting?"

He decided to give the subject of no bras a miss and hurriedly gulped his cold coffee.

Christine's face creased, and tears welled up in her beautiful blue eyes, held for a second and then came tumbling down her cheeks. "This is my best dress," she wailed, looking utterly miserable, "do you want me to go home and change?"

"No, of course not, I just thought I'd mention it for the future," he tried to be jocular "I hope you don't mind!" "Well I do, I'm very upset. Can I go back to my work now?" she asked abruptly

"Yes, of course."

She left the room, sniffing. He sat back in his chair. Great he thought, I made a complete mess of that.

He was in the middle of drafting an affidavit when suddenly the door to his office was flung open, and Joan, his father's secretary, marched into the room.

Without a word, she stalked over, slammed a file on his desk tossed her head and tutted shaking her head in that maddening way women do. Turning, she slammed the door on her way out, all without uttering a word.

What the hell's going on, he thought, getting up and walking into the secretary's room. They were all there in a huddle, standing round Christine who was blubbering. None of them was working.

"Now, look what is going on here," he shouted. They all jumped. "Would you all kindly get on with your work, and Joan don't you ever come into my office slamming things down and banging doors again. I simply will not tolerate it." There was a stunned silence. He turned to Christine. "Pull yourself together and stop being silly. I expect this room to be buzzing with activity from now on."

He went out, closing the door quietly.

They all exchanged glances and went back to their desks.

Christine turned to Joan and expostulated, "well, that didn't help much. Why did you have to poke your nose in?"

Joan started feeding paper into her typewriter mechanically. "Thank you very much, young lady that will be the last time I stick my neck out for you. It's just that I wanted him to know that we were all behind you and that he had no right to make disparaging comments about your clothes," she muttered in a hurt tone.

"I'm sorry, Joan, it's not that I'm not grateful. I just don't want to lose my job, because I like working here. I've learnt so much since I came here, and I enjoy the variety in the work."

"He will probably forget all about it by tomorrow," said Joan; after that Christine stopped sniffing and blew her nose loudly.

David was fed up. Bloody women! That damned secretary Joan had broken his concentration. It was nothing to do with her anyway. He went off in search of Elizabeth and his father for moral support. He found them going over a file together.

"What on earth was all that about?" asked Christopher. David told them what had happened. They both put their hands to their faces, quite smartly to hide their amusement, and burst out laughing.

"David, really, what do you expect?" chortled Christopher, "don't' worry, it will soon blow over."

"Now, Elizabeth where were we? Oh yes, I quite agree with you..."

David became aware that he was not going to get any sympathy from those two and slunk back to his office.

The next day Christine turned up in a large dress, which looked two sizes too big for her. David pretended not to notice.

After lunch he was in the middle of a letter to the insurance company on a personal injury claim, when his 'phone rang.

"It's Mr. Peterson in reception, Mr. Markham." Clare sounded worried. "He is demanding to see you."

"I'll come down, Clare."

He reached for his jacket.

Mr. Peterson was the estate agent whose assets had been frozen by the Court the previous week. As he entered the reception area, he heard Mr. Peterson say.

"I don't bloody well want to sit down, you stuck up cow. I want to see this bloke who's trying to ruin my business." Clare was clearly on the brink of tears.

David thundered "Mr Peterson, will you please come this way."

He ushered him to the spare interview room.

Peterson was overweight, early thirties, and red in the face, giving a distinct impression of high blood pressure.

"I'm Mr Markham. What do you want, and why are you upsetting my staff in this unnecessary manner?"

"I'll tell you something, Mr. Smartass bloody Markham. You have tried to ruin me, oh, yes you have!" Peterson was wagging his finger and foaming at the mouth in a most unseemly way. "Frozen my bloody bank accounts, that's what you have done, because of that bitch!

I've got a big commercial deal going through at the moment, and, if you ruin it because I can't get to my money, I'll have you, I'll sue the bloody pants off you!"

"Very nice", said David. "Have you finished because if you haven't, I will call the police and have you thrown out, you realise that you've already caused a breach of the peace!"

"I'll have my solicitor, I'll bloody have him." Peterson looked fit to bust as he left slammed the outside door as hard as he could. The large oak door took the assault without a groan.

He poked his head round Elizabeth's door. She was intent on the telephone.

"There is no way I am prepared to advise my clients to release the keys, until the balance of the purchase money is in my client's account. That's the law, and you know it. I see no purpose in continuing this conversation." She slammed the receiver down. Looking up, she saw David.

"Are you having a bad day as well?" asked David.

"You could say that. Why do men shout at women when they can't get their own way? That Solicitor really is a rude pig. He goes on and on, taunting me, and being supercilious. He won't budge me by bullying tactics. I stick to the rules. After all, I don't make them!"

"Sure, darling, but if you need any help, I'm here, although you sounded to me as if you were coping perfectly well. I bet he wouldn't shout at me."

"I bet he wouldn't," she said, "what was that terrible commotion in reception? I could hardly hear myself think."

"Mrs Peterson's husband came into the office behaving in a most offensive way and frightening the girls. I simple threw him out!" He laughed, brushing his hands together, as if flicking a fly.

"Give me a kiss." He bent over the desk and kissed her. "Compensation for working together." he said, closing the door as he went out.

The phone rang. Elizabeth wearily picked it up. "Yes Sally?"

David's secretary handed him a message, putting on his coat he went to the Police Station, where they were holding one of his clients. On arrival he asked to be taken directly to the cell. Bob Hart was the son of one of his old existing clients, a bit of a rough diamond, but the family had always been very loyal to David and his father. Bob's father had, in the past, had a couple of speeding offences, but nothing serious.

He found Bob lying in the cell on a wooden bench, staring at the ceiling. The door clanged shut and locked behind him.

"Now Bob, what have you been up to?" asked David. Bob sat up at once. "Hello Mr. Markham thanks for coming so promptly. You're never going to believe this!"

"Try me".

"They are going to charge me with dishonestly handling cars."

"What's the evidence?"

Bob hung his head in obvious embarrassment, and his voice dropped to a whisper. "You see it was like this, I had two cars parked outside my mother's house, both with the same number plates. The local Policeman noticed as he drove past."

"I bet he did" laughed David. "I can't believe it, is it true?"

"Yes, Mr. Markham I'm afraid it is, it was very stupid of me."

"What else?"

"Well, they came back to my house, and found more sets of numbers plates in the garage. Bloody stupid, but there we are."

"What you're saying is, you've been stealing cars, changing the number plates, and selling the cars on with false documents. It's called ringing them, isn't it?"

"Yes, but they were only old bangers, nothing expensive".

"You don't honestly think that will help you, do you?" said David. Bob shrugged his shoulders.

"You can't have done this on your own. Who were your accomplices?"

Bob just stared at him by way of a reply.

Now, let's see about that statement, and then, if you will excuse, I must be getting back to the office."

"Thank you very much, Mr. Markham."

The following morning Christine brought in his coffee, giving him a charming smile. As she turned her back, he noted she had reverted to her original way of dressing. He smiled, and gave up............

"The housing department is on the line Mrs Markham," said Sally.

"Oh yes, put them through."

"Good afternoon Mrs. Markham, we've got your letter here and I have now got out the file in relation to Jean Brown. There does seem to be quite a history to Miss Brown and Mr. Big. You see, we gave them a council flat some time ago, but we had to evict them for non payment of rent, and the damage to the property was very bad indeed."

"Well, she's finished her relationship with Mr. Big and she's got the twins to look after. She really does need some help"

"That's all very well, Mrs. Markham, but we've got 3000 people on our waiting list, and we have to be very careful before we allow anyone to jump the queue." said the voice in a dreary monotone. Elizabeth wondered, unkindly, if he had a peg on his nose.

"So there is no hope?"

"I wouldn't say that Mrs. Markham, I have been conferring with one of my colleagues, and we have a two bedroom ground floor flat coming up shortly, which we may be able to offer to Miss Brown. I will have a word with the Social Services first and come back to you."

"Thank you very much," said Elizabeth, "I look forward to hearing from you."

When Elizabeth got home from work, having collected the children as usual, she found Jean much better. She cheered up even more when Elizabeth told her what the council official had said. The week staying with the Markhams had done Jean the world of good. She still had a nasty puffy eye, and her cheek and ribs were as painful as ever. The pain killers prescribed by the hospital had helped. Mrs Fraser had taken her one afternoon to see the Gynaecologist. After careful examination, he had told her she had internal lacerations and had asked her to take three salt baths a day for a week, and he would see her again in a week's time. Hopefully, with care, she would heal completely.

Jean had telephoned the hospital every day, and at last they seemed to be making some progress. Only that day they had been moved out of the intensive care unit. Geoffrey still seemed to be the weaker of the two and was still causing concern to the doctors.

Jean had also enjoyed helping Mrs. Fraser around the house. Keeping Robert and John occupied had helped take some of the pressure off Mrs Fraser.

What a dream it would be for her to live in a house like this, she thought. There was so much space, and the views out to sea were breathtaking. There was a secure fence all round the garden, with access onto the cliffs through a locked gate.

A couple of times she had taken herself off and sat on the grass slopes of the cliff, drinking in the fresh air, the view, and the peace. She really was very tired and had made such a mess of her life in the last few years. She knew there was no way she could repay the Markhams kindness. She felt that the only thing she could do was to be genuinely grateful to her. These tranquil thoughts took her mind away from the worry about the twins and the certainty that one day soon she would have to face her parents!

CHAPTER ELEVEN

The Cave

Jack Big had made his way along the coast to Robin Hood's Bay. It was a large bay, aptly named, with a history of smuggling for centuries back. In a copse on the hill, there was a shack, where he used to play when he was a boy. Coming from a fishing family, he knew practically from birth how to survive out in the wilds. His uncle George sometimes had gone there with him after he'd had a row with his Aunty. George would often tell him things he didn't understand and drink a lot before falling into a drunken slumber, leaving him feeling bewildered and lost. No-one came here these days, only him, it was far too remote.

It was all very different from the days when the trains still ran along the cliff between Whitby and Scarborough with lovely scenic views across sea.

The network of railway links across the North Yorkshire moors had first been approved by George Stephenson in 1833. The same year the work on the railways started. Trains ran busily between Pickering, York, Scarborough and Whitby. Between the wars the lines were popular as they ran along some of the most scenic routes in the country. Unfortunately, the line was closed down in 1965.

The shack was placed between the old railway track and the cliff face. Well hidden by undergrowth, it was very difficult to find. It was about ten foot square, with a small window. Jack kept an old trunk in the corner, covered by some worn sacks. In the trunk he had bedding, consisting of a blow up lilo, sleeping bag and two blankets. Behind the trunk was wedged a small camping stove and two one gallon cans of paraffin, which were full. In another corner he had his fishing gear, and in an old cardboard box there were tins of provisions with a can opener. He'd forgotten nothing. It was as if, unwittingly he had been preparing for this occasion. He had made himself completely self sufficient and could hole up here for weeks without anyone knowing. He planned to sleep by day and go out by night and fish. He wasn't afraid he knew the sea's uncannily violent ways so well.

Months ago he had carefully stolen an old small "coble" boat and hidden it, in one of the coves. It meant climbing down the rock face to get to it, but that presented no problem to him. He would row out to sea by moonlight, and he would eat like a king. The boat was thought by his mates to have been sunk at sea in a storm, he'd done a lot of clever play acting on that wild night. He stood on the edge looking down at the cliffs in the dark. It was not a pretty bay, at night at all but rather menacing. The rocks were brown and jagged, and Jack felt the whole damp misty atmosphere wanted to draw him into its clutches, never to return.

Jack shivered he seemed to feel something or someone pass over him. Long ago there had been several murders in the Bay, and fights over the contraband after it had been landed. Two ghosts were supposed to haunt the bay. His uncle had also told him several chilling stories. But he liked the bay, it suited him.

He had not intended to knife his friend. He'd actually had

so much drink inside him he could hardly remember what happened. All he knew was that, after leaving Jean he had bumped into old Joe, who had been sleeping where he had fallen, Joe told him about the knifing and that the Police were looking for him, for questioning. Jack had not waited around, but had made his way straight to the shack under cover of darkness. He had decided to lie low for a few days and then go and try and find Joe to see what the score was with his mates. He felt he'd had some rotten luck recently; nothing seemed to go right for him. He would have to do some careful thinking and planning to try and get out of this mess.

Jack worked his way down the cliff in the dark. The rocks were jagged and he had to lever his body along various small crevasses protruding from the cliff face, before finally dropping down onto the beach.

The descent completed, he walked along the beach. The cove recessed between the rocks for about twenty feet, at the end of which was the entrance to a narrow cave.

As he edged his way into the cave, he clutched the walls for support, only to find them slimy and running with water, draining off the headland. As he moved further into the blackness of the inner reaches of the cave, a chill ran down his spine. He could hear small animals scurrying away from their usual habitat as he approached. For an awful moment, in the darkness he thought the boat had gone. As his eyes became accustomed to the blanket of darkness he saw a shape. He quickly lit a match there she was, covered with sacking just where he had left her. Moving the sacks he pushed her gently into the shallow water. He climbed inside and felt all round, dry as a bone, she was still seaworthy. Replacing the sacking, with grateful reverence, he decided to come back tomorrow night and try her out on the open sea, and maybe catch a few fish. He noticed the cave had become much wider and rounder. Clambering back up the cliff, he quickly made his way to the shack, pulling out the bedding he covered himself. Unable to sleep, his nerves on tender hooks he lay awake pondering on his plight.

CHAPTER TWELVE

Barbara

The following day David telephoned Barbara and agreed that she and her boyfriend Sebastian Durrant would come on Saturday morning and take Carol and Robert out for lunch, returning late in the afternoon for tea with the rest of the family.

Carol was very excited, and her excitement infected Robert. At about 8.30 in the morning, she heard the sounds of the piano and went downstairs to find Carol already dressed in her best blue dress. She had brushed her beautiful shoulder length hair until it shone and the blue Alice band matched her dress. She was very proud of her black patent shoes, set off by her new white socks. She was already beginning to play some quite melodious pieces on the piano, and Elizabeth hoped her enthusiasm would be sustained. It was bad luck for Carol that Pip already played very well for her age, and was obviously very musical. Pip was already on grade 3 which was the same grade as Carol, and this was beginning to cause a little bit of conflict between them. Her hands being small were unable to stretch an octave which held her back a little.

Elizabeth took out of her pocket a handkerchief and

handed it to Carol. "Here is one of my lace hankies for you to put in your little handbag. I'll go and sort Robert out. Don't get dirty, Carol, please!"

"No, I promise, Aunty Elizabeth, I will sit here." She carefully put the pretty hankie in her red handbag and resumed her playing. She wanted to feel her Mummy's arms round her so much.

Elizabeth found Robert tearing round the bedroom pretending he was an aeroplane. He had managed to put on his underpants and socks and had then got bored had decided to play with John.

"Come here Robert," Elizabeth said sternly. "Come here let me dress you, your mummy is coming to see you today." She proceeded to dress him in matching pale blue short trousers and shirt, with a little check tie and favourite blue jumper, with an engine as a motif. She brushed his mousey hair as best she could, but it was a mass of natural curls which just bounced back with more vigour. His blue eyes shone with excitement and naughtiness.

"Did you brush your teeth?" Elizabeth remembered to ask a bit late. He nodded vigorously.

Pip, overhearing the conversation, came sauntering in from the landing, and interposed imperiously. "No, he didn't, he just ate the toothpaste, and I saw him!"

"Oh, never mind now," said Elizabeth wearily. "Let me dress John. I want you both to cover yourself at breakfast to protect your clothes otherwise I will have to change you again."

"What a fuss," said Pip, "can I put my best dress on too, then?"

"Well ok, if you want to."

"And me," said John, stabbing himself in the chest vigorously with his finger.

"You don't wear a dress, silly," Elizabeth chided, "Come

here and give me a cuddle". He ran into her arms, giggling.

Pip stood staring critically at herself in her bedroom mirror. No matter how much she ate, she didn't seem to put on any weight she thought. Opening her wardrobe she chose a pink dress with smocking at the front. There were two ties, which made a nice bow at the back. She preferred to wear knee length socks, because everyone always teased her about her skinny legs. She put on her brown sandals, which were not her best, a gesture which she felt summed up her feelings towards the day. She was determined at least to be comfortable. Sitting on the bed, she thought it was going to be a simply horrid day. She could feel it already.

John was being thoroughly impish this morning. He kept rolling on the floor giggling, and deliberately getting himself in a mess.

As Elizabeth tried to dress him, she had to resort to a smack on the back of the leg which had a sobering effect.

In order to prevent any disagreements, she dressed him in similar clothes to Robert. He was not as tall as Robert, who in fact was six months older than him. She doubted whether he would ever be tall for his age. He was a typical little boy, who was already getting into all kinds of scrapes. He always seemed to have muddy knees, and only yesterday came into the kitchen happily showing everyone the worm he had dug up and put in his pocket. Carol thoroughly disapproved, and went stomping off to her bedroom, leaving Elizabeth to try and extricate the wretched thing from his pocket. He simply couldn't understand what all the fuss was about.

As Elizabeth tried to comb his unruly locks, she mused how unfair it seemed that the girls should have straight hair and the boys curly. Wrong way round, she decided. She inhaled deep breaths to try and prepare herself for the rest of the day, which like Pip she felt, would be simply awful.

As the time drew near for Barbara to arrive, the children pulled chairs up to the window watching for her car; which is where they were when her Morris Oxford Traveller came slowly up the drive. Barbara stepped out of the car. She was wearing expensive knee high leather lace up boots, a black leather mini skirt, and a tight red jumper. Her hair, which was dark brown, was long straight and heavily fringed at the front.

Her makeup was very pale, her eyes heavily outlined with black eyeliner and lips painted pale pink.

She was quite tall, 5ft 10 in her two inch heels.

Turning she dived back into the car, presumably to get her handbag. Provocatively, and quite deliberately, showing her red knickers as she bent over, causing Elizabeth to seethe. Barbara stood up, smiling obsequiously and artificially at David as he opened the front door and put his hand out to greet her. There was an obvious iciness between them.

Sebastian, long, gangly and wraithlike, unwound himself as he got out of the car. His hair hung in long greasy tendrils on his shoulders. He had on a green silk shirt and the neck handkerchief round his neck spotted red and tied at the front, he reminded Elizabeth of a gypsy. His sage green corduroy jacket was well worn, with leather elbow pieces. His legs seemed to go on forever, and were wrapped in a tight parcel of denim, which presumably was supposed to pass for jeans. How he managed to get into such tight trousers was only a matter for conjecture. His leather brogues were well worn, and a little bit of a giveaway, one would have expected him to be wearing boots of some kind.

Carol ran screaming shouting and crying into her mother's arms. Robert stood back a little with John, unsure of the situation chewing on his lip.

Barbara bent down and picked up Carol, swinging her around and letting her kiss her, however she obviously became increasingly embarrassed as Carol refused to get down or let go, until in a strangled, but highly affected voice she said. "Carol, darling, you simply must get down mumsy cannot hold you any longer. After all, you are a big girl now."

She put Carol down unceremoniously. Sinking down on her haunches, balancing carefully, she put her arms out to Robert who was still very unsure of her, it was after all months since he had seen her. He took one step forward and stopped.

"Come on my darling give your mumsy a big kiss." Robert still refused to move, his eyes unblinking. She moved forward and grabbed him, picking him up in her arms and trying to kiss him. He strained back, nearly falling backwards out of her arms, and pushing his hands into her heavily made up face trying to keep her from kissing him.

"Charming", she muttered, and put him down, whereupon he ran straight into Elizabeth's open arms and hid his face in her chest.

Barbara stood up. "Sebastian, for goodness sake give me a cigarette!" Sebastian was still standing awkwardly outside the front door. As for David he found he was full of a mixture of emotions, he could hardly contain himself. He found himself saying to the outstretched hand of Sebastian, "Please forgive me, David Markham, please come in, I would like to introduce my wife, Elizabeth".

Barbara had singularly failed to acknowledge Elizabeth

Elizabeth stood up, still holding Robert, she found herself looking into heavily browed coal black eyes, which gave nothing away. She shook hands politely with him. She saw that his nose was pointed, and slightly bent. As he smiled he showed straight square teeth. She noticed the mouth smiled, the eyes however did not they remained watchful; he was at the most twenty three years old and seemed to be totally unprepared for the day's events. He lit a cigarette and handed it to Barbara.

Barbara by now was standing leaning on one leg, picking at her nails, looking bored, and wanted everyone present to be aware of this. David undeterred and determined to be polite at least as an example to the children, introduced Elizabeth's children to both of them. Pip came forward and smiled shyly, John just sat and looked. You could have cut the atmosphere with a knife.

Sebastian politely said "how do you do", to the children. But it was all Barbara could do to acknowledge them, which she did by nodding her head. She seemed suddenly to remember herself, and directing herself at Elizabeth said, "Well Elizabeth how are you?" and promptly answered the question herself. "Well, I hope. Good, now, if we are going, we had better go. I understand Robert is also coming with us, that will be nice, especially as we have made such a good start this morning", the final comment being made through gritted teeth.

Sebastian looked completely out of his depth.

"There's a good girl, Carol, You've got your coat". Carol stood smiling by her Mother, looking lovingly up at her.

"Now, come on Robert dear, let's make the best of it", she practically grabbed him from Elizabeth's arms, snatched his coat from the chair, and strode to the door, momentarily forgetting the restrictions of her tight mini skirt and looking thoroughly ruffled. She bundled the children into the back of the car, wound down the windows, and shouted at the group in the doorway.

"I'll bring them back after lunch".

Elizabeth could hear Robert crying, a strangled sort of cry, as they drove away.

They shut the front door, both completely stunned by the tornado of emotions which had just entered their house. They fell into each other's arms, "Come here you two, let's have a cuddle".

Pip and John gladly ran into the protection of their arms, very upset by the scene which had just taken place, which they simply could not understand. David said, "Let's all have a nice cup of coffee". They all went into the kitchen, he filled the kettle and, as he was plugging it in, he said, "Well, what do you make of that, at least our matrimonial clients can't accuse us of having no experience in problems over access".

Elizabeth felt utterly drained. She ranted "She is completely unbearable and has the maturity of a sixteen year old, with no sense of responsibility as far as the children are concerned. There was no real show of emotion, indicating that she had missed the children or remorse at her behaviour".

David sat down at the kitchen table munching on a biscuit. "The trouble is, what effect, will the meeting have on their emotional stability. It is all so difficult. One has a duty to protect them as they are too young to look after themselves, but it is so easy to do the wrong thing. If we insist on regular access, she might not come at all. Although that may in the long run have a more stabilizing effect on the children, it would be unfair as they have a right to see each other until they are old enough to decide for themselves. I feel I must try and have a private talk with Barbara when she comes back, what do you think?"

"Well, clearly, I'm not keen on her coming here occasionally when it suits her, disrupting the house and mincing off again when she feels like it, leaving us with all the responsibility of bringing up the children and dealing with their emotional bewilderment at being dumped. There is a limit as to how much I am prepared to tolerate. How would it be, as a suggestion, if I had a word with her, as long as I can keep my hands off her"?

"No, I would like a word with her first, I don't feel I

acquitted myself, very well this morning, and need to make amends, now let's go out for lunch, it will do us all good".

"That's a super idea darling. I can lay for tea in the dining room before we go. I'll make the sandwiches and cover them up. What happens if they get back before us?"

"Too bad," said David, "they can wait. I think we all deserve a treat, and the children are all dressed up and raring to go, aren't you?"

"Oh! Yes, Daddy," cried Pip," where are we going?"

"Come on, let's help Mummy get the tea, and then we can go. We will jump in the car and find a new place for lunch".

"I'll help with the table" said Pip.

"What can I do", wailed John.

"You can sit up here, and help Mummy make the sandwiches".

He always loved sitting on the work surface and chatting to her. "Can I have a new pair of shoes, Mummy?" asked Pip. "We'll see, darling", she said stroking her cheek lovingly.

The drove into the countryside and found themselves in a small village they had not been to before. It was so tranquil, just what they needed to calm them down after the morning's turbulence. They found a restaurant with beamed ceilings and bowed windows either side of centre door. The lattice windows had old fashioned bulls-eye glass which distorted their view as they tried to peer through. Inside they found a vacant table by the inglenook fireplace.

The fire roaring in the grate was very welcoming away from the bitter wind outside.

They had all enjoyed a good meal.

David leaned back in his chair, stirring his coffee, feeling replete, "there's nothing like a sustaining meal to make one feel better, and more able to cope with the trials and tribulations of life", he said jocularly, chucking Pip under the chin.

"What are they?" queried Pip.

"Now, little lady," David said leaning forward and tugging at her ponytail gently, "nothing for you to worry your pretty head about. I thought you wanted some new shoes?" he winked at Elizabeth and went on "I saw a shoe shop down the road before we parked the car".

"Oh goody! let's go", she jumped down and started pulling at her coat on the coat rack.

"Steady, you'll pull the whole everything over", cried Elizabeth grabbing the stand, which had already started to rock.

"Oh, come on Mummy, let's go, you are so slow", pleaded the excited Pip.

On the way home, they stopped at a farmyard gate and watched the chickens and ducks striding around the yard. The children were delighted.

When the two geese let out their warning noise, the children in response replied with squeaks and giggles.

CHAPTER THIRTEEN

Aftermath of Barbara

Whether subconsciously intentionally or not, they arrived back at the house later than they had originally intended, to find Barbara seething in the car.

She got out, imperious as ever. "Really, David," she remarked very loudly, "I think this is a bit off, we have been waiting for half an hour".

"We do have our own lives to lead, Barbara. Perhaps you would all like to come inside". David strode off towards the front door key in hand, taking command of the situation.

Barbara followed, tossing her head and muttering under her breath, leaving poor Sebastian to help the children from the car. Barbara flopped down in an armchair unasked. "Well that was a great success, I must say. They have both been crying all the time. Robert refused to speak to anyone, I take it he can speak?" she said sarcastically, "and Carol has nearly driven me mad crying and asking me not to leave her".

David thought to himself, "I would like to break your calculating uncaring neck", but he was determined not to lose the advantage and instead said; "Would you please come into the study? I would like a word with you".

"Oh, I say, look who's giving the orders" she said stupidly, getting up and following him.

"Please sit down", David pointed to a chair. She sat down, returning his gaze coldly. David launched forth with such passion that the tone of his voice did not invite, or indeed perceive, that interruption would be tolerated.

"I consider your behaviour since you arrived this morning to be intolerable, to put it mildly. Bearing in mind your education and upbringing, you should know better. Your parents, I am sure, would be thoroughly ashamed of you, as indeed I am that I ever got involved with you in the first place. You deliberately set out today to make a spectacle of yourself and upset everyone. Since you walked out on the children, I really had to struggle with them until I met Elizabeth. My Mother was desperately ill, and I could not worry her with my troubles. If it hadn't been for Mrs. Fraser, I don't know what would have become of them. Robert has obviously settled down quicker because he was so young, but in the early days there was such a tortured look in his eyes, it tore me apart. Carol was crying herself to sleep every night, it was terrible. A Father simply cannot compensate for a caring Mother, however hard he tries.

You have not bothered about the children in two and a half years. One would have thought that at some point you would suffer with remorse over your neglectful behaviour towards the children, but no, you have to compound it today.

There are unwritten laws in the civilised world as a precedent for a decent and honourable way of life, which most of us try to abide by. You have broken all the unwritten laws, and most of the written ones, in my book. There would seem to be no salvation as far as you are concerned. Robert really doesn't know who his Mother is. It is hardly surprising he didn't rush to you this morning. You have got to do some serious thinking about your attitude otherwise you will make those children emotional cripples, which I simply will not allow". He was pacing the room, and as he reached his desk, he slammed his clenched fist down so hard, that he made a book fall onto the floor. She jumped.

He continued, hardly drawing breath, pulling his hands through his hair, "I thought that instead of having access agreed through the Courts, it would be much better for the children if it could be dealt with in a civilized way between us. Well, that is clearly out of the question, unless you can persuade me now that your future intentions for the children are honourable and responsible. I propose to withdraw access, and we will fight it out before the Judge in Chambers. I'll introduce conduct into the case.

Your parents will love that, their little darling. What's the matter with them don't they care about their grandchildren?" he shouted, suddenly remembering "Let me tell you, you are very lucky I did not strike you today, because I came very near to it, but you are simply not worth soiling my hands".

He sat down heavily at his desk. She seemed afraid to move, sensing that she had gone too far, but was unrepentant. He looked at her as if seeing her for the first time. She clearly was a very selfish woman who was completely incapable of seeing anyone else's point of view. She sat on the edge of her chair, her hands relaxed in her lap.

"Now you have got all that off your chest, I am sure you feel better," she said pulling herself together patronizingly. His hands twitched.

"I cannot understand why you refuse to see my point of view. That part of my life with babies is over I am into a new phase of self discovery, and learning about one's inner self. It's all so fascinating". David couldn't believe his ears. She went on.

"It is unfortunate I know, but I don't have any feelings

left for the children. Oh, I shall always be interested in their welfare, and progress, but the nappies, dental care, school visits and piano practice, are really, not for me anymore. My dear chap being a Mother is so restricting and boring. It is hardly surprising that most women end up looking so dull, because they are dull. Not for me. I wash my hands of it. Over to you I am quite happy never to come and see the children again, if that's what pleases you. I promise you, I certainly wouldn't bother to go to Court and fight to see them, you must be joking", she laughed coldly.

"Sebastian and I have this wonderful meeting of minds, he's stinking rich you know, doesn't look it, does he?" she sighed and ran her hands through her hair, stretching her body backwards in the chair. "No darling, I've had it I gave up all those years looking after Carol. I want to be free now free as a bird on the wing, to do exactly what I please.

It's all so exciting, and quite honestly I don't see eye to eye with Carol anyway. We've never really got on, so it's all probably for the best. Now that's all out in the open, Seb and I will just disappear. If you do want to contact me urgently, the best thing is to write to my Mother, you know the address".

David, for the second time that day, was unsure of his feelings. On the one hand, it would be great for him not to see Barbara again, but on the other hand, Carol would present a problem. "She is wicked and selfish", he thought. But he knew it was no use to pursue the matter any further.

"Very well", he said, "I can't pretend to understand your motives, and all that drivel about meeting of minds I simple do not understand or want to, but I would ask one favour of you. That is not to rush off, but to stay and have tea in a civilized way, and then disappear. That way, it will help me to deal with Carol".

"All right", she said, "I suppose that won't be too painful, except darling Elizabeth is so righteous, she reminds me of my missing conscience," she giggled.

Opening the door David guided her out by waving his other arm. "Come on, let's make the best of the next half an hour, and don't ever criticize Elizabeth to me again", he hissed in her ear.

They went into the television room, and found Sebastian lounging, in one of the chairs.

He was amiably talking to Elizabeth about nothing in particular, with the occasional interruptions from the children, who were playing happily round them, all still on their best behaviour.

Elizabeth looked up expectantly as they came in, but David gave nothing away, and instead smiled sweetly at her, as if giving her a sign, and asked her to put the kettle on, as perhaps they could have tea straight away. She rose her face wearing a mask over her emotions, and went into the kitchen.

The table was laden with a profusion of goodies. The sandwiches, of egg or ham, had all the crusts removed and were bite size. There were two cakes, a Dundee and chocolate sponge. Sausages on sticks, chocolate biscuits, and homemade scones filled with cream and jam, and the centrepiece, was a three coloured jelly of orange, green and yellow stripes. It was on a stand, and looked so pretty. Carol grabbed her Mother's hand, and said, "You must sit next to me".

There was a false jovial atmosphere throughout the meal. At last the meal was over.

Barbara chucked Carol under the chin, "And we must be going now".

"Oh no", wailed Carol, "can I come with you? When will I see you again? Can I come and stay with you?"

Barbara stood up, ignoring her as if she hadn't heard.

She picked Robert up and kissed him. He did not pull away, but neither did he respond. She hugged the weeping Carol and kissed her as she was going through the door. "Now you must be a good girl, and I will contact you when I can, but I am going abroad, and will be very busy. Bye, David, it's been fun." David nodded his head but did not reply. He felt it was safer. Anyway he was beside himself with rage. Carol had retreated to the stairs and just sat on the bottom stair, weeping silently.

Barbara waved from the car, and muttered to Sebastian under her breath, as the window was open, "Come on, for Christ's sake let's go!

"Ok,ok." he replied, "I don't think I have liked your behaviour at all today. I'm certainly glad you're not my mother. You really were a cow, and for the moment I would prefer it if we drive back to London in silence if you don't mind!" "CHARMING" she cried.

They pulled away, watched by the silent group at the front door. As the car went down the drive, Carol had to be physically restrained from running after it.

Elizabeth asked "What on earth happened between you two?"

"I'll tell you later", David replied crossly, "in the meantime, I must look after Carol. Carol, come with Daddy into the study for a chat".

CHAPTER FOURTEEN

Poor Carol

Placing his hands under her arms he picked her up and sat her on his knee, "Here you are darling, have a big blow into my handkerchief, and when you feel a little better, we will have a talk". Carol sat up, her face sopping wet, and blew really hard into his handkerchief.

"Gosh, you must feel better now after that big noise!" he said lightly. She laughed in spite of herself, and then started laughing and crying.

"Come on", he said, "just lie back here on my shoulder for a while quietly". She complied, starting to feel safe again. Her sobbing soon stopped.

She sat up, "I'm ready now, what do you want to tell me, it's about Mummy isn't it?"

"I'm afraid it is. I'm in a hopeless situation, you are still very young, but old enough to understand certain things and I feel that you are entitled to be told the truth. You noticed your Mother didn't say anything to you. She just left it to me"

"I suppose what you're going to tell me, is that she doesn't want to see me anymore", a stifled sob erupted unexpectedly.

"More or less darling, without watering it down that's it. She feels she wants to be free to go where she wants. She thinks you are better off here. I tried to ask her to come and see you regularly, but she doesn't want to, leastways at the moment, she may change her mind."

Carols big blue eyes looked at him, getting bigger.

He put his arms round her and cuddled her to him. "I'm sorry darling, but I care too much for you to mislead you... If I told you that she misses you and is going to come to see you on a regular basis, and she failed to turn up you would feel even more let down. If she changes her mind, well, we'll have to cope with that when, and if it happens. But, in the meantime, as I have said I felt I had to tell you the truth. She simply doesn't want to be bothered with bringing up her children".

Why did she have us, then?" Carol mumbled.

"That's a perfectly fair question. As I've already told you, you were conceived in her tummy before we got married. She wanted you at the time there was no question of her not wanting you. I just think she has always been spoiled by Granny and Granddad and feels she can do what she wants. She is basically irresponsible, I think".

"What does that mean?" Carol asked.

"Well, it means that when you make a decision, and certain things happen in consequence, like having children, you cannot just change your mind, you must stand by your first decision, and look after the children to the best of your ability. After all, any parent can only do that. As you quite rightly say it's not your fault". She put her arms round his neck.

He continued, "I'm sorry poppet, I always seem to be the one to give you bad news, but I haven't had a chance to talk to Elizabeth since I spoke with your Mother. I know she is very upset as she has grown very fond of you. I think you have got to be big and strong and put your mother to the back of your mind. Otherwise, you will just make yourself ill and it won't make any difference. From her attitude today, she doesn't care. Is there anything else you want to ask me?"

"No Daddy, I think I knew all along what she felt, she made it quite clear today when we were out. She was kissing and cuddling that awful man, she changed when she spoke to us and made us feel very in the way and not wanted. That's really what started me crying. She told me my hair looked awful, and she didn't like my dress. She blamed Elizabeth, and laughed about her. She was dragging Robert around by his arm, and he was just crying because he was frightened, I'm sure of that".

"Well, next time, if there is a next time, we will ask her to stay here, so we can make sure you are looked after".

"Thank you Daddy, I wish I didn't love her, but I do".

"You probably always will, but you will have to learn to live without her. Now let's go upstairs and look at that homework".

Carol's bedroom, carefully furnished by Elizabeth, was decorated in strawberry pink and white. She had a single four poster bed, with a white lace canopy. There was a fitted wardrobe with a kidney shaped dressing table. The bedspread, curtains and drapes round the dressing table were in the same matching material. She had a little desk and chair her books were all neatly put away in the book shelf. The wallpaper was essentially white with occasional pink roses. The carpet was in a toning pink, and there was a white fluffy rug by her bed. Her bedside chair was shaped like a teddy bear and she only just fitted into it, but she refused to either to get rid of it or agree it was too small. Although her room was not a double, it was a good size for a single and was situated on the corner of the house, with one window overlooking the sea, the other the garden.

David stood, looking out of the windows, "You really do have a delightful view from this room".

"Yes I know, I love my bedroom; that's why I quite like being here, also I feel it's mine, if you know what I mean"
"Yes darling, I used to feel just the same. Look as I can't fit in the chair, I will have to sit either on the floor or on your bed".

"I will pull the cover off and you can sit on my bed", she said warmly.

"How many subjects today?"

"Four", she said.

"Ok, let's get started, and don't huff if I correct you".

She gave him a wry smile.

*****

Elizabeth sat in the drawing room sipping her whisky. The room had a pine polished floor off white furniture and rugs. She collected Porcelain figures which were dotted round the room on various pieces of antique furniture.

David had put Carol to bed after he was satisfied she was calmer. The decision over her home seemed to have taken her mind off things. On entering the drawing room he found Elizabeth sitting on the settee reading a book, he noted the large whisky in the tumbler and hoped it was diluted with water but said nothing. He was becoming increasingly worried about her drinking. He sighed, she really was a very beautiful women. Utterly and completely graceful at all times without making any effort, so different from Barbara. Elizabeth looked up as he entered.

"Phew I did not enjoy today! I need a drink." He said as he poured himself a stiff gin and tonic. Ignoring the tongs in the ice bucket, he took some ice with his fingers, dropping it absently into his glass.

"I feel completely drained", he said.

"So do I. What on earth happened between you and

Barbara?" She raised her hand in protestation. 'I don't know why I asked that because if there is likely to be any friction between us in consequence, I would rather leave it until I feel stronger".

He bent over her, and gave her a long gentle kiss as if she herself were made of Dresden.

"My darling, I quite agree, but I think I would like to tell you what happened, just to get it out of the way, if you don't mind".

Elizabeth sat silent while he related the interview with Barbara. Somehow she was determined to stay calm. The day had been quite harrowing enough. There was no point in getting upset any more about Barbara. When he had finished, she said "I am not surprised in the slightest.

Nothing that callous women does would surprise me. For my part, I hope we don't have to see her again, but I have a horrid feeling that she only means what she says at the time and that if the mood takes her, she will not hesitate to come here again regardless of the upset she causes which she clearly enjoys anyway. I'm so glad you had a long chat with Carol and that she seems to be taking it all very sensibly, considering her age".

David went on to tell her what Carol had told him about her day.

Elizabeth sighed, "Oh dear, she is most concerned with how she looks. I do hope she won't take her Mother's remarks to heart and lose confidence in herself again I've been trying to build it up. I know what I'll take her to my hairdresser for a grown up assessment of her hair. That way she will feel she is getting independent advice. Come on darling, let's not talk about it anymore, and enjoy our evening.

"There's something good I want to see on the television!"......

CHAPTER FIFTEEN

Jeans Flat

Jean Brown couldn't believe it when Mr Pebbles, the man from the council called to inform her that after careful consideration of all the facts, the Council had decided that her case was sufficiently urgent for her to be given priority over others on the waiting list and she was to be given a two bed roomed flat. At the same time he warned her that they would be watching her to make sure she did not damage the flat; as she was on their list as a bad tenant. She had assured him that she now lived firmly on her own and that she only wanted a decent place in which to bring up the boys.

After Mr. Pebbles had shown her the flat he'd handed over the keys and left. He gave her a rent book and told her the day on which they would be calling to collect the rent, and she was to make sure that she did not fall into arrears, as before. Suitably chastened, she assured him there was no way she would jeopardise losing the flat.

It was a ground floor flat, in a block of six maisonettes on a fairly new council estate. There was a small garden to the rear which had been divided into two. One part was for the upstairs flat.

There was a separate tarmac area. Each flat had its own dustbin and washing line. The flat, although it had been previously occupied, was comparatively new. There was a lounge, two bedrooms, a kitchen and a bathroom.

Jean wandered from room to room drinking it in. The kitchen already had an oven and fridge, which must have been left by the previous tenant. The heating was electric storage heaters, so she would have to be very careful. The walls had been freshly painted in magnolia. The floors were covered throughout in plastic blue tiles. Jean hugged herself; for the first time in a long while she felt happy. She would now set about furnishing it, which wouldn't be easy.

She left the flat and returned to her room and started planning how she would furnish the flat. Bending down she pulled out one of the drawers in the battered chest. Feeling at the back she removed a brown envelope and tipping the contents onto the bed she counted it; one hundred and fifty two pounds.

She had been putting the odd few pounds by for months, and on several occasions, when Jack had returned the worse for drink she had left him where he fell and raided his wallet. He never bothered to check it before he left, she was sure he didn't miss the few pounds she purloined. When he was drinking he didn't know what he spent anyway. There was no way he would demean himself by asking his friends either, she was certain.

She already had a bed and a cot for the twins. Buying a local paper she noted when the next cheap sales were taking place.

She had great fun bidding for her furniture. Now the flat really was beginning to feel like home. She asked a friend to help move her furniture from the rented room.

She put a single bed in the twin's room as well as their

cot. They would soon be big enough to sleep in a bed. She had it all planned out.

She had been lucky with the suite, it was rather old fashioned, and the fleck colour was a bit nauseous, but it was in good condition, and she had secured it for twenty pounds. A few cushions would cheer it up, she decided. The carpet pieces for all three rooms had been the most expensive, and had set her back fifty pounds.

Never mind, it would be warmer for the children. The things she needed for the kitchen seemed endless, but as usual she settled for the basics, and purchased some second hand saucepans; buying a job lot in an old cardboard box which was knocked down to fifty pence, the contents of which no-one had bothered to check. There were various plates with different patterns, but all perfectly serviceable. The council, for some reason, had said that they would pay for a new kettle, if she gave them the receipt which she jumped at. She wanted to keep a little money in reserve and set about finding a new hiding place.

She bought some provisions for the larder and decided she would try and buy something, every week, like flour or pasta, to keep it stocked up. She had also bought some net curtains for a few pounds and with wires had put these up straight away to give herself some privacy. Curtains would take a little while, but she would do it.

She had been to the hospital that day, and had a long talk with the doctor, who welcomed the news that she had been re-housed, and the children would have somewhere decent to come home to. They had been in the intensive care unit for two weeks before they were moved out into the ward. The nasal-gastric tubes hooked in the stomach to feed them had been removed, and they were now feeding normally thank goodness. After the initial worry about Nicholas, the x-rays had shown that no permanent damage had occurred to his spine. He might have a weakness in his lower back later on in life, but there was nothing to worry about. He should be perfectly normal. He had suffered contusions to the arms and legs, and had broken both legs, which were still in plaster. Hopefully, the plaster casts would be removed shortly. He was always pleased to see her, giving her a lovely warm smile, and giggling when she cuddled him. The doctors were still concerned about Geoffrey. He had been in a coma for a while, and there was always a worry of infection, and septicaemia setting in; lying in a prone position because of the other wounds was not helping his recovery.

He had broken a leg and an arm, and these were in plaster like Nicholas. He had developed a cold today, and had been moved away from Nicholas which upset him. His temperature was up again but he seemed far more content when Jean was around. Although children run temperatures very easily, because of his condition, and what he had suffered recently, he was still giving cause for concern amongst the staff.

Jean decided she would go to the hospital on an earlier bus in the morning. She hadn't heard a word from Jack since his disappearance, and was very relieved. The police had been round to see her a few times, trying to get some lead on Jack. Hopefully, he had left the area.

CHAPTER SIXTEEN

The Docks

On Monday morning, Elizabeth felt compelled to go down to the dockyard. She drove inside the marked gates, parked the car and walked along the quayside. There was only one coble boat unloading its catch onto the quay. One of the men waved to her, the others gave occasional good humoured wolf whistles. She went into her father's office, the staff seemed pleased to see her and told her that her father was not around this morning, but that her brother Michael had only just popped out for a few minutes and would be back shortly as he was in the middle of preparing the banking.

She wandered off looking for him. She thought he might be talking and walked in the general direction of the sheds housing groups of men filleting fish. They worked at speed and soon the fish boxes were piled high, nearly touching the ceiling.

She wanted to find out if any of them knew where Jack Big was.

She had received an update on the condition of the two men injured in the fight with Big. Taffy was still very ill suffering with a collapsed lung, and Billy was out of hospital, but his jaw had been so badly broken that it had to be wired in to place. His food could only be taken in liquid form through a straw. She shuddered at the thought.

Although the men obviously had differences of opinion, in the main they tended to stick together against any outsiders, especially the police. She knew that, but she felt she must try

She went into one of the filleting sheds, belonging to her father, the men looked up from their work and nodded at her by way of recognition, or said "Hello, Miss Elizabeth", which is what they had always called her since she was a little girl. They were all very well aware of the latest position on all fronts including her befriending Jean Brown and helping her after the accident. Needless to say, they had views.

She directed her questions at Tom, one of her father's oldest employees, who had always stayed very loyal to the firm through thick and thin.

"I wondered, Tommy, whether you have heard anything of Jack Big, since his disappearance?"

Tommy became immediately absorbed in the fish he was gutting. He was clearly embarrassed to speak in front of the other men.

She said "It's all right Tommy I just wanted general information that is why I have asked you the question in front of the other men".

Her eyes did not waver from him, although she was aware that all work had stopped round them, they were all waiting intently for Tommy's rely.

"No, Miss Elizabeth, I have heard nowt. I know there are quite a few men in the yard who would like a word with Jack, apart from the police. That must have been a terrible fight, because both Billy and Taffy are still very ill, and it's their families that suffer. Billy's wife has just had a babe and needs his money, aye that she does. Dammed social is not enough to keep a bird alive, especially when you have been used to being provided for by your man. I shouldn't wonder if the lad never goes to sea again, he's that bad Miss, a fisherman's life is a hard one; you have to go out in them boats to understand. He has to be physically fit; otherwise it's such an extra burden on the rest of the crew if he don't pull his weight. There's young Billy, always did talk too much, did that lad, but none of us wished that upon him, nay, lass." The men chuckled at the thought of Billy and his chattering.

"Also, Miss, Jack's got his mates as well, who feel he has been hard done by, and that the fight was not all his fault. The trouble is, he's such a big bugger and when he's been drinking, it's best to keep right out of the way. But at sea you couldn't wish for a better bloke, he'll not grumble on the hours he works. Then this happens and makes him look a right B. Oh. Sorry Miss I'm forgetting myself". He had spoken with passion and his face was flushed. Going back into his shell he resumed gutting the fish.

"That's all right, I'm a grown up girl now. In my job, I sometimes come across very unsavoury language. Thanks, Tommy, anyway it looks as if the men are divided into two camps by way of loyalty".

"Yes, that's about it, Miss, I'm sorry I can't tell you anymore". A feeling of gloom settled on her.

"That's all right, thanks anyway, sorry to interrupt your work. I was trying to find my brother I understand he's around this morning".

She turned and walked from the shed. The men turned on Tommy, and one man spoke for them all. "What the bloody hell did you have to tell her anything for we don't want her sort poking around down here, I know her father employs us, but that doesn't mean he bloody owns our souls, and if I know Jonas he wouldn't want to neither what with the villains round here and all". They all laughed.

George, the spokesman, continued. "You know very well that, if and when Jack Big shows his face there's going to be a great deal of trouble. The men would want to have their say, so to speak, that's before the police get involved. Any road the less we say to anyone the better, we'll sort it ourselves."

The men broke up, slapping George on the back for standing up to old Tommy.

Elizabeth walked idly to the end of the quay she found a bench and sat looking out to sea. She thought the waters around here could certainly tell some tales about the men who fished their lives away. What did they say in the old days, that the coble boats were made of wood and rowed by men of steel? Today it was more like boats of steel and men of wood. Still, it was a very hard life for them who wanted to try their hand at it, and she wished them luck.

She jumped as a hand was placed on her shoulder. "Michael, how lovely to see you, it seems ages", she stood up and kissed him on the cheek. Michael was a younger version of his father, just a bit taller. He was twenty six years old and was still single. He had his own house, but still spent most of his time at home, being looked after by Mum.

"Aye, lass, it's grand to see you, it certainly has been too long. It's just that our paths don't cross normally during the day, and I know you are very busy with the practice and the children, and I don't like to trouble you".

"It's no trouble, now you promise me you will come round and have dinner with us, I know David would like it. We'll set a date before I leave, then you will be no excuse.

Now, I came down to see whether there is any more information about this man Jack Big, you know the one involved in the fight." Michael nodded by way of acknowledgment. She continued, "I have spoken to Tommy, but other than to say there is bad feeling between the men, who are divided as to what actually happened, or if he does, he has decided not to tell me".

Michael shifted and looked down at his boots as if examining them. "I have heard all about what Jack has been up to, plus the fact that you have been getting involved with his woman, I really don't think it's very sensible, especially when he returns, which he surely will, and finds out about the accident. You know how people love to exaggerate and distort the truth. You have got quite a few enemies around here at the moment. There are many men and their missus who would like you knocked down off your pedestal as they put it, so you must be careful".

Elizabeth was surprised. "You know I didn't run those children down. Jean pushed the pram was in front of me".

"I know that, love, but do they? I feel they believe what they want to believe. Let me walk you to your car. You can rest assured both Dad and I have our ears closely to the ground, and as soon as we hear anything, we will let you know first, promise".

They had been walking side by side. She opened the door to the car, reached inside and took out her diary, "Now let's agree a date for next week shall we, how about Friday?"

"That's fine, about seven thirty".

"You know you can come when you like. If you finish early, come round and you can help me put the children to bed".

"O.K." he laughed, "I'll see what I can do".

She drove back to the office, still deep in thought. It was very strange about the complete disappearance of Jack Big, someone must know where he is or who might be harbouring him.

She was not in the mood for the office today. Four house

transactions were completing, and although she had tried her hardest to prepare everything, something invariably went wrong at the last minute, creating tension and upset. She felt she should be getting used to it by now.

CHAPTER SEVENTEEN

Trip for Provisions

Jack Big had been holed up in the shack for two weeks, and was getting restive. He had ventured out once into town late at night, and had managed to find old Jo, propped against the wall down and alleyway, in a drunken slumber.

After shaking him back into consciousness, he told Jack that things were still bad, and it would be very foolish for him to show his face for the time being. Jo had told him about the injuries to Billy and Taffy. He also told him that their friends were after him to settle the score on behalf of their mate, before the police got to him. This shook him. He knew only too well how the men stuck together, and liked settling their own scores privately.

Jack also learned about the accident with Jean and that the twins were in hospital, badly injured. This had upset him more than he thought possible, 'a solicitor, knocking his children down in cold blood'.

He wanted to go and find this woman, and make a scene, but self preservation prevented him from doing so at the moment. He would bide his time.

Why hadn't Jean mentioned the accident to him, perhaps she had something to hide. I'll wring the truth out of her, he thought. Come to think of it, he couldn't remember whether they were in their cot or not, he was too drunk on that dreadful evening. It was all a blur. He hadn't had a drink for two weeks, and was surprised how sharp his brain had become. But he still missed his drink.

The shack was too small to stay in, and he didn't like being there in the day in case hikers or snoopers came by. So he spent most of the days lying in the boat in the cove, covered by his oilskins for protection against the damp and cold. The cave walls were running with water, and he had caught a dreadful cold. There had been two storms and he had had to drag the boat further into the inner reaches of the cave for safety. Otherwise most nights he went fishing, enjoying lying in the boat watching the stars.

His peace had been interrupted on one day, when a family emerged seemingly joy riding around the cliffs in a small boat with an outboard motor. They had stopped at the mouth of the cave, and there was noisy discussion amongst them as to whether they should explore this large unexpected opening. Eventually, much to his relief, they decided not to, as they were without lanterns or torches.

They weighed anchor and ate their lunch deep in conversation; discussing the history of the cliffs around this part of the coastline. The father appeared to be a geologist and talked learnedly to his son about the rock formations.

Eventually they chugged away, agreeing that they would revisit the cave on another day, with equipment to explore it properly. The fact that they made no mention of when they would return worried Jack even more.

His general provisions were getting low, and it would soon reach a point when he would only be left with fish and fresh water from the spring. The paraffin had run out, and he really was beginning to suffer from the cold.

As he lay there, he thought it might be possible for him to travel down the coast towards Whitby and pull in at a little cove. There he could make his way to the nearest village, where he should be able to buy provisions, without drawing too much attention to himself weather permitting he would start rowing his way down the coast tomorrow, very early.

The next day he made three unsuccessful attempts to set off down the coast for his badly needed provisions, each time he had been forced to turn back because the storm the previous night had churned up the currents and at times the waves were still six foot high.

After two days the weather at last seemed to be abating and, although there was the odd high wave, he felt he could chance his luck once more. His stores by now were in a desperate state.

The next morning he changed his mind and decided to go down the coast in the opposite direction towards Scarborough, partly because of the wind. He wanted to aim for Clowton Wyke or Hayburn Wyke where he should be able to find a village shop. He also wanted to find out if possible whether Billy and Taffy had recovered from their injuries.

There were plenty of coves along the shoreline, where he could take shelter, if it proved necessary, and to rest at intervals.

The outboard motor was nearly empty of petrol, which meant he would have to row most of the way. He thought it would probably take him several hours. He put the rest of the provisions in the boat, and set off. The skies were grey and the wind swirled round him. He thought as he pulled away, that the weather would probably brighten up later. He was cheered by this, as the distance grew between his boat and the sanctuary of his cave.

As he rowed, he mused on the word Wyke. He had found an informative book in the shack, left there by his

Uncle. As he rowed he had nothing else to do except study the coastline.

At Hundale Point were huge slabs of sandstone with brilliant examples of ripple marks, which had born the ravages of time. The book claimed that the marks were made over one hundred and fifty million years ago. This passage of time was beyond his comprehension.

The sandstone was remnants of a huge river delta, which in those days covered this part of the North East Yorkshire Coast. There is a very famous broad ledge, below the cliff edge at Hayburn Wyke, but above sea level. It was named locally as the "undercliff", and as it was hardly ever visited by anyone, it was a haven for wildlife. The trees which grew there, gave the animals and birds habitat.

Badges, foxes and even deer, could be found on this boulder strewn platform. The bay itself was completely secluded, with vegetation growing down to the shore. There was also a spectacular sight of a twin waterfall, cascading over a rocky ledge into the sea.

At last, tired wet, and hungry, he reached his destination, Hayburn Wyke. He pulled his boat well out of the sea, hiding it behind some rocks and trees. It was a very steep climb from the beach. He then had to traipse across a wood, over a stile and continue uphill through the field. A track led him through farm buildings, which brought him out in front of the local hotel. He had tried to tidy up his appearance as much as possible, but in the circumstances this had proved somewhat difficult.

He had made a rather pathetic attempt to shave before he left. Cold water and a blunt blade didn't help. He now had a growth of stubble, and felt thoroughly dirty all over.

There were quite a few visitors around, people taking their spring holidays, he supposed. He had met one or two on his walk up from the cliffs. He had nodded genially as he passed, hoping they would hardly notice him. He made his way towards the village shop and hung around outside for a while, waiting until the shop was empty.

He went in. It looked as if no one was there. Slowly a head raised itself above the counter, muttering. Eventually, the back straightened up to reveal an older man of about sixty five, wearing very thick horn rimmed glasses. Jack visibly relaxed. He handed his list to the man.

The shopkeeper took it and smiled with pleasure at the amount wanted. "Good order". He said.

"Stocking up my caravan", Jack replied.

"Very good, lad Aye, I'm pleased to see you. We have had a hard winter, and business has been very slack. It's hardly worth opening some days. Still this order will cheer the wife up. I think you'll need a cardboard box for all this. Ah! Here we are". He blew the bits out of the bottom of a box. He was breathing heavily with the exertion of collecting all the goods. Jack helped him load up the box, grabbed a local paper and threw it on top.

"Well, how much do I owe you?"

The old man took some time to add it up on a brown paper bag. "Would you like to check it lad, I sometimes make mistakes?"

"No, that be all right. It sounds right to me any road. Here you are, this seems the right money. Well I hope business picks up for you and you have a good summer".

"Thank you kindly, lad, thank ee, and good luck to you".

"I think I need it," Jack muttered, as he closed the door behind him, waving a cheery goodbye.

He started to feel better and not quite so nervous. However, he was ravenous. He could hardly sit down in this hamlet and start devouring the contents of his box. He looked round frantically for somewhere where he could eat shave and freshen up. He saw an old man tending his garden and decided to chance his luck.

He ambled up to him, resting his box on the old man's gate. The old man looked up, straightened his cap, and hobbled over. Jack saw he was a man of great age. He cupped his hand to his ear.

"Did you speak to me, son? I'm afraid I can't hear very well. You will have to speak up".

Jack shouted back. "No, I was just resting my load and looking to pass the time of day. Do you mind if I sit down and talk to you?"

"No, of course not, be my guest nice to have some company for a change."I get very lonely these days since she passed away.

"I was admiring your garden. You certainly take good care of it. It must look a picture in the summer".

"Not much else to do with my time. Old age is not funny son, comes to us all one day you know. Would you like a cup of tea, I was just going to make one?"

"If it would not be too much trouble, I would, thanks."

"Best come into the house".

Jack had to stoop quite low, to get through the small front door of the mid-terrace cottage. This greatly amused the old man, who was considerably shorter than Jack, even in the days when he could stand up straight.

"I think my little house is a bit small for you, lad," he chuckled. "You had best stand still in the living room. Don't move around neither, lest you knock something over".

Jack tried to straighten, but his head hit the ceiling. He sank onto his hunkers in front of the little coal fire. The old man bustled round his small kitchen, whistling to himself.

He suddenly boomed "My name's Ben, what's yours?"

"Jack".

Jack was trying to get round to the subject of a wash and shave. The room was so full of furniture and knick knacks that there was very little free space at all. There was a tiny wooden table, with two matching hard chairs. Either side of the fireplace nestled two little arm chairs. Jack was afraid to sit in one in case he broke it.

Ben shuffled in, looking for him and, finding him on the floor, chuckled. "Here you are, laddie, git this down yer"!

Jack sat on the floor supping his tea, the old man sat at the table. Jack looked at him with a cheeky grin. He had his story ready. "I got up real early this morning, like, to come up this way, as I had to sort out my caravan. Well, I didn't have much time for a wash and shave before I left. I am expecting my girlfriend this afternoon, and would like to make myself presentable before I see her. I suppose you wouldn't let me have a shave here, would you?"

Ben giggled, "You young things think of nothing else but sex. I suppose I was just the same at your age, although my Ada wouldn't like to hear me say it, even though she's passed over. I still keep her knitting in her bag, by her chair over there, you know can't bring myself to throw it away.

Oh! Forgive me going on. You're not interested in my funny ways. Yes, son, of course you can wash and shave. There's still some water in the kettle. Help yourself".

"Mighty kind of you, I thought I could sense someone with a kindred spirit to mine!"

He winked at the old man as he went to get his shaving things from the box. He shaved in the kitchen and then went out in the back yard and had a good sluice down. He got wet through but felt much better for it. He noticed the old tin bath on the wall and realised that, the poor old feller hadn't got hot water. Still has his weekly bath in front of the fire, no doubt. He seemed happy enough.

He went back into the house through the back door, and thanked Ben profusely for the tea and the wash. Ben told him that if he was ever passing again, he would be welcome to call in and see him. Ben waved goodbye from his front door, and Jack ambled off, whistling, down the road.

He turned the corner, and went in search of a drink. The Pig and Whistle looked inviting so Jack entered and placed his box of shopping in the window seat. He went to the bar, trying to control his eagerness. Whatever happened he mustn't draw attention to himself in any way. He must just present himself as an ordinary passerby. He ordered a pint of beer, which he downed in one; it hardly touched the sides of his throat. He immediately asked for another one, explaining he was very thirsty. He also asked for a large whisky.

The woman behind the bar was engrossed in conversation with two other people, whom she seemed to know fairly well. She paid very little attention to him, and he took his drink to the window. He reached down into the box for the local paper. He scanned the pages for any news of Billy and Taffy, but found nothing, which made him feel very frustrated.

He called for the menu and ordered tomato soup with roll and butter, and double fish and chips with peas. The bar lady said dryly "Well, lad, you're certainly not on any new fangled diet. Won't be long, sit yerself down".

When the soup came, Jack was quite glad that it was piping hot, which served to restrain him from scavenging the bowl indecently. He savoured every mouthful of the meal. He thought it was the best food he had ever tasted. It was, after all, the first proper meal he'd had in weeks. He downed one last pint of beer, and with his box under his arm, made his way down the road.

It was a long hard row back to Robin Hood's Bay he would use the outboard part of the way, but he wanted to be sparing with the petrol he'd bought in the village. He now had to give some serious thought as to his next move. He didn't feel he could go on with his present existence for much longer. He was also running out of money.

CHAPTER EIGHTEEN

Robin Hood's Bay

Michael was looking forward to his flying lesson. He had been working very hard recently and needed a break.

He leaned back in the seat as he drove to Teeside airport to meet James his instructor who was twenty eight, two years older than Michael.

Usually, Michael had one hour in the air preceded by about forty five minutes briefing on the ground in the classroom. At the briefing, James would go through precisely what they were going to put into practice when aloft. It was very expensive to keep a plane up, because of the fuel. The more he concentrated at the briefing, inwardly digesting the technical details, the quicker he would learn to fly; depending on the instructor, and his personal aptitude, he could end up flying solo after ten to twenty hours flying time.

Michael had only clocked up four hours so far and was finding the manuals a bit of a slog. There were four Principles of Flight; Air Law, Radio Telephoning and Meteorology.

On principles of flight he seemed ok, but the meteorology he found boring, yet he knew it was vital for him to master it.

In his Morris 1300 G.T., it took him three quarters of an hour to get there.

James met him at the door of the flying school, smiling broadly, whilst shaking his hand. They were about the same height. He suggested they went straight into the briefing room for some peace and quiet. On the last flight, Michael had managed to take off and land the plane solo under James watchful eye. Although James had told him he was quite pleased with his progress, the danger was for Michael to become over confident. James thought that some pupils had to be taught a lesson occasionally. A few spins and downward spirals usually made them sick and did the trick, but he didn't say this to Michael. Michael was anxious not to rub James up the wrong way. So they actually got on very well.

This morning, they were planning to fly out to Robin Hood's Bay. This meant that the flight path had to be carefully planned by Michael as an exercise. Fylingdales Ballistic Missile base was very near Robin Hood's Bay. The Ballistic Missile early warning station on Fylingdales Moor formed a very important part of the national defence system. Light aircraft were precluded from going over the base so Michael's route took them in a large L shape.

James checked his calculations, approved them and then went to file the flight plan. They walked together over to the Cessna 150. Michael completed his ground checks, and James approved them. By now Michael was feeling very much at home. It was a small plane, a two seater with one propeller. James decided to take off straight away. They taxied down the run way, and the nose lifted. It was a beautiful day, a cloudless blue sky, perfect flying weather. As soon as they were in the air, Michael took the controls. He had quite a few turns to make today, and he wanted to concentrate. It was easy to see Fylingdales from the sky. The Radomes rose in the air like huge white golf balls. They were each 154 feet high and weighed 100 tons from the sky looked a fine sight.

Robin Hood's Bay was also clearly visible from the air. Michael started to make his turn; as they reached the Bay he noticed a rowing boat right beneath him, dangerously near the rocks. He wondered what on earth a boat was doing out at this time of day. Especially since the sea was still very choppy after the recent storms. He hoped the person in the boat knew what he was doing. He thought of contacting the Coastguard and mentioned it to James. They circled the boat again to see if there were any distress signals. It seemed OK, so James said he wouldn't bother to report it, but would note it in the log.

Just then a fighter plane screamed from their right straight at them, directly across their path.

Michael's immediate reaction was to let go of the control column and raised his arms protectively. The plane began to zigzag crazily. James by reflex grabbed his own control stick and managed to right the plane. There was a deathly silence between them as both men were extremely shaken. Their hearts were still pounding after their narrow escape when a second fighter plane came so close its downward draught affected the little Cessna very badly, and it shook and rattled violently.

"That's it!" exploded James. "I am definitely going to file an official complaint. We have to keep to the rules, but these air force pilots do what they want. They don't tell the civilian airfields what they're doing. They should have known we were here. It's disgraceful we could both have been killed.

He pressed the transmitter button. "Teeside Approach, this is Golf Mike Delta".

"Mike Delta, Teeside Approach, go ahead".

"I would like to file an air miss report Teeside Mike Delta. Two Buccaneers crossed right to left at 300 yards; can you trace them on radar? I will fill in an air miss form when

I land. Returning to field now, estimating 56, request joining instructions".

"Roger, Mike Delta, maintain VFR report, field in sight. Left base, join runway 26. QSE 1007".

"Mike Delta, will report field in sight QSE 1007."

He pressed the transmitter button. "I think that was the right thing to do, don't you"?

Michael felt at that moment that he could never master all the technical jargon.

"I certainly do, I think you were jolly good. I completely lost my nerve. Still, I will try and be ready next time and hang on to the controls like grim death."

"That's the spirit. Now do you feel sufficiently recovered to fly us back to the airport?"

"I certainly do!"

"Good chap. As soon as I'm off duty I would like to buy you a beer".

They flew on, laughing together.

CHAPTER NINETEEN

The Fight

Jack had looked up, and seen the light aircraft circling above. He kept his head down and continued to row, hoping the aircraft would ignore him and fly off. He tried to keep the boat stable. The last thing he wanted was for some keen pilot to call out the coast guards to rescue him. Their attention was hopefully distracted by the jet fighter.

He reached the safety of his cove, and with the last remnants of his energy, pulled the boat as quickly as he could, into the cave. He hadn't forgotten the earnest geologist and his family. Having stored his provisions away, he made himself a snack before bedding down for the night.

He felt he could stand the suspense no longer. He had to know what the score was. Tomorrow, at first light, he would make his way on foot back along the shoreline to Scarborough. Once there, he would be bound to find someone to tell him what the news was. In any event he was prepared to face the men they would definitely have strong opinions but he'd had enough of his own company. With his mind full of this, he fell into a deep slumber.

At first light, after giving himself a strip wash and close shave, he set off for Scarborough docks. He even managed to give his hair a wash, which it badly needed. After the success of yesterday he was in good spirits as he walked along. There was a fine drizzle, and the air was full of the smell of spring. Everything was starting to burst forth with growth. The birds were in full song, and several rabbits scuttled across in front of him as he walked. On the high ground, the heather stretched for miles, like a glorious mauve blanket although it grew on rocky ground, and he had to tread carefully. It would be all too easy for him to sprain an ankle through carelessness.

He reached the docks and took cover behind one of the large sheds. The boats would be returning shortly, since the sale of fish always started on the quay at five thirty every morning. He peered from behind the shed and noticed several cobles, with crews he knew, tying their boats up. It was nice to see their faces again. He wondered if anyone would be pleased to see him. He had to confess he did have an awful sinking feeling in his stomach.

The sun was coming up and started to shine on him, making him feel vulnerable. He moved backwards into the shadows and bumped straight into Archie.

"Bloody hell, where the ell did you come from?" Archie gasped.

"Hello, Archie nice to see you. I thought it was time I came back to face the music. Any road, I want to know how the lads are, also about my babes. I can't hole up forever you know!"

"Well, mate, if I was you I would get your head down and come further round the back here, out of the way. If the lads see you there is bound to be trouble, and I for one won't want to be involved. I've got a wife and kids to think of, besides a bloody great mortgage. You don't seem to realise, lad, feeling is running very high against you amongst the men. We're all pretty hard men here, but what you did was wrong. Getting blind drunk is one thing, injuring those lads the way you did is another, then to run off."

Jack sat on a box, well out of sight, "I know, I know, don't you think I've gone over it in my head a thousand times. I know I drank far too much, but they needled me all evening. I was tired, they owed me that money, but they wouldn't pay it over. They just kept egging me on, thought it was funny like they did. Well, you know I have a quick fuse. No one takes the piss out of me. I still wish I could make amends in some way".

"What the hell are you going to do? You can't stay hidden here. The police are looking for you"

"I know that. I'm not staying on the run forever. If only the men would let me speak to them and put my side of the story. I think I've got a good defence, because of the provocation. Taffy started the fight, you know, he threw the first punch. I defended myself, lad and I'm going out there into the yard to talk to the men. The auction of fish will finish soon".

"Bloody ell; well don't say I said anything. Don't drop me in it, please" whined Archie.

Jack stood up. Archie crouched behind the boxes of fish, indicating he intended to stay put. Jack slowly walked into the middle of the yard, where all could see him.

One after another, different men recognised him. They nudged each other and turned to face him started to move towards him, forming a ring. One or two were dispatched to tell the other men who were working elsewhere. No one would want to miss this confrontation. They stood in silence forming a circle around him; the power of their united presence was formidable. Some of the men were smoking, some were chewing gum, some just spat as a gesture of their feelings.

There must have been about fifty of them standing around him, a voice from the back of the men called out,

"Well, what do you think you are doing here, Jack Big? You've got a bloody cheek, just walking in here without a by your leave, aye that you have".

Someone else called out, "you're a bastard, Jack, we don't want the likes of you here, bugger off!"

This prompted all the men to start to shout out comments, which merged into a rebellious noise.

Jack raised his arms to try and quieten them.

"Look men," he shouted above the noise, "I have no quarrel with any of you. There are always two sides to any argument. Billy and Taffy were winding me up all evening. A few of you were there. You must have seen that it wasn't me that started the fight or throw the first punch. Those two were begging for trouble that evening. They were just spoiling for a fight."

The men continued to shout abuse at him. The atmosphere was getting more and more heated. "That didn't call for you using a knife, Jack, that's out of order you've ruined that poor young bugger's life. You're not going to smooth talk your way out of this one. A man your size should know better!" The owner of the voice turned and walked away, disgusted, with his head down. Jack shouted again, his heart pounding, his hands were running with sweat.

"You can call me what you like, but at least I have come back to face the music. I would like to see the lads, too."

Bob Spatt had been standing at the back of the men. He pushed his way through them, his eyes only on Jack. He was the largest man in the yard by a long chalk. He stood six feet seven inches, with a fifty two inch chest. His hand spread was two inches bigger than Jack's.

He was known as the gentle giant, a quiet peaceful man who kept himself to himself.

The men hardly noticed he was around most of the time,

because although he was large, his movements were always unobtrusive. He never made a fuss. He was a true loner, who lived alone with his cats and read a great deal. He was never bored with his own company. Even tempered though he was, no one ever thought of crossing him.

Jack started to inch back slowly. "Now, look, Bob, I've got no quarrel with you. We've fished together, and you are a good mate to have." Bob stood his ground, with his arms folded in front of him. Tears slowly rolled down his cheeks.

"Taffy is married to my sister", he said, "You've put her through hell. I can't forgive you for that. What with a new babe in the house and him on the social for weeks. She has very little to be happy with you about, Jack. It follows that neither have I. It's time, Jack Big that you were taught a lesson, in the language you understand". He moved further forward.

Jack knew there was no way out. He was surrounded by men, who were now rubbing their hands together and muttering to each other about the impending fight. Most of them were quite relieved that Bob was doing the job for them as they didn't fancy taking on Jack. A lot of the men shook their heads. They never thought they would live to see the day that Bob resorted to violence.

Jack knew he had to defend himself, but he'd no appetite for the fight. Fighting someone in cold blood was entirely different from fighting when you were full of drink and out of control.

Bob immediately hit Jack in the solar plexus with a left hook, his right hand swept up with an upper cut to the jaw. Jack went reeling backwards, badly winded. He got to his feet, bent double, trying to regain his breath. Blood trickled from the corner of his mouth. He knew Bob was finished talking, and he would have to defend himself. The men were shouting things like, "good job, just what the bastard deserves."

Jack charged at Bob, butting him in the stomach. Bob took a step backwards, grabbed Jack by his shoulder, and threw him back on his feet.

Jack threw a punch which hit Bob on the side of the jaw. The next blow Bob blocked, and Jack's defences were to put his hand to his face. He aimed a low kick at Bob, which missed and sent him off balance. He grabbed at Bob as he fell, and both men ended up grappling on the floor. The men surrounding them had to move as they pitched forward. They blindly fell into a ten foot stack of boxes full of fish. The boxes scattered, shedding their contents all over the two men. Fish was cascading everywhere. They stood up, slipping, sliding and cursing.

Bob had received a direct blow to his left eye, which was beginning to close. As Jack weaved low to strike another blow, Bob lifted his boot and kicked him a blow to the side of the head, which knocked Jack out cold. He lay there, spread-eagled amongst the cod, plaice, haddock and crabs!

Bob stood up and shook his head. He spoke to the throng. "It gave me no pleasure to do that. I want you to know that, men. I just knew it had to be done. Now, if you will all leave me be". He pushed his way through them and made his way to the toilets to clean himself up. His head throbbed, and he wanted to get some ice on his eye.

Two men walked over and gleefully emptied the contents of their ice cold buckets of water over Jack. Jack shook his head and looked round, remembering what had just happened. The men, seeing there would be no more entertainment, lost interest in Jack and dispersed, laughing, back to their work.

Jack leaned on his elbows, trying to see straight. He felt his jaw. He didn't think anything was broken. Bob certainly could pack a punch. He was drenched to the skin.

He became aware of various sets of uniformed feet standing over him. He looked up to find six constables standing grinning down at him. "You bastards you shopped me" Jack shouted after the retreating men, who grinned back in reply.

He hated the police they were bound to know about his record going back to his teenage years. He would receive no assistance or help from them, that he was sure of. He was pushed headlong into the back of the police van. Some of the policemen were abusive to him, making rude and personal remarks. He supposed he did rather stink of fish.

An older policeman was having none of it, and said to the men, "Eh, lads, there's no need to go on so, we're not judge and jury, it's our job to take him in, so let's be doing it, without any more trouble".

At the Police station, they unceremoniously took his finger prints and photograph. He was frog-marched into a cell and left there. He decided that there was no point in making a fuss. Now they had him in custody, they would do precisely what they wanted with him. The likes of him had no rights.

In fact, he was to be pleasantly surprised. The police men, who had spoken up for him in the van, had obviously had something to say to the Sergeant concerning the behaviour of his men. A young constable appeared and left him a meal on a tray although he didn't say anything at least he wasn't aggressive or rude. They left him alone for several hours.

Sergeant McVane entered his cell, just as it was getting dark.

In the early evening he was formally charged, the first count being grievous bodily harm to Billy and Taffy.

Count two, grievous bodily harm and rape against Miss Jean Brown, on the same date, and third was possession of an offensive weapon.

Jack had already been asked whether he required a Solicitor to be present, but he had declined. He considered there was no point. He would be up before the Magistrates in the morning and they had told him the police would apply for him to be remanded in custody pending his trial. Jack thought for the time being the best place he could be was in prison to be left to nurse his injuries. At least he could ask to be put in solitary confinement if he felt threatened. He considered he would have plenty of time to get his defence together. He intended to plead not guilty his story would be he was provoked into acting in self-defence. He knew how he would deal with Jean.

The following morning, Jack appeared before the Magistrates. He was remanded in custody for seven days.

He had to wait in the court cell until after lunch, when he was handcuffed to a prison officer who completely ignored him and put him in a cubicle in the Black Maria. He had to draw his knees up there was not enough room to stretch out. It was extremely uncomfortable. He imagined it was meant to be. When he eventually arrived at Hull prison he was handcuffed again whilst waiting in the induction centre.

A form was then filled in, with his name, age, address and details of the charges. He was then taken to the showers. A Prison Warder handed him his kit; brown for remand prisoners, grey for convicted men. He was given a number, which he had to memorise, and taken to his cell. This number went on the door of his cell which was for three inmates.

Two sets of hostile eyes greeted him. They both turned their backs on him, facing the wall. Jack thought this is a great beginning.

He undid his bed pack and laid down on it. He still had not been told exactly how the lads were, or about his twins.

No doubt the Duty Solicitor would put in an appearance and he would ask the Solicitor to apply for Legal Aid. I suppose an emergency certificate could be issued like last time. He sighed.

CHAPTER TWENTY

Bad News

Jean caught the seven thirty bus to hospital. The day before, she had purchased a small cuddly toy for Geoffrey and Nicholas, which she had tucked safely in her shoulder bag.

As Jean entered the ward, Sister emerged from her office "there you are, Miss Brown. I would like a word with you" her manner was business like, but kind. Jean followed her into the office and sat on the edge of a chair clutching her bag.

Sister sat at her desk, her face showed genuine concern. "I want to speak to you about Geoffrey. He is causing grave problems at the moment. Mr Lee the paediatrician will talk to you when he does his rounds".

"What has happened? Please tell me", pleaded Jean. The sister looked at her appraising her carefully, unsure as to whether she should continue or leave it to Mr. Lee. She decided that having alerted the Mother so far, it would only be kind to tell her what she knew.

"It is not, of course, simple, Jean, things rarely are. Because of the injuries to his legs Geoffrey had to lay flat for some time, which meant the lungs were vulnerable to becoming congested.As you know he caught another cold which has gone straight to his chest, and we fear septicaemia has set in.

He was taken down to the intensive care unit in the middle of the night, where everything possible is being done"

Jean put her hand to her face and began to cry. "Is he going to die?"

Sister put her arm round her, "let's not think of things like that at the moment, but it is certainly serious. Now, you stay there, and I will get you a nice cup of strong tea. When you feel up to it you can go and see Nicholas. He is having his breakfast. Mr. Lee won't be here much before ten anyway".

She left the door ajar.

Jean sat there, staring into space, with tears rolling down her cheeks. Hugging herself, she rocked backwards and forwards on the chair. She couldn't believe it she had come such a long way since the accident. Getting her own flat and preparing it for the boys return, her spirits had been raised. Now suddenly she was terrified again, for Geoffrey, herself and for Nicholas.

Sister returned, "Now come on, drink this". Jean drank her tea, blew her nose and asked to see Nicholas. He was lying in bed, gurgling happily at the shadows he could see on the ceiling. He smiled and waved his arms when he saw Jean. She bent over the cot and kissed and hugged him. She gave him one of the teddies, which had a little bell inside. He laughed with delight, clutched the teddy and took it immediately to his mouth. He was looking so much better. She sat beside him, letting him grasp her finger.

For a moment she was completely lost in her own thoughts, and jumped when a figure in a white coat suddenly appeared beside her. There were several men with him, junior doctors she presumed, standing respectfully behind him. They looked as if they were standing to attention in his presence.

"Mrs Brown?" he enquired.

"No, Miss Brown"

"I am sorry, Miss Brown. I'm Mr. Lee I wanted a word with you about Geoffrey". His face looked grave. Sister pulled the curtains round the cot, leaving the other men outside. Jean felt her knees starting to shake. He sat on a chair, took her hands in his and looked straight into her eyes.

"I'm afraid I have some very bad news Jean. Geoffrey suffered a cerebral embolism about an hour ago, I am afraid he's....

"No", she cried, "he can't be dead, I only saw him yesterday. He had a cold I know" She started to get hysterical and tried to pull away.

He went on steadily but kindly, still holding her hands tightly. "I am afraid it happens sometimes.

He caught another infection, and septicaemia set in, the infection went straight to his brain. He had already suffered a great deal from the injuries after the accident, we did all we could. Sometimes patients respond to antibiotics, but he was too small for too many drugs, and his heart couldn't take it. I am so sorry. I thought he was making a good recovery too. If only he hadn't caught the second infection".

Jean was completely numb all over. She was hazily aware of Mr.Lee extricating his hands from her gently and slowly rising and leaving the cubicle, sister coming over and putting her arm round her. She tried to stand, but then blackness engulfed her.

She woke up to find herself in a bed, and it was some moments before the horror of the truth came flooding back. She opened her mouth, and in the distance she could hear screaming then figures in uniform, then blackness. The next feeling she had was something warm on her face, and opened her eyes to see the sun streaming in the window. The sky was a beautiful blue. She turned her head, to find Elizabeth sitting beside her. She propped herself up on herself up on her pillow. Elizabeth said "I'll call the nurse". She whispered "What on earth happened to me?" she pressed a bell and a kindly nurse appeared.

"Well now, first things first, after the shock of hearing about your poor darling little boy, you fainted and suffered shock. The doctors gave you a little something to let you have a good sleep. That was two days ago".

"Where's Geoffrey? I must see him. How is Nicholas? I must get up".

"All in good time, whilst I am on duty you will do as you are told. You will first have some tea and breakfast. Then I will come and help you get dressed and see how fit you are. Now, talk to this nice friend in the meantime, who has called to see you."

Jean slumped back on the pillows, her eyes streaming with tears again. "I suppose you heard what happened?" she said to Elizabeth.

"Yes, I went round to your flat, you weren't there, so I came on here, and they told me the terrible news about Geoffrey, I am so sorry. I felt I just had to be here when you woke up". Jean thought I should be grateful, but I can feel nothing

"I don't feel like talking if you don't mind. Would you please go?"

"Of course", said Elizabeth, and quietly tiptoed out of the room. The nurse came bustling back again.

"Now where's your nice friend gone."

"I told her to go I don't want to see anyone".

"Well that's understandable, but I suspect you need all the friends you can get at the moment. You will need someone to talk to, it's the best healer, you know. Now eat this cereal, and I will get you some toast."

"I don't want it".

"Listen my girl, you haven't eaten for two days, and you're suffering from shock. Unless you eat, you will collapse again, and I for one will have no sympathy with you, if you refuse to try and help yourself. Now stop being naughty, and eat.

I'll go and get the toast and a boiled egg".

Jean started to eat automatically, and found to her surprise that she was very hungry. When the nurse returned with the toast and egg, she ate that as well without complaint. She felt so guilty. How could she eat with her little boy lying in the morgue? Such a waste, he had never hurt a fly poor little darling. How her heart ached! The pain felt as if a large stone had got lodged in her chest, it made her feel breathless.

She sat on the side of the bed as soon as she tried to stand up she felt dizzy and promptly sat down again putting her head in her hands. The nurse returned and noticing her white face, said.

"Now, take it easy. Come on, let's wash and dress you. I suppose you think I'm heartless, but it's my job to get you well. After all you have darling Nicholas to think about. He needs you, you know. He's going to miss his brother.

O.K., I know he will get over it, being so young, but he will always miss his brother. I feel desperately sorry, but unfortunately that won't bring him back. Have a good blow and dry those eyes. If you want to see Geoffrey I will arrange it." Jean nodded utter defeat showing in her eyes.

"Ok. Just sit there".

A little while later she was leaning on the nurse's arm as she was taken into the hospital mortuary. It was very cold. Geoffrey looked perfect, just as if he was having a blissful sleep. His hands were clasped across his chest, and he was holding a little white rose.

She broke down completely, sobbing bitterly. The nurse tried to guide her out, but she pulled back, murmuring "just a little longer". She touched his hand and face they were quite, quite cold. She bent over and kissed him, and with her tear she made a cross on his forehead. "He was never christened, you know," she whispered, "I never got round to it, will it matter, I hope God won't mind."

"No, my dear," the nurse replied "They are all little angels to him".

Jean straightened up, and nodded. The nurse's arms went round her and with her head resting on her shoulder she walked slowly from the mortuary.

She sat beside Nicholas, holding his fingers and looking lovingly at him. She felt transparent, divided between the love she felt for Nicholas, and the pain she felt for Geoffrey.

A woman appeared by the cot and pulled up a chair. "I am from the administration office, and wonder whether you feel well enough to discuss the arrangements for Geoffrey."

Jean turned and said "Yes, of course."

"Here is a card with the name and address of the undertakers, unless you want some other firm to deal with the funeral."

"No."

"Geoffrey will be collected this afternoon, and I will make the arrangements. They will want to know whether he is to be cremated, or buried, and of course, where". She was a kindly bespectacled, middle aged woman, who was doing a job that not many people cared for.

She was dressed soberly. Jean put the card in her handbag, "Thank you, I will contact them direct, tomorrow, when I have had time to think!"

The administrator handed her another form.

"If you are on welfare, read this form and it will tell you about the death grant. My name is Mrs Watkins, and if you need any further help, please don't hesitate to ring me."

Jean mumbled her thanks and turned back to Nicholas.

*****

She stood alone at the crematorium. The nurse, who had taken her to the mortuary, was standing behind her a kind gesture which she greatly appreciated. The chapel seemed so cold and bare. Catering for all denominations, it lacked its own identity.

The organ music came from a recording which was getting worn. She did not recognise any of the tunes. The tiny white coffin looked so lonely. There was a posy of white rose and forge-me-knots on top, with a card which read,

"TO GEOFFREY THE PUREST AND MOST INNOCENT BABY WHO WAS NOT ALLOWED TO LIVE, YOUR LOVING MOTHER."

She stared straight ahead, she had taken the pills the doctor had given her, and there were no tears left she was drained of all emotion.

Slowly, during the last hymn, the roller began to move, and the little coffin disappeared through the curtain. Jean caught her breath. The Vicar was standing at the door. He had a tear in his eye as he held out his hands. She stared steadily back at him, as if in some way blaming him. He clasped his hands round hers.

"Are you all right, my dear?"

Without blinking, she said "I will never be all right again." He whispered, "God will look after Geoffrey, he is in safe hands."

"I am sure he will do a better job than I did," she muttered. She retrieved her hand and walked away. She did not see Jack, handcuffed to a warder, standing at the back of the chapel.

CHAPTER TWENTY ONE

Elizabeth Perplexed

ELIZABETH sat at her desk, unable to get on with her work. She had found out about the death of Geoffrey from her Mother. Her visit to Jean in hospital was intended with the very best of intentions, and, although she expected Jean to be upset, she was not prepared for the cold dismissal. The funeral was today and she had wanted to send some flowers at least, but she had a funny feeling that the gesture could be misinterpreted. Up till now she had thought the twins were making a steady recovery. The dreadful feelings of guilt over their injuries still overwhelmed her, but had not been so acute recently as the twins seemed to be getting better. Now, with the death of Geoffrey, she felt plunged into an abyss of confusion, guilt and misery.

It was the wrong time of the month for her and she had backache and that dreadful dragging feeling in her lower tummy. Reaching for her bag she went to the rest room to see if she could make herself more comfortable. She hated taking pain killers but this morning she thought, anything to stop this dull ache. She combed her hair and reapplied her lipstick, feeling a little better she returned to her office.

She decided it was probably best to leave Jean for a few days to come to terms with her grief, and then perhaps she would be able to speak with her again.

She knew she must try and pull herself together and get on with her work. She looked at her watch and rang for Sally.

"You haven't forgotten your appointment, Mrs. Markham?"

"No, I know I have got to be on site for the meeting in an hour's time. It will take me twenty minutes to get there, so make sure I leave on time, please. The plan is for us all to return to the client's offices for lunch, followed by a meeting in the board room. The architects and accountants will also be present. Hopefully they can all put together a feasible deal. If you need me urgently, here is their number. Ask the receptionist to interrupt the meeting if necessary.

"She took the coffee from Sally and gulped quickly burning the roof of her mouth she cursed and added more milk. "Sally, would you be kind enough to get my briefcase ready with the files and of course a notebook.

Elizabeth put her head in her hands not knowing what to do. Sally poured her another cup of coffee, putting it on the desk beside her. "What's the matter?"

"Oh, it's the twins and the accident I really must stop thinking about it, it's beginning to affect my work. Did I hear DTM return? She always referred to David with his initials when speaking with staff it seemed less formal than Mr. Markham.

"Yes, I think so, if there is nothing else, I will go and get on," said Sally, leaving the room.

Elizabeth put her nose round David's door. He was removing files from his briefcase. He turned, "darling, come here," Without a word, she crossed the room, and nestled into his outstretched arms. "I started to feel a little better about the twins, but now I feel worse than ever. I don't want to move from the protection of your arms, I want to stay here forever." She whined.

David kissed the top of her head, "Now come on, you can do better than this. It wasn't your fault and you know it. I realise the whole thing is awful, but we have to carry on. You have a meeting shortly, haven't you?" She nodded. "Would you like me to go for you, I'm very tied up today, it would mean juggling appointments, a bit but if it would help I would be pleased to do it."

"No", she sighed, "you are a darling to offer, but of course I must go. After all, ninety per cent of the details are in my head anyway."

"Right then, give me a kiss and let's both get on", he said, more briskly than he had intended. By the time she closed the door, David's head was buried in a file.

Men were so different from women she thought; they very rarely allowed their emotions to affect them when they were working, whereas women have jumbled emotions floating through them all the time, which they had to control, subdue and try and understand all at once. Unfortunately, this was not always possible.

The meeting had gone fairly well. She would have to work on the details later whilst they were still fresh in her mind. Perhaps she would take the file home, she thought as she drove along to her client's office. If the planners agreed, it could be a very nice development which would of course mean, overall a good fat fee for the firm.

It was nice to have a lunch prepared by someone else for a change. Her clients employed a trained Cordon Bleu cook to prepare their meals daily. Elizabeth had enjoyed the French onion soup, followed by Coq au Vin and vegetables. Cheese was offered which she declined. She had been the only woman at the meeting, apart from the secretary taking notes. She was quite used to this, and none of the men seemed to mind. The lunch was slightly marred by the architect, Simon Bird, who had made a pass at her. He was more effusive than was normally acceptable, and suggested `entre nous` that they should have lunch together shortly to discuss the project in detail, as he respected her views. This was not the first time such a proposition had been made to her.

Laughing lightly she had told him that lunch would have to be sometime in the future, but if he wished to speak to her in the meantime, he could always ring her or call to see her at the office by appointment. She felt he had taken the hint and would probably not present any more problems, so long as she was careful.

The meeting had certainly succeeded in taking her mind off the twins, as had thoughts of their next holiday.

It was Easter shortly, and David had surprised her with tickets for the family to fly to Malta for a week. This would be her third visit to the island, and David's fourth. They were going to stay in the Sunny Isle Hotel, in St Julians. There was a lot of political unrest in Malta, the country wanted to be independent, and it was felt that the British Armed Forces would be withdrawn within months.

There was a wonderful sleepy pace about it. The people were very friendly. They had suffered very much at the hands of the Germans in the last war. The resistance came basically from the ordinary people, who had put up with everything the Luftwaffe could throw at them.

Yes, it certainly would be fun to see their old friends there again and to show off each other's families. The children were very excited. John and Robert had not flown before, but Elizabeth was sure they would take it all in their stride, children usually did. The temperature would probably be in the low seventies if they were lucky, so she was going to pack some warm clothes, just in case. It certainly would not be hot enough to swim in the sea. The sea usually warmed up from the end of May to October. Perhaps, if they all enjoyed their visit, they could go back in the summer holidays when it would be really hot. Carol and Pip were very anxious to get a tan, to show it off to their friends.

Elizabeth parked her car, retrieving her somewhat battered briefcase. It was a present from her parents before she went to university, an act of faith by them in her capabilities. Her initials were stamped on the inside hide. It was friendly and comfortable and had encompassed in it over the years a veritable cocktail of human problems.

It was five o'clock, and she was dying to get home and change into something more comfortable. Robert and John had spent the day with her parents. Carol and Pip were having piano lessons after school. One of the Mothers was bringing them home a group of them took it in turns.

If she hurried, she could be home before them. If they stayed to tea with their friends, which they sometimes did, this would give her even more of a breathing space.

Sally had put the post on her desk to sign, already franked to save time. In a separate basket, she had placed two complicated letters with the relevant documents and a note attached saying, "please check carefully".

Elizabeth was standing by her desk, signing the post, when Sally came in with a cup of tea. "Just off, I thought you would like this".

"Bless you, my dear, sorely needed." She drained the cup. Sally's face was expectant.

"Yes, Sally, good meeting, could be a very interesting site, a lot of work for us but rewarding if the clients are happy. I will tell you more tomorrow, Ah! Here are my messages!

She scrambled through them, making relevant notes.

"Right, see you tomorrow.

"Goodnight and thank you." She scuttled back to her car and then home.

The warm bubbles of that relaxing bath already seemed

very enticing. It all depended on whether the children were home first, and her luck had run out. She didn't mind really. She was just being a bit selfish and felt like being self indulgent. David's door had the engaged sign up, so she didn't bother to interrupt him before she left the office. The sooner he finished, the sooner he would be home, she thought.

CHAPTER TWENTY TWO

David in trouble

As a result of the Matrimonial Causes Act of 1969, David's life as a matrimonial lawyer, and for that matter all matrimonial lawyers, had been made easier and cheaper for the client.

The old stringent rules about condonation and the like had gone for good. Now, because of the new legislation, undefended cases were heard in the county court where Solicitors could represent their clients without needing to instruct a barrister. David also felt that his clients liked dealing with the same person throughout the case.

David had had two undefended divorces that day, his first under the new provisions. The preparation of the cases was very important in order to respond effectively to any awkward questions the Judge might raise. Luckily, he had two sensible clients, who had answered his questions without any prompting. All solicitors knew that it was a mistake to think you could tutor your clients beforehand. Some people simply went to pieces in the witness box.

The two cases were concluded in about ten minutes, much to the relief of all concerned.

He had a nucleus of permanent clients who always seemed to have new problems, for which of course he was very grateful. One of his clients, a Driving Instructor, had four personal accident claims going at the same time. She certainly made the claims inspectors a bit jumpy.

David was a tenor for the local choral society, and tonight they were rehearsing Handel's Messiah which he felt he couldn't miss. If he went straight there he could eat afterwards. It would also give him time to prepare his case for tomorrow.

The door opened and his Father came in.

"How did it go today?" he asked, sitting in the other wing chair usually reserved for clients. "Very well, the clients behaved superbly, answered all my questions. The Judge was a bit distant, but not unpleasant, and granted the decrees with no trouble, so I am very pleased. First time for me, a bit nerve- wracking how was your day?"

"Oh! I had quite a pleasant day getting on with my paper work. Amazing how much there is to do in some of these probates, especially when they keep changing the laws. I had an old client who came to see me today. He has a problem over one of his boundaries. Apparently one of the farmers is up to his old tricks again; the old business over ownership of the ditches. It's very simple. As far as I am concerned the person with hedge on their side owns the ditch, and vice versa. I will probably pop out and have a look myself.

David told him about his case tomorrow. "Sounds interesting if I have a moment I will creep in the back of the Court and listen to you on your feet. Goodnight, David, see you in the morning."

"Goodnight, Father, drive carefully."

*****

Elizabeth was in a foul temper when David got home. Carol and Pip and returned from school quarrelling. Apparently Pip had overrun her piano lesson and had kept Carol waiting. This infuriated Carol, who proceeded to upset Pip by calling her teacher's pet. Pip retaliated, and they had had a fight. By the time they got home they were both sulking and refusing to speak to each other. Tossing of heads and banging of doors

John and Robert were the reverse, returning from the afternoon with their granny, over-excited and full of energy. Elizabeth had left them for five minutes in their bath, and they splashed so much that the whole carpet was sopping wet. Using bath towels she had tried to soak it up, but it was still very wet she felt she would have to revert to lino at this rate. The little monkeys had found two empty shampoo caps and were competing as to how many capfuls they could ladle out of the bath.

She had bundled them into bed unceremoniously, with no bedtime story as a punishment. Feeling sorry for themselves they had both started to cry. Her head thumped.

To top it all she had just sat down with her paper when David phoned to say he was going to his b... choir practice straight from work and would eat later. Eating late did not agree with her, but she felt it rude to eat without him. In consequence, she had prepared the meal and was starving hungry by the time he got home at ten. She had thought he might be home at nine, and the waiting the extra hour had done nothing to calm her temper.

She blasted him as soon as he entered the house. Partly because he came in, grinning stupidly, trying to ingratiate himself, with his tail down, knowing or feeling he had done wrong. He could see that with one look at her face, although he wasn't quite sure why.

"What time do you call this?" she shouted. "I have had

a hard day as well today, you know, in fact I would go as far as to say I have worked far harder than you, which is not unusual. Not only have I done a full day's work, with a tough meeting thrown in, but as usual I have had to deal with the children and look after them on my own. They are your children as well you know. When was the last time you bathed them and cleared up their mess? Come on, tell me! You can't, because it was so long ago!"

"Darling, don't you think you are over reacting, I'm only forty five minutes late."

"No I don't, and please refrain from using that patronising tone with me. Save it for your clients.

"That remark is simply not worthy of you."

"I don't care!" she screamed; "the accident, your ex-wife, the children and their problems, the job, the office, the house everything. I have had enough. I am going to pack my bags and leave".

David slumped down in the kitchen chair, his head in his hands in disbelief. "I can't believe this is happening. Now you are making me angry, bloody angry in fact. I have had the temerity to spend three hours on my hobby, and the heavens descend. Well, it's not good enough." He slammed his fist down on the table. It was laid for dinner and the cutlery jumped in the air, landing crazily at different angles. Two glasses fell over. He watched as one rolled round on its side and fell splintering into many fragments on the ceramic floor.

He went on, "Many men spend hours playing golf or go down the pub or to their club all evening, not me. I only play golf occasionally and never go out without you, and this is all the thanks I get."

She turned measuring up to him, her face still contorted with rage. "How dare you, how bloody dare you, who the hell do you think you are, you pompous fool.

If it's such an effort for you to be with me, then don't bother. I can manage perfectly well on my own, probably better."

"You cow." He took hold of her wrists.

"That is a technical assault on my person", she shouted into his face. "Let me go at once."

"Don't be stupid", he said as he released her wrists, he gently pushed her back and turned away. She raised her clenched fists and beat him on the back. "Don't you dare turn your back on me, I'm going to my room and please do not follow me."

"You'll be lucky", he said.

She ran from the kitchen, locked the bedroom door and flung herself down on the bed. I hate him I hate him she thought as she punched the pillow in rage.

She lay back exhausted, staring at the ceiling, her heart beating quickly. She rolled over and started to cry, feeling very sorry for herself. Just at that moment she felt used, abused and unloved. Gradually her mind started to clear and feelings of remorse crept over her. She was still hungry and wanted her dinner. She really also wanted a cuddle as well. David had not followed her up to the bedroom. She had hoped he might. She stood up and looked in the bedroom mirror. What a sight, smudged mascara, red eyes, no lipstick and tousled hair. First things first, she went to the loo, straightened her clothing, and brushed her hair, enjoying the gentle massage which helped to sooth her.

She wiped the mascara off her face and put on some fresh lipstick. She unlocked the door and crept down stairs.

David had taken the stew out of the oven and was sitting with his back to the kitchen door, eating his meal and reading the Times. Men, she thought, impervious to everything except their stomachs.

She leaned back against the door waiting to be noticed.

He felt her presence and turned. His face gave nothing away. "So you have come down" he said, returning to his meal.

"Well, it looks like it, doesn't it I don't think you love me at all."

He put his knife and fork down with a sigh and looked at her. She started to weep again, consumed with self pity.

"Come here silly," he said, patting his knee. She slowly went and sat on his knee with her head bent, picking at her nails. A tear ran maddeningly down her nose, tickling her on its way and hanging on the tip before dropping into her lap.

"Don't you think you were a bit hard on me?" he said, gently. He put his hand on her shoulder to pull her to him. She resisted. "Now, come on."

She fell against him and promptly melted into his arms.

He kissed her, and they both laughed together, their kisses became more passionate, and he pulled away saying, "Hey can't a fellow eat his meal in peace. Please, may I finish, and by the way you are heavy, my thighs have gone to sleep."

She got up and helped herself to some stew. Pulled her chair close to him, they ate in silence, with only eyes for each other. "You are a silly Billy I thought you would be glad of a few hours peace and quiet."

"I don't really enjoy being without you," she said. "The children were awful this evening." She related the events of the evening to him. "Come on let's clear up together, and then its bed for us my girl." He patted her bottom affectionately. "Watch it", she smiled, "otherwise we'll never make it up the stairs."

He put his hand inside her blouse, stroking the soft folds of her warm skin as she was putting the food back into the fridge. "I really do fancy you" he said huskily as he kissed her ear. She squirmed, "come on, let's hurry up."

They ran giggling up to their bedroom. She lay back in his arms. He ran his hands through his hair and exhaled.

"There now, wasn't that a lot of fuss about nothing?"

It wasn't what he said; it was the tone of voice he used which annoyed her. The anger within her started to rise again.

She sat up fuming. "You have no conception of how deeply I was upset this evening, have you?" Without waiting for a reply she went on, "your returning home late was the tip of the iceberg that brought to the surface all the upsets and irritations I have been feeling for sometime I don't think you understand basic emotions at all".

He sat up. "Just because I don't go round shouting and screaming about my problems all the time doesn't mean I don't feel anything. You women think you have monopoly on emotions, and I for one am getting heartily sick of hearing and reading about it!"

She grabbed her nightie and put it on in front of him, her nakedness suddenly making her feel very self conscious. "I am going to sleep in the spare room." As she closed the door, David fell back on the pillow, rolled over and fell immediately asleep.

She lay in bed unable to sleep. The trouble was that once that she had stirred her emotions into such a state of frenzy, it was some days before she felt normal again. She eventually drifted into a restless sleep.

There was a polite, but cool, atmosphere between them over breakfast. The children were very subdued. It was either because they had been scolded yesterday or because they had heard the row which would obviously have upset them. Pip toyed with her cornflakes and, without looking up, said, "Why did you sleep in the spare room last night, Mummy?"

Elizabeth put down her toast, and Pip looked up into the direct gaze of her Mother. The look in Elizabeth's eyes did not encourage the question to be repeated.

"Sorry, Mummy", said Pip and continued with her breakfast.

Elizabeth spoke to David. "I will not be coming to the office today. Please inform Sally. I was supposed to have a half day, but I don't feel like putting in an appearance at all. I have enough work in my briefcase to keep me busy should I feel so inclined, which is unlikely at this moment in time."

"Very well, I will take the girls to school if it helps."

"That would be very kind," she said politely.

She rose to put the plates in the dishwasher. David got up at the same time. "Come on you two, you will have to hurry, as Daddy's already behind schedule, say goodbye to Mummy."

The children were clearly disturbed by the atmosphere but did as they were asked.

She heard David's car drive away and she turned her attention to the boys, who were watching her carefully. She immediately started to relax. She said out loud, "Mummy has a whole day off to be with you two, let's have a nice time".

Their confidence returned, and they both came and climbed into her arms. "OK. let's start with me reading you a story."

They sat as close as they could to her, one each side, and every now and then she stopped to give them a kiss and a hug.

They had a lovely day. After buying the provisions, they went to the beach and had a happy time throwing pebbles into the sea. Lunch at the Wimpy bar and then she bought them both a pair of new shoes, which they wore immediately. Their feet were growing so quickly. They had helped her choose a jumper each for the girls. Having picked them up from school, they all went to her friend Joyce for tea. She had children of similar age.

Elizabeth had deliberately not contacted the office during the day, which she normally would have done. Just for once they would have to do without her.

*****

David was feeling thoroughly out of sorts, having dropped two silent children off at school. He hated upset, especially when it affected the children.

Elizabeth certainly had a great deal on her plate at the moment, but he really hadn't meant to upset her yesterday. He would give up the choir if it helped. He wanted to make it up with her, but decided against ringing her in case she was still cross with him. He turned to his papers he really must concentrate on his case his client had the right to expect the best from him.

He was also relieved that Christine was being more sensible about her dress.

She had a new boyfriend who made her wear a bra and, thank goodness, not such tight clothing. It made him feel a lot better. Christine was certainly a temptation to any man.

As he filled his brief case with his books he toyed with the idea of getting rid of her again, and then headed off to Court.

When he returned he had a stack of second post to deal with. After lunch there had been an urgent call from a female client. She had been attacked and badly beaten by her husband and was phoning from the hospital. The police had confirmed the violence and felt in the circumstances that a non-molestation order would assist in this particular case. David usually felt that some non-molestation injunctions were a waste of the Court's and client's time, as minor matrimonial disturbances usually settled down after a few days, and rushing off to Court could alienate the clients even more.

In a bad case such as this he was left with no choice. He had to drop all his other work and make an immediate emergency application to the Judge for a restraint order against the husband. An emergency application to the judge meant he also had to drop everything to deal with it. This did not usually please the Judge. However, after hearing the details from David the Judge had granted the order for seven days when the husband would actually appear before the Court to explain himself. This temporary order restrained the husband from having any contact with his wife for seven days. David felt that at the full hearing he would succeed in obtaining an application for the husband to be ordered to vacate the matrimonial home for good, thus ending his wife's misery.

David turned the car ignition off and walked quietly into the house, unsure of the reception he was likely to receive.

As he walked into the hall, he was met by Elizabeth flying down the stairs. "Darling, it's so good to see you", she hurled herself into his arms and kissed him generously. "Oh, I have really missed you today and I am so sorry for being, well, you know", she trailed off.

He clasped his hands round her waist and swung her round in the air, drinking her in. "Well, this is a very nice welcome home for a chap. I wasn't sure what kind of reception I would get. I have had a hell of a day. I won both cases, tell you later. Give me another kiss". He stood back, she was wearing a blue chiffon cocktail dress her hair was sleek and shiny.

My, you look beautiful tonight". Elizabeth smiled widely with delight. "Thank you darling, I have had a lovely day with the children, did us all good. They went to bed like angels, gave me a chance to dress for dinner".

"What are we having, I'm starving?"

"Simple but nice; courgettes stuffed with prawns covered in a wine and cream sauce, steak, gratin dauphinois and salad. I have made your favourite crème Brule for pudding".

"That sounds smashing and not at all simple is it ready,

I am starving. I only had time for a sandwich at lunchtime".

"It certainly is. Well, I have to cook the steak and warm the courgettes, but that won't take long. I have already decanted a bottle of your favourite burgundy, just as you like it. Let's have an aperitif first"

She slid her arm through his and guided him towards the drawing room. David stood and watched as she poured them both a dry sherry. He raised his glass.

"A perfect end to an interesting day", he sighed with contentment. He kissed her very gently on the nose. "I love you so much let's have a nice cuddly evening.

CHAPTER TWENTY THREE

Jean goes to the Police

Jean was sitting alone in the flat when she suddenly realised she had not moved from the settee for two hours. Following the funeral of Geoffrey she was still in a confused state. Chain smoking, food had hardly passed her lips for the past forty eight hours, only endless cups of coffee.

When she had moved into the flat she had found a part time job at the corner shop. It gave her a few extra pounds a week over and above the social security money she received. She enjoyed the work it got her out of the flat, when she wasn't at the hospital. Seeing different people had cheered her up. Since Geoffrey's death she could not summon the energy to do anything and had simply not turned up.

Geoffrey's death had left her consumed with a burning hatred, mainly against Jack, who she felt had let her and the twins down very badly. But also for Elizabeth Markham, whom she felt had killed her child. No wonder she had wanted to make friends with me, she thought as she switched the kettle on again. I'm sure she didn't really care as she pretended to she was just worried about her own skin.

Professional people did not really take to people like her,

tarnishing their unblemished character. Well, it was all going to change now. She was going to see that Elizabeth Markham got her just deserts and suffered just as she had made her Geoffrey suffer. She could not bear the thought of anything happening to Nicholas she started to weep again. Her mind went back to the day of the funeral.

After the funeral she had walked in the garden of rest. Other people were there, either walking or just sitting quietly, like her, on one of the benches. It had rained during the service, but now the weather had cleared, the clouds had parted to let shafts of sun stream through, revealing a perfect blue sky behind. The layout of the garden had been planned with care, and gave an ambience of tranquillity. Some of the bushes were in full bloom, which she thought Geoffrey would like, he loved colours. She had requested his urn to be buried in the garden. She would have a tree planted and a plaque placed on the wall behind it in his memory.

The wind was very cold even for April and she had hugged her anorak round her tightly trying to keep warm; she could not remember how long she had been sitting on the bench time seemed to have stood still.

Jack had obviously been in the chapel throughout the service; she had only noticed him when she was sitting on the bench.

He had turned and looked at her over his shoulder as he was led away. Their eyes met, she turned aside weeping.

Somehow staying there had made her feel closer to Geoffrey. Thoughts kept floating through her mind, how she had failed him in so many ways. If only she had the courage to return to her parents. They would probably welcome her with open arms. No, on reflection, she thought she had created a divide too wide to breach at any rate just at the moment.

*****

She rose from the settee, still in a daze and nearly fell backwards from weakness, her head was spinning. You are so stupid, she thought, the nurse had been quite right to reprove her. She had to keep her strength up for Nicholas, so she must eat. She went into the kitchen and foraged around in the fridge. She found a hard piece of cheddar cheese and a slice of old luncheon meat curling up at the edges. She put the two together in a sandwich and rammed the unappetising food into her mouth. She surprised herself again she immediately started to feel a little better. At the back of the cupboard she found some cornflakes. A bowl of those with yet another cup of coffee, made her feel quite full.

She now knew exactly what she was going to do.

As she entered the ward there was a festive air, all the children who were well enough were playing games and laughing.

There were presents and birthday cards around a little boy, who although he couldn't move from his bed was smiling and enjoying the others fun. Nicholas was sitting up in his cot, propped up by pillows he smiled at her as he continued to bang two bricks together happily, biscuit crumbs were all over his bed. Sister appeared by her side.

"How are you, my dear?"

"I'm fine, or as well as can be expected in the circumstances", Jean managed to smile.

"That's the spirit", sister countered slightly awkwardly. "Well, I know you will be pleased, Nicholas is coming along in leaps and bounds. We are delighted with his progress and are hoping to discharge him shortly, if you feel you can cope". Jean smiled for the first time in ages. "That is brilliant news, can I hold him?"

"Of course you can, just be a little careful with him".

Sister watched as Jean picked up Nicholas who was very excited and squealed with glee. Jean sat down clutching him to her, rocking him gently and supporting his back.

"Now, don't upset yourself or Nicholas, please you will spoil the fun and they are all having such a good time. You sit there and I'll get you a piece of birthday cake."

Sister reappeared. "Would you like to give him his tea, my dear, although I'm not sure he will eat much, too many biscuits and cakes. You'll be surprised what they can eat when they try."

Jean laughed in spite of her inner feelings of turbulence.

She bent and kissed him all over his face he giggled and nuzzled into her. Jean found herself helping with feeding the other children as well. So many sweets, Nicholas had managed to get chocolate from ear to ear. After settling him down for the night she waved to Sister and left.

Scarborough police station was in the middle of town, just a short bus ride from the hospital. The desk sergeant looked up as Jean walked in and nodded at the constable beside him, who rose and approached the counter. "Good evening Madam, how can I help you?"

"My name is Jean Brown and I want to know what is happening about my twins being knocked down in cold blood by Mrs. Elizabeth Markham. I suppose you know one of my babies has just died as a result of the accident." Her anger and hatred had returned, and her resolved hardened. The constable was completely taken back by the violence in her tone. He had no personal knowledge of the case.

On the other hand the desk sergeant, who was listening, chewing on his pencil thoughtfully, was only too aware of this particular matter. The involvement of a solicitor had caused some consternation in the station. The constable began to look flustered he was probably no more than nineteen years old. He had yet to fill out physically as a man. Having only been out of police cadet school for six weeks, he was somewhat green when it came to dealing with the general public.

The sergeant rose to his feet, overweight, short, about forty five, greying at the temples. Putting down his pencil he muttered. "Leave it, John, I will deal with the lady."

The constable stepped back, grateful to be relieved of this situation. He sat down within earshot hoping to learn from the sergeant. As he pushed back his chair, to get up, one of the legs got stuck in a hole in the aged linoleum which was worn through where the chair had been in the same position for years. The pile of waste paper was mostly due to attempts by various constables throughout the day to produce cogent and correctly spelt reports to be sent upstairs for scrutiny by the inspector. The police force was run very much like the army. There was a serious pecking order, which meant the lower echelons had a hard time.

"Sergeant Williams, at your disposal, Madam" he smiled at Jean, although it was more of a wince. He was suffering from indigestion. He had had a large fried tea of sausages, eggs, bacon, beans and chips, treacle pudding and two cups of tea to wash it down. He decided it was definitely the treacle pudding causing his distress. He tried to wriggle his trousers into a more comfortable position. He looked at the clock on the wall he would certainly have to go to the gents soon. He went on, "I think I know the case you refer to, Madam, if you would take a seat over there, I will get my constable here to locate the papers".

Jean's fist came down on the desk. "I'll not be put off I want some action now".

"All right, Madam, all in good time, please sit down."

Jean decided to sit down on the hard bench without making any more fuss and looked miserably round the police station. They certainly missed this place when it came to dishing out comfort, she thought.

A smartly dressed man in a dark suit clutching a briefcase entered, walking very quickly, through the swing doors to the desk and asked for directions to Robin Hood's Bay.

As John was busy, another constable came to the aid, producing a large scale map he set about showing the man the way. Having giving him the necessary assistance he left; meanwhile John had returned to his original position, bent double over the filing cabinet searching through the papers trying to find Jean's file. "Come on, come on!" muttered the sergeant testily, "we haven't got all day".

"Sorry, Sarge, but the papers are not in alphabetical order "he wailed.

"Well, they should be" the sergeant replied querulously. "That's your next job, son, you can set about getting this filing cabinet in order all four drawers. If you keep at it you should finish before this shift is over".

"Yes Sarge. Thanks". The young constable acknowledged mournfully. "Here are your papers!"

The sergeant relieved him of them without comment. He lifted the barrier and turned to Jean. "Would you like to come into the interview room it's more private".

Jean stood up and followed him.

Sergeant Williams sat down opposite Jean, placing the file on the table. His trousers still felt very tight. He wondered if she would notice if he undid the top button; on reflection he thought she would. He strained to pull his girth in.

"There is a note on the file stating we are waiting for a report from the hospital doctors. I thought you were friendly with Mrs. Markham". He spoke tentatively.

Jean was ready for this and exploded, she was so anxious to put her side of the story. "I suppose you know, Geoffrey died a week ago. It is all the fault of that woman. Oh! Yes! She wanted everyone to think we were friends, well, we are not. She came to my house, saying it would be better for me and the twins if no fuss was made. She made it clear if I refused to give evidence, the police's case would be weakened, and she would be able to fix me up with a flat and help financially, on the side of course, as the boys grow up. Well, it all seemed very tempting to someone in my position. I have had a lot to contend with. Here she was with her clever talk, fine clothes and large house persuading me not to give evidence against her. After all, if we were friends I could hardly stand up in court and speak out against her, could I? Well, I worked out what she was up to, and I am not having it!" Once again she banged the table by way of emphasis. She continued, raising her voice.

"I want that woman locked up for killing my Geoffrey and injuring poor Nicholas. What about damages? I should be entitled to some money for the injuries. You see I went to see the Citizens Advice Bureau!" She leaned back in her chair folding her arms with a self satisfied smile on her face.

"These are very serious allegations you are making against Mrs. Markham, Miss Brown. Are you prepared to make a statement to us and repeat what you have just told me, in Court, under oath?"

"I am!"

"Well, we will have to go into details a little more specifically when you make a statement with dates, times and places."

Just then the sergeant's stomach made a rumbling noise, like the sound of the bath water dispersing down the plughole. It went on for a good half minute and was too loud for him to disguise. He stood up, colouring profusely.

"If you would excuse me a moment madam?" Closing the door to the interview room behind him, he darted a quick look at the desk and reception area. No one around, all clear, he thought. He ran across the office to the gents toilets, unbuttoning his trousers and pulling them down as he did so. John who was still labouring over the filing cabinet, raised his head just enough to see the amazing apparition run past, and collapsed in helpless laughter on the floor.

Jean was, grateful for a breathing space to put her thoughts in order. She was glad he had popped out to the toilet she supposed. She knew she would have to get times and dates correct. This shouldn't be too difficult as she had already given the matter a great deal of thought. She had worked herself into such a state she was absolutely determined to see the matter through. She thought that the sergeant was behaving a little strangely.

Just then the door opened and he returned, looking considerably more comfortable. He resumed his seat.

"Now, madam, if you are ready to give a statement I will get a constable to come and take it down. We will then have it typed and ask you to check it before signing it, to satisfy yourself that the contents are correct."

Jean nodded. "I am ready as soon as you are". She returned his steady gaze.

CHAPTER TWENTY FOUR

The Arrest

They all felt much better for the week's holiday in Malta. After arriving home in the early evening it was mutually agreed that David did the unpacking whilst Elizabeth put the children to bed.

The shower refreshed her and she decided to put on a pale blue leisure robe, after all she did not expect to see anyone.

She picked up the weeks mail from the hall table and settled down in the drawing room to open it. The handwriting on one of the envelopes caught her eye, she opened it and gasped. It was from Jean and it read...

"Dear Mrs Markham, Please do not call round to my flat, I never want to see or speak to you again, signed Jean Brown."

David appeared carrying a large armful of clothes. He took one look at her downcast expression.

"What's the matter with you?" She handed him the letter without speaking. David took it, read it, and sighed, as he said. "Oh, dear, what on earth is she up to?"

Elizabeth just shook her head silently and carried on opening the mail David cupped his hand under her chin, making her look at him. "Cheer up darling

Would you mind if I popped down to the office just

to see what has been happening while we were away". She smiled weakly.

"No, of course not, darling"!

Bending over he kissed her forehead, "Don't worry. I won't be long". She heard the click as the front door closed. She slumped back in the chair, staring into space and remained there for about half an hour without moving. The sound of the door bell made her jump. She put her hand to her thumping heart as she went to answer it. Tying her robe more securely round her waist and muttering to herself, "I bet David's forgotten to take his key," she flung open the front door to find two police officers on the step. She couldn't help but notice both men looked her up and down. Automatically, her hands went across her body protectively.

"I am very sorry I thought you were my husband forgetting his key". The policemen shifted uncomfortably. "No, madam, but you should be a little more careful when you open the front door you don't know who may be on the other side. Is it all right if we come in for a moment and have a word with you madam?" She nodded.

They entered the hall, closing the door behind them. "Would you mind if we waited for your husband to return?

"Yes, and yes, of course. Please sit down, my husband has gone to the office. He should be back shortly. In fact, as you know I thought you were him. Would you please tell me what is the problem?"

"All, in good time madam, we'd rather stand if you don't mind, spend too much time these days sitting down".

Elizabeth found she was reacting to their formal behaviour. She felt weak at the knees. "I hope you don't mind if I sit down." she gratefully sank onto one of the hall chairs.

The two officers stood with their hands clasped behind their backs. No one spoke, the atmosphere was terrifyingly still. They remained in this position until David appeared about five minutes later.

As he burst through the front door, he said, "What on earth's going on?"

One of the constables replied "Glad you are back, sir, now we can get on with it."

He turned and directed himself at Elizabeth. "Mrs Elizabeth Markham, I am arresting you on a charge of causing death by dangerous driving on the 10th of March 1970 to Geoffrey Brown. Anything you say may be taken down and may be used in evidence against you."

Elizabeth slid off the chair like a rag doll in a complete faint. David picked her up and carried her into the drawing room and then laying her on the settee; he turned to the senior officer. "I'm sure she will recover in a few minutes. I would like to come with her to the station, if possible. The two men nodded.

"Would you be able to hang on while I call Mrs. Fraser and ask her to babysit for an hour or two? She only lives round the corner?"

"Yes, just as long as it doesn't take too long."

After phoning Mrs Fraser, David went over to the Sheraton desk in the drawing room.

Pulling open one of the drawers, he rummaged for the smelling salts he knew were in there somewhere. Putting his arm round Elizabeth to support her, he sat her up, waving the smelling salts near her nose.

"Come on, old girl, got to pull through. Now, take deep breaths. You have got to get dressed and go down to the police station. I am coming with you; Mrs Fraser will babysit whilst we are gone. I won't leave you."

Elizabeth opened her eyes and stared at David, whilst her brain was busy remembering what had just happened.

David was distressed at the sight of her ashen colour.

Her heart was pounding, her head was splitting. "Could I please have a brandy?" She gulped it down too quickly and coughed and spluttered. Composing herself quickly she said. "I think I can trust my legs now." She leaned on David as he guided her up the stairs to dress. As she passed the constable standing in the hall, she managed to say in an incredibly dignified voice. "So sorry to keep you waiting"!

Once in her bedroom, some of her old fighting spirit returned as she yanked her dress unceremoniously over her head. Whipping the brush through her hair, she foraged in the wardrobe with her feet for a pair of shoes. A splash of lipstick, and she was ready. David held out her coat. She put it on, and grabbing her handbag, she positively ran down the stairs. She had now got a complete grip on herself.

"I'm ready", she announced.

"Just a quick word with Mrs Fraser before we go, you don't mind".

She ran into the kitchen. "Mrs Fraser, you are a darling, it's very kind of you to turn out at this time of night. I hope they won't keep me..." her voice trailed off. Mrs Fraser squeezed her arm. Walking back to the hall Elizabeth said

"Right let's go".

"I'll follow in my car", David shouted as he unlocked the garage door.

Elizabeth was escorted into the charge room after her fingerprints and photograph had been taken. Sergeant Williams accompanied by the Inspector and a constable sat opposite her. The Sergeant seemed to be a bit nervous but managed to repeat the charge. "You are released on bail to appear at the Scarborough Magistrates Court for the preliminary hearing on the 6th of May, in two weeks time. Have you anything to say?"

Elizabeth replied, "No, I have already made a statement."

"Should you wish to alter your statement, at any time, please let me know, but of course you already know the procedure, madam you are not planning to leave the country in the near future?" he said awkwardly.

"No, Sergeant, I'm not".

"Well, I need not detain you any more I wish you goodnight". With that, he left the room, followed by the Inspector. Elizabeth turned and left the charge room only to find David sitting on a bench in reception.

They drove home in silence. When they arrived, Mrs. Fraser had the coffee ready, and with her impeccable discretion, silently withdrew and went home.

Stirring his coffee, he looked glum "That's not all the bad news. I knew there was trouble brewing here was a letter from the Law Society, awaiting our return. It would seem that Jean Brown has written to them complaining about you, accusing you of unprofessional conduct by misusing your position as a solicitor. They require an explanation". Elizabeth felt her inner strength growing. It would seem she was under attack from all sides. Well, she would have to draw herself up to her full height and stand up for herself.

"Well they will have to be informed of the impending prosecution against me. Presumably, the committee will then wait for the result of the hearing before deciding on what action, if any. It's going to be quite difficult for the Police. They will have to find local magistrates who don't know me. I would have thought the trial itself would have to be heard out the area. The Old Bailey is possibly the safest bet".

"I agree, but we will have to wait and see" David said as he sipped his coffee. He went on as if thinking out loud. "I want to know why the police now feel so confident!"

*****

The headlines from the local paper blazed at them over the breakfast table, the following morning.

LOCAL SOLICITOR CHARGED WITH CAUSING DEATH BY DANGEROUS DRIVING.

There was a large picture of Elizabeth. The article went on to give details of the accident and personal information about her.

"Well", said David, leaning back in his chair. "They didn't waste much time, did they?"

Elizabeth white and drawn sat sipping her coffee. The children ate their breakfast in complete silence. Suddenly John, sensing the strained atmosphere, burst out crying. David reached across and picked him up.

"Come on, old chap", John clung to him sobbing. "Look", David felt the need to restore confidence, "It's all going to be all right".

"But we don't understand," said Carol, "what's happened?"

"Well, I will tell you, but you must promise not to chatter to your friends, even if they ask, which I'm sure they will; promise?" He looked from Carol to Pip.

They both said in chorus, "We promise, Daddy".

David proceeded to outline briefly the events leading up to Elizabeth being charged.

Mrs Fraser popped her head round the door.

"Mrs Markham, the press are at the door waiting to speak to you, and there is also a gentleman on the telephone". Elizabeth looked up.

"I was half expecting them! Please tell them I have nothing to say at the moment but I will issue a statement later on today". She raised her eyebrows at David for approval. He nodded. Mrs Fraser said, "Leave them to me"!

David resumed his explanation to the children.

"I'm not saying it will be easy for you when you go back to school, but you must refuse to discuss anything I have told you with anyone. I will speak with your Headmistress before term starts."

Carol and Pip's eyes shone like beacons from their innocent faces.

"Poor Mummy", said Pip, "I do love you", John feeling the atmosphere had settled and a little of the tension had been dispersed, remembered he was still hungry, slid off his Father's knee and resumed his seat at the table and proceeded to finish his breakfast.

A familiar figure burst into the kitchen and walked straight over to Elizabeth, who rose and ran to greet her. "Mother" she exclaimed.

Elizabeth put her arms round her. The loving protection of your mother never really waned, regardless of how old you were. Hilda took Elizabeth's arms from around her neck, and gently held them in front of her. They looked lovingly into each other's eyes and then fell into each other's arms again. Hilda stroked her hair.

"Come on my girl, I've come to take the children away for a few days to give you both some breathing space."

Jonas kicked off his wet shoes as he came into the kitchen. Elizabeth looked up. Extricating herself from her Mother, she flew into his open arms.

"Daddy, you as well"!

Tears welled in his eyes, as Elizabeth wept on his shoulder. He cradled her, rocking her backwards and forwards.

"There, there, my pet, you have a good cry on your old Dad".

"I'm sorry", she said, "I am making a fool of myself; self

pity I suppose. Useless emotion, never helps, it's just so nice to see you both"

She blew her nose loudly.

"Aye lass, well you know we are all behind you. It's not going to be easy, especially with the practice and all. Some clients are going to be upset".

David stood up and waved for them to follow him into the sitting room. They all traipsed through, the children followed, clasping their grandparents hands confidingly.

"I do realise, Daddy" Elizabeth answered, "that there will obviously be some clients who may go elsewhere, and it concerns me a great deal. David and I intend going to the office first thing to explain everything to Christopher.

We haven't had time yet, and we don't want him to find out from a third party. Let's hope he hasn't read the local rag this morning". She flicked her hair back from her face and continued.

"I will issue a press release shortly, which hopefully will stop a bit of the harassment. After all, they will be looking for anything newsworthy up to the trial. It's possible they may contact you."

Jonas shifted in his chair. "Well, you know there'll not get much joy from us. Your mother and I will tell them to bugger off, perhaps not in those words, but you know what I mean".

"I certainly do," Elizabeth said, laughing in spite of the misery she felt.

The children were standing in the hall with their overnight cases, clutching their favourite cuddly toys. They looked so desolate and glum. Elizabeth went over to embrace them. She knelt down and cuddled each one in turn.

"Mummy's sorry, but she didn't do anything wrong you must believe me. I love you all so much".

"And we love you", they all mumbled. Tears were running down their cheeks.

"Come on, cheer up, you will have a nice time with Granny and Granddad. Mummy and Daddy will try and sort things out. I will ring you this evening before you go to bed."

David helped them load up the car. Jonas slipped the Volvo estate into gear, and the car went slowly down the drive. The children's noses were pressed to the windows waving and smiling bravely.

David, standing at the door, saw a man hovering in the drive. He gesticulated to him, waving him off the property, grabbed Elizabeth and pulled her inside the house, closing the door firmly. "Right, the first thing is that statement I suggest short and sweet.'Mrs Elizabeth Markham intends to plead not guilty to the charge and has nothing further to add at this stage.' I think that is all that is needed."

"It sounds fine to me", said Elizabeth.

"O.K.", David moved down the hall, "I will just phone the office. Oh! There is the phone now. I'll get it", he shouted to Mrs. Fraser.

CHAPTER TWENTY FIVE

Heart Attack.

After the children left Elizabeth went straight upstairs and lay on the bed. Two minutes later David came haring up the stairs two at a time, nearly knocking over the flower arrangement on the landing.

"It's my father", he gasped. "He's just collapsed at the office. The ambulance is on its way. I must go, sounds like a heart attack".

"I'll follow", shouted Elizabeth. David grabbed his jacket, flew down the stairs and, leapt into the car and tore off with wheels spinning.

Elizabeth put her head in her hands. She didn't feel she could cope with any more traumas. She took a few deep breaths to try and calm down. She had started to hyperventilate, it always happened to her when she was stressed. Feeling giddy, she sat back on the bed. Poor Christopher, she must go to him at once. Unfortunately, from experience she knew that if she hurried she would probably collapse. Having showered and dressed, she put on a navy and white dress with a pleated skirt. She found she needed to hold on to the wardrobe for support. After a final glance in the mirror she went to find Mrs. Fraser, who had just finished clearing the dishes away.

"I suppose you heard, we think Christopher has had a heart attack or a stroke. I must go".

"The family seems to be going through a bad patch at the moment. Poor Mr. Christopher, such a lovely man, gentleman of the old school".

"I must be going."

"Dear, oh dear", muttered Mrs. Fraser as she watched Elizabeth drive away, "whatever's going to happen next".

David arrived as the ambulance men were carrying his father out of the office on a stretcher. Christopher was conscious, but his face had the pallor of death about it. He saw David, and, retrieving his hand from under the blanket, he held it out and David clasped it.

"So sorry, what a time for me to make a fool of myself"!

"Nonsense, I'm coming with you". David's secretary, Christine, was hovering by the door of the ambulance looking anxious. David leant out and handed her the press release, which he had managed to scribble out.

He said urgently in a hushed tone, "Phone that through to the local paper, and that's all you tell them, or anyone else who asks, until further notice. See you later", He closed the door and went to his father's side.

The ambulance pulled away. His father lifted his head, and tried to talk.

"Leave it Dad just rest, I want to get you to the hospital as quickly as possible".

One of the ambulance men was sitting beside Christopher, with his hand on his wrist, checking his pulse. He suddenly banged the floor with his foot.

"Come on, Harry, put your foot down and get that siren ringing". The ambulance started to zig zag crazily weaving between the morning traffic. Christopher seemed to have lost consciousness.

"Make sure the cardiac unit have been alerted I'm going to give him some oxygen, don't like his colour!"

"It's already done mate first thing I did." His colleague shouted.

David held the canister still while the ambulance man held the mask to his father's face. At last they arrived and the doors were hurled open by a waiting team. Then they were all running with the trolley through the swing doors, white coats flying, a nurse climbed onto the trolley as they ran, and, sitting astride Christopher, started massaging his heart.

A Doctor came running down the corridor his bleeper going. He caught David's arm. "Are you a relative?"

David nodded, "Son"

"Well, take a seat over there, nothing you can do, we'll do all we can", he shouted, as he disappeared through the swing doors. David was left pacing the corridor.

It was at times like this he wished he smoked.

When Elizabeth arrived at the office, she was met by a stunned atmosphere. She found the girls were carrying out their duties in a most perfunctory way. Joan was sitting at her typewriter, crying unashamedly.

"Joan, I hope you are not too upset?" Joan looked up, snuffled and fled to the ladies.

"Whilst we are all here together, I can talk to you. It is obviously dreadful, Mr Christopher collapsing this morning. I am going straight down to the hospital. As for my problems, whilst my arrest last night came as a surprise, I have been half expecting something to happen, especially after Jean Brown estranged herself from me. You all know my side as to how the accident occurred. We must, of course, all pull together for the sake of the practice. However, if anyone of you wishes to leave because of possible embarrassment, then I will quite understand". She paused for some response.

They all shook their head.

"No, we are all ok." said Christine, "we'll hold the fort until you get back".

Elizabeth smiled gratefully, and swept out.

*****

She found David still waiting in the hospital corridor. "Any news"?

"No, doctors and nurses keep coming in and out but ignore me completely. I feel so useless!"

"I'll get you a coffee from the machine". He drank his gratefully; he had been completely devastated by the events of the last twenty four hours.

At last a pre-occupied Doctor emerged from the unit.

Elizabeth broke his train of thought by demanding,

"Would you please tell us what is going on? She practically whispered. "My husband has been here for two hours and we are very worried"?

The Doctor turned towards them.

"Your father has suffered a coronary heart attack. He has arrested once. He will shortly be transferred to the intensive care unit. You can see him for a few minutes, but please keep talking to a minimum we don't want him stressed in any way." Just then his bleeper went.

"Excuse me, I'm may be wanted urgently".

He ran to the nearest phone in the corridor and dialled. He then dashed off in the opposite direction, without a further glance at Elizabeth or David.

David felt the tears starting to well up, first his Mother, now his Father, who was still comparatively young. He could kick himself for not contacting him last night, however late, to let him know about Elizabeth, and to reassure him. In the long run it may not have helped, but now he would never know. He put his head on Elizabeth's shoulder. "These last few months have seemed like a terrible nightmare." He said dolefully.

Another doctor swished past, a nurse appeared and came over to them and whispered to David.

"You can come in for a few minutes, don't be frightened by all the wires, they are very necessary".

David rose and followed the nurse. The room was fairly small and full of equipment. The doctors were still waiting for a bed to become available in the intensive care unit. His father was lying on the same trolley that he had arrived on. David bent over and kissed him on the forehead, then took his hand and squeezed it gently. There was a flicker of a squeeze in return.

"Come on, Dad, you can pull through. I don't want you to worry about anything, everything is under control, concentrate on yourself and rest, you look tired. I love you very much, as we all do".

Outside David turned to her.

"I must get back to my office, when can I visit again?"
"Well, anytime, depending on his condition. We have your telephone number. If there are any problems we will phone you immediately."

"Thank you", David said, as he took Elizabeth's arm and led her away. He turned.

"I really am most grateful to the nurses and doctors for the efforts they have put in this morning to save my father". She smiled and was gone.

CHAPTER TWENTY SIX

Jack meets his Solicitor

Jack Big's cell mates were Micky Smith and Sean Winder. They had been on their guard with him at first, but eventually they slowly started to acknowledge his existence, with the occasional grunt, and odd word. A disturbance on the wing caused by an inmate slashing his wrists finally broke down the barriers and a conversation on mutual misery and the unfairness of life ensued.

*****

Jack had made a formal request for a solicitor to represent him and he picked Mr Basil Newcomb from a list presented to him.

The key turned in the lock and the steel cell door swung open. "Big, your Brief is here, move yourself". Jack swung his large frame down from the top bunk.

Winking at the other two, he followed the warder on to the landing. He wondered as he walked down the endless corridors what this geezer would be like, in any event, he felt that all lawyers were fuddy duddies covered in cobwebs and had very little idea of what real life was all about.

Basil Newcomb was a bespectacled man, twenty-five years old, with thinning hair. He was rather a timid man and didn't know why he had opted to specialise in criminal matters, because most people frightened him anyway. His mother had been so powerful and demanding that he had been left introverted and unsure of himself. He stood up as Jack entered the visitor's room. No special room had been allocated for the interview; they had to mingle with the other prisoners and their visitors.

He put out his hand to Jack. Jack noted the wet clammy handshake and wiped his hand involuntarily on his trousers. The warder nodded to Newcomb completely ignoring Big, and sauntered off.

Mr Newcomb opened the conversation.

"I understand you have been charged with GBH I would like to hear from you what actually happened?"

Jack looked him straight in the eye, "If you read it properly, you will see. It says GBH on two counts plus rape and carrying an offensive weapon".

"Yes, I see, but how will you plead?"

"Not guilty, of course".

Mr Newcombe's eye twitched, it always happened when he was nervous. "By that, you are saying that you didn't do any of it?"

"Well, I'm not exactly saying that, can't really after what happened to Billy and Taffy. It's just that it wasn't my fault, so I don't think I'm guilty, if you get my drift".

"Yes, yes, I see. Perhaps we can go through the events carefully". Newcomb shifted in his chair, produced his notebook and prepared to take notes.

"Tell me about Billy and Taffy?"

"Well, it's like I said, I don't know how they got in such a bloody mess. After all, they provoked me and hit me first. I just defended myself, it weren't my fault".

Mr Newcomb broke into a sweat. He'd only been qualified a few months and felt his inexperience was showing. Beads of perspiration were forming on his forehead.

"Yes, yes, I see, but you put them both in hospital with serious injuries. You are claiming self defence and provocation, but what about the knife wound?"

"I don't know where it came from!"

"But you did use it?

"I can't remember".

"But you must".

"No, I can't"

"Yes, yes, I see".

Jack started to get angry, this man annoyed him.

"I wish you would stop saying 'I see', you are getting on my bloody nerves."

Mr Newcomb dropped his pen. He blew his nose loudly and mopped his brow.

Jack wondered how he'd got this mushed up effigy of a human being to represent him.

"No, I think we will have to get a barrister."

"I think we will, an all".

"Do you know someone, or will you take pot luck with my choice?

"Pot luck, it seems that sort of a day".

Newcomb looked up, obviously missing the irony. Jack grinned to himself.

"Never mind mate, you carry on writing", said Jack.

"Now, what about Jean Brown, there is a charge of GBH and rape against her?"

"I know that".

"Well, what have you to say?"

"Didn't do it, did I? How can you rape your girlfriend,

I ask you". He leant back in his chair. He went on, his voice taking on a confiding tone.

"No, she's just a lying slag she's got it in for me because I won't marry her".

"But you did go and see her after the fight?"

"Aye"!

"Was she all right when you left?"

"Listen, mate, when I go with a woman they're always all right know what I mean!"

Jack fell about laughing at his own joke and nudged Newcomb's elbow in a friendly way. Newcomb concentrating on his writing was caught unawares. The elbow he was leaning on slipped off the table and he lost his balance and nearly cracked his chin on the table. The Warder moved forward quickly. Other visitors and inmates turned their heads to watch the commotion.

"Big, sit up and behave otherwise, I'll bang you up!" Jack sat back in his chair, touching his forelock in mock salute to the warder.

Newcomb recovered his equilibrium.

"Well, no doubt they will have medical evidence in support".

"I don't care about that she could have been with another bloke for all I know".

"I suppose so;" it took Newcomb another uncomfortable hour to take a detailed statement from Jack, finally he looked up.

"Would you please sign this application form for legal aid? Once legal aid has been granted I will send the papers to a barrister, who will want a conference with you, well before the hearing. I will be in contact with you. Here's my card, should you want to get in touch in the meantime".

We haven't exactly got a phone in the cell, you know".

"You certainly like your little joke. Anything serious and the Governor's office will contact me. Well, nice meeting you Mr Big I'll say goodbye for now". He and left with his briefcase under his arm.

Jack stood up and stretched. The Warder moved towards him bringing with him another screw with whom he had been conferring with. He muttered at Big under his breath. "Move your bloody self".

'Here we go', thought Jack.

They went into the corridor two other warders were already there. They nodded at each other, and moving as one pushed Jack into a small empty cell. His arms were grasped either side. He knew what was coming. The warder, whom he had cheeked, said.

"Mr bloody smartarse needs teaching a lesson. He hit Jack hard in the solar plexus, but Jack had stomach muscles like iron. He hit him again. Jack held his breath, grimaced and withstood the blow.

"Christ, you're pushing your luck, sonny!"

With that, he brought his boot up between Jack's legs. Jack moaned and crumpled on the floor, which is where they left him.

CHAPTER TWENTY SEVEN

Michael's Hunch Pays Off

Michael, Elizabeth's brother latest obsession was to know where Jack Big had been hiding for the missing three weeks after the stabbing. His curiosity had been roused by the man in the boat he had seen from his plane out at Robin Hood Bay. Whoever it was must have been a good sea man otherwise he would not have dared to go out in the aftermath of the previous storms. Michael had known the whereabouts of the fishing fleet on that particular day, and they were nowhere in the area. He had asked various men whether there was someone fishing in that locality, but they knew nothing.

He decided to take a walk up to the Bay, once there he could take a look round, but did not to mention the germ of an idea forming in his mind to anyone. He tried to put himself in Jack's position on the night he had injured Taffy and Billy. Undoubtedly, Jack would have travelled on foot that night so he couldn't have gone that far.

On Saturday morning he set off at the crack of dawn. It was a beautiful day, and the sun glistened on the heather.

"By heck, it is a grand day" he said out loud as he set off at a steady pace.

The exercise would do him good anyway. At last the Bay came into sight.

Robin Hood's Bay was used by smugglers over the centuries. He stood looking around from the cliff; it was a sheer drop down to the beach. As he slowly negotiated a path down he noticed a shack which was partly hidden by the undergrowth on a protruding shelf. On further investigation he found evidence of habitation. The path to the padlocked door was trampled flat. Peering through the window, he could make out shapes in the darkness, which clearly told him someone had been living there. Now for the boat! He followed the flattened grass to the cliff edge, wondering how anyone could have got down from there. Accidentally, he pushed against some bracken which gave way, revealing a pathway down the rock face. It was risky descent and meant jumping from rock to rock. He knew when the tide was due to turn and checked his watch. The currents and tides along this coast changed with great speed. He decided to risk it and scrambled down his boots gripped well but he tore his jacket on a jagged rock and cursed silently under his breath. At last he was at sea level, and he sat down on a rock trying to regain his breath.

"What the hell am I doing down here, I must be nuts", he exclaimed. Standing up, he surveyed the long bay; knowing there were many caves; he had to find one that Jack would have thought was well hidden. Scrambling along the boulders, he noticed a trickle of water running into an opening, which ran between two huge rock formations.

He rubbed his chin thoughtfully, at high tide the gap would be wide enough for a small boat to go through.

Taking the torch out of his pocket, he edged his way into the cave. Two disturbed gulls swooped noisily over his head.

It opened up and got larger as it recessed. At last he

reached the back which was in complete darkness, the ground was bone dry and sloped upwards. His torchlight caught the edge of what looked like tarpaulin. He pulled it back. There it was the boat. At further examination he stopped with amazement. He recognised the boat which belonged to him and his father. It was supposed to have sunk months ago. "Well I'll be damned, it looks like the morning had been worthwhile after all," he exclaimed.

He decided that later on, he would bring some men with another boat, and tow it back to the harbour. His eyes had now become accustomed to the dim light and he sat down chuckling, taking in the surroundings; so this is where Jack Big had spent most of his time, the old fox. Pretty gloomy to be in here for long, but then Jack was an odd man, and a wanted man's priorities would be bound to change. Michael realised he must make a move, before the tide cut him off. He re-covered the boat securely with the tarpaulin and edged his way out. One look at the sheer rock face was enough he decided to return by a more normal route along the shoreline. He was suddenly feeling rather chuffed with himself.

*****

The children had soon forgotten the gloom of home, and their boisterous spirits returned. Jonas and Hilda had driven them down to the yard in the morning; they seem to find it such fun investigating all the sheds peering at the fish in boxes and chatting with the men.

Jonas shouted, "come on you lot get in this spare boat and I'll take you out in the bay." Secure in their lifejackets, they had a whale of a time. John and Robert had ropes tied round their waists as well as the life jackets, so that Hilda could keep them near her. It had not taken Robert long to discover a box of fish which had been left on the boat, and was having an enjoyable time poking the eyes of the dead fish; he laughed as they slipped from his grasp until Granny caught him and dragged him away, scolding and wiping his hands at the same time. It was lovely for Jonas and Hilda to have the children to themselves for a short time, but by heck they were exhausting.

*****

Michael returned to his parent's house just in time for lunch. As he entered the kitchen he took off his boots and hung up his oilskin jacket. He had worked up quite an appetite this morning having walked so many miles. He kissed his mother on the back of the head as she busied herself at the stove. The children ran into the kitchen and took their places at the table expectantly.

"Hello, you lot", he laughed. "Had a good time this morning, have yer?"

"Yes thank you", Pip replied.

"Aye, we did that", said Jonas. "We took the boat out with four of them, and by heck, we brought four back, can't be bad". He laughed merrily at his own joke.

"Don't tease them", Hilda chided, "They don't understand."

Jonas turned to Michael.

"Well, what have you been up to son?"

Michael was bursting to relate the morning's events.

"I don't know whether you remember me telling you about the two Buccaneers which nearly collided with the Cessna, on my flying lesson a few weeks ago", Jonas nodded.

Well, just before that incident, I noticed a small fishing boat in the bay; it was hugging the coastline. I thought at the time it was because of the bad seas, but now I feel the person in the boat was trying to hide. At first I was concerned that it might be someone in distress: I then decided that only an experienced fisherman would risk going out on such a day. Lately I got to thinking I have always been intrigued as to where Jack Big had been hiding for those weeks before he was caught. So this morning I tried to put myself in his shoes that night, and walked along the cliff to the bay".

"Trying to retrace his steps, as it were", mused Jonas. Rubbing his chin thoughtfully. Michael then related exactly what he had found that morning.

"Well, I'm blessed", exclaimed his father, "that boat will be worth a few hundred. Well done, good comes out of evil in the end. We'd best tell the Police that we are reclaiming the boat".

"Aye, I'll do that later, and then I will take you lot over the park for a spot of football".

"I can't play", said Carol loftily.

Michael chucked her under the chin, and whispered, putting his face close to hers.

"Never mind Miss high horse, you only have to try and kick the ball and run!"

"Enough talk, eat up otherwise it will all be cold", Hilda snapped. She was privately sick of hearing Jack Big's name. That man was nothing but trouble!

CHAPTER TWENTY EIGHT

Barbara Stirs Up Trouble

Elizabeth had arrived at her office at seven thirty that morning. With all the recent problems her work was very much in arrears. She would have liked to have laid low for a while to let the dust settle, but, with Christopher lying ill in hospital and David, quite rightly, by his bedside, she felt she had no choice but to get in early and work through the files piled on her desk.

Elizabeth sat and mused over her coffee she had just made to take a break. She and David would have to split Christopher's work load between them on the basis he would return to work when he recovered, if not....

The phone rang and made her jump.

"Mrs Markham, I have Berry's the builders on the line, they insist on speaking to you personally".

Here we go, she thought; they were the developers I had lunch with the other day, over their latest proposed project.

"Put them through. Hello!"

"Good morning, is that Mrs. Elizabeth Markham?"

"It is".

"Hector Foster here, M.D. of Berry's, we met the other day. My colleague Henry Wright introduced us".

"Yes, Mr Foster I remember, good morning, and how can I help you".

There fell a pregnant pause. The gushing confidence had gone from his voice and was replaced by tentative nervous and embarrassed vibrations down the phone. Eventually he replied.

"I'm sure you must realise that we have all read the local papers".

He paused again, and there fell another silence, Elizabeth refused to help him by saying anything. He continued.

"It places us in a most difficult position after all we have our good name to preserve. I,I mean the board, feel that in the circumstances we will have to take our business elsewhere".

"I quite understand", Elizabeth interjected with immense dignity.

"To whom would you like me to send the papers?"

He coughed.

"We have not, actually, appointed other solicitors to act for us. After all, we have always been more than satisfied with the service we have received over the years from your firm, not that we can find any fault with you now. It's just that we are concerned. Mind you we are all sure of your innocence, but as you have told my board on many occasions, Courts are funny places, and one can never truly predict the outcome".

"As I am sure, you must appreciate Mr Foster I cannot discuss my affairs with you, or anyone else for that matter. As I have already said, I quite understand. May I suggest that as soon as you find other solicitors you telephone my secretary, give her the details, and the papers will be forwarded without delay, as soon as you settle any outstanding costs. I can guarantee you that!"

He still sounded unsure and upset.

"Thank you, for all you have done for us in the past, good bye!"

She replaced the receiver; her hands were clammy, she wiped them carefully on her lace handkerchief. Was he going to be the first of many, she thought.

*****

Christopher had been in hospital for two weeks. He had remained in the intensive care unit for four days before being transferred to the ward as he was now out of danger. The doctors were pleased with his progress.

Elizabeth and David had been putting in a twelve hour day at the office. Her mother had been a brick, helping with the children, but she had her own job to contend with and had also run out of annual leave. Thankfully, the girls were back at school, but that presented the problem of collecting them.

She went into David's office.

"Got time for a coffee and a chat? All we seem to do recently is work and sleep."

"Yes, of course darling, sit down, I will go and make it. The girls are very busy."

She kicked off her shoes and sank back in the chair. David returned with the coffee and sat down opposite her. "Come on, put your feet up on my knee and I will give them a rub. Which of your many problems is troubling you?"

"I do think we should make contingency plans regarding Christopher. He, thank goodness, is on the mend, but I doubt whether the doctors will permit him to return to work for at least three months. They will obviously want to discharge him as soon as possible, probably in another two weeks. We can't let him go home to an empty house. I think he will have to stay with us for the time being".

David went to speak. She raised her hand.

"Please let me finish I have already thought we could convert the study into a bedsit, it has a lovely view over the garden. That's if he doesn't want to sit with us in the sitting room."

David put her feet on the floor, leant forward and taking her face in his hands, kissed her gently on the nose and then the mouth.

"At a time like this you are still prepared to take on more. What can I say, except I love you; I must admit it has been worrying me, but I didn't like to mention it".

"You should mention anything that worries you. Now you will have to make these suggestions to him, very tactfully. He will not like it at first, he values his independence too much, but I am sure he will come round in the end."

David sipped his coffee thoughtfully.

"I will speak with the doctors first and then to father. Are you coming up today?"

"Yes, later on".

"All right, I will tell him, I know he will be pleased to see you."

"There is one other thing I think Mrs. Fraser needs some help, she is stretched to the limit at the moment. I don't want her giving notice. Do you think we can afford to employ, say, a young girl to help her in the morning and help her with the cleaning?"

"Darling, do what you like, you know you don't have to ask". She smiled.

"I was only worried about the extra expense."

He stood up and went into the office kitchen with the dirty cups.

Elizabeth had welcomed the deluge of work like a gift, anything to take her mind off the trial. Every time it flashed into her mind, the thought of being found guilty made her heart pound.

David returned.

"Now, my girl, a word with you about your case, I feel you must be represented by an independent firm of solicitors to get some impartial advice. I have already, tentatively, approached the clerk to the barrister Norton Biggleswade who is a silk in Lincoln's Inn. I know him by reputation although I have never instructed him, which is probably all to the good.

"Have you a firm of solicitors in mind, my mind's a blank?"

"Leave it to me. Yes, there is a good firm of solicitors in Lincoln's Inn. I have had dealings with a couple of the partners. I'll give them a ring myself and make the first possible appointment. As we are so short staffed would you mind going down to London to see them on your own?"

"No, of course not, in some ways I would rather see them initially on my own." She smiled bravely. "What's their name?"

"Lanthanby and Twist!"

*****

David had gone home at seven thirty to relieve Mrs. Fraser. It was agreed that Elizabeth would visit Christopher on her way home.

Elizabeth immediately saw Christopher as she entered the ward. He smiled broadly and put his book down. "Elizabeth, my dear, how kind of you to come."

She kissed his cheek.

"I am so glad to see you sitting up and taking notice, I hope you're behaving yourself with the nurses," she joked.

"Some of them are not bad, that one over there keeps

giving me the eye". "You're obviously getting better," she said laughing. "Did David speak to you about our idea?" He reached down and patted her hand. "Yes, he did, and I don't see how I can possibly refuse". "Good, well that's all settled. When are they going to discharge you?" He shrugged his shoulders and exhaled. "Doctor, says he would like me to stay for another week, at least". "Well, I'm pleased you are not rushing back; I have brought you the latest law journals and magazines to read. Unfortunately I will have to love you and leave you, there's so much to do".

Damn she could cut off her tongue sometimes, what a thoughtless thing to say. Christopher looked miserable. "I'm so sorry, my dear".

"Take no notice of me, please, we are managing, it's just the other business as well, and no, I am not discussing that either at the moment, so you can take that expectant look off your face. If you want to help, please rest, relax and get better. That will make me very happy. Now I must fly". She kissed his forehead and was gone.

"Lovely girl", he muttered and started to babble to his neighbour in the next bed.

Elizabeth drove slowly home. It was a damp and dreary evening. The roads were slippery. She decided she would pick up some fish and chips on the way. She seldom felt like cooking in the evening these days, she was always so tired. One thing was for sure Mrs Fraser would be pleased to hear they were getting more help round the house. Perhaps she might know of someone looking for a job.

As she drove along she wondered where the committal proceedings would take place. The prosecution would have to persuade the magistrates that they had a prima facie case against her. If satisfied, the Magistrates would commit her for trial at the Assizes before a Judge and jury. She was dying to know what evidence the police had against her. As her father was a magistrate in Scarborough, and she had previously practised in York before joining David and Christopher, it was unlikely, that either of these two Courts would be used.

Reaching in her handbag for her handkerchief, she noticed with distaste the blue form, handed to her by Sergeant McVane giving a date in ten days when she was to go to court.

As part of her bail she had to surrender her passport and report to the police station every day. She had been very lucky to get bail, because a murder charge normally meant being held in custody. She shuddered at the thought.

She pulled up outside her father's shop and went inside.

"Hello, Mrs Markham, what a pleasant surprise it's right nice to see you. Sorry about your problems!"

Betty swung the chip basket with skilled dexterity, emptying with one swish the sizzling chips into the draining part of the unit. She was short and rounded, like a plum. She didn't walk, she waddled. Having been with the firm for years, she ran the shop practically single handed. Any louts who crossed her were likely to feel the back of her hand. She could certainly live up to the reputation, "fish wife", if suitably provoked. Her hair was dyed blonde, and being naturally curly, it seemed to be trying to eject the hat plonked unceremoniously on top. She laughed a lot, and her deep throated chuckle was infectious.

"It's nice to see you, Betty, you're looking well. My that food smells good, I'm ravenous".

"Aye, you look right peaky, my girl, you look as if you need fattening up, not quite like me though!" she bellowed and slapped her ample hips.

"I pride myself on my cooking. What'll it be cod, haddock, plaice, or I could pop you in a nice piece of skate?"

"Sounds good, one large skate and one large cod, please."

"It will take a few minutes, but you know the best fish and chips is straight out of the pan. Your father came in earlier, works too hard and I told him so, not that he takes any notice of me. He likes my savloys, never eats fish, funny for a fisherman."

Elizabeth felt tired and wanted to go. She had noticed, a couple who had just come into the shop, whispering to each other. She was sure they were talking about her, or was she just getting paranoid. They kept looking her way. Betty made her jump.

"Here you are, love, penny for them. Off you go and look after yourself, girl. No good ruining your health".

"Thanks Betty, goodnight".

At home David got up to greet her.

"Great, you have bought some food with you. I've spoken with the solicitors. Mr John Lanthenby would like to see you tomorrow afternoon at 3.30 if you feel up to it".

"No, but I don't think I have much choice". She threw her coat on the chair and got the plates out. They munched in silence for a while. David leant forward.

"Why don't you stay the night at the club, you look all in, and it would give you a break, and you could get the early train back in the morning?" "No, thank you. I would rather come back. At least I can work on the train, quite useful. I forgot to tell you Berry's the builders have taken their business elsewhere, sorry about that. I suppose more will follow".

She finished gloomily.

"Not necessarily, most of our clients are pretty loyal". The phone rang in the hall. "I'll get it said Elizabeth, probably Mrs. Fraser" she called as she walked down the hall to the phone.

Elizabeth picked up the phone.

"Hello!"

"Hello! is that Elizabeth, its Barbara Johnston-Bloice here", said the voice imperiously. Elizabeth sat down, her pulse quickened and her mouth felt dry.

"Yes, Barbara what do you want?" The maddening, syrupy voice continued. "It looks as if you have got yourself in a mess, if what I read in the papers is correct".

Elizabeth fumed. "Barbara, what do you want?"

"Well, I'm bored at the moment Sebastian has gone off and left me. Oh, not properly, he adores me too much for us to part. No, some family trust he has to sort out. We have just returned from the Middle East. I've got a marvellous tan. At the moment, I'm kicking my heels".

"How interesting, but I don't see". Barbara interjected.

"No, my dear, you wouldn't see, would you".

That patronising lilt, Elizabeth dug her nails into her hand. David had come into the hall and was standing beside her. He indicated he would take the phone, but she shook her head.

"I got to thinking about the children and realised I quite missed them, my dear; if the case goes against you, you surely could go to prison. You would then be struck off by the Law Society, conduct unbefitting, don't they say, lowering the tone of the God like profession. If that happens, and one never knows, then what will happen to my darling children? I'm not sure I would want them living with a convicted criminal; I suppose I would have to come and take them away and employ a fleet of nannies to look after them. Where's David, I've done with speaking to you".

Elizabeth face had drained, and she was completely white.

"I haven't finished with you, not by a long chalk. To use the word Mother to describe you is a complete misuse of the word. You are a conniving, selfish, self-centred cow. Your treatment of the children has been appalling. I can assure you, that David and I will never relinquish the children to your so called care without a fight. It should not be difficult to persuade a Judge that you are an unfit Mother".

She shouted down the phone with more conviction than she felt.

"Even you must surely have noticed, with your small brain, the chaos that you caused on your last visit. You made a complete fool of yourself and upset the children terribly. Robert hardly remembered you, and you made them both cry, even for the two short hours you were alone with them. Wearing skirts up to your knickers, you looked absolutely ridiculous and pathetic, trying to act like a teenager instead of a grown woman, what Sebastian sees in you I have no idea. As to the case I haven't the slightest intention of discussing any minute part of it with the likes of you. I wouldn't lower myself".

"My, my, we are in a temper". The taunting voice interrupted, "May I speak to David?"

"NO, YOU MAY NOT".

Elizabeth shouted into the receiver, slamming it down at the same time. She got up and started striding up and down the hall, she was still shouting mainly to the air.

"How dare she ring up talking about removing the children, because I am, or will be a convicted criminal if she was here, I would strike her!"

She lashed out at the hall stand with a kick.

David sat down.

"Why didn't you let me deal with her, I'm used to her".

"But you're no good at dealing with her, are you?"

He looked hurt.

"I just meant it would have prevented her going on at

you in her inane way if I had taken the call. I shouldn't take any notice of her she probably only wants to cause mischief because she was bored".

"That is precisely what she said.'I'm bored'".

"Well then, let's clear up the kitchen and take a nice chocolate drink to bed. By the way the Blakes, have cried off from the dinner party on Saturday, something about another engagement. I'll ring Tony and Jean in the morning to see if they can make up the numbers at short notice, or would you rather cancel the whole thing?"

I'm too tired and upset to think, but on balance, no, we must keep up appearances. We don't have to flaunt ourselves, but hiding won't help."

CHAPTER TWENTY NINE

London

Mrs Fraser was in at eight as usual. Elizabeth brought her up to date with the latest events.

"Do you know anyone who will help in the house?" she enquired?

"Not off hand, but I will think about it, I must say it will certainly help me if there's another pair of hands, especially if I'm to give Mr. Christopher the attention he deserves. I'll stick a card in the Post Office window".

"Thanks, I must fly".

Elizabeth drained her coffee, grabbed her briefcase and fled.

In the office, she quickly left instructions for Sally, sorted out the files she could work on in the train and stuffed them into her briefcase. She could hardly lift it it was so heavy. "Sorry this is so heavy", she turfed out two law books and put them on the table. "I will have to manage without them"!

"You're ready for the off. Here give me that I'm coming with you to see you safely on the train. You can get a taxi from the station, straight there. I don't want you lugging this briefcase too far. My it still weighs a ton."

"I always get taxis in London, you know that. Come on, otherwise I will miss the train!"

She waved goodbye to David as the train pulled out of the station, and settled down with her papers in an empty carriage.

She spread files about hoping no-one would join her.

This worked until she had to change trains at York when she was joined by a man, who sat quietly reading his book much to her relief. The train arrived punctually at Kings Cross; a porter seeing her struggling relieved her of her briefcase and carried it to the waiting taxi rank. She asked the taxi driver to take her to the Waldorf Hotel in the Aldwych just off the Strand, where she could enjoy a peaceful lunch before her meeting. Sitting back in the taxi, she took in the atmosphere of London's city life. Stony faced people were charging about with great purpose, but they all looked so grim. The men seemed to have the same uniform appearance. The fumes from the car exhausts were suffocating, she closed the window firmly.

The taxi pulled up outside the main entrance of the hotel. The doorman stepped forward, touching his hat as he opened the door. She deposited her briefcase with the hall porter, retrieving a notebook and pencil in readiness for her interview with Mr Lanthenby. She would collect the briefcase later on in the afternoon. The head waiter greeted her warmly and found her a quiet table for lunch.

The halibut was superb, poached in a cream and wine sauce. The chocolate mousse was just a naughty indulgence. She left in good time to walk round the corner to Lincoln's Inn.

She entered through the large gates into the inner sanctum of Lincoln's Inn, New Square. The Porters on duty at the gates smiled politely as she passed.

The Georgian grandeur of the stately buildings was very

impressive, brimming full of earnest barristers beavering away in every square inch of workable space.

Each 'set' as they were called consisted of twenty, thirty, fifty barristers. They would range in seniority from the newly admitted to the experienced junior barristers, with usually up to twelve Queen's Counsel, or silks as they were referred to, as the senior members. One of the QC's would be head of chambers. The senior clerk was their contact with the outside world. It was to them all the barristers in chambers would look to promote them to firms of solicitors and negotiate on their behalf a good fee for the work, depending on their specialities. The success of a good 'set' of chambers was mainly down to the senior clerk and his good counsel; an inefficient or lazy clerk could soon ruin the business.

It was therefore easy to see, by working in this protected environment (no member of the general public was allowed to speak to a barrister direct, unless it was in the presence of their solicitor) how the barristers could easily become divorced from the realities of life. And they went on to be appointed to the judiciary it is no wonder they are sometimes reported as being out of touch.

A quiet peace reigned within the square, whilst London jostled, screamed and yelled outside.

Lanthanby and Twists only entrance door was in a little side passage off the square in Butt Street. Elizabeth soon found the black door with the shiny brass plate and doorknob. Pushing gently, she went inside.

The reception was gloomy, not like her office at all. Two girls were chatting behind a desk in the corner.

She mentioned her name and one asked her to take a seat. She sat, waiting expectantly.

A tall man came down the stairs and conferred quietly with the girls behind the counter. His hair was grey, and his broad shoulders filled his well cut suit. He turned to face her and held out his hand.

"Mrs Markham good afternoon, my name is John Lanthenby."

His face relaxed into a broad open smile, showing a flash of healthy white teeth. His demeanour was commanding and she felt he had great presence. She immediately felt at ease and grasped his extended hand he led the way up some stairs and along a corridor. She dutifully followed him into his office which overlooked the square.

"What a nice room!"

"I like working up here tucked away, especially with the view. Please sit down". He resumed his seat behind the desk. Elizabeth perched on the chair which he had indicated which had certainly had seen better days.

"Mrs Markham", he smiled understandingly.

"Your husband outlined brief details of the case yesterday on the phone. I wonder if you would be kind enough to tell me what happened in your own words".

Elizabeth sat back in the chair and started at the beginning. He made notes, interrupting her occasionally to verify certain details. She handed him the letter from Jean, which he read and then placed carefully in the file. When she had finished, she felt quite drained. A thoughtful silence fell between them.

"I have written out a detailed statement which I will leave with your for further reference." She leant forward and placed it on his desk.

Lanthenby sat back in his chair, chewing on his pencil, pondering. He suddenly seemed to jerk back into life.

"You must be thirsty I'll ring for some tea".

He lifted the receiver and muttered into it. A tea tray for two appeared almost immediately. He resumed his train of thought.

"Now, we have the photographs and measurements, taken by your husband on the day of the accident. I will of course need to visit the scene or locus, as it was called, and see for myself. Let's see now, you have to appear in court in nine days time to renew your bail. We could fit a site meeting in later on that day. I doubt very much whether the prosecution will be ready for at least two months. If you agree, I will send instructions round to Norton Biggleswade; the barrister, whom your husband suggested. Good choice I thought. I will give some thought to a junior and speak with Norton."

Elizabeth decided to keep quiet and leave it to Lanthenby as it was a fact that a QC like Mr Biggleswade couldn't appear in court without a junior barrister as well. It was therefore helpful if they both got on together.

"Yes, well, I will certainly form my own opinion when I meet him. I agree that instructions should be sent to him as soon as possible.

"I must say this seems all very unfortunate for you, it would appear that you are a victim of circumstances. I'm sorry to drag you all the way to London, but I'm sure that you, more than any of my clients, appreciate the value of a face to face meeting."

He stood up. "Well that's that, I don't think I need keep you any longer".

Elizabeth rose "I am most grateful to you for seeing me at such short notice, and I feel much better for an impartial viewpoint. No doubt Mr. Biggleswade will want a conference. Anyway, I know I can safely leave that to you to arrange".

She shook his hand, and he ushered her out into the afternoon sunshine.

Looking at her watch, she noted it was four thirty. She realised that she was about to walk into the London rush hour. Feeling weak from all the emotional turmoil, she decided not to let the congestion upset her.

Completely lost in her own thoughts she mounted the steps of the Hotel. A man came running down the steps and collided with her, nearly knocking her over.

She bent to retrieve her handbag, which had been knocked from her hand on impact. The man grabbed her arm, offering profuse apologies. As she straightened up, she found herself looking straight into the face of her ex-husband, Andrew Birch.

"Well! she exclaimed, "Of all the people to bump into, what on earth are you doing here Andrew?"

Equally surprised, he replied.

"I may well ask you the same thing. How are you? You are looking great. Come on let me buy you some tea".

"You gave a good impression of being in rather a hurry".

"It's true, I was, but I can sort that out with a quick phone call, I can't just walk off without having a chat, now can I?"

"I suppose not," she smiled weakly.

"You have caught me at a good moment I wouldn't mind avoiding the rush hour!"

She knew they did rather a good tea at the hotel and sometimes there were tea dances. Thank goodness, this afternoon was not one of them. With David it would be fine, but not with Andrew.

Andrew made his phone call, and Elizabeth called David. She explained that bumping into Andrew would hold her up, but she would be on the first available train and would ring him from the station.

She ordered china tea, Andrew asked for Earl Grey. An awkward tension had settled between them.

He looked quite well, in fact better than she had seen him in years. She muttered, for something to say.

"You're looking well, how's the drinking?"

"Given it all up, haven't touched a drop in months. I feel so much better, and I have been attending AA meetings regularly which have helped a lot. How are the children?"

"They are fine, really they are!"

He suddenly leaned forward in his chair confidingly. "Look, you want to get back, and I would like to hear more about the kids. I haven't been well enough to come to see them. I wasn't going back to York until tomorrow, but, if I make one more phone call, I can probably get round that and travel back with you this evening. We could have dinner on the train!"

He smiled ingratiatingly, and seemed rather pleased with himself.

Elizabeth pondered for a moment.

"I was going to work on the train, but I suppose I have to eat sometime", she said ungraciously.

"That's you, always working, give yourself a break." She smiled weakly.

"Good, that's settled then, excuse me" He rose and strode off in the direction of the telephones in the hall.

Elizabeth slowly exhaled, emptying her lungs, trying to release some of the tension. The last thing she expected or wanted was to bump into him. Never mind, it was too late now.

Andrew's medium height and athletic frame re-appeared again. She wondered how successful his computer company was these days. He had always kept up the maintenance payments without any apparent problems, although he hadn't seen the children for ages.

Picking up her briefcase he said.

"Come on let's brave the traffic it's going to be deuce difficult to get a cab this time of the evening".

Over dinner on the train they settled into a fairly relaxed

conversation. She told him about the children, not forgetting Barbara. She also felt that in the circumstances she should refer briefly to the impending trial, as he had probably read about it in the newspapers anyway. If he already knew, he showed no sign of it, and let her carry on.

He in turn told her about his company and the reasonable success he had been experiencing recently. His eyes were much bluer than she remembered, probably because they were marred in the old days, by his constant state of inebriation. Andrew boasted about what his company were achieving, she doubted whether they were strictly accurate but decided it didn't really matter to her anyway. He then asked about seeing the children, if she didn't feel it would upset them.

It was agreed that after talking to David about it, she would contact Andrew with a couple of suggested dates.

He still lived in the Mock Tudor house they had bought together when they were first married, six miles outside York.

The journey passed quickly. The British Rail dinner had not acquitted itself very well. She had a slight tummy ache. A feeling of relief came over her as the train pulled into York station and she was able to say her goodbyes to Andrew. Her connection to Scarborough left on time, and she settled herself in the carriage, waving cheerily as the train pulled away.

Thankfully David was on the platform to greet her it had been an exhausting day; he hugged and kissed her, "Ok" he said.

"Yes, not bad, I will tell you all about it when we get home".

CHAPTER THIRTY

Christopher

The children were very excited at the prospect of Granddad coming to live with them. They had all been told he had been unwell and that they must not make a noise outside his room until he felt better.

Christopher in turn was delighted to be out of hospital, it was such an un-restful atmosphere what with being woken at some ungodly hour in the morning and the constant comings and goings in the ward. Even at night the nurses sat at their desk whispering in a constant maddening drone making it impossible to sleep!

David had arrived on time to collect him; driving home through the town and seeing people about their daily business had cheered him up already. There was a cold north wind blowing and David noticed his father catch his breath as he helped him from the car.

Elizabeth had made the study very welcoming. There was a settee, an armchair and a single bed. The desk had to be removed to make more room.

"Christopher" she exclaimed and hurried forward to greet him.

"Come on let's pop you into bed for the time being".

"Is it really necessary, my dear? I've had enough of bed?"

"Yes, it most certainly is - doctor's orders. When and only when he says you can get up, will I allow it".

"Well, that seems to be that, better do as I'm told".

"Do you want some help undressing?" she enquired.

A look of thunder crossed his eyes, momentarily.

"Ok ok, only asking", she raised her hands in a defenceless gesture.

Christopher undressed and climbed into bed, he was surprised how tired he felt considering the short time he had been up.

Elizabeth brought in a cup of coffee only to find him dozing, so she tiptoed out again.

She was due to attend the court on Monday, the first of her bail appearances. Her case had been transferred to Harrogate, after a great deal of fuss.

She met John Lanthenby on the steps of the court. He had already tried to have a word with the prosecuting Solicitor, who was most unhelpful and would tell him nothing. The Police required further time to prepare their case and the Magistrates granted them a twenty eight day adjournment. 'Dam' Elizabeth thought as the cameras flashed as she was leaving the Court.

They drove to the station to meet Norton Biggleswade who had decided to come as well as his junior. It had not been considered necessary for him to attend the preliminary court appearance. She was looking forward to meeting him.

A man came racing up the steps at Scarborough station, jacket unbuttoned, hair tousled and in need of a cut she noted. This small eccentric looking man turned out to be Biggleswade himself. A breathless Junior Barrister called James Mcguire followed him; together with trainee 'pupil' Tony Marsh who was carrying his bulging briefcase. Biggleswade rushed forward, hand outstretched "John!" He bellowed.

"Norton, good to see you" they chimed. John introduced Elizabeth, who was given the same gusty handshake, and a probing stare into her eyes.

"Let's go", he shouted, taking charge of the group, and climbing into the passenger seat of Elizabeth's car.

They drove out to the village where the accident had taken place. Norton slowly and ponderously walked up and down the street, taking in every detail, especially the visibility from both the pedestrian and drivers angles and the position of the speed restriction signs. Notes were taken. They then decided to adjourn to the nearest pub for a talk and a sandwich.

When they were seated in the bar, Norton carefully went over the details. James made one or two observations but otherwise remained quiet.

Norton continued.

"It seems on the face of it that their case is very fragile. We will just have to wait for the hearing and see what evidence they produce, if any. The prosecution are certainly exuding an air of confidence, but they are obviously keeping their ammunition for the committal proceedings."

He went on to ask for an expert Surveyors report to be obtained, dealing with the technical aspects such as stopping distances and the condition of the road surface, and a set of photographs.

Elizabeth drove them back to the station and left the four men on the platform. She thought, as she drove along, that it had already been an expensive exercise, so she hoped it would prove helpful. She knew that it usually assisted the Court to have an accurate picture of what had happened. She was anxious to get back to the office before closing time, if possible, and then straight home to make sure Christopher was all right and to reassure him about today's events.

*****

Christopher had settled in nicely and was getting on with Mrs. Fraser like a house on fire, whom he now called Patricia. She fussed round him, and he loved it. He was not only allowed to get up now, but the doctor had encouraged him to take half an hour strolls, depending on how he felt. He was especially enjoying Patricia's home cooking. Her stews were scrummy. He was trying to persuade her to cook him some apple dumplings, but she refused on health grounds. He spent happy hours wandering along the cliff paths near the house, sitting on a comfortable wooden bench and sat staring out to sea ruminating on past events and the direction his life was now taking. He was also beginning to acquire a healthy tan.

"Do you know", he said one morning to Patricia. "This is the longest break I have had from work in forty years I of course have taken the odd two weeks, but never as long as this"

"Well, it shows that you should have been more careful and taken holidays more often. The work will be there after you're dead and gone, so what's the point in slaving away? If you hadn't worked so hard, you probably wouldn't have ended up in hospital".

"I suppose you are right. The trouble is once on the treadmill and its jolly difficult to get off. Besides, I love my work, don't have to do it, you know." He stood up and stretched.

"I'm getting restless, it's time I thought of getting back to work."

*****

"No, Father, I absolutely refuse to let you come back to work yet," David exploded.

He took his son's hand.

"Look David...... I haven't pestered you about the work because I didn't feel I could help. Anyway, now I feel I can, so you must let me. I'm beginning to get bored sitting around all day. You and Elizabeth both look exhausted, don't think I haven't noticed. What with all the problems and my workload as well, it's too much for you both. I will be sensible, I promise".

David exhaled slowly. He knew he was defeated. The practice was very busy, and he could certainly do with another pair of experienced hands.

"All right, I'll tell you what I will do. You can work from here for the time being.

I will bring some files home; on the strict understanding that if you feel the slightest bit tired or under pressure you leave the work and rest... the phone is connected internally to the office, so you need not feel cut off in any way. What do you say?"

"To be honest, I don't like it but I will give it a go."

"Great, you can start tomorrow!"

Christopher settled behind the Times, he was unable to stop the small grin that had spread across his face. David hadn't put up much resistance; they must be very busy; it was nice to feel needed again.

Maggie Smith the young girl from a local village was now living in. She was mainly employed to look after Robert and John, but also helped Patricia with the household chores. She was just sixteen had come from a large family of seven children. Having her own room for the first time in her life made her happier than she had ever been before. She adored the children, especially the two rascals, John and Robert. She was treated as an older sister, which was gratifying. Having been used to helping her mother care for her brothers and sisters, these two were a doddle. She loved the large house with its beautiful garden and views, and she got on well with Mrs. Fraser. In the main she made herself scarce when Mr. and Mrs. Markham were home. They obviously wanted some privacy, and she in turn could retreat, with a clear conscience, to her room. Christopher was enjoying working again. He found he still tired easily and was grateful to be able to have a rest after lunch. Joan, his secretary, had bucked up no end when he had spoken to her on the phone. He knew that she didn't like working for anyone else.

His visits to the kitchen talking to Patricia while she was cooking had proved both interesting and illuminating. It seemed she had been hiding her many talents. She had no children of her own and, being a widow for some five years, and had long since felt that it was unlikely anyone would be interested in her as a person. He had found that she was an accomplished pianist and had given many recitals over the years, purely as an amateur, but, even so, he knew that one had to attain a reasonable standard for the general public to come and listen.

She also painted water colours. After a great deal of cajoling he had persuaded her to bring a couple of her pictures to the house. He had been most impressed, and thought they were really very good, she told him that she had quite a few more at home. He had presumptuously invited himself to tea with her. Patricia had been a little taken aback, but secretly flattered. She promised that she would invite him shortly, and then he could look at her amateurish brush work to his hearts content.

"You never know," he half joked, "You may have enough pictures for me to organise a small exhibition for you one day."

She smiled shyly, with obvious pleasure.

"Oh, I don't think so, Mr. Christopher".

"We'll see".

He had found in Fred, the gardener was a most amazing character his accent was so thick that Christopher could hardly understand a word he said. Although he was obviously very old it was quite impossible to tell how old, and unthinkable to ask. He was permanently bent double from years of gardening.

He seemed to coax the plants through the earth and encourage them to flourish, even against the salt winds of the sea, no easy task. Endless rock formations filled the beds, which was his way of giving the plants some protection from the prevailing winds.

The greenhouse was his panacea. Here everything flourished under his care. Of course, David had set the seeds but then left it all to Fred. David fully appreciated Fred's natural gift and understanding of the fundamental needs of the plants. He came in three mornings a week and got through an inordinate amount of work in that time.

CHAPTER THIRTY ONE

Jack meets Martin Forbes

Jean stood and looked down at Nicholas who was lying on the settee surrounded by a bed of cushions. She was so happy to have him home with her. He had to be watched as he was now trying to sit up and often rolled over surprising himself as much as anyone else.

She had made friends with a divorcee from a flat in the same block. Leonie's ex-husband had signed the rent book over to her, which enabled her to stay there with her daughter Elaine. Leonie was the same age as Jean, and their children were also very close in age, Elaine being only a month older than Nicholas. They were both glad of the friendship. Bringing up a small child on your own presented lots of problems. Making friends with Leonie had allowed Jean to resume her old part time job at the corner shop, but now they could both enjoy the fruits of this job. Leonie babysat whilst Jean worked and vice versa. The old ladies had been delighted to employ Leonie as well, for a few hours a week in the afternoon. The arrangement worked well for all concerned.

The police had informed Jean that Jack intended to plead "not guilty", which meant she would have to testify against him in court. She damned him for his bloody mindedness. In her own mind she was quite satisfied, that he knew he would probably be found guilty and that he wasn't going down without making everyone's life, in the meantime, as difficult as possible.

She had been suffering from blinding headaches recently, and had gone to see the doctor, who had put her on a course of tranquillisers for her nerves. Nicholas had to visit the outpatients department twice a week, and the health visitor was on her doorstep seemingly every other day. The old doubts of being an unfit mother were very much with her. She felt she was being watched by the social services whom she felt were getting ready to pounce. The terrible guilt she felt over Geoffrey was almost too much to bear.

The committal proceedings against Elizabeth would shortly be listed for hearing in the Harrogate Magistrates Court and Jean was not looking forward to giving evidence against her. Still, she had burned her boats and couldn't go back now. What was done was done. Anyway, if Elizabeth was found guilty, then perhaps the social workers would leave her alone. She felt happier as the thought passed through her mind.

*****

Jack's legal aid certificate had been granted. Basil Newcomb had instructed a barrister by the name of Martin Forbes. Forbes had a reputation of being a middle of the road criminal Barrister, with a moderate practice in the local Chambers. He had requested a conference, which he had arranged through the prison authorities.

Sean and Micky were still cell mates of Jack. Their cases had not come up for trial either. They were all very restless. A confined cell, forcing them to lie on their beds for most of the day, was not a healthy place for young able bodied men, especially when they were all technically "not guilty" until their cases were proved against them. There was surely something fundamentally wrong with a system which locked people up, sometimes for months, only for the courts to find them innocent. They were then released by the establishment with a polite cough and insincere apologies. The mental scars these men would bear for being locked up and treated like convicted criminals was immeasurable. It was true that, they could bring proceedings against the Police for wrongful arrest, and no doubt damages would be paid. But for truly innocent men, nothing could compensate for the personal and emotional torture and humiliation which they had suffered. On the other hand it was unlikely that the occupants of Jack's cell would qualify as such victims as they were both hardened criminals.

One of the perks of remand prisoners was that visitors could bring gifts of soap, toothpaste, cigarettes and personal items for hygiene, but not of course razor blades. Jack didn't have any visitors, except old Joe on one occasion, who arrived too drunk to be compos mentis and was sent packing by the screws.

Sean's girlfriend came regularly, and Micky's wife visited once a week when she could get a babysitter.

There was a perpetual theme in prison, and that was 'escaping'. With this in mind in order to keep fit, the men did press ups and any physical jerks they could manage in the confined space of their cells.

As time passed Jack was getting very restless. It came harder to him than most, being cooped up. He was used to being in the open in all weathers.

His Counsel was due at two thirty, and he was quite

looking forward to it. He intended to prolong the interview as long as possible; anything to keep out of the suffocating cell.

Martin Forbes looked up from his papers as Jack was ushered into the interview room. He did not get up, but shook Jack's hand and indicated to him to sit down, then resumed his reading. Jack sat, his muscled arms crossed in front of him, and waited. Mr. Newcomb was sitting beside Forbes, a pen poised ready to take instructions from Forbes. Why Newcomb acted in such a subservient way to Forbes was beyond his comprehension.

Forbes eventually put his pen down and sat back, with his hands in his pockets, surveying Big for the first time. Jack began to feel uncomfortable. It was obvious to him this man Forbes was a totally different force to be reckoned with than Newcomb. Forbes then changed his position, leaning forward with his elbows on the desk, bringing himself even closer to Jack.

"It seems to me, Mr. Big that the cards are stacked against you, yet I understand from Mr. Newcomb that you wish to plead not guilty to ALL the charges"

"That's right", Jack replied.

Forbes went on, "If that's the case, I do have to warn you that if the Judge feels you are pleading not guilty just to waste the courts time and you are found guilty, he may award a much heavier sentence."

"He can't do that."

"Oh, yes, he can, and he will. It happens all the time; not officially, of course." A grim smile settled on his face.

Jack picked his teeth. "I thought you were supposed to be on my side?"

"Of course I am," his public school accent echoed round the room. "So if you still wish to maintain your plea, we had better go through the sequence of events. Would you in your own time take me through the precise details of what happened the evening in question I warn you to be sensible and try and remember every minutiae detail. If you are not then I doubt I can help you".

Jack realised he was not going to get away with glib comments. This Forbes bloke seemed serious enough. If anyone could help him get out of this mess, he could. He started at the beginning during which Forbes made copious notes, and occasionally raised his hand, indicating to Jack to wait before continuing. Jack told him about the money owed, and the argument that ensued with Billy and Taffy.

He surprised himself by remembering the names of the witnesses in the pub; the fight that followed, and the production of the knife from the inside of his boot, strapped to his leg, where he always kept it.

Mr Newcomb shook his head at Martin Forbes in disbelief. Jack flashed him a warning look. "I thought you wanted the truth," he shouted.

"Please control yourself Mr. Big." Forbes snapped. "We must know the truth, otherwise – I repeat – we can't help you. Once we know exactly what happened, we will see what kind of defence you can plead, if any." Forbes noticed the flash of hope spring to Jack's face. "No, that does not mean we make up a story and lie to the court. That wouldn't do at all. You seem to think this is a game. Well it certainly is not. The charges against you are extremely serious. I want to see whether I have sufficient ammunition to persuade the prosecution to reduce one or both charges to actual bodily harm, which does not carry such stiff penalties. It may mean pleading guilty, but we will have to see."

Jack was about to protest.

"Please, Mr. Big, do me the courtesy of finishing your story, I will then advise you. If you don't want me to represent you, you can dismiss me, and either find someone else, or act for yourself. I must warn you again that the prosecution are going to come very heavy on you, and you can't dismiss them! He almost shouted; let's not waste any further time, please we must get on with it"

Jack found himself skating over the details of his treatment of Jean. He suddenly felt ashamed. He finished by telling them about the shack and the fight in the yard.

"So your version is that you always made love to Jean roughly, and she liked it. I understand she suffered cracked ribs and a fractured cheekbone. How do you account for that?"

"Well, it's difficult for me to say." Jack shifted uncomfortably in his chair. "I hadn't seen her for a while. She may have another bloke. Does anyone know when she went to the hospital? If it wasn't the same night, then that surely must prove it wasn't me." He sat back, feeling rather pleased with this deduction.

"I take your point, but unfortunately it doesn't prove anything of the kind, the retort was immediate. Now how about changing your plea to 'actual bodily harm' on both counts, and 'not guilty' to rape? That is of course if the prosecution will agree!"

Jack stood up and paced the room. "What does that mean, exactly?"

"It means the Courts only have power to award a much lighter sentence and the fact that you have pleaded guilty and not run a spurious "not guilty" plea will be taken into account. You might get eighteen months, with remission nine or ten. If you go down on grievous bodily harm and rape, the sentence will be a long one, for at least five years."

"Bloody hell, it don't seem as if I have much choice, I leave it to you!"

"Good man! Committal proceedings are on Monday.

I will speak with the prosecution then. You are lucky they seem to want to deal with you rather quickly maybe local pressure. Well, goodbye, see you on Monday, and try and look presentable!"

The Barrister stood up, gathering his papers together. Newcomb, who had remained silent throughout the whole interview, grunted at Jack and followed Forbes through the door. The warden pressed the bell, and the large iron door swung open, letting the two lawyers out into the sunshine and fresh air.

*****

First thing on Monday morning, Jack was banged up inside the prison van and driven to the Court together with the other prisoners appearing that day. On arrival they were each handcuffed to a policeman and taken down to the cells.

Martin Forbes came bustling into the cell."Good morning, Mr. Big, all the interview rooms are busy, so we will have to talk in here." Newcomb entering behind him nodded at Jack and said a polite good morning. Forbes perched on a court bench."I have had a word with the prosecution, and they won't play ball. They refuse to reduce the charges to the lesser ones. They feel confident they can make them all stick, so we go on with our plea of 'not guilty' unless you want to change your mind." Jack shook his head.

"I'm afraid you're in for a bit of a wait. The Magistrates will hear the 'guilty pleas' first, so I will come back later. I'm on in another court", he told Newcomb.

"OK."Basil replied, "See you later". He remained with Jack in the cell.

Turning towards him said. "I do hope you are pleased with Mr. Forbes, he will do his best for you!"

Jack sat up. "What's he mean, in another case. Is he working for someone else this morning?"

"Yes, happens all the time; barristers and solicitors diving from one court to another. Sometimes the courts are held up waiting for them to finish in another case."

"Greedy buggers, isn't one job at a time enough for them?"

"It doesn't quite work out like that, and it would take too long to explain. Now, if we could turn back to your case. I'm afraid these types of committal proceedings tend to draw things out. The law is changing next year to shorten them, thank goodness, but this of course, does not help you. It's really like two hearings. The court will go through the evidence today and maybe run into tomorrow. The magistrates will undoubtedly find there is a case to answer, and sent the papers for trial before Judge and Jury at the quarter sessions. Then the whole process is repeated in more detail."

"It's all gibberish to me any road," said Jack.

"If you will excuse me, I will go and see how the list is moving". Newcomb summoned the police officer to let him out.

Jack was taken up to the dock at two-thirty. He'd been offered lunch, which he had refused; he didn't feel much like eating. The courtroom was packed, but he couldn't see anyone he knew.

The magistrates came in, and everyone stood up. The bench consisted of two men and a woman. They were all late middle-aged, with grey hair and blank expressions on their faces. They stared stonily at Jack as he was jerked to his feet by the officers either side of him.

The clerk read the charges out. "How do you plead?"

"NOT GUILTY, SIR."

The prosecution opened by outlining the events leading up to the point where the alleged attack took place on the night in question. The Magistrates and the Clerk made notes.

The first witness, Billy was called. He shambled into the courtroom and uneasily read the oath from the card. The prosecution started. "Are you William Holden Bull of 6, Mew Cottages?"

"I am, sir".

"Please address yourself to the Magistrates?"

"I am sir," Billy repeated, half turning his body.

The awkward thing about courts is that every witness automatically wants to speak to the person addressing him, yet you have to answer in a sideways direction.

"Would you tell the court, in your own words, what happened on the night in March?" Billy looked helplessly round and started mumbling. The Chairman leaned forward, "You will have to speak up, Mr. Bull, the bench can't hear you" He spoke kindly. Billy cleared his throat and tried again. He told a story similar to Jack's version, except that he left out any reference to provocation on their part.

He finished by telling the court that Jack had left them both unconscious in an alleyway.

The prosecution prompted. "Did Mr. Big, the accused, make any attempt to help you afterwards?"

"No sir"

"Were you injured? If so, tell the court about it?"

"I was, sir, my jaw hurt bad and later at the hospital they told me it was badly broken, and they wired it up."

"Did you suffer any other injuries?"

My hands were badly cut and I had bruises all down my legs".

The Chairman asked, showing genuine concern. "Is your jaw better now?"

"It is, sir, but I still suffer from pain and headaches, sometimes."

"Are you back at work?"

"Yes sir".

The prosecution stood up again and addressed the bench. "I have no more questions of this witness, sir. I don't know whether you have?"

The Chairman conferred with his colleagues shook his head and then inclined it towards Martin Forbes who was already on his feet.

:Mr. Bull, just one or two questions. On the night in question, were you engaged in an argument with the accused?"

"Well, we had a bit of a disagreement, like, but it weren't much". He looked nervously at the chairman.

Forbes went on. "Mr. Bull, I don't, I am sure, have to remind you, you are on oath.

I put it to you, not only did you have a heated argument with Mr. Big over money you owed him, but that you and your friend asked Mr. Big to come outside and started a fight by hitting him first?"

There was a deathly silence in the courtroom. Billy looked confused. He had not realised that giving evidence for the prosecution was going to be anything like this. He broke out into a sweat.

"Please answer the question", thundered Mr. Forbes.

"Well", Billy stuttered. The chairman leant forward again, and said crossly, "Please speak up!"

"I admit that there was a discussion about money."

"Did you owe Big money or not? I put it to you you did!"

"He thought we did, so we must have", Billy said lamely, "but we didn't start the fight, he jumped us as we were leaving the pub to go home".

Forbes glared at him, gently fanning himself with his papers. "How much did you have to drink that night?"

Billy stumbled again, and chokingly replied. "Do you mean alcohol?"

"I do."

"About six pints, sir".

"I put it to you that it was nearer ten, with whisky chasers."

"No, sir, definitely not".

"No more questions", he addressed the bench, "Have you any questions Sir."

The chairman was staring at Bull very hard. "No thank you," he managed to mumble.

"Very well, you may sit down". Billy scuttled back to take his seat next to his wife. She patted his hand, comfortingly. She hadn't taken her eyes off Jack since he was brought up from the cells. Billy glanced at him, caught his eye, and looked away.

Taffy was called next. He came into court and was duly sworn in. He was more positive and quickly got through his version of what happened. The prosecution repeated. "If you were injured, please tell the court?"

"Aye, well he rammed this knife into my ribs, which pierced my left lung. Normally, this heals itself in time, I'm told, but in my case something else was damaged, and the damn lung is quite useless now. I've got to go through life on one lung. All through him!" He shouted, pointing at Big in the dock.

"All right, Mr. Drummond that will do, and please don't use offensive language in my Court." The Chairman intervened.

Taffy rounded on the bench. "It ain't me on trial today; it's that creature over there. I only came along to make sure he gets his just deserts and is sent away for a long time." His face had reddened, and he looked as if he was about to leap across the Courtroom and have a go at Jack. Instead, he glowered at him. Jack stared moodily back.

The Chairman was trying to attract Taffy's attention.

He stood up and leaned so far over the bench that everyone thought that he looked as if he was about to fall headlong on top of his clerk seated below.

"Mr. Drummond, Mr Drummond, please look at me. Taffy dragged his eyes slowly away from Big and stared motionless at the Chairman, who was called Mr Truthful, a name he didn't like bandied about the Court. He continued, having at last attracted Taffy's attention.

"I will not tolerate unseemly outbursts in my Court. If you do not agree to behave I will have you removed to the cells and hold you in contempt, until you apologise, WELL?"

Taffy nodded vaguely; the Chairman looked fit to bust. "Yes or no?"

"Yes!"

Very well, continue".

"I have no more questions", said the prosecution, wanting to get Drummond out of the box as soon as possible.

Forbes had enjoyed the show. A barrister's dream is an out of control witness. He decided he would save his best attack for the main hearing. He asked the same questions as Billy, with one additional one. "Is it not a fact, Mr. Drummond that you are very friendly with Mr. Bull?"

"Yeah, he's my best mate".

"Would it not be fair to assume that, although you were not in court to hear his replies, you carefully agreed what to say"?

"Come again, I don't understand the question".

Forbes exhaled loudly. "Did you agree with Billy what you would tell the court?"

"Well, we might have discussed it. So what?"

"No more questions", Forbes sat down.

The Chairman conferred with his colleagues, and looked at the court clock. "11am. tomorrow", he asked both Counsels. The Clerk continued to write fiercely, it was his job to note everything down.

The following day the Court resumed and Jean Brown took the oath. She surveyed the courtroom. She was terrified. The prosecution invited her to tell the Court in her own words the sequence of events on the night in question. She gave evidence, clearly, surprising herself. She faltered when she came to the help she had received from Elizabeth Markham. She tried to skate over it and hoped the Court didn't take much notice. The defence's tactics were not to cross examine her.

She sat in the courtroom for the rest of the hearing, her eyes carefully averted from Jack. Eventually, all the witnesses had checked and signed their statements.

Then Mr. Forbes stood up, "On behalf of my client I would like to plead 'not guilty'. I reserve his defence".

The Chairman addressed Jack. "Stand up". Jack shuffled to his feet. 'We are satisfied that there is a prima facia case on all charges.

"You are committed for trial at the York assizes at a date to be fixed; and you will be remanded in custody in the meantime"

Jean turned to look at Jack, but he was already disappearing down the steps, to the cells below. She was very uneasy about today. The real truth about Elizabeth homed in on her thoughts.

Jack had to wait in the dingy cell until the Courts ended for the day at five o'clock. He was then driven back to the prison in the same uncomfortable vehicle.

CHAPTER THIRTY TWO

Andrew Visits

Christopher was getting better every day though David still felt it necessary to limit his work load. They had agreed that Christopher could return to work, but only on a part-time basis. David and Elizabeth had just managed to take on a newly qualified assistant solicitor, who was helping tremendously with the extra work.

Trevor Potts was six foot four, thin and lanky. Educated at the local grammar school, his deep bass voice was very masculine and edged with a strong North Yorkshire accent. His mop of brown hair was continually falling over his left eye, which meant that he was constantly tossing his head in order to see, quite an endearing characteristic to some ladies, Elizabeth thought. His most outstanding feature were his pixie ears.

"Quite extraordinary", was Elizabeth's first comment, after the preliminary interview. She especially liked his warm genuine smile. He lacked experience and had not yet decided in which area of the law he wanted to specialise.

Christopher's relationship with Patricia was definitely blossoming. As promised, she had invited him round to tea. He was delighted to be shown the collection of her paintings which were dotted round the house.

The four storey semi-detached Victorian house was in the town, fairly near to Elizabeth's house. It was tall and narrow, one of its features being a solid oak staircase, with a small gallery on the first floor. The furnishings were chintzy, and each piece of furniture looked as though it had been selected with extreme care. The whole clever effect was of a home where one could relax. The garden was protected by a six foot wall, and was full of herbaceous flowers, all neatly growing in the immaculate borders. Yellow roses covered one whole wall, whilst the far wall had runner beans trailing up it.

Christopher had recently taken her to a piano recital, and she in turn had invited him to a friend's latest art exhibition. David and Elizabeth were both delighted that they were getting on so well.

Following his encounter with Elizabeth, Andrew had telephoned as agreed and was coming the next Saturday for lunch. This time the children were all staying firmly with them, they were taking no chances. Pip and John showed vague interest, but pretty unconcerned about the whole impending visit.

Somehow, Elizabeth was feeling much better about his arrival than the feelings she had encountered before Barbara visit. She felt at least she could cope with him.

He duly arrived at twelve thirty on the dot. Instead of rushing to the children he sat in the drawing room and let them come to him when they were ready, which they did mainly out of curiosity.

He had brought them all a present, and thoughtfully including Robert and Carol.

"My, you are improving", Elizabeth laughed, but was secretly pleased that the other two were not excluded. The children crawled all over him and made him get down on the floor, playing with their cars and toys. The day went off without a hitch, and he took his leave at six o'clock. As he was getting into his car, he turned and smiled.

"Thank you both very much, it's quite the happiest day I've had in a long while. Can I come again?"

"Of course", said David, "Just give us a ring".

"Oh! By the way, I didn't mention the case, Elizabeth, but you are obviously going through hell. If there is anything I can do to help, you only have to ask".

"That's very kind", said Elizabeth, "Goodbye".

CHAPTER THIRTY THREE

Jack's Fortunes Change

Waiting for a final hearing date to be given was wearing Jacks nerves down. The claustrophobic atmosphere of the prison was destroying him. The air in the cell was putrid. Sean and Micky felt the same, but seemed more able to contain their emotions.

He was now sure that he was going to be convicted and sent to prison, he didn't know if he could take it. Recently he had started sweating profusely, for no apparent reason and the tears would roll down his cheeks involuntarily. He knew he was losing his grip but was helpless to do anything about it. All he could do to take his mind off the trial was to read endless novels, and talk with the others about their problems.

The warders had noticed deterioration in Jacks mental state but other than noting it in their report they had chosen to do nothing about it.

One of the strange things about prison life was you never saw the governor until you were due for discharge. In the films, the Governor is invariably portrayed as interviewing all the new inmates, and then keeping in reasonable touch throughout their term.

In reality, he was never seen.

He didn't even carry out an occasional round of the prison to make sure his men were doing their jobs properly.

The probable excuse was that he was too involved in the administration. Without, the comfort and positive evidence of the Governor, the men felt even more stranded.

Jack woke in the middle of the night delirious; he was shaking and his body was bathed in sweat. Involuntary screams were erupting from his body. Sean and Micky in an attempt to control him had wrestled with him and in the end had been forced to resort to sitting on him. Jack simply tossed them off.

"For Christ's sake man, shut it, otherwise they will throw you in the padded cell!!" shouted Micky.

The door, burst open and two Warders, came in.

"Big, shut it", they shouted. It made no difference; Jack was in a world of this own.

"He can't man; can't you see when a man's ill? It's been coming on for days, you know that", said Sean.

"All right Big, we'll get the Doctor, but you better not be shamming".

The light was turned out as the Warders left the cell. Jack continued to thrash, mumbling incoherently in the darkness.

Doctor Sleamen, arrived twenty minutes later. He took Jack's pulse and temperature. He darted a look at the warders.

"How long has this man been in this condition?"

The Wardens shifted uncomfortably. "It's only just come on".

"That's not true, Sir", intervened Micky. "He's been unwell for days off his food.

They know". He poked his thumb towards the Warders; "they just chose to ignore it".

"Shut it", bellowed the taller of the two Warders.

"On the contrary", Sleamen said in a resigned tone, "I will have to make a report and these men have been more helpful than you, and what's more I want it noted", he turned to face them so that he could make a mental note of their numbers, "that these prisoners are not to be punished for speaking out. I am going to give this man an injection to sedate him. He is then to be moved as quickly as possible to the prison hospital. One of you stay with me, the other go and get a stretcher and more men, he will be heavy to carry".

The Warders could not fail to notice the doctor's contempt for them; he dismissed them by turning his back on them without another word and speaking with Jack.

Sleamen had been in the prison service for twenty years. He had great sympathy with the prisoners in the main and mild antipathy towards the warders. There was no doubt in his mind, if this man had come to see him in surgery days ago, he would have been able to prevent this breakdown. It happened a lot in prisons.

Prisoners, for the first time in their lives developing genuine phobias at being shut in confined spaces. A great many were on tranquilizers for the whole of their sentence. The man in front of him was obviously an outdoor man. Marvellous toned muscles. Poor bugger, he would probably rather die than be stuck in here for long.

The injection had taken its course and Jack had settled into a deep slumber.

Sean and Micky let go of their hold on him and returned to their bunks. Six men arrived with a stretcher and Jack was carted off to the hospital.

The prison hospital wing was very small, consisting of thirty beds. The turnover, not surprisingly had to be very fast. The other patients in his room were two men cut in a fight, sporting a labyrinth of stitches; one recovering from a hernia operation. A man with a broken pelvis the fifth had just reacted badly to the removal of four wisdom teeth.

Sleamen liked the cosy little unit, this was his domain. He held surgery once a day. The men had to get permission to see him. He shook his head, surveying Jack's unconscious body before him. This enormous healthy man locked up in a cell ten by six with two other men, only similar comparison was polar bears in a zoo, and they usually lost their minds as well. He would keep him sedated for a couple of days and see.

Jack came round on the third day having been kept sedated by Sleamen; he sat up and surveyed his surroundings. Hospital, how did he get here? He carefully moved his toes and fingers, and then gently under the clothes he touched his body.

It seemed all there, what on earth has happened to me, he thought, as he sat bolt upright.

Sleamen came out of his office accompanied by his male nurse. He raised his hand as he walked indicating to Jack to stay put.

"Now then Big, take it easy".

Jack blinked. "Could you please tell me what's happened?" Sleamen reached his bed. He sat on the edge. "I hope you are not going to give me any trouble".

"No, of course not, I don't understand", He clutched his throbbing head.

"You have had a bit of a breakdown. I want you to be a good chap and rest tonight. Tomorrow, I'd like a talk with you, before I send you back to your cell. Daren't hold on to you any longer. Nurse here will bring you some food. I'll see you at eight o'clock sharp in the morning". He rose and went back to his office.

Jack sat back on his pillow. He could remember feeling clammy and shaking, but nothing after that. He looked round the ward the other men were either reading or asleep. No one paid any attention to him. He started to doze in a fitful sort of way.

The following morning the male nurse told him to get dressed and present himself outside Sleamen's office at eight.

He found himself shaking as he tried to stand; he was surprised how feeble he felt. Sleamen motioned Jack to sit down. "My assessment of you young man is that you are suffering from a form of claustrophobia".

Jack raised his eyebrows.

"Fear of confined spaces, in the circumstances there is very little I can do about it. I am going to put you on a course of tablets that will help to keep you calm. If you start feeling panicky, try taking some deep breaths.

"Your cell-mates were very helpful, you ought to thank them."

"All right, Big off you go".

Jack was escorted back to his cell.

Dr Sleamen settled down to his report. He didn't quite know why he had taken a shine to Big. He recommended in his report that Jack should be given some manual work to do. After all he added in his P.S. he hadn't been convicted yet!

Once back in his cell, Jack sat down on his bed and put his head in his hands. "No matter what the consequences, I have got to get out of here", he mumbled.

Sean and Micky looked at each other. Sean volunteered, "Well, we do have an idea

The three heads bent together in collusion.

Three days later, when they went to slop out, in the morning, the Senior Warder called Jack over. "Aren't we the favoured one, you've been assigned to a working party. As soon as you have eaten your breakfast, I want to see you", he could not keep the note of sarcasm out of his voice.

Jack replied, "thank you sir", He didn't let the screw see any change in his countenance, but as he walked back to his cell, his heart leaped for joy.

He was sent to join a party of six men assigned to dig trenches for the new underground electricity cables. Apparently, one of the men had fallen sick and this had given him a chance. He knew nothing of the doctor's recommendation.

Outside in the fresh air, even the fine continuous drizzle that did not abate on the first day, was a pleasure, it felt good to use his muscles again. Working up a healthy sweat and filling his lungs, fit to burst. The other men treated him with suspicion and ignored him. He didn't give a dam. He was too big for them to annoy. He was enjoying himself so much, he left them behind. The warder wandered over.

"Ease up man. I know you're pleased to be out of your cell. But you'll kill that lot; they are not used to this pace." Jack grinned, and wiped the sweat from his forehead with the back of his hand.

"Thank you, sir. I hadn't noticed, I'll slow up a bit". He eased up allowing them to catch up, but not quite.

I'll not get tired at all working at this sloppy pace, he thought.

Jack behaved himself impeccably that week, because he had forced the pace, the team had completed twice the length they had dug the previous week. Jack had cracked it; he was assigned permanently to the outside digging party. He ignored the men's gibes at him. He could put up with a lot, anything rather than stay shut up in that cell twenty four hours a day!

CHAPTER THIRTY FOUR

Dinner Party

Where oh where, was the practice going, thought David as he sat in his office. He had employed Trevor Potts but was that because the work load had increased or rather, with his father part time and Elizabeth in a state, they were working inefficiently. He would have to consider the accounts very carefully when the year ended the fees earned would then give him a clearer idea. He wished the trial was over no telling what harm it was doing to the practice. Still one had to be positive in life and forge ahead.

That morning he had visited a client in hospital. Miss Ingram who had been badly burned in a car crash, her parents had come to see him about making a personal injuries claim weeks ago, but she had been too ill to give proper instructions. Her injuries were horrendous. Most of her upper torso had suffered first degree burns, the scarring would be terrible. If the burns had been any more extensive then she clearly wouldn't have survived, the doctors had said. How could money possibly compensate for the suffering and permanent scars she would no doubt have to contend with for the rest of her life.

At this moment in time the plastic surgeon didn't know

exactly how many operations he would have to perform.

Thankfully his battle with the estate agent was over.

Christine entered his office breaking his train of thought.

"The photo copier has broken, Mr Markham!"

"Have you called the engineers?"

"No, Mr. Markham, as this one's very old, I wondered whether you would like me to order a new one?"

"No, I certainly would not. Kindly get the service engineers to come forthwith".

"Yes, Mr. Markham", she sighed as she tottered out of the room.

Those heels must be four inches high, he thought.

Elizabeth came in. "Got a minute?"

"Yes, just having a mental breather myself". Elizabeth stood at the window, surveying the traffic, with her hands on her hips. She turned, He gave her his hand.

"You know I told you the builders Berry's have taken their business elsewhere, well they have just recommended one of their friends to me. Very odd don't you think?"

"It shows they must still have faith in us, they'll be back."

She continued. "As a result, I have a meeting this afternoon, is it all right if I take Trevor along for the experience".

"Yes, be my guest".

"What are we going to do about Christopher, he seems to be getting through the work, but seems rather entrenched at home.

The house feels sometimes, full of an inordinate amount of people. It now, looking back on it was very peaceful with just the kids and us", she sighed and went over and sat on his knee.

"I know darling, I was thinking the same, but just let's leave the status quo, just for the time being".

She got up "by the way, I've just been told the committal

proceedings are to be heard next Wednesday".

"OK, we'll speak about it later, don't forget the dinner party on Saturday", he called after her.

"Don't worry I won't".

*****

"Well, how are you settling in?" Elizabeth quizzed Trevor as they drove along.

"I'm enjoying the variety of work very much, as you know; I was stuck, doing Probate during my articles."

"You didn't like it?"

"Well, it was a bit limiting. Not much pressure!"

"Oh", she laughed, "You will soon have more than your fair share of that, I can promise you."

They pulled up beside the architects Land Rover and the builders, Pearson Brothers Volvo Estate.

Elizabeth got out of the car giving a cheery wave to the group awaiting her.

The twenty four acre site stretched before them. It was on a hill, if planning permission was granted, the residents would be able to enjoy superb views she thought.

They put on their gum boots and traipsed about over the land. They agreed with the clients they would look at the deeds and let them know of any problems, especially if rights of way needed to be moved. It was agreed to adjourn the meeting until the architect had prepared some rough plans for discussion. They said their goodbyes and were glad to get back to the sanctuary of the car. The moors were certainly throwing up some dreadful winds this afternoon.

*****

Elizabeth had given instructions to Mrs. Fraser for the dinner party on Saturday. Maggie, living in was a great boon. She could help with the serving and do the washing up. One of the minus points about entertaining was the debris afterwards. Patricia was as happy as a lark these days, and didn't mind staying late, because she could always pop in and chat to Christopher. There were definitely plus points, with having Christopher under the same roof. For all her comments to David she would miss his company, when he went home.

The children had been despatched to her Mother for the night.

It was five o'clock and Elizabeth was checking the last arrangements for the dinner. She went through her mental list.

The dining room table was laid, flowers on the table, butter in silver dish on the table. Courgette mousse in fridge, Salmon en croute in fridge, waiting to be cooked, new potatoes washed salad and vegetables ready.

Chocolate roulade, nearly finished, hazelnut meringue needed wedging together with double cream, raspberry coulis to make, fresh fruit salad prepared in fridge. The poor fridge was groaning. There was undoubtedly a great sense of achievement when it all started to come together.

"Right, Patricia you carry on and finish the roulade, before it cracks. I'll whip the cream for the meringue. Maggie you can start clearing up the kitchen, it looks as if a bomb has hit it. I think the floor will have to be washed yet again, it's a bit slippery?"

Maggie", she called as Maggie appeared from the dining room, "Put the dishwasher on when it's full. I want it empty for kick off."

Patricia wiped her hands. "If you don't mind, after I put the salmon in the oven, I'll hand over to Maggie. I'd like to go home, my feet are killing me. I think Maggie can cope, turning out to be a good little cook. Mr. Christopher is coming round to my house for a bit of supper, so he won't be in your way."

"There's no question of that, but I'm sure he would rather be entertained by you". She winked at Mrs. Fraser, who blushed.

At six thirty Elizabeth went up to change. The guests would start arriving at seven thirty. David came out of the bedroom as she mounted the stairs, yawning and tying his dressing gown cord round his waist.

"I was just going down to sort out the wine, see you in a minute."

Elizabeth felt like being a little light hearted; even if it was ostensibly superficial and part bravado. She had thought of cancelling this evening, but had decided against it. She put on a royal blue taffeta dress which came just above the knee. She took special care with her makeup, after she had put pearls round her neck and wrist. She swung round in front of her bedroom mirror. The skirt billowed out. "At least", she said to her image, "you'll go down fighting".

David had changed whilst she was in the bath and had already gone downstairs clad in his dinner jacket.

Elizabeth grabbed a pretty pinny as she went into the kitchen, and took the salmon out of the oven. "Perfect", she exclaimed, pleased with herself, "I hope it tastes as good as it looks" she muttered Maggie was sitting down with her feet on a stool reading a book. Elizabeth surveyed the immaculate kitchen. "Well, young lady, you seem to have everything under control.

I would be grateful if you would stay and clear away, until after we have finished the cheese course, after that I should sneak upstairs, I'll deal with the coffee!"

They smiled at each other like conspirators as the door bell rang!

Sally and Tom Powers, builders by trade, were the first to arrive. Followed by Anthea and George de la Mare, he was a barrister in the local set of chambers. David had settled them in the drawing room and was getting a round of drinks when the bell rang to admit, Major Ronnie Thompkins and his wife Rosemary.

He was an army dentist attached to the Lancers.

The dinner went without a hitch, the mouse with just a hint of fresh mint, was different. The salmon, with her special concoction of rice in the middle was very well received. Most guests tried two of the puddings. Maggie added certain grandness to the occasion. Elizabeth went into the kitchen after the main course to find her flagging. She looked very tired. "Come on you have done enough, clear this lot away and then take yourself off to bed. You can have tomorrow morning off, as you have worked this evening and have a lie in". She started the coffee peculator and returned to her guests.

The evening was going too well she thought. The Major was busy regaling everyone with stories of Northern Ireland. George was countering with escapades at the bar, puffing on his cigar.

Anthea, his wife simpered and hung on his every word. Sally, Tom's wife went into peals of laughter at the slightest thing.

Her well endowed figure bounced beneath her low cut dress, giving the constraining part of the dress, a hard time. She kept playing with her shoulder length hair sending the occasional kiss to Tom, across the table. He was not adverse to this. Elizabeth felt they would not be going straight to sleep when they got home, she was sure of that.

The conversation flowed. Not once did any guest refer

to Elizabeth's impending trial or her involvement in the Jack Big's case.

At last they were all going.

As he shook his hand at the door Tom put his other hand on David's arm. He winked confidingly. "It's been a lovely evening", he leaned forward, "good luck to you both". David smiled back and nodded, while the lusty builder continued to pump his hand so vigorously, the joints were shaking in David's shoulder.

"Phew, glad that's all over", said Elizabeth flopping down into a chair.

"You did brilliantly, darling, the food was marvellous, everyone seemed to enjoy it. Let's go to bed".

"I must clear up the kitchen".

"Oh, come on leave it until the morning".

"No, David, you don't seem to realise how hard everyone has worked.

It simply isn't fair. I'll go and get out of this dress, take off these excruciatingly uncomfortable shoes, and get on with it. You can go to bed".

"Don't be a martyr, I'll help", he said peeling off his jacket, "give me and apron".

CHAPTER THIRTY FIVE

Elizabeth in Court

ELIZABETH sat in the dock. She refused to look anywhere but straight in front of her. Smartly dressed in a grey check suit with a matching blouse, she found her mouth was dry and her palms clammy. Oh God, she thought, the sheer humiliation of it all. She viewed the forthcoming proceedings with icy clarity.

Biggleswade had decided to keep his options open. He still wanted the substance of the prosecution's evidence. He contemplated running a defence in this lower Court, in the vague hope of persuading the magistrates that there was no case to answer, but there would be a very slim chance of this tact succeeding.

Elizabeth was already on her feet, as the door opened and the Magistrates filed in. The Chairman entered the courtroom first. Leonora Snoop was middle aged her neat suit covered a thin and spiky body. Her temperament was usually pretty even, but this morning her equilibrium had definitely been disturbed. The milkman had forgotten to leave her any eggs for breakfast, and someone had parked in the space reserved for her in the Court car park. She took her seat.

Placing her spectacles on her nose she noticed Elizabeth standing in the dock. She only hoped the day would improve.

Her fellow Magistrates were Frederick Smith, a greengrocer by trade, who had been on the bench for years and was held to be a respected member of the community. Sitting on the other side, Graham Benjamin took up his pen. He was a newcomer to the bench; at forty six years of age he was hoping the cases today would not take too long; his wine business needed him, he had had to leave some urgent problems this morning. Sometimes it was inconvenient to sit at court, but one couldn't cry off at the last minute.

The charge was read out by the clerk to the court; Elizabeth stood and answered, "Not guilty". She resumed her seat. She knew that Christopher, David and Michael were all in Court. Her mother preferred to stay away. David was sitting next to John Lanthenby, whispering with him. Norton Biggleswade sat in the front row, with John Mcguire beside him.

James Crosby, the solicitor for the County Prosecution Service, was sitting at the other end of the row. He got to his feet and quickly gave the magistrates the details of the case. He ended "The prosecution will seek to prove without any shadow of doubt that the accused was exceeding the speed limit at the time of the accident".

He called his first witness, a Sergeant Thompson from the accident re-construction unit. He opened his note book.

The next witness was an unknown man who smartly went into the witness box and swore the oath. The defence were all agog. Elizabeth made a mental note of every detail of his gangling and angular looking appearance. He was aged about forty with horn rimmed, thick glasses, perched on a thin long nose.

His face was set in heavy lines around the jowls. His black hair which had been sleeked back with grease clung to his head. As he gripped the box, she saw the long pointed fingers with engrained dirt under the finger nails. His jacket was misshapen with age and sported leather patches on the elbows. He looked thoroughly unsavoury.

James Crosby faced the witness. "Would you tell the court your name and address?"

He replied in a grating whining tone of voice. "Clive Hope, 14, Monk Drive, Thesby near Scarborough". He sounded confident and full of himself. Crosby continued, "How can you assist the court?"

Clive Hope spoke as if well rehearsed. "On the 14th of March, I was driving in my car from Whitby to Scarborough. I was overtaken by a red Porsche travelling very fast. I knew I was approaching a village and a restricted zone, so I was slowing down".

"At what speed would you say the Porsche was travelling?"

"Well," he smiled ingratiatingly, showing yellow teeth stained, from years of smoking. "I'm not an expert, you understand, but in my opinion, the car passed me doing more than eighty miles per hour".

Elizabeth heart stopped.

"How far from the village were you?"

"About half a mile".

"Did you have the Porsche in your sight at all times?"

"I did".

"Was the Porsche applying the brakes, were the brake lights on making any attempt at slowing down?"

"Yes, I did see that".

"At what speed, in your judgement?" He coughed politely. "Would you estimate the Porsche entered the thirty mile per hour area?"

"At about seventy miles per hour".

What speed were you doing?"

"Just above thirty, but of course, slowing down, as I have already explained to the court."

The prosecution solicitor sat down saying, "I have no more questions".

Biggleswade was completely left-footed. He glanced at Elizabeth and she had indicated she had never seen this man before. Biggleswade stood up. "I have no instructions in respect of this witness, or should I say I have no questions at this stage."

Crosby was on his feet again and addressed the bench. "Madam Chairman, I don't know whether you and your colleagues have heard sufficient evidence. If not, I can call Jean Brown the mother of the twins."

The bench conferred. "We would like to spare the mother any unnecessary upset if possible. Unless there are strong objections from learned Counsel we have heard enough."

Biggleswade wanted to play it cool. They had to find out more about this independent witness. He knew very well that the court placed great reliance on the evidence of independent witnesses, as; in theory they had nothing to gain and were merely there to assist the court. "I do not object, Madam". After the witnesses had signed their depositions Elizabeth was committed for trial at the Old Bailey.

Biggleswade stood up and formally reserved her defence and asked for bail to be extended until the trial. The Chairman looked at James Crosby who half stood up and stated he had no objections. "Granted", said the Chairman.

Elizabeth, Christopher and Michael waited whilst Biggleswade conferred with Crosby who had a self satisfied smile. He always liked unnerving the other side.

"My client knows nothing of the independent witness!"

Biggleswade told him.

"That's not my problem", Crosby muttered as he collected his papers together and swept from the Court.

David was white. "I'm not happy at all," he said. Catching David up Biggleswade said "at least the technical evidence does not seem very strong. Come back to the Hotel round the corner. Biggleswade and his entourage followed. I want to read the depositions John; I will pop into the stationers and take photostat copies, if I may, before I hand them to you, Biggleswade, chose not to join them, and returned to London, waiting further instructions from John Lanthenby.

Christopher stood rubbing his chin. "I know that witness's face, but for the life of me I can't place him. I will think on it".

David replied "Yes, the face does seem familiar. We will have to undermine the validity of his evidence otherwise we could be sunk".

Elizabeth turned, "I promise you all, I was not speeding, and I have never seen that horrible man or his car in my life!"

Jean had been relieved at not being required to give evidence this morning. She had been outside the court, waiting in the corridor when Elizabeth came out of Court, their eyes met, yet still there was no animosity emanating from Elizabeth. She looked more upset than anything. Jean went home, and flung herself weeping onto her bed.

CHAPTER THIRTY SIX

Jacks Schemes

Jack and his confederates Sean and Micky were planning their escape. Sean's girlfriend made a habit of bringing a fresh tube of toothpaste on each visit; this was permitted, except each tube contained a tiny small hacksaw blade. It took ages to collect sufficient blades to make any attempt possible. They made a small pocket in the side of one of the mattresses, into which the blades were slid as and when received. They prayed they would not have to change cells otherwise other prisoners would be the beneficiaries of their efforts so far.

It was a ten foot drop from the window to the street below. The window was not very large, so they decided they would all have to start losing weight which was quite difficult because of their stodgy diet. They made a concealed cut to test the strength of the blades in order to make an estimate the time it would take them to remove the bars. They were old, rusty, and not that thick. It would probably take a few nights of solid work to cut through two of them.

*****

Shortly after the hearing in the magistrates Court, John Lanthenby wrote to Elizabeth giving her the date in July her case was listed for hearing. The Judge's list varied on a daily basis; so that the date given was approximate as the trial before might take longer than anticipated to complete. Elizabeth did not know how she had got through the next few weeks without completely cracking up.

Compressed lips of non-discussion had settled over the office staff. David had staunchly refused to be drawn by Elizabeth into discussing contingency plans, in the event she was convicted. He knew that it would lower her morale even more, and anyway, he hadn't the faintest idea what he would do if the unthinkable happened. Twice he had found her in the bedroom sobbing inconsolably. He didn't know what to do, except hold her and assure her that everything would be all right, which he wasn't one hundred percent sure about at all.

The Judge's list had collapsed, (the prosecution had withdrawn from the previous case because of insufficient evidence) so Elizabeth was called for the following day

Staying at their club in Sloane Street they were at least amongst familiar surroundings. Elizabeth refused to leave her room in the evening.

She was getting paranoid about people looking at her. She only toyed with the scrambled eggs she had sent to her room and eventually fell into a fitful sleep in David's arms. She had kissed him, and he had whispered endearments into her hair.

They got to the Old Bailey at nine thirty to find John and Norton Biggleswade waiting for them. Biggleswade came forward.

"Ah, there you are, my dear, just one or two questions about Miss Brown". He walked beside her down the corridor; he fiddled with his wig as he walked as if it irritated him.

David looked helplessly at John for support.

"Come on, old boy", said John we'll do our best, got to tear this man "Hope" apart though!"

The Old Bailey Judge was called Maurice Featherstone, Biggleswade knew that he was hard of hearing in one ear and had instructed his junior, John McGuire, to reserve their places and stack their papers on the side of his good ear.

Treasury Counsel, Nicholas Riddle and his junior came haring into Court. When he saw Biggleswades papers in situ, he realised he had made his first tactical error.

Elizabeth went to surrender to her bail and was taken down and locked in the cells. She was white when she said goodbye to David, but managed to hold back the tears which were threatening.

The Court duly assembled. Elizabeth head held high walked up the narrow stairs to the dock, flanked either side, as usual, by two female warders. Elizabeth noted with relief that there was only one member of the press there, and he looked pretty junior.

Mr Justice Featherstone came into Court, attired in his brilliant red robe and short grey wig. All in Court rose and bowed deeply, not taking their seats until his Lordship, having returned their bows was himself seated. The jury shuffled into the court. As they came in, they stared around, this being for most of them their first time in a courtroom. They seemed more bewildered than the rest of the assembly.

Biggleswade stared at them, making a careful mental note as each one was sworn in. There were eight men and four women. A motley bunch, thought Biggleswade. Still, juries always looked pretty unimpressive at first glance they sometimes surprised him as the case unfolded. He could see no reason to object to anyone. He looked at Elizabeth, who knew what he wanted, and nodded her agreement.

The jury sat down, glad to be out of the limelight.

The judge leant forward and addressed them briefly on their duties. They all nodded, indicating that they understood.

"Very well", said Featherstone, "Let's proceed". He put his spectacles on and made a careful study of Elizabeth with a guarded expression on his face he knew that she was a solicitor. She stood up, her black suit looking very sombre. "Mm", grunted the Judge, adding "Yes" expectantly.

The clerk got to his feet and read the indictment.

"Elizabeth Markham", he boomed, "You are charged that on the 14th of March 1970 you drove a vehicle dangerously causing the death of a child. How say you?"

"Not guilty my Lord", her voice was both audible and firm.

Nicholas Riddle, tall with greying moustache, opened the case; addressing the jury, he took them through the events, outlining all the details. When he came to the pram and the twins, there was a gasp from one or two of the women, and all eyes turned to Elizabeth. Elizabeth stared straight ahead. He went on with his opening speech for the rest of the morning.

Featherstone made notes as he went along. Judges always took a careful note, as they would have to refer to these accurately in their summing up speech to the jury later on, at the end of the trial. Their notes also helped to resolve any conflict during the case as to the evidence already given.

Featherstone wanted to get away early that day, so he only allowed a thirty minute adjournment at lunchtime, forgoing his usual lavish lunch, perks of the job. He allowed himself just enough time to eat his sandwiches and have a coffee.

At half past one when the Court re-assembled, the first witness called was Sergeant Thompson. Biggleswade had his own expert to call later on to challenge some of his figures and conclusions.

Sergeant Thompson repeated to the Court the same evidence he had given previously, on which he had not been cross examined until now. Riddle finished by asking him.

"In your opinion, was the accused driving dangerously?"

Thompson shifted uncomfortably. "Well, as I've said, the skid mark was not that long, which could be for several reasons". He thought about his superiors. You got a terrible wigging back at the station, if you let the prosecution down in Court. "It would be difficult for me to say it were dangerous."

"Was she speeding?"

"I think so".

"No more questions, thank you".

Biggleswade got slowly to his feet. Sergeant Thompson held his breath.

"Now, Sergeant Thompson", he clasped his hands behind his back. "The jury heard what I consider to be most inconclusive evidence by you. Would you not agree?"

He shuffled, and looked down at his notes, as if hoping some help would spring from them. "No, Sir".

"If, as my client will say, she was not exceeding the speed limit, it would be difficult for you to categorically prove otherwise on your own evidence would it not?"

"Yes, Sir, but it may be, she did not apply the brakes in time". He added hurriedly.

"From your findings, would you say that my client could definitely not have been travelling at a speed in excess of thirty miles an hour?"

"I would think so, Sir"

"Yes or No?" thundered Biggleswade.

The sergeant blushed pink. "No".

"Thank you, no more questions". He looked at the Judge who shook his head indicating he had nothing to add.

Clive Hope was called to the witness box, dressed in exactly the same clothes he had worn in his previous Court appearance. He trotted out what seemed a well rehearsed story. Biggleswade stood up.

"Mr. Hope, I have one or two questions to ask you". Hope smiled inanely, little knowing that Biggleswade was his enemy.

"Mr. Hope, you have told the court a story; anyway, it sounds like a story to me, as you seem to have got it word perfect".

"I don't know what you mean", Hope spluttered.

"No, I'm sure you don't". Biggleswade spoke without sincerity. "Are you sure that, you saw the accused's car entering the restricted zone at a speed in excess of seventy miles an hour?"

"I am, sir".

"You see", he went on slowly; "We have just heard from the previous witness that the accused could not have been travelling at that speed".

"Well, he's wrong. I know what I saw".

"I forgot to mention, Mr. Hope that the previous witness was a sergeant from the traffic re-construction unit. With respect, it's his job to know".

The witness looked down at the floor.

"Mr Hope, I cannot see from the police report, anywhere where your name is mentioned. Did you not speak to the Police?" There was a silence.

"Please tell the Court what you saw?" He suddenly snapped. The change in tone made Hope jump.

"Well, like I said, she passed me, and then the accident happened."

"What did you do", shouted Biggleswade.

"I, I drove off", he stammered.

Biggleswade sensing the theatre of the moment threw his pen on his papers. "You drove off, after noting the accused speeding recklessly, you saw an accident in consequence, and you just drove off?" He turned to the jury shaking his head, in disbelief.

"Yes, Sir".

"Without seeing whether you could help or speaking with the police?"

"Yes, Sir".

"This surely must put your whole evidence in jeopardy. Have you anyone who could verify you were on that road on that day?"

"No, Sir".

Biggleswade blew his nose. "I must confess I'm puzzled by your sudden appearance in this case. Tell me," he said quizzically. "Do you know the accused? She is a practising solicitor in Scarborough".

"No, Sir".

"Her husband or his firm?" Biggleswade had the scent, like a bloodhound.

"I know the firm", Hope replied in a barely audible voice.

Featherstone cupped his good ear. "What did he say?"

"I put it to you, Mr Hope, that on the day in question you were not there at all. For reasons of your own you have come to this court today with nothing but a tissue of lies. I trust you know the penalty for perjury you weren't there, were you?" He bellowed.

Mr Hope did not reply, but hung his head. Biggleswade slowly and triumphantly resumed his seat.

Riddle realised the hopelessness of pursuing this witness.

"I think you had better sit down Mr Hope, no doubt the police want a word with you".

Hope slunk out through the Court.

It all came back to Christopher. He cursed himself for not remembering earlier. Hope had been on the other side of a probate action some three years before. His collusion with witnesses and perversion of the truth had led to the action being dismissed by the Court, with costs awarded against him. He did not benefit from the estate and had to sell his house in order to pay the costs after the hearing, he had sworn he would get even with the Markhams. "And by God", Christopher said out loud, "he nearly succeeded".

Elizabeth had never seen him; it was well before her time. David had only seen him once in the waiting room when he attended their office.

After that the Court adjourned for the day. Elizabeth fell into David's arms, laughing with relief. "Wasn't Biggleswade good?"

Excellent", said David. They had a short conference with Biggleswade, who told Elizabeth that she was not out of the woods yet, despite Hope's annihilation. David was anxious to get back to the club in order to phone the office. Poor Trevor was coping single handed.

They were all back in their places at eleven- thirty the following day. The Judge had kept them waiting for an hour. He had been hearing two urgent applications which had priority.

Without further delay Jean Brown was called to the stand. Her hands visibly shook whilst she read the oath from the card.

She was wearing a pink dress, and her hair was tied back in a pony tail.

The eyes of the Court were upon her. Sympathetic waves emanated silently from the Jury.

Riddle stood and read out her name and address.

"Miss Brown, in your own words, please tell the Court what happened on the 14th of March?"

To begin with she spoke falteringly, but she gradually became more fluent.

"I was taking my children with me to catch the bus. I had started to cross the road, when this car, a red Porsche car, came from nowhere. It struck the pram, and as a result of the injuries, Geoffrey died and Nicholas was badly injured.

"Do you see the driver of the car in Court?"

"Yes".

"Would you kindly point her out?"

Jean raised her hand and pointed directly at Elizabeth, who met her gaze without flinching.

"At what speed do you think the car was travelling?"

"Very fast indeed, otherwise I'd have seen it!" She took out her handkerchief and wiped her eyes.

"Please don't upset yourself; I have just one more line of questions. Did you have any personal contact with the accused after the accident?"

The Judge thought, leading question, oh well, never mind.

"Yes".

"Please tell us about it". Jean was scathing about her various meetings with Elizabeth being careful not to dwell too much on the kindness that had been shown to her.

"I have no more questions of this witness". He looked towards Biggleswade who was already on his feet.

"Miss Brown, I note you are not married. Is the father of the child present?"

"No, my Lord."

"Where is he?"

"He's in prison awaiting trial", she whispered.

"Do we know what he's charged with"? He was now playing with her.

"I think its GBH and rape".

"Against whom?"

Featherstone said wearily. "I suppose there's a point to this line of questioning?"

"Indeed, my Lord, all in good time".

"Very well, please proceed".

Jean replied in a whisper. "Me, my Lord".

"Who?" boomed the Judge?

Biggleswade said loudly, "She said ME my Lord".

"Oh, you, Mm, all right", he muttered into the hand he was leaning on as he resumed writing.

"Perhaps you could assist the court by telling them the father's name and what sort of man he was?" continued Biggleswade.

"His name is Jack Big and he is a fisherman".

"Go on".

"There's nothing else to say".

"Good God, woman, the man is in prison accused of raping you and you can tell us nothing".

"May I remind learned Counsel", intervened the Judge, "that Miss Brown is not on trial, and to the best of my knowledge, we are not here to try a rape case".

"I'm sorry, my Lord", Biggleswade persisted, "but I am only trying to get to the facts of this case. I am afraid that, I am going to have to crave your indulgence by persisting with this line of questioning".

"Very well", replied the Judge sighing.

Jean was becoming uneasy. She hadn't bargained on being cross examined.

"I repeat the question, Miss Brown, what is Jack Big like?"

"Well, he is a large man, who sometimes had bad temper fits".

"Yes and what happened then?"

"He sometimes used to hit me".

Exasperation was now flowing from Biggleswade. "I put it to you that he used to beat you, and on the night of the 13th he had beaten you again, and you had taken sedation tablets?"

"That's not true".

"Be careful, Miss Brown aren't you one of the key witnesses in the impending trial against Mr. Big?"

"Yes", she said.

"All right, we'll leave that for now. You have already stated that after the accident the accused visited you at home. Did she not try and help you?"

"Yes, she came round all right, but only to try and save her own skin. She said that if I didn't give evidence against her she would help me financially and get the council to give me a flat".

Featherstone peered over his glasses, "Are you quite sure Miss Brown? I doubt whether the accused would have the kind of influence over the local council to get them to give you a flat!"

"That's what she said, my Lord", said Jean triumphantly.

"Did Mrs. Markham befriend you?"

"Well, she tried, but I would have none of it".

Biggleswade sighed, "Miss Brown was, or was it not Mrs. Markham, who came to your aid after you had been raped and beaten by Jack Big, and further was it not also the case that her husband took you to the hospital for treatment, and called the police, and that she and her husband asked you to stay with them in their own home until you felt better?"

Jean could feel the Judge's unwavering eyes on her. He was definitely formidable. "Well, I admit, she did turn up at the right moment".

"Did you stay in her house?"

"Yes, clever of me, I thought to play along with them, after what she'd done, don't you think?"

"I do not think anything; I am not a witness in this case. Did you get a flat after all?"

"I did, all through my own efforts, no thanks to her".

"I put it to you, Miss Brown that Jack Big beat you up regularly and the night before the accident was just another example. You took too many tablets, became confused, and momentarily wanted to vent your anger on the children. You saw an easy way out. You noticed the Porsche coming slowly along and deliberately pushed the pram in front of it; stepping back onto the pavement to save yourself didn't you?" His voice was rising. "You killed Geoffrey, by deliberately pushing his pram in the path of the accused's car?"

"NO", Jean screamed, IT'S NOT TRUE!!!"

The courtroom fell silent.

Biggleswade sat down.

Riddle stood up. "Just one further question Miss Brown. Did the accused offer you a specific sum of money if you did not give evidence, or did she vaguely offer assistance for the boys?"

"The latter".

"I see. No more questions, thank you".

Jean blew her nose, wiped her eyes and glared at Biggleswade as she left the witness box.

Various members of the public gave conflicting evidence of what they had seen. No one seemed to agree.

The prosecution witnesses were over. The following morning the defence called Elizabeth to the stand.

*****

Biggleswade was on his feet. "Are you Mrs Elizabeth Markham of "Charlene", Willows End, Scarborough?"

"I am, my Lord".

"Are you by profession a solicitor of the Supreme Court?"

"I am".

Elizabeth was wearing a navy dress and jacket, with white piping and a matching polka dot handkerchief protruding from the pocket. Her navy and white shoes were high and feminine. She looked vulnerable, but very pretty as she stood in the witness box waiting expectantly.

"Would you please tell the court what happened on the 14th of March?"

Her voice rang out clearly and positively across the court. She had everyone's attention.

"I was driving from Whitby to Scarborough in no particular hurry. In fact I was enjoying the drive. It was a lovely spring day, and the countryside was coming alive. As I approached the village, I noted the restriction signs, and slowed right down. As I passed the speed sign into the village, I was travelling at the exact speed limit. I could see a woman ahead with a pram. Suddenly the pram was in my path, there was nothing I could do. I immediately put the car into an emergency brake, pulling on the handbrake at the same time with all my strength; but I had no chance. I simply had insufficient time to stop".

"Did you pass a cream Anglia car, driven by Mr. Hope?"

"I did not; the road was clear behind me and in front".

Featherstone was enjoying hearing the accused speak. Her intonation and diction, was easy on his good ear. She was also very attractive, which made her also easy on the eye. I believe her, he thought, it looks a bit like a set up to me.

"May we now pass on to Miss Jean Brown, the mother. Why did you go and see her and what transpired?"

"Whilst I felt at the time, and still do, that I had done all

I could to prevent the accident. I was obviously deeply upset, and also very concerned about the injuries to the children. No one would tell me how they were. I was beside myself with worry. So much so that as soon as I found out where she lived, I went to see her.

At first her reception of me was extremely hostile, which, I felt was understandable. I eventually persuaded Miss Brown to let me in for a chat. She told me about the children. She then became upset and started telling me about the social workers not being pleased with her; that Jack Big, her ex-boyfriend had returned and given her a beating. She had taken a sleeping pill when he left, and in the morning she took another sedative. She said that she was confused and upset and at the time was hating the children. She was then concerned that the social services would remove the children into care, if they came to the conclusion that it was a possibility that she was responsible for the accident, because of the drugs she was on and her irresponsible attitude in the past. Miss Brown broke down crying at this point.

"I was completely flabbergasted, but it made sense. She must have seen me coming, I couldn't understand why she did not wait for me to pass before crossing the road. Now, it started to fall into place. She begged me not to tell anyone. I returned later and drove her to the hospital and she let me see the twins. They were in intensive care", her voice dropped. "They looked so fragile, poor little mites".

She clasped her hands to make them steady.

"You went to see her again?"

"Yes, I called in, with the family on the way back from church. I found that Jack Big had returned, and she was in a terrible state.

My husband took her to casualty; he then brought her home where she stayed for a week, being looked after by my house keeper, Mrs. Fraser at home".

"Did you at any time offer her money, and try and persuade her not to give evidence?"

"Of course not. In fact in the canteen at the hospital, the first day we met, I explained most carefully, that I had only come to see her because of the children's welfare and that the police might take action against me; in which case I would deal with them in the proper manner. I was not there to sway her. Because of my job, I knew that by going at all, I was making my position vulnerable, and I told her so. My concern for the children, however outweighed the risk, and I am still glad I went."

"What about the flat?"

"Yes, I did ring up the council, but that was all. It has already been suggested in this court that it is extremely unlikely that I would have any sway with the council at all which of course is true. Yes, I did say I would help with the children, if I could", she went on. "What I meant was, with four children at home there were bound to be cast offs and toys, and maybe some of these would help her. It was an open gesture with no hidden meaning."

"Is there anything else?"

"After poor Geoffrey died, her attitude changed to open hatred towards me."

Elizabeth fumbled in her handbag.

"I produce this letter". McGuire had handed Biggleswade the letter which Jean had sent to Elizabeth, on her return from holiday, in which she stated that she never wanted to speak to Elizabeth again.

Biggleswade handed the letter to the Judge with copies for the Jury. He read it slowly aloud he then sat down; well pleased with the way in which Elizabeth had given her evidence.

Nicholas Riddle stood up.

"Mrs Markham, we have heard evidence that you were speeding. How fast were you going?"

"Thirty miles an hour. I felt the police officers evidence was very inconclusive and indecisive, and I would prefer not to comment on Mr. Hope's.

The Judge frowned.

"I have already told the court, I was not speeding"

"Very well. Now, your version of what was said between you and Miss Brown cannot be verified so it's your word against hers?"

"That's correct".

"Presumably, you feel that because of your professional standing we all should believe you and not Miss Brown?"

"I don't think that at all, and I consider it a particularly unworthy thing for you to suggest". Elizabeth retorted.

"Oh, dear, I must remember not to offend you in future", he taunted.

The Judge snapped. "That will do".

Riddle now chastened, continued. "I put it to you, the suggestion that Miss Brown admitted to you that she had pushed the pram into your path on purpose, is pure fiction and a tissue of lies."

"It is the truth", Elizabeth said levelly.

"No more questions". Biggleswade saw no reason to re-examine and sat down heavily.

Elizabeth returned to the dock, looking neither to the left nor right.

Biggleswade next called Mrs. Stroud, the social worker. She took the oath. "Mrs Stroud it's very kind of you to spare the time to come. Would you tell the court about Jean Brown and Jack Big?"

"Yes, they have been known to us for some time. They lost a flat once, due to damage and rent arrears. I have always kept a careful eye on Miss Brown during her pregnancy and after the babies were born. We were always concerned because we knew about the violent rages of Mr. Big. It seems we weren't careful enough". She sighed.

"Was she depressed?"

"I'm afraid she was frequently depressed and seemed to me to be virtually living on tranquilizers and cigarettes".

"Yet you allowed her to take Nicholas home?"

"Yes, well, she seemed to me to have turned over a new leaf and was really trying. Apart from that, Jack Big is safely in custody. We do visit almost daily".

"Thank you, Mrs. Stroud".

Riddle stood up. "Would you say Miss Brown is a good mother?"

"She has had her moments, but will always need supervision in my view."

Biggleswade addressed the Judge. "I don't know if you have any questions for this witness, my Lord, but if not perhaps Mrs. Stroud could be released, she is very busy".

"Yes, I think so". Featherstone replied."Why not".

Biggleswade's next witness was an independent expert who gave evidence on the skid marks and measurements of the car and pram at the point of impact. Tony Jones was an engineer who spent part of his time in court dealing with cases such as this one. He really couldn't see from the documentary evidence how she could have been speeding. On his calculations, she was travelling at a speed below the limit, and he told the court so.

Norton Biggleswade addressed the jury. He was very pleased with the way the case was going. He could not see how the Jury could do anything but return a verdict of 'not guilty'. Having got Mr. Hope to admit his perjury and personal vendetta against the Markhams he was no longer a threat. The problem was Jean Brown, bound to make the jury feel compassion, having lost a child. After all it was still her word against that of Elizabeth. He was therefore careful and gentle in the way he tried to demolish her evidence, to the jury. Nevertheless, Elizabeth thought that his speech was eloquent, forceful and full of passion.

In his address to the jury on behalf of the Crown Jean's barrister Riddle made great play of the fact that Jean had not cracked under brutal cross examination and was therefore, presumed to be telling the truth. Why, he asked, should any woman want to harm her children, particularly in such an extraordinary way? He tried to say the police evidence had conclusively proved she was speeding, but sounded unconvincing even to himself. If the Judge was against him, in his summary he felt they would lose the case. The jury would find her not guilty.

Featherstone looked at his watch, and then at the court clock. "I think this would be a convenient moment to adjourn until tomorrow morning" he said. It was four thirty and he was tired. He reminded the jury not to discuss the case with anyone overnight.

CHAPTER THIRTY SEVEN

The Eclipse

Jack Big was on the run. The escape had taken place two days previously. Having eventually managed to file through the bars, they had left them in place until they were ready. The escape had been geared to a certain shift of wardens and time of day. Three o'clock in the morning was the quietest time, when the wardens usually settled down in their room for a sleep and were at their least vigilant. Jack had only just managed to squeeze his frame through the bars. Even then he badly grazed his shoulder on the window ledge. He had jumped first. The fifteen foot sheer drop was a long way. But using a sheet tied to a bed had helped break the fall. Continuous work outside had made him very fit.

Sean jumped next. He landed badly and broke his ankle. He couldn't walk, and decided it was hopeless for him to try. He promised Jack that he would wait a suitable length of time before giving himself up. Jack thought of knocking him out to make sure he kept his promise but thought better of it.

Micky had lost his nerve completely and decided to stay put. Jack was furious with them both for holding him up, and swore at them as loudly as he dared, before turning on his heels and disappearing into the night.

Sean decided to wait until slop out time before giving himself up; this would give Jack several hours start. He daren't even have a fag, his ankle had swollen to twice its normal size, it was throbbing and he was shivering with the cold.

Jack had made straight for the moors. Obviously he could not return to the shack. He had enough money to buy provisions to last a couple of weeks. His plan was to get right out of the area and change his identity, but first he wanted to see Jean and Nicholas for the last time. "I'm sure she will be pleased to see me", he muttered to himself, with an evil smile on his face.

He was worried that her place would be under surveillance, after his escape, so he knew he had to bide his time. After two nights on the moors, he decided to risk it. Approaching the flat with care; sure enough, there was an unmarked police car parked thirty yards from the flat. Stealthily he crawled to a rear window, luckily it was unlocked. Easing it open, he jumped inside. Crouching low, he looked round to get his bearings. This must be the lounge, he thought, not bad. He crawled along the floor and there before him lay Jean in bed fast asleep. He could see her swollen eyes.

She had been crying, a handkerchief was clutched in her hand.

He found Nicholas asleep next door. He crawled to the cot, putting his hand through the bars he stroked Nicky's forehead. A tear welled in Jack's eye. My God, what a lovely child, he thought. Nicky turned over and gave a little whimper. Jack stayed for a few minutes watching him, and then went back into Jean's bedroom.

He put his hand over her mouth. She was bolt awake in an instant, her eyes wide open. Recognition dawned on her she knew only too well who it was. Ever since the police had informed her of his escape she had half been expecting him to turn up either at home or at work, she had hoped with the police outside he would not be stupid enough to try to see her. She had been wrong.

"I've come back to see you, Jean, for the last time. I couldn't leave without saying goodbye, now, could I, especially as no doubt you were hoping they would lock me up for years, when you give evidence against me. I was glad, that you felt so much for me".

His voice was menacing, and his face then broke into a terrifying leer. "I'm going to remove my hand. If you make one sound, I'll do you in. I might as well it won't make much difference to the sentence I've already earned!"

He took his hand away. She stared up at him, stupefied with fear. She managed to say hoarsely. "What do you want?"

"I want you, that's what I want, you're the only woman, I've ever wanted. It's been a long time, aye, that it has".

"Oh, no Jack, not again, I can't stand it".

"That's too bad, but if you do as you're told it'll be all right. Trouble with you lass, you always argue, besides I'm not drunk this time, I wish I was".

He started pulling his clothes off. She cringed at the thought of what was to come. Her flesh crawled. He pushed her over and fell on the bed beside her, tearing off her nightie with one wrench. She immediately clutched her arms across her body trying to protect herself, and drew her legs into the foetal position.

"Oh, Jean, why do you hate me", he groaned. He started kissing her, holding her jaw so that she was unable to turn aside. His hands were all over her and he gradually got rougher. The tears were coming, she could not help it. He mounted her and was lost in his own self gratification.

Suddenly her brain became razor sharp. She would put

the plan she had long nurtured into operation. Stealthily she reached below the mattress. Dropping one arm over the bed, her fingers closed on the handle of a six inch stiletto knife. She had practically stopped breathing, not once did she remove her eyes from Big. He was engrossed, with his gratification eyes closed, busy pumping into her. She felt nothing, the pain had gone, and instead the adrenalin was flowing all through her.

The knife had been placed there quite deliberately for just this occasion. Ever since his last visit, she had sworn to herself that she would not let it happen again, and she meant it. Slowly she brought up the arm holding the knife to her side. She lifted up her fore-arm, with the blade in the upright position, her elbow still on the bed. She waited, not daring to move a muscle.

He was reaching his climax; the veins in his neck were standing out. She held the knife still and bolt upright as his great body came crashing down. The stiletto slid straight through his stomach wall. A split second passed a look of horror, mixed with disbelief and realisation of what had happened, crossed his face. He pushed himself up and felt for his stomach.

"You bitch, you bloody bitch", he moaned feebly

He rolled onto his back. Jean flung herself headlong onto the floor, well out of his reach. Momentarily he had forgotten about her. He grasped the handle and started to pull the blade from his stomach. Jean ran to the doorway and crouched down, stuffing her hands in her mouth, to stifle an ear piercing scream which was threatening to erupt from her. She did not want to alert the police, they might save him.

The blood was pumping out of his body. He tried to staunch the flow, ineffectually, it was useless. He tried to get up, but fell heavily back on the bed.

"You've done for me, Jean", he uttered in a whisper.

Jean was weeping silently, uncontrollably. "It's your fault, Jack, you wouldn't leave me alone. After your last visit, I swore that I'd never let you beat, humiliate and degrade me again. The knife has been there ever since, waiting for you. The worst thing is, I'm not sorry!!"

She watched him struggling to stop the blood. Slowly, blood started to trickle out of his mouth. He tried again to speak, but collapsed, his body jerked, and his head lolled to the side. He was dead.

Jean rose to her feet, wrapping her arms round her protectively. She took another nightie from the drawer and put it on. She felt cold and was shivering. Crossing the room, she went into Nicky who mercifully was still sleeping; but then Jack had been very quiet because of the police outside.

Picking him up, she cuddled and kissed him. He nestled into her breast. "My baby", she crooned, "I have to leave you". She placed him with tender love back in his cot and covered him with his Noddy quilt. Everything had now become clear to her. She knew exactly what she had to do. Going to the table, she found a notepad and tore off a sheet of paper. She sat down and wrote:_............

TO WHOM IT MAY CONCERN

It is quite obvious to me after what I have been hearing in Court these last few days that it is unlikely anyone would believe my story against Jack Big. His defence lawyer would try and say that I was a women scorned and had made it all up to get my own back on him. Even if the facts are clear in your own mind, they keep drumming at you with the version they want to hear, so in the end one can get tricked into agreeing with them. Well, tonight I did for Big. I planned it, but only if he attacked me again. Well, he did, and it's done.

As I write he lies there with the life poured from him. I killed him, and I'm glad I did. If he got off, he would have soon started on Nicky, and I couldn't bear that. I've already done enough damage to him and poor Geoffrey, thanks to Jack. I feel bad about Elizabeth Markham and the lies I have been telling about her. She was a good friend to me. All she has said in Court, is completely true. I was mentally deranged on the day of the accident. Momentarily, I was blaming the twins for all my problems and my inadequacies in dealing with Jack and them, I suppose. Make no mistake in understanding me; I pushed the pram in front of Elizabeth's car. She didn't stand a chance. I agreed with the Police about the car travelling behind her. He wasn't there.

I never saw him. I don't know what his game is or what he's up to. When Geoffrey died, why did I turn against her? Simple, I was scared. After all I had pushed the pram. By the time this letter is found, I will be finished. I won't mess this up. I have enough sleeping tablets saved up. What's the phrase? Oh, yes, they will say I committed suicide whilst the balance of my mind was disturbed. Well, it's not. I feel very calm and strangely at peace. Quite simply, I have had enough of this life. I hope God will forgive me, for he alone knows what I have been through. I would have made a mess of bringing up Nicky. I know I would. This is my last request, and it is directed at Elizabeth Markham. If she could find it in her heart to forgive me, I would like her and David to adopt Nicky and bring him up. I know it's a hell of a thing to ask, but in a strange way his rightful place is with her. She would make a better mother than me. Nicky would have a better start in life. I am happy for this letter to be published. Please, Elizabeth I beg you, please help me for the last time. I would like this letter shown to Nicky when he's old enough, if you agree.

Nicky, I love you and always will. Forgive me, I just couldn't make it on my own. I will always be watching over you. God bless, Jean.

Slowly she got up from the table, stubbing out her cigarette and immediately lighting another. Going into the kitchen, she took the sleeping pills from the cupboard, dividing them fastidiously into two piles. She walked round the flat, reflecting on the happenings of the past few months. She paused at the door of the room, where Jack lay in his own blood. How things might have been, so different if he had been a decent fellow she thought.

Returning to the kitchen, she crushed one pile of tablets and swallowed them with the aid of a glass of milk. She gagged, but managed not to be sick. Sitting down, she just waited. The effects of the tablets started to work very quickly. Feeling very drowsy she went to the sink and crammed the rest of the tablets into her mouth, she forced them down with some water.

She gripped the sink with her hands, willing herself not to try and save herself. Her mind floating, she thought just one more look at Nicholas. Her body slid slowly to the floor she dragged herself, crawling towards his bedroom. Reaching the door she could move no further. She passed into insensibility and the deep ravine of death. The last thought which passed through her mind was of her sleeping baby.

*****

Jean should have left for court on the first train to London. She had insisted on coming home each night. Leonie had been looking after Nicky for her during the day. When she hadn't emerged at first light with Nicholas, Leonie had fallen asleep again.

The policeman who had been watching the flat knew that Jean should already have left for Court and had become worried when she failed to appear. He had knocked on Leonie's door, as he knew she had a key. It was eight o'clock she let herself into the flat.

As she went inside she heard Nicholas crying. Going towards his bedroom she came across Jack and Jean and fainted.

*****

At ten thirty that morning the Courtroom was full. The Judge's clerk and approached both Counsel asking them to attend the Judge in his private room.

The Judge was sitting at his desk in his gown, but not wigged.

"Good morning, gentlemen, I don't know whether you are both aware of what happened of last night. Must be something in the air at Scarborough", he muttered under his breath.

Mr Riddle raised his eyebrows, indicating to the Judge that he knew what had happened. Mr Biggleswade looked expectantly at the Judge and said firmly "No, Judge, I do not know!" He then momentarily glared at Riddle.

Featherstone leant forward. "I'm afraid this man Jack Big escaped from remand. He broke into Miss Brown's flat, who apparently killed him and then herself. Small child involved dreadful business. Here is a transcript for you both of the suicide note, which Miss Brown left last night. It was not possible in the time to get the original to court."

"Gentlemen in the circumstances I shall direct the jury to bring in a verdict of not guilty. They nodded and went back to court.

The Judge dismissed the jury and discharged Elizabeth from the dock. They all filed out into the corridor. Biggleswade shook Elizabeth by the hand "My dear, you look all in, you have had a terrible time. May I suggest", his eyes twinkled", that you get this husband of yours to take you away for a few days break".

"Goodbye and thank you for all you have done for me. Do you think the jury were really on my side?"

"Yes, and so was the Judge, if his comments in chambers were anything to go on".

He said goodbye to David and Lanthenby, and, turning he marched off back to his chambers and a waiting mountain of paper work, Mcguire scurried after him, laden down with his brief and books.

Elizabeth took herself off to the ladies. Locking herself in, she sat down. She took deep breaths to calm herself. She knew she was not far away from total collapse.

Poor Jean, what a terrible ordeal she must have gone through. Standing up, she brushed her hair and re-applied her lipstick. She just wanted to get away home and to bed as soon as possible.

CHAPTER THIRTY EIGHT

Christopher Goes Home

Nicholas Brown had been taken into the care of the local authority. Jean's letter had somehow been leaked to the press. Dramatic stuff, they loved it. As it happened they portrayed Elizabeth as being wholly innocent, completely vindicating her. She knew however there would always be some people who preferred to think the worst.

Both the household and the practice had started to settle back into their normal routine's, after several months of disruption. The atmosphere in the office, was one of relief, it was all over. Christopher had resumed full time work. Joan was tickled pink to have her master return. He was still being careful and had promised not to take any work home.

Christopher sat at his desk, drafting yet another will. Joan had just brought him his morning coffee. Replacing his pen in the silver ink stand, he swung his chair round to view the office garden. He sipped his coffee thoughtfully. He was wondering, about the future of his relationship with Patricia Fraser.

She certainly had brought some warmth back into his rather sterile existence. He found her intelligent and surprisingly well read. They always had so much to talk about and had mutual interests.

He had invited her to his house for the whole day on Saturday and was looking forward to it enormously.

She had never been to his home before and he was a little apprehensive as to her reaction, when she saw it.

He had moved back home soon after the trial. He would have like to have gone before, but had not wanted to rock the boat in any way. The strain of the trial on Elizabeth and David had been incalculable. Afterwards they had gone away for a few days. He had remained until their return, to help with the children, As soon as they had returned he quietly packed his bags and went home.

It was nice to be amongst his own belongings and familiar surroundings once again, part of him really. After a few perfunctory noises, Elizabeth had not put up any real resistance to him leaving probably glad to see the back of him. But it worked both ways, he coveted his privacy and was delighted to be able, once again, to do precisely what he wanted, when he wanted!

CHAPTER THIRTY NINE

A Frisson with Barbara

Elizabeth yawned and stretched as she sat at her desk, remembering those few blissful days away. They had stayed at a hotel in Madeira, hailed as the best on the island. The hotel was built on a promontory overlooking the sea. The views were spectacular. In her opinion the island was like paradise. It had highly fertile land, the weather was equable, in consequence the islanders were almost entirely self sufficient. Madeira had always been a favourite with the English, especially the wealthy Victorians who used to winter there, returning from their winter sojourn they brought with them specimen plants, for their orangeries.

They both had badly needed to draw breath, and get some balance back into their lives.

Hardly leaving each other's side, they constantly re-affirmed their relationship by physical communication.

Christopher had kindly stayed until they returned and had happily scuttled off to his own home. She knew he was dying to go, so she didn't try and dissuade him.

She looked at her watch; she would like to finish at lunchtime today. The children were on holiday and she had half promised to take them down onto the beach for a picnic.

Her phone rang. Sally trilled, "It's that man from Berry's the builders again!"

"Oh yes", sighed Elizabeth, "put him through".

"Good morning", said the confident voice. "Hector Hillborn of Berry's the builders".

"Yes, I remember, Mr Hillborn, I thought my secretary had passed all the papers to your new solicitors."

"Well, yes, that's true, the problem is, Mrs. Markham, we are not very satisfied with them. They have sent an enormous bill for very little work, and they are so slow in sending out draft contracts. You know we must keep our cash flow going to survive. Now, that all your little problems are over, we wondered if we could return to the firm of Markhams with our business?"

Elizabeth thought unkindly, what a horrid little creep, but said. "Of course Mr. Hillborn, delighted, perhaps you would give written instructions to your solicitors accordingly.

Once I receive all the papers, may I suggest we have a meeting, and you can then bring me up to date"

"Oh, that's a relief. I thought you might say no. I'll get on with it straight away, and then wait to hear from you. I might get them delivered to you by hand".

"That will be fine, goodbye Mr. Hillborn and thank you for calling".

She replaced the receiver and poked her tongue out at it, in an involuntary childish gesture.

She went through to Sally's office. "Well, they want to come back now I have been proved innocent. Ah well, we can't afford to turn away any business. The papers may be delivered by hand, in which case make up the files and put them on my desk, I'm off now!"

It was a beautiful day, and it was great to be leaving the office at lunchtime. Her pale lemon cotton dress was sticking to her as she walked to the car.

She found the children all roaming round the garden in their bathing costumes. Maggie was trying to organise a game without much success. They raced across the lawn towards her.

"You all look as if you're enjoying yourselves", she laughed. "We went in the sea", shouted Robert, "it was cold." "It wasn't baby, it was lovely and warm", crooned Carol.

"What have you done to your knee, John?" asked Elizabeth.

"I was racing up the steps of the cliff to the back gate, when I tripped over". Deciding he was now upset about it, he came closer for a supportive cuddle.

"Right, Mummy will go and change, and then we will all go back down onto the beach."

"Can we have an ice cream?" Pip said excitedly.

"Later, the biggest one I can buy".

"Whoopee," they all jumped up and down, clapping their hands.

It was an idyllic afternoon, not a cloud in the sky, and temperatures were in the mid-seventies. The children spent hours running in and out of the waves.

Barbara and Sebastian came sauntering up the beach. "Hello you lot," she called.

Elizabeth looked over her sunglasses and groaned, "Oh my goodness", she stood up. She was amazed how hostile she felt towards Barbara. "I would have thought after our last conversation, we had little to say to each other!"

"My dear girl, I wouldn't lower myself in talking to you, I have come to see my children!!"

Just then a figure appeared at the top of the steps from the house. "Thank goodness, David's here", Elizabeth whispered under her breath. "Who's that with him it can't be, it is, Andrew oh, this should be interesting," she thought. She raised her arm and waved at David. He returned the waves, and shielding his eyes against the glare of the sun, tried to recognise the figures standing with Elizabeth.

It was quite a steep descent from the garden, thirty one steps to be precise. As he drew nearer, he said to Andrew over his shoulder.

"Oh, my God, it's bloody Barbara and Sebastian. I hope you'll be a good chap and back up Elizabeth, Barbara has treated her in an unspeakable way. What on earth can she want, trouble I suppose"?

"Well, old boy, there's only one way of finding out, they're all waiting expectantly for us, it seems".

They reached the beach, both kicking off their shoes and removing their socks.

Barbara, was dressed in black hot pants, low cut top, no bra, bangles up her arms and eyes heavily lined in black, she came simpering up to David.

David stood motionless, hands on hips. "I can't exactly say this is a pleasure, Barbara, but unexpected certainly. That I am sure is how you planned it".

"Oh, David, you do malign me. We went to the house first, but no-one seemed to be around, so we thought we would check the beach. I just wanted to see the children are all right. After all, Elizabeth's murder charge was somewhat unsavoury, don't you think? I was worried, as any mother would be, as to whether the poor little mites were suffering."

"You weren't worried about the children you came because you're just bloody nosy. You knew very well the jury returned a verdict of not guilty."

"Yes, but only after Jean Brown committed suicide, poor thing, what else could they do".

"It may interest you to know, you scheming bitch......."

"Steady on, old boy", intervened Sebastian, suddenly

creaking into life. David ignored him. "The jury had already decided on their verdict before the judge summed up".

Barbara continued, "Well, mud always sticks; she'll never live it down. There will always be some people who will hold her, 'Guilty as charged'".

David screamed. "Go away, and never come back, I never want to see you again!!"

Sebastian stepped forward. "That's enough of that behaviour, I insist you apologise, at once."

"You can go fuck yourself". David stepped back, swung his right arm, hitting Sebastian a heavy blow to the jaw. Sebastian, completely taken by surprise, keeled over backwards and lay spread eagled on the sand.

The children, who had started listening to the conversation at first had soon got bored, and raced back to the sea, encouraged by Maggie. They now ran over and peered down at the motionless Sebastian.

"Is he dead?" asked John.

"No", said Andrew who had gone over to check he was alright. "That's a shame", he replied, and they all ran off giggling, except Carol, who stood twisting her fingers.

Her mother had yet to acknowledge her, despite her bogus claims to caring, thought David.

Sebastian sat up, leaning on his elbows and shaking his head. "That was quite a punch, never been hit before, I hope my teeth are intact". He carefully poked his tongue round his teeth. Andrew took his arm. "Feel strong enough to stand? Here, lean on me".

Sebastian looked up. "Thanks old boy, who are you, don't think I have had the pleasure".

"Andrew Birch, Elizabeth's former husband, father of Robert and Pip."

"Ah, makes sense now, Sebastian Durant, friend of

Barbara's." He smiled weakly and extended a hand.

David had put his arm round Elizabeth and wandered off down the beach, deep in conversation. Andrew found himself stuck with Sebastian and Barbara, who was temporarily silenced. She had never seen David like that before. Carol edged her way forward and tried to hold her hand. Barbara pretended to fiddle with her hair.

"Mummy, it's nice to see you", she said quietly.

"It's lovely to see you, darling. My goodness, your hair, it looks simply dreadful. I suppose that style was Elizabeth's idea, she has no taste, you mustn't listen to her".

"As a matter of fact", Carol said tearfully. "It was my choice, and I like it, and I'm fed up with you coming here, upsetting everyone and then going. Why can't you be nice?" She ran off to Pip, sobbing uncontrollably.

They clutched each other confidingly, and walked into the waves, until the water was knee high. Turning, they both glared at Barbara, and then sat down in the water, deep in conversation.

"Well", Barbara said tersely, "I wish I hadn't come". Sebastian turned. "You know very well you were itching to cause trouble and upset Elizabeth. You can't stand the fact that they are happy and she is a damned good mother to them all, despite recent events. I for one am getting heartily sick of your silly emotional games. I want no part of it. In fact I hadn't told you before but I'm off to the Amazon next week, joining an ecological expedition. Seems my degree wasn't a complete waste of time, after all. Anyway, I don't know how long I will be away, maybe a year. I am unsure at this stage whether I want to resume our relationship on my return, but it is very doubtful".

"Charming, absolutely bloody charming, thanks for telling me now". She stormed up the beach in the opposite direction.

"Quite all right, no more than you deserved", he muttered.

Andrew had rolled up his trousers and was wading in the waves with John and Robert. They were all pleading for ice creams, giving in, he took them by the hands and headed for the ice cream van. Barbara looked the other way, and they ignored her.

Elizabeth and David sat on the rocks letting the waves lap at their feet. "It's so difficult for me to fight back, because there is always an element of truth in what she says. I will never get over the trial, the horrors of it will live with me for the rest of my life".

"I know darling, but you have to accept it could have happened to anyone. You were simply in the wrong place at the wrong time."

They looked down the beach, the children were all chatting to Andrew, eating their ice creams. Barbara was wandering down the beach. Sebastian was sitting on the bottom stair of the steps, staring into space. "Come on, we had better go back. I'm not apologising to Sebastian because I am not sorry. In any event he should not interfere. As for Barbara she can go to hell, but I must change out of this suit. I want to enjoy what's left of the day with you". Putting his arm round her, he kissed her deeply. She put her arm through his and the meandered up the beach, little knowing what had transpired between Sebastian and Barbara.

Barbara had now worked herself up into a real spiteful temper. She always seemed to lose the fight with that bitch, even though she didn't say anything in retaliation, like today. Well, she'd get them. She changed her tempo, speeding up her stride, and marched towards the "idyllic couple" she muttered under her breath.

When she was ten feet from them, she stopped and

shouted in a most unseemly way. "I've decided the children would be better living with me, their mother; on my return to London, I am going straight to my solicitor, I will instruct him to apply to the court for "care and control" to be transferred to me, unless you want to give them to me now."

She paused, no one spoke. "No, I thought not". She turned on her heel, shouting over her shoulder. "We'll see who has the power and the last word round here".

Sebastian languidly started to rise.

"And you", she shrieked, "Can go to hell. If you are leaving me to go to the Amazon next week and don't want to see me on your return, you can get lost as of now. You can find your own way back to London, it's my car, and I'm not giving you a lift". She suddenly remembered the children. With forced maternal effort, she called to them.

"Come and kiss Mummsy goodbye, you will soon be living with me again". Her voice sounded sickly and phoney.

Carol and Robert stood up in the water, waved, and sat down again, turning their backs on her.

"Goodbye, sweeties". She blew a kiss into the air, turned on her heels and marched back up the beach in the direction from which she had arrived.

Elizabeth and David burst out laughing. Andrew saw the funny side and joined in. Sebastian flung his sun glasses in the air by way of expressing his relief, she was gone.

"I need a drink, come on Andrew, I'll lend you some shorts, we'll go and change and bring down some plonk. Sebastian, I hope you will join us?"

"Why not, it's been a bad day". He said rubbing his jaw.

They all enjoyed the rest of the day. Maggie took the children, kicking and scuffling, off to bed, and Elizabeth cooked an impromptu barbecue. They all got a little drunk, and then Andrew offered Sebastian a lift back to York station. If he missed the last train, Andrew had said he could spend the night with him and travel down with him the following day.

Elizabeth enjoyed ruminating and expressing herself before retiring for the night, otherwise the events of the day would go round in her mind all night, tending to keep her awake.

"It's not that I'm not concerned about Barbara applying to remove the children, we knew she could try it at any time, and we will fight her, it's just her continually having a go at us. Her behaviour was hysterical today, how can she expect anyone to take her seriously when she behaves like that.

Poor old Sebastian got a sock in the jaw for nothing."

They fell on the bed laughing. "I've never seen you hit anyone before, darling, or even think of it. I was really proud of you. I think he took it in good part.

Nice of Andrew to give him a lift to the station, they will probably spend the night together and have a good chat. I think Sebastian feels he got off lightly and is well out of it. As for Andrew, I don't think he could believe his eyes or ears. I quite like him now he's sober".

"Darling, that's enough, come here".

CHAPTER FORTY

Tulham Manor

Christopher lived at Wykeham a few miles outside Scarborough. He had inherited 'Tulham Manor' from his father which had been in the family for over a hundred years. It stood well back from the main road in its own grounds of seven acres, and a further seven hundred acres were farmed. He employed a farm manager, Arthur Young, who lived in a tied cottage. He had worked for him for twenty years and as a way of thanking Arthur for his loyal and devoted service he had also made sure that Arthur and his wife would not have to leave the cottage after he retired. They could stay there until they both died.

Roughly half the farm was set to pine forest, and the rest arable. Some two hundred sheep were also kept in order to graze the land which was too rocky to cultivate. Sheep were excellent animals at foraging for their food.

The Manor had been built by his Grandfather in 1865 in the middle of the Victorian era. The hall was vast by today's standards, square with a beautiful oak sweeping staircase leading up to a galleried landing.

The doors and panelled walls were in oak, whilst the floors were of pine, all preserved in their original colour, only the floors had darkened a little with age and years of polishing. A Red Indian carpet covered the large expanse of the hall floor, over which the crystal chandelier hung some fifteen feet above suspended from the first floor ceiling.

To the right of the front door through double doors was the drawing room, some forty feet long. The fireplace was Adam and the ceiling had ornate intricate mouldings. An off-white Chinese rug covered most of the wooden floor. The pastel colours from the carpets were reflected in the decor and the furnishings. A grand piano stood at one end covered with framed family portraits.

To the left of the front door, double doors opened into the panelled library, overlooking the front of the house. There was a further set of doors on this side, which went straight into the dining room to which the kitchen also had immediate access through the butler's pantry. At the far end of the dining room, a concealed door led into the orangery, a thirty foot conservatory housing real fruit bearing orange and lemon trees. This is where his specimen plants thrived.

Christopher loved coming into this room in the mornings when he was at home. It caught the early morning sun, and even in the depths of winter he could enjoy its sunny and tropical ambience.

Upstairs were eight bedrooms, two with canopied four-poster beds. There were three bathrooms, which used to be too large to heat properly, so everyone froze in the winter. The first renovation he and Anne-Marie had undertaken was to install central heating. Christopher did not know how his father had survived without it. He must have been very hardy.

Christopher remembered as a child always feeling cold and running from one warm part of the house to another.

He supposed that to the outsider Tulham would seem

very grand, but to him it was just home. He could have been a farmer, but in order to make a good living he would have needed to extend the acreage. He had preferred to practice the law. After all Arthur looked after everything for him very well. Even his wife Ann-Marie had insisted on practising as a GP. The village doctor had left on the outbreak of war in l939, just after she qualified, so she came to the rescue and then refused to give it all up when peace came. His father was alive then and ran the farm.

When Christopher had come out of the Navy in 1945, he wanted to resume the law. He felt lucky that he was one of the first to be discharged. He had already seen six years active service. Having qualified in 1935, he managed three years in private practice, before the war temporarily curtailed his career. As an officer in the Navy, he had started his service on destroyers and later transferred to frigates, mostly running convoys in the Mediterranean and the Mid-Atlantic.

He had been discharged with what was considered to be the respectable rank of Lieutenant Commander.

His Father had lived on his own until his death in 1959. He was killed in a riding accident just after his 70th birthday. Christopher felt that he should never have been hunting at all at his age. He was unsaddled as the horse reared, kicking him in the head, as he fell. He had never regained consciousness.

As Tulham was in trust for David, Christopher could hardly sell it, even if he wanted to.

Originally Anne-Marie had not wished to move from their cosy four bedroom house, but had been persuaded in the end. She manfully took on the large house and tried very hard to keep it in good repair. Some of the pictures which hung in the hall and library were valuable. How valuable he did not know, but anyway there was no question of selling them.

Most of the income from the farm went on the upkeep of the house and grounds. In the main the seven acres were laid to formal gardens, parts of which had been planted in an imitation of Capability Brown style. He enjoyed the luxury of a full time gardener, Jo Morritt. Although he worked under the nominal supervision of Arthur, he actually hated any interference by anyone in what he considered his domain.

The azalea and rhododendron walks were Christopher's favourites out of all the specimen shrubs. Polygoneum, primula and golden rushes grew at their feet.

The herbaceous border had a large variety of venerable plants, much coveted today.

Christopher was nervous and unsure as to what Patricia would make of the Manor, which David had only referred to as his "Father's home".

His housekeeper, Jenny Lynch, came in daily and employed extra help when needed, which wasn't often. He had done very little entertaining since Anne-Marie had died.

He had asked Mrs. Lynch to prepare a cold table.

There was iced cucumber soup, salmon in aspic with salad, and fresh strawberries and cream from the farm. She was returning to cook them a roast for dinner.

Christopher drew up outside Patricia's house punctually at the appointed time of eleven o'clock. She was ready and, having pulled her front door firmly shut, walked down the path, smiling warmly to greet him. He got out and opened the passenger door for her. As she got into the car she was aware that she was blushing slightly like a young girl on her first date.

During the drive they mostly discussed the weather. Christopher noted a small intake of breath as they entered the property through the ten foot iron gates. He brought the car to a standstill outside the front door.

She looked round in genuine amazement.

"Is this where you live?"

"Yes, I'm afraid so".

"I had no idea".

"There is no reason why you should. Come on, I'll show you round the garden, or the house first if you prefer".

"Oh, I think the garden".

"Right, please take my arm", he said cheerily.

They strolled round the garden. She was very knowledgeable about the names of the various plants. The walled rose garden was a picture. The second part of the walled garden housed the vegetables. It looked immaculate. All the plants were strong and healthy and well cared for. They all seemed to stand to attention as if on parade. Patricia laughed in spite of herself.

"I think I am going to enjoy today, I'm impressed".

"Jolly good, I want you to have a good time, you deserve it for looking after me so well".

He took her into the house through the conservatory into the kitchen. He thought she would like to see the kitchen anyway. It was at least twenty foot long, with a well worn refectory table in the middle. There was a four oven Aga and various other cooking appliances, the main feature being the enormous pine dresser covering the whole of one wall. The blue Willow Pattern china looked so pretty.

Patricia counted twenty-four dinner plates, before being gently ushered into the hall. He then took her round the whole house and let her take her time, absorbing each room.

They found the cold buffet, suitably covered, laid out on the dresser in the dining room.

"Would you like a drink before lunch, Patricia?"

"I certainly would, I'm famished after all that walking".

Christopher laughed, "That's the ticket, and would you

like me to make us a large glass of Pimms?"

"Sounds smashing. Can we have our drinks on the terrace?"

"Of course, come on".

They lunched in the conservatory, with the doors open out of the breeze. They both had a little snooze in the drawing room after lunch.

Patricia was delighted to be allowed in the kitchen to make the afternoon tea, scones, jam and china tea. Christopher insisted that she used the magnificent silver.

Over tea, Christopher explained briefly the history of the house and farm. He ended by emphasizing that the running of the house and farm was a continuing responsibility. He told her of the family trust created by his grandfather, which meant that David would inherit it all when he died. The tax had been taken care of so far as possible.

"Well, I still think you are a dark horse. You never let on a thing about this house when you sat talking with me in the kitchen, trying to get me to make apple dumplings".

They burst out laughing.

"Does it matter?"

"No, of course not", she replied.

"I'm a little uneasy about Mrs. Lynch cooking for me. I think I can hear her in the kitchen now". She started to fidget.

Christopher leaned forward in his chair.

"Mrs Lynch is more than happy to cook the evening meal, and I would consider it an honour if you would just sit back and enjoy it, for once".

"Right, sir", she said in a naughty mocking voice."I'll behave. One more wander around the garden?"

"Come on", he held out his arm.

When they came in again they played Lexicon until dinner. Mrs. Lynch came in and informed them that everything was ready for them in the heated trolley, before she left them alone.

The dining table looked lovely. A large silver rose bowl stood proudly in the centre, full of old fashioned roses giving off their marvellous scent. The wine glasses stood fragile and exquisite. The silver cutlery was solid with beautiful carved handles. A tempting plate of hors-d'oevres was on the table. Patricia peered nosily into the heated trolley, making Christopher laugh. Roast lamb, with all the trimmings.

"Chablis?"

"Yes, please".

They spent a long time over dinner. It was now Patricia's turn to ask the questions, and she hardly stopped. Her excitement was bubbling over. After coffee and brandy in the drawing room, he let her poke about in the library and then drove her home, correctly, at ten thirty.

As he nosed the Jaguar home after leaving her, he felt very pleased with himself.

Henry was there to greet him his tail wagging.

"Where have you been? Out shooting with Arthur I'll be bound. You look worn out, come on, let's go to bed".

When he got into bed, he picked up the photograph of Anne-Marie which he kept on his bedside table. He studied it and, kissing the glass gently, laid it on his chest.

Henry settled down beside the bed. Strictly speaking, he was not allowed in the bedroom at all, but they soon found that they were company for each other.

His hand slipped under the empty pillow beside him. Here he kept Anne-Marie's nightdress case with a clean silk nightie inside. He fingered the delicate white lace trim surrounding the pink case which had become worn over the years; Anne-Marie had always kept her nightie in this case.

A lump started to grow in his throat. Having it there brought him some measure of comfort. He often slept with his hand resting on it. Every morning, he carefully replaced it in a hidden drawer. Every night he put it back in its right place beside him. He didn't know why he hid it from Mrs. Lynch. Anyway, it was no one else's business, he decided, as he turned and fell into a blissful sleep.

CHAPTER FORTY ONE

The Inquest

The Coroner's inquest took place a week after Elizabeth's return from her holiday in Madeira. Both Jean and Jack were going to be dealt with by the court on the same day in view of their joint and violent deaths. The Coroner's Court was actually run by the Coroner's Officer who was a fulltime policeman from the local Constabulary. The Coroner was a local G.P. called Hugh Stirling. There would be a jury of eight people.

Elizabeth felt that she should attend the hearing, although there was no need for her to do so. She made her way to the Court, feeling rather depressed by the thought of all the gory details coming out in public.

The rain, which had long been expected, fell without mercy in a cloud burst. Because of the long dry spell the ground was too dry to absorb the water, so that the streets were soon flooded to a depth of several inches. The sewerage system was simply unable to cope with the sudden deluge quickly enough, and the sewers were soon overflowing.

The water had seeped into the carburettor of Elizabeth's car when she was forced to drive through part of the road which had flooded deeper than she thought. The engine spluttered and died. Cursing silently at her luck, she abandoned the car and made her way to court on foot, wading through the water.

Thank goodness she had remembered to put her wellington boots in the car.

Leonie Claxton, who had found the bodies, was called to the stand first. A tall willowy blonde, she took the card and read the oath with a shaky hand. She spoke with a lisp which may have been exacerbated by the nervous state she was in. She tucked her blonde hair behind her ears and looked expectantly at the Coroner. Mr Stirling leant forward and asked her to tell the jury how she came to find Jean Brown and Jack Big.

Slowly, she explained briefly how the relationship between her and the deceased had been formed and how, over the months, they had got to know each other quite well. She went on to tell how she would never forgive herself for falling asleep when Jean had failed to knock on her door, as agreed, to leave Nicholas in her care before catching the train to Court in London. She felt that if she had gone to find out why Jean had not left for London straightaway, it might have been possible to have saved Jean's life. She was full of remorse.

She really could only help the Court by reading Jean's occasional comments about Mr. Big, whom she had never actually met before finding him dead in the flat. Leaving the stand, she took a seat at the back of the Courtroom, weeping silently.

The Pathologist took her place reading the Oath clearly. He had done it all many times before. He spoke unemotionally, confining himself to the facts.

The knife, which was produced to the jury, had entered Big's stomach at an angle, puncturing the stomach wall. It had twisted in the body on entry, thus extending the size of the cut. Death would have finally been caused by asphyxiation.

"In other words", his voice rang out "He drowned, in his own blood as his lungs filled".

This very blunt remark had the effect of making most of the assembled company swallow and feel slightly sick.

The Coroner looked up.

"Perhaps you would explain to the jury your theory as to how the knife entered the body and whether Mr. Big was standing or lying down at the time?"

"It was evident from examination of both bodies that sexual intercourse had taken place shortly before death. I think it is possible that the deceased was actually on top of Miss Brown involved in the act of intercourse when the knife entered his body. The twisting of the knife was the result of a heavy body falling, presumably unwittingly, onto it. After all, Mr. Big was a very powerfully built man. In my opinion there is no way that a woman could have overpowered him".

"Do you think a third person could have been involved?"

"In my opinion no. I am satisfied from the position of the entry point on the body that it happened as I have already told the Court".

"Perhaps you would be kind enough to wait there".

The Coroner turned to the jury.

"In this unusual case it seems difficult to split the two deaths into two hearings. I feel you should hear the evidence about Miss Brown as well".

He spoke again to the Pathologist.

"Would you please give your report on Miss Brown"?

"Yes, of course. The time of her death was about three hours after Mr. Big. The cause of death was barbiturate poisoning. The levels recorded in her blood were sufficient to kill three normal people. It would seem that she was very determined to end her life".

Leonie was recalled to the box. She told the Court how

upset Jean had been over Elizabeth Markham. It seems that she had told the whole story to Leonie, who went on:-

"She knew she had pushed the pram into Mrs. Markham's path and had effectively caused the death of Geoffrey. She was torn between her terrible guilt over Geoffrey combined with her false accusation against Elizabeth, and genuine fear of being arrested herself and being sent to prison. She told me that is why she turned against Elizabeth to save her own skin. She hated herself for doing it. I found her to be a kind, generous person. She just seemed to have dug a hole she couldn't get out of. Every time she tried, the hole just got bigger and deeper, if you get my meaning. I must repeat now I could kick myself for falling asleep when she didn't arrive with Nicholas that morning. If I'd gone down at five, who knows, I might have saved her".

The Coroner said, "Thank you, Miss Claxton".

He turned to the jury and asked if they had any questions for her. They all shook their heads.

He then read out a copy of Jean's suicide note and passed copies to the jury.

The Coroner asked for confirmation of the validity of the handwriting and signature. His Officer stood up.

"Yes, sir, Miss Brown's mother is present in Court".

"Very well, thank you. Now members of the jury, you have heard from Miss Claxton, the last person to see Miss Brown alive and from the Pathologist. The suicide note has been verified as having been written by Miss Brown. You may also feel the note explains everything. You may also feel beyond doubt that your verdict should be that Miss Jean Brown premeditatedly killed Mr. Big and then took her own life. I feel that she did so whilst the balance of her mind was disturbed, despite her insistence to the contrary".

The foreman of the jury confirmed their agreement,

repeating the exact words of the Coroner. After the usual expressions of condolences to the relatives, the Coroner ended the inquest. There was the usual perfunctory, so called service at the Crematorium, and, as sods law dictates, they followed each other into the burning embers, united again in their mutual destruction.

Elizabeth had noticed Jean's mother in the Coroner's Court, and again in the Chapel. She looked a faded colourless woman who seemed older than her years. She was very short, probably about four feet nine inches. Her pale blue coat was worn, and the black hat with the short scrunched veil which had a dent in the middle. It looked as if it had spent many years at the bottom of the wardrobe. She shuffled when she walked, always looking down.

Elizabeth noticed she was alone.

After the service Elizabeth made her way over to her and introduced herself. The woman shook her hand in a desolate way and said drearily,

"I knew it would end like this. She would never listen to me or her father. Oh! what's the use". She turned away.

Elizabeth held her arm and pulled her gently to a standstill.

"Please stay and talk a little and accept my condolences over the loss of your daughter. You know, for all that happened I really rather liked her. Where is your husband, did he not wish to come?" and then remembering her place, mumbled

"I'm sorry; it's none of my business".

Mrs. Brown looked at her, her pale blue eyes showing a glint of steel.

"You are correct in one assertion; it is none of your business. Since you asked, my husband is dead. He died six months ago. He would not have come to her funeral he wanted nothing more to do with her after she took up with that man. You know she was a very bright girl, passed all her 'O' levels with good grades but insisted on leaving school at sixteen. My husband wanted her to go on to university, but as soon as she met that man everything changed, we seemed to have become nothing to her. It broke his heart".

"Although I cannot say I knew your daughter intimately, she spoke about you. What she said to me was that she wanted to come home when she was in trouble but was too ashamed to do so. She was very proud of her flat, and I am sure that if Big had not returned she would have got her life more in order and then contacted you. I am sure of it.

"Maybe, if you say so, but it's all in the past now, I am just a lonely old woman with nothing to look forward to.

"There is always Nicholas. You have a right as his grandmother to bring him up if you so wish. That's if you feel you could cope".

"She wanted you to bring him up. Anyway, I must be going, I can't discuss that now".

"I'll bring him to visit you one day".

Mrs. Brown grunted and turned away again. Once more Elizabeth caught her arm.

"Where can I contact you?"

The grey woman found a pencil and scrap of paper in her bag, scribbled and, without further verbal contact, walked away.

Elizabeth thought, great, she seemed pretty concerned.

*****

Elizabeth had had long discussions with David over the request in Jean's suicide note. Adopting a child was a very serious step to take, and it might well be that when the child was old enough to understand, he would not necessarily be in agreement with them adopting him.

David felt they had more than enough on their plate already but bearing in mind their reasonably secure financial position, that aspect at least would not be a problem. It was just the emotional side, and their own personal energy.

Elizabeth still felt very bad about the accident and also a certain amount of maternal protection towards this small unwanted little boy. Obviously they knew it would be a commitment for life. It was at last mutually agreed the Social Services should be approached. Jean's mother would have to be contacted to see if she wanted to care for him and if not, whether she had any objections to them looking after him. In view of her attitude at the funeral, Elizabeth did not think that she would present a problem. Months later, after case meetings and interviews with the Social Officers, Nicholas was placed with them as foster parents to begin with. His progress would be carefully monitored and, in time, probably after two years, they could apply formally to adopt him.

Maggie was going to remain as part of the team. Her help had proved invaluable, and even now, after Christopher had returned home, Elizabeth didn't know what she would do without her. The children were thrilled she was staying, and so was she.

Three months later Nicholas arrived in the arms of a Welfare Officer. They had been very pleased with the offer by the Markhams for possible adoption. It wasn't their position or middle class background, the most important aspect was the feeling that they would love him and bring him up as one of their own, not making him feel different from their own children.

The nursery had been made ready, and Robert and John were bursting with excitement at the thought of a younger brother. Elizabeth and David had told them all about Nicholas, and they all loved him a bit already.

He was obviously going to take a little while to settle down. After all, he had been moved around several times in his young traumatic life. Elizabeth had taken a few days off work to be with him. It was lovely to have a baby again to cuddle.

David knew it was unreasonable, but a little more of her attention was diverted from him.

CHAPTER FORTY TWO

David weakens

David had taken to working late recently. He had several Court cases coming up which needed peace and quiet to prepare. The house was bedlam at the moment what with the baby throwing the household into disarray. A baby crying was not conducive to concentration. The only time the office was peaceful was at five- thirty when the doors were closed.

Trevor had been staying late helping him, but tonight he had sent him home with four files to work on. David wanted all the papers put in order. A meeting could then be arranged with the other solicitors so that the bundles of papers to be presented to the Judge could be agreed.

David felt tired. He was thirty-nine yet his recent surfeit of life made him feel like fifty. He hoped the arrangement with Nicholas was going to work. He was satisfied that Elizabeth would make sure it did. She was certainly very determined.

Standing up, he went into his father's office and helped himself to a gin and tonic. He sank back in the chair, letting the gin seep into his body. He thought he was alone.

The door opened a fraction, and Christine came in. David sat up wearily.

"I thought you had gone home" he said.

"No, I was just finishing that long Affidavit. It's easier to get on with it without interruption after the office closes".

"I agree. Would you like a drink?"

"Yes, please, it's been a long day, and I am tired. You sit still, I'll get it. Give me your glass. I'll recharge that for you".

He numbly handed her the glass, watching her bending over peering into the cupboard. She pulled up her skirt and went down on her haunches to reach the tonic at the back of the cupboard. Her long blonde hair fell over her face. She tossed her head, flicking it back so she could see.

David felt a strangled feeling in his throat. His trousers were becoming uncomfortable. Standing up, she poured a generous measure of gin into each glass, equivalent to a triple, and brought it over. What the hell, he thought, no bra again. She bent forward to hand him his drink. His eyes wandered to her cleavage. As he reached for his glass his hand brushed her blouse. The warm soft flesh beneath seemed to come alive at his touch. He looked up into her face, his hand ignoring the glass. He found that he had cupped his hand round her.

"Oh God I want you," he groaned.

Taking his hand from her breast, she whispered, "I'll go and bolt the outside door".

He took his jacket off and gulped the gin. He found himself gripped in the release of months of pent up passion for her. Both hands went inside her blouse; his tongue plunged down her throat. She gasped.

"Clothes, clothes, always in the way" he muttered. The trousers and skirt fell to the floor, and so did they. It felt like the first time for him. He stood up surveying her. She laid hips gently rolling on the floor. He gulped his drink, not taking his eyes off her, and, like a man possessed, exclaimed.

"I want you again".

They climaxed. He didn't care, he'd enjoyed it and, by God, she'd asked for it.

CHAPTER FORTY THREE

Christmas

The preparations for the Christmas festivities were nearly complete. Elizabeth was determined that they were all going to enjoy themselves. It had been such a traumatic year she would be glad to say goodbye to it. The office was closing for the ten day break from Christmas Eve until the first working day after the New Year.

Snow had started to fall on Christmas Eve which delighted the children. The eight foot tree was decorated with handmade ornaments and small gifts. Below the tree were parcels of all shapes and sizes. It had been such fun decorating the house.

The larder was full to bursting. Yes, Elizabeth thought, we are all going to enjoy ourselves.

The office party had finished at four o'clock, sending the office staff home rather tipsy.

The children had carefully pinned their names to the empty pillow cases, laid with great ceremony in front of the drawing room fireplace. An orange and a half a pint can of beer was also waiting, together with various carefully scrawled notes addressed to Father Christmas.

It seemed the only night in the year the children didn't mind going to bed.

David had tried to forget the incident with Christine. Christmas and the New Year celebrations had passed by without incident. The office had opened with a buzz of enthusiasm on the 2nd January. He decided that his approach to Christine would be cool and distant. He hoped that she would realise that his aberration was a moment of madness not to be repeated. However, her presence continued to arouse every fibre in his body which he tried desperately to suppress.

By the end of February he was beginning to relax a little, as Christine had been behaving perfectly normally towards him.

It was a cold Tuesday evening and the rain was beating against the office window.

The staff had gone home, and he was going through the accounts before the Auditors arrived. The client account had to balance to the penny, which, thankfully, it always did.

His door opened a crack, and the impish face of Christine appeared. "How did you get in?" he demanded, feeling instantly annoyed and cornered. "I locked the door? "Simple, I had my own key cut". She smiled triumphantly, holding up the key in her left hand.

"Look" said David standing up. I think you had better go".

"You must be joking, you can't push me aside that easily. I want to talk to you".

"What about?" She undid her coat and let it fall to the floor, revealing her perfect figure beautifully swathed in a black velvet dress. Her only adornment was the ostrich feathers along the neckline. She sat down demurely on the edge of one of the leather chairs. Her face beamed with knowing confidence and determination.

David felt trapped. He decided he must make some feeble effort to take control of the situation in which he now found himself. He moved away from her and sat down defensively behind the desk. The distance made him feel a little more comfortable.

"Now, listen Christine, what happened between us before Christmas was completely wrong and madness on my part for which I take full responsibility. I am very sorry if I have caused you any distress, but such a transgression must never occur again. I'm sure you understand that. After all, I have a wife I love dearly. I have obviously considered asking you to find employment elsewhere, but decided against it on the basis it would not be necessary if we could both put the incident behind us". This was not strictly true. He felt that if he had asked her to leave, it would invite the very confrontation he was trying to avoid; it now seemed with conspicuous failure.

A flash of steel came into her eyes, but only for a second, as she remembered her powerful position. She knew that he was saying what he felt he ought to say; she was very confidant.

She stood up, and so did he, thinking she was leaving. Instead, she walked round the desk, taking his hand in hers and looked straight into his eyes.

"I hear what you say, but I do not believe you mean a word of it. You want me now as we stand here. I can feel the heat coming through your hands. These last two months I have hardly been able to contain myself. You have been acting like a man wearing a chastity belt, who has lost the key". She threw back her head, laughing at her own bad joke.

"Even if I left, which incidentally I have no intention of doing, I am sure that you would eventually seek me out". She put her arms gently around his neck and kissed him.

David removed her hands. He didn't trust himself to speak. He felt that his voice would make a strangled sound which would betray him. He cleared his throat loudly.

"I really must ask you to leave," he demanded.

She took his head in her hands and proceeded to kiss him. His arms at first were limp by his side but, as the passion stirred in him to an unbearable level, he found himself responding, at first gently, his hands caressing her buttocks; and then as if gripped by forces beyond his control, he took her barely moving from where they stood; she wrapped her legs round his waist, a suspender broke under the strain.

He laughed as he put her down, burying his head in her blonde hair.

"It's no good; I have tried very hard to resist you. I think I'm falling in love with you" he said stupidly. "But how can I possibly be in love with Elizabeth as well?"

"Oh, let's not talk now. Come back to my flat for a coffee".

"I don't think I should. I will have to phone Elizabeth". He reached for the phone, his heart beating loudly. Elizabeth answered promptly.

"Darling" he tried to sound normal "I'm going to be longer than I thought. Don't wait for me to eat. I'll pick up something and bring it back to the office".

As he was speaking, Christine put her hand inside his trouser pocket and started to fondle him, at the same time kissing his ear. He tried to push her away, but the more he tried, the more forceful her movements were. He was terrified Elizabeth would suspect something. His emotions were torn, and he had completely given up with his body. Elizabeth's disappointed voice sounded down the line.

"All right, darling, I understand. I'm tired. Try not to wake me when you come in".

"Of course not" he nearly squeaked. He replaced the receiver.

"That was out of order, young lady".

Christine ignored him, imprisoning his mouth in a kiss. She spoke out of the corner of her mouth.

"Come on, we're wasting time".

Her flat was clean and modestly furnished. Inevitably they retired to the comfort of the double bed immediately. Her appetite seemed insatiable, and every time he thought she had drained him of all emotion she found another way to tease him into action and more passion.

*****

He sighed with relief as he slid into bed beside Elizabeth, praying she would not wake up. He was dead to the world, when a hand landed on his tummy working its way down. His eyes shot open, and it took him a few seconds to remember where he was. Elizabeth ran her hand through his hair.

"Darling, I missed you, I want a cuddle".

"I'm absolutely bushed, darling, I don't know whether I can oblige. I must be fresh for the Judge in the morning". He broke into a sweat.

"You are a bit hot, you may have a temperature". Elizabeth muttered as she heaved herself on top of him. God, he thought, women have no mercy.

Despite the rigours of the evening he found himself responding to her loving touches. As he climaxed, she rolled from him.

"Well, I must say I have known better, darling".

"Really" he replied "I wonder why?" He turned over, looked at the clock, muttered "Oh God! Four o'clock "as he fell soundly asleep.

******

The shower was warm on their bodies as they soaped each other. The confined space limited their movements. Stepping outside gave them more freedom. Lying on the floor soaking wet, they slithered and slid on and off each other. The droplets of water which fell from one to another were very erotic. In the end, they laughed so much that they returned to the shower. Christine hung on to the shower head as their fired bodies temporarily burnt themselves out. Wrapping themselves in towels they flopped down on the bed.

Christine lit a cigarette, and lay back on the pillow, blowing rings of smoke into the air.

She suddenly announced "I'm pregnant!"

David sat bolt upright.

"You're what?"

"Darling, you heard. How do you think babies are made?"

"This is madness, I never intended this" he blustered. "I thought our affair would burn itself out in a few months. Why aren't you on the pill? I assumed you were?"

She was now feeling upset. "Well you assumed wrong. Anyway, the pill upsets me. You could have used something, but you are always so wrapped up in yourself you would never think of that. Well, this time you have got caught out".

"I have a feeling that you did this deliberately. We must find a doctor who will help you have an abortion".

"David, let's get this quite clear. I fully intend to have this child. There is no question of an abortion".

"Well, I don't know what you expect from me but I have equally no intention of leaving Elizabeth. A divorce is unthinkable".

She leaned back on her elbows, examining her painted toe nails as she raised her right leg in the air.

"Yes, well I thought you would say that. I will now tell you precisely what I want you to do. You will buy my silence. I want a small house purchased in my sole name and maintenance for me and the child. A Trust Fund must be set up for the benefit of the child's education. You will see the child on a regular basis. He, or she, will be told nothing of your other family, at least until it is as old as possible. I will, of course, live out of the immediate area, but near enough for you to come and stay and be a proper husband. I suggest that for the purpose of the new community we both change our surname to 'Barker'".

David was looking at her in complete amazement. He found his jaw had dropped, and he was actually gawping.

"That was quite a speech, obviously well rehearsed. Why didn't you tell me before, for goodness sake? I don't know where you think I am supposed to get the money from".

"Firstly, the reason I waited was because I knew you would react like this, and I wanted to be sure. Secondly, your father has plenty of money in various Trusts. I have been doing some checking up in the dead files and documents in the safe. You keep them so carefully preserved in immaculate order, a good rule of the Law Society; it helped me a great deal. It all makes interesting reading".

She decided not to tell him that she had taken photostats of the various documents and secured them safely in a bank deposit box. She had used the last few weeks to think carefully and prepare herself, before dropping the bombshell. She had no intention of being cast aside like an old boot, as they say the flavour of last week. No, she wanted security and intended to play her hand well.

She ran her hand sensually down her leg, feeling in complete command of the situation.

"Have you seen a doctor?"

"No, as a matter of fact, I haven't".

A minute feeling of relief flooded through David. He smiled nervously.

"Well then, you can't be sure, maybe it's a false alarm. Without positive confirmation we may be in the clear".

She got up and walked over to where David was standing looking aimlessly out of the window. The towel wrapped round her slipped open, revealing her body. She looked up at him.

"Can't you see how my breasts are bigger; they are also far more sensitive. I wish you would not keep referring to the unborn baby as if it were a terrible demon. Don't you understand, I love you and want you. I want to have your baby. I'm glad it happened and am very proud. I wish you would be just a little bit pleased".

David looked down at her, his mind was racing. How could he have been such a careless fool. The last thing he wanted at the moment was another child. He already had a house full of them. Christine was obviously far more calculating than he thought, but he was fast learning that all women were born like this anyway. They single-mindedly set out to get what they wanted. Well, she seemed to have it all worked out. He knew, as she stood before him looking up to him lovingly with her perfect white skin and baby blonde curls covering her womanhood, he knew that he could and would never let her go. Placing his arms inside her towel, he pulled her gently to him. They stood naked together in the centre of the room. He crooned to her as he rocked her, stroking her waist length flaxen hair.

"My baby, of course I'll look after you. I don't think I can live without you, but I mean it when I say I am not leaving Elizabeth, now or ever. If that's not good enough for you, I will not be blackmailed. You can blow the whistle and tell Elizabeth, and I will take my chances with her. Our relationship is very strong. However, I can, see your way working. As long as we act with discretion then no-one will get hurt".

"When you tell Elizabeth I am pregnant, please say that it was my boyfriend who has done a runner, and that I don't want to pursue the matter with him".

"You really have thought of everything".

"A girl in my position has to. I will always be the loser because I will never be Mrs. Markham, but I would rather share a little of your life than none at all".

"Now, when is the baby due?"

"In six months time".

"Gosh! Well, that doesn't give us much time. Have you found a house?" He ran his hand through his hair, trying to think quickly.

"Yes I have, and I would like you to see it. David, I am serious about the Trust Fund. I want a Deed of Trust drawn up before the baby is born incorporating an agreement to pay maintenance until the child is eighteen also maintenance for me until the child is at least in full time education, when I can return to work. You know the law as it stands is an ass when it comes to protecting unmarried mothers or common law wives for that matter.

They get nothing in the event of a break up, regardless of the length of the relationship; unless they have contributed financially then they only get back what they have paid. I want the Deed of Trust watertight so that, if we part, it cannot be broken in any court of law. At least you cannot make the excuse that you did not understand the significance of the Deed!"

David laughed "My God, you're intelligent. I'm no match for you. Come here and let me kiss those beautiful breasts. I must be going".

He dressed quickly. Looking at his watch he exclaimed

"Nine thirty". He had promised Elizabeth he would be home by nine.

He reached for the front door handle.

"As a matter of interest, what were you proposing to do,

my young madam, in the event that I decided to send you packing with a flea in your ear?"

She smiled. "There is no fury as that of a woman scorned. I would have been left with no alternative but to make your life as uncomfortable as possible if you had refused to honour your responsibilities. Oh, I know there will be those who will say it was my fault and that I tried to trap you. But remember, it takes two to tango. I seem to recall that you could hardly contain yourself at the time. It was as much your responsibility as mine to make sure a child was not the product of our emotions. Even if you assumed I was on the pill, if you were really concerned you could have taken your own precautions, or not played at all. Some people don't conceive for years - I had no idea we would be so fertile together".

"Ok, ok but that doesn't answer my question. What would you have done?"

"Blown the gaff with Elizabeth and brought a paternity suit against you in the local Magistrates Court. If you contested that, I would obtain a Court Order to force you to have a blood test. Does that answer the question?"

"Yes, I'm afraid it does". A wry smile crept across his lips. He kissed her on the nose and closed the door behind him.

He drove home, sunk in his own gloomy thoughts. What a bloody mess. He felt completely drained and desperately in need of a stiff drink.

He pulled up outside the Blue Boy Public House, hardly aware of what he was doing. Inside, the airless hot fug of smoke hit him. His eyes started to smart from the smoke, even as he stood at the bar and downed a large scotch. He called for another, drank it in one, put the money on the counter and left.

On the road, he felt a little more relaxed as the scotch seeped into his bloodstream. He decided that there was only one way to play this latest disaster at the moment and that was Christine's way. He needed time to think and to adjust to the idea of running two households. He didn't know whether he had the stamina.

Elizabeth's sexual appetite was pretty healthy, and Christine was bordering on his idea of a nymphomaniac. He doubted whether she would ease up much during her pregnancy, at least not until it could be harmful to the child. In the meantime she, no doubt, would think up ingenious and different ways to satisfy her insatiable lust.

He found Elizabeth in the drawing room, not in the best of moods. She glared at him as he came in.

"Really, darling, this is too much, a quarter past ten. I wanted to talk to you sensibly this evening. Everyone seems more important than me". She sounded hurt.

"Now you know that simply is not true. What is it you want to discuss?"

"It is much too late now, I am tired, and I'm going to bed. One day, when you can spare me a couple of hours of your precious time, I will tell you, but not until then" she said sarcastically.

"You have every very right to be annoyed. I have been neglecting you recently. How about going out for dinner tomorrow evening?"

Sounding a little appeased, she called over her shoulder as she walked into the kitchen, "Ok but I bet you will find something better to do, and cancel".

"There's no chance of that" muttered David to himself. "The juggling act is beginning so I had better get in practice."

CHAPTER FORTY FOUR

David Explains

Barbara had wasted no time following her threats on the beach. Her Solicitors, the eminent London firm of Ross Proctor & Pryck, had written immediately, informing David that they would be making an application to the Court for custody, care and control of the children to be transferred to Barbara with David being allowed reasonable access. She was also making a further application for a lump sum and maintenance for her and the children. Considering her financial position, David did not take this threat seriously, merely a try on.

A hearing date had now been set for the following week. John Lanthenby had been instructed to act for David. The children had been seen by the Welfare Officer who felt the children should be returned to their mother. Both Elizabeth and David were amazed when they read the report. They now felt uncertain as to the outcome and just wanted to get the hearing out of the way. It was just more emotional strain on everyone, which, is precisely what Barbara intended.

*****

David went for a walk along the promenade while he was waiting for Elizabeth to get ready. He hoped he would be able to get through this evening without giving anything away. He felt sure that once he had got over the initial lies, it would become easier as time went on. He did not want to hurt Elizabeth in any way. He loved her very much, and she had already gone through a great deal.

The restaurant was fairly empty. David had booked a quiet table in the corner. He reached out and held her hands across the table.

"You are looking very beautiful tonight. I love the pink dress it shows off your pale complexion beautifully".

Elizabeth sat back in her chair. "I'm not sure whether this is a good time to discuss my idea with this wretched case hanging over us, but here goes anyway. I would like to open another office of Markhams".

David initially was flabbergasted but he quickly recovered and was interested to hear what she had to say. He was quite satisfied in his own mind, that she would have thought it through in great detail, before even mentioning it. She went on to tell him that she was feeling a bit frustrated with her career and wanted to prove herself on her own. She felt that four solicitors in their small office was a little top heavy and another office would obviously broaden the number of clients the firm could handle. Some premises had become available in Filey, and she would like him to look at them and say what he thought of them.

To start off with she would base herself there, with Trevor coming over to help when required. She would probably take Sally with her. The only other staff she would need would be a receptionist. She could then think of more staff as the work increased.

"Mmm" said David "You seem to have thought it out in

some detail. I'm not sure that I would want to open another office for at least a year".

"By the time the office has been bought and decorated and fitted out, it would probably be getting on for a year before I could open anyway. I just wanted to see your reaction. If you agree in principle we can approach Christopher together. Now, what have you been up to?"

David's heart missed a beat; however, he could tell from the innocent expression on her face that it was a harmless remark with no underlying meaning. He quickly recovered his equilibrium.

"Nothing much, only work as you know. Oh, there is one thing Christine told me today she is pregnant".

He waited for the response.

"I'm not surprised I thought she was she's had that look about her for a while. How many months is she? When is it due?"

"I think three months, I don't know the date I left that sort of thing to you, women's talk" he added trying to seem abstracted.

"Is her boyfriend going to marry her?"

"I don't think so she told me she wanted nothing more to do with him and intended to bring up the baby on her own".

He surprised himself by the casual tone of his voice. His clammy hands were clasped tightly together under the table and his heart was beating rapidly.

Elizabeth went on "well, it's quite an obligation for a young lady on her own. I'll have a word with her tomorrow". She leaned back in her chair gathering her handbag. "Nicholas has developed a nasty cold. Can we go? I don't want to be too late.

*****

"Sally, would you please come into my office". Elizabeth replaced the receiver she was feeling decidedly testy this morning, probably P.M.T she thought. Sally came in carrying more files. Seeing there was no more room on the desk she placed them carefully on the floor. She looked expectantly up at Elizabeth.

Elizabeth barked "Would you please tell me why the Land Registry have raised all these requisitions on this new registration. Surely by now you should know what's required and should be able to get it right first time".

Sally hated being reproved, and the tone of her voice in reply was not the slightest bit conciliatory.

"I was under a lot of pressure at the time, and I forgot to send a certified copy of the mortgage".

"Well, from the letter that's not all. Please deal with it and be more careful in future I do hate work having to be repeated, it's such a waste of time".

"Is that all?" There was a pink flush to Sally's cheeks.

"Yes, for now. Oh no, would you please send Christine in. I would like a word".

Sally closed the door firmly, just resisting the temptation to slam it. She was feeling miffed. Pick, pick, pick. What about all the things she got right, nothing was ever said about that. Having made herself a coffee to try and calm her rebellious feelings, she asked Christine to go and see Elizabeth, warning her that E.M. was not in the best of moods.

Although Christine had been expecting Elizabeth to summon her and had primed herself, now the moment had arrived her nerves of steel seemed to have deserted her. Tying her hair back into a pony tail she knocked on Elizabeth's door.

"Come in, Christine, and sit down". Christine did as she was bid.

"Mr. Markham has told me your good news. Are you

pleased? I must say you're looking well".

"Yes, I am pleased, thank you, and I feel well except for the odd morning sickness".

"Well, that must be expected". Elizabeth replied, unable to keep the note of experience out of her voice.

She went on "I also understand that you don't want to marry the father and that you intend to be a single parent family. Are you sure you can cope? It really is difficult for me to say this, but have you thought of an abortion?" she asked tentatively.

Christine looked at her levelly, her eyes unblinking.

"I have never considered an abortion although it has been suggested to me". She was actually thinking of David.

"It is out of the question. I'm afraid I would not dream of killing an innocent child. I am in the process of buying a house, only a modest one to begin with. My family are helping me finance it" she lied.

Leaning forward she looked deep into Elizabeth's innocent open eyes. "Unfortunately, Mrs. Markham the father cannot marry me, so there we are. I'd rather not talk about it if you don't mind".

"No, no, of course not. I just want you to know if you need any help. You only have to ask".

"Is that all Mrs. Markham?" She got up to leave.

"Remember, you only have to ask". Elizabeth was already dialling out as Christine closed the door.

Christine returned to her desk. Self satisfied bitch, she thought. If only she knew, that patronising smile would soon disappear.

David thundered into Elizabeth's office.

"I don't believe it of all the rotten luck, the case of Andrews is warned on the same day as the hearing against Barbara".

Elizabeth patiently put down the file she was reading

"As you have already instructed Counsel in the Andrews case, Trevor surely can cover?"

"No, he can't, he's in another Court altogether. I will have to send one of the secretaries to sit behind Counsel. Goodness knows what the client will think. I will just have to explain I'm double booked". He went out, grumbling.

"What a day" Elizabeth muttered to herself. She turned her attention once again to her work, tracing the plan with her finger. "Now where is this right of way supposed to lead to?"

CHAPTER FORTY FIVE

Custody Hearing

As David's divorce from Barbara had been obtained in London, it followed that any ancillary actions would also be held there. As the proceedings being brought by Barbara concerned children under age, the hearing would be heard by a judge in chambers. This meant that no members of the public or press were allowed to be in Court, only the parties to the case and their legal advisers. The door was actually barred, and an usher stood outside to prevent intruders walking in who did not understand the rules.

The judge would be wearing a suit, wigs and gowns were for matters held in open court. It was for him to decide whether to hear the case in his private room or in the actual Court. He had decided this morning to hear the case in the Court room.

"More space", he said to his Clerk. "When emotions run high I find my private room becomes stifling. The limited space between people is not enough for them easily to contain their emotions".

Elizabeth and David were seated in Court behind John Lanthanby, when Barbara came into Court. She was hardly recognisable. She was wearing a demure knee length navy suit and a white blouse. Her face was devoid of make-up except for a token of pale lipstick.

Her dark hair was pulled back severely into a French pleat. Her solicitor, Mr. Proctor of Ross Proctor & Pryck, showed her to a seat behind him in the same row as Elizabeth and David. About ten feet separated them. David squeezed Elizabeth's hand and whispered in her ear "Bit of a difference, dressed up, or rather down, all specially for the Judge, I hardly recognised her".

Elizabeth returned the squeeze by way of acknowledgment. They then stared straight ahead.

Proctor had already spoken with Lanthanby outside the court to see whether the Markhams would capitulate and relinquish the children. Of course the answer was a clear no, so the hearing went ahead.

Judge Thompkins entered the Court. He smiled generally at all present, wanting to relax the atmosphere a little. Fighting over children was one of the most serious and unpleasant kinds of work with which he had to deal. It was such an important matter for him to have to decide on. To get it right was even harder. After all, he was faced with the parents on the day, in the way they chose to present themselves to him. The custodial parents were both solicitors, he noted. He had read the papers before coming into Court. One affidavit referred to unseemly behaviour by Miss Barbara Johnson-Bloice, and was countered by an equally unpleasant attack against Mrs. Markham.

It referred to an accident with some twins. One unfortunately had died, and the mother had committed suicide. And then there was the proposed adoption of the orphan, Nicholas Big. He remembered reading about the case in the newspapers at the time.

Finally, there was the all important Welfare Officer's Report.

He looked up

"Mr. Proctor, you are going to address me first".

"Yes your Honour. I appear on behalf of the plaintiff Miss Barbara Johnston-Bloice, and me friend Mr. Lanthenby appears on behalf of Mr. David Markham". He fingered his papers. "I don't know whether your Honour wishes me to read the Affidavits".

"No, that won't be necessary. I have already read them".

Proctor continued "My client is making this application for custody care and control to be transferred to her,

Your Honour may think, a little late".

The Judge who was writing merely grunted. "Yes, please continue".

"After the marriage failed my client suffered very badly with her nerves. Because of strain you realise.

At that time she felt it better the children should remain with their father. But, after recent events, she now feels the environment they are being brought up in is extremely unhealthy. Mrs. Markham works, and the day to day care of the children is left to two hired helps.

I understand that one is a cleaner come cook, and the other a young unqualified nanny. My client feels that the children need the love and support of a full time mother, which, of course, she could and would give them. As you will see from the affidavit my client is of some substantial means, so there are no problems on that score.

I would now like my client to give evidence". He turned and inclined his head to Barbara who stood up and nervously made her way to the box. She took the oath in a whisper that was barely audible. The Judge leaned forward and said kindly, "Miss Johnson-Bloice, it is very important that we can all hear what you say. Would you please remember to speak up"?

Barbara looked at him feigning timidity and nodded. Her hands, resting on the box, fingered a delicate lace handkerchief. "God, she's acting" David muttered under his breath, his blood rising.

"Would you please look at his Honour and tell him why you feel the children should come and live with you?"

Barbara spoke beautifully and sincerely:

"It has always been a great source of personal regret to me that I let the children out of my control in the first place.

You see, I was so upset by the divorce, I suffered from depression and was really in no fit state to look after them or make any decisions". She flung her head back confidently. "I am now much better and want my babies back with me where they belong". She wiped a mock tear from her eye.

The solicitor continued to take her through the details given in her affidavit.

The Judge said "Just one question. Do you feel well enough to look after the children yourself, or will you employ a nanny?" The Judge watched her carefully.

"Oh yes, I feel very well. No there would be no need for me to have a nanny I could be a proper mother to them"

"Thank you" the Judge acknowledged the reply.

Lanthenby stood up.

"Miss Johnston-Bloice, do you think you are being wholly honest with this Court?"

Suddenly Barbara was on her guard. Her eyes had taken on a cat-like look which she failed entirely to mask.

"Of course I have been honest with the Court. How dare you suggest otherwise".

"As you will know from the Affidavit sworn by my client, your behaviour towards the children over the last two years can hardly be said to be consistent with that of a loving mother"?

"I don't know what you mean. I have always been there if they wanted me".

"Miss Johnston-Bloice, will you agree that on a visit last year, the first since the divorce after several months, the children were most disturbed and upset. You also went to great lengths to spell out to my client you wanted nothing to do with the children or their upbringing. You went on to say, did you not, that you would never bother to go to Court over them"?

"That is a complete lie, the children were delighted to see me, and I certainly said no such thing".

"I have just been handed this picture taken on your last encounter with my clients. I crave the Court's indulgence to allow this exhibit, as in my submission it helps the Court get the general picture; sorry for the pun".

The Judge looked over his glasses. Proctor took one look at the picture and leapt to his feet objecting.

The Judge overruled him, and the picture was passed to Barbara, who visibly paled.

"Is that a photo of you, if so it's a little different from your dress today?"

Her eyes flashed with anger. "It is a photograph of me. May I ask who took it?"

"It was taken by your daughter Carol, while you were engaged in a tirade against Elizabeth Markham. As you can see from your body language, it would seem that you were certainly not involved in a calm discussion".

Barbara made no reply.

The Judge studied the photo and handed it back without comment.

"I put it to you, Miss Johnston-Bloice that you have only a passing interest in your children, which comes and goes depending on your mood of the moment. I also suggest that you would certainly not look after the children yourself, as you have assured this Court, but, to use your own phrase, you will employ a fleet of nannies and other help. Finally you have only brought this action out of spite to cause further upset, especially since your relationship with Mr. Sebastian Durrant is over, I am given to understand!"

"Barbara nearly exploded. Gesticulating with her hands by way of professing amazement at the allegation being made, she turned to the Judge

"I am at a loss. Words fail me. Surely you, your Honour, can do something to prevent these dreadful lies and allegations being made about me in Court".

The Judge felt that he was being involved in party tricks of which he wanted no part. His voice was tinged with exasperation "Miss Johnston-Bloice, this is not an open hearing. Everything said in this Court is privileged and cannot be reported or used elsewhere. Mr. Lanthenby is only presenting his case to the best of his ability. As far as I am concerned, he has done nothing wrong. Would you kindly answer the questions"?

"None of it is true, it is all a pack of lies," she shouted.

A silence fell upon the Courtroom. David looked down. He was thoroughly ashamed of Barbara's behaviour.

Proctor rose and stiffly invited his client to return to her seat.

David gave evidence next. After swearing the oath, he was taken through the events concerning his children, Carol and Robert, since the divorce. He told the Court that the only way he managed to care for the children in the early days was with the help of Mrs. Fraser. He had met Elizabeth some time after the breakup of the marriage. Lanthenby asked David to tell the Judge about Barbara's failure to come and see the children regularly, which with Barbara's constant and unwarranted attacks on Elizabeth had affected Carol the most.

Judge Thompkins adjourned for lunch. Over lunch, he pondered about the contents of the Affidavits in conjunction with the Welfare Officer's Report. The Welfare Officer was of the opinion the children should be returned to the care of the mother.

He had visited her house and was impressed with her intentions. He had believed her failure in the past was a small aberration and should be overlooked. Carol had told the Welfare Officer that she wanted to stay with her father and was fed up with her mother and the upsets she kept causing. The last visit by her mother had a lasting effect on her. The Welfare Officer had dismissed these as emotive ramblings of a young girl who clearly needed her mother's guidance.

The Judge meditated as to whether the Welfare Officer had been taken in by Barbara. After all in her own home she would have no one to upset the balance of her act, if indeed it was one.

Would he have been completely taken in by her had it not been for Lanthenby's attack on her which clearly seemed to have unnerved her.

The Court re-assembled at two o'clock. Proctor was on his feet just about to launch into cross examination of David, when a Court usher came hurrying through the Court and whispered to the Court Associate sitting below the Judge, who promptly rose and conferred quietly with the Judge for some minutes, during which Judge Thompkins nodded several times. He then signalled to Proctor to sit down.

"Something, or rather someone, has come forward who wishes to address me over this application. Since I wish to hear what he has to say in this delicate matter, I have decided that Mr. Johnston-Bloice, Miss Johnston-Bloice's father, be allowed to give evidence. I understand that neither of the advocates are aware of his request". They both looked at each other and concurred.

"Unless either of you gentlemen wishes to address me, I will have Mr. Johnston-Bloice called".

Both advocates shook their heads and David returned to his seat.

Mr Johnston-Bloice entered the Courtroom. He was a tall distinguished looking man, wearing an impeccably tailored suit, of which the tailoring was the important part, in order to hide certain embellishments which came with too much good living and the advancement of years. He was obviously a man used to making decisions at the highest level.

He ignored everyone in the Courtroom, including his daughter and directed himself totally to the Judge, as if he were the only person present. Speaking with great command and authority, he said "I have come here today because I feel I might be of some small assistance to your Honour in this matter which concerns my daughter and my grandchildren. It is with deep regret that I have to inform you that there are times, far too many in fact, when I have been deeply ashamed of my daughter's behaviour".

Barbara's lips tightened and her eyes bulged in their sockets. Proctor started to grapple with his papers.

Johnston-Bloice continued "I cannot pretend that I approved of the match with Markham. I did not. I have, however, the highest regard for the responsible manner in which he has dealt with my grandchildren. My daughter's behaviour since the divorce has been everything I abhor. Not only did she dump the children, but she went on to behave like the irresponsible spoilt and idle rich man's daughter that she has now become.

To my own knowledge she did not suffer a breakdown of any kind after the divorce. On the contrary, she went gallivanting off around the world with various men of ill repute. I should know, I picked up the bills, and I will probably also be asked to pay the costs of this case. My wife and I have not seen our grandchildren for some two years, which has been a cause of great distress to us, and I would like that put right if possible.

If I cut my daughter off, she would not have a penny of her own and in my view is quite incapable of supporting herself. I feel, no, I know that she brought this action out of petulant spite and probably boredom. On more than one occasion she has told my wife and I that she wished she had never had any children. I know that she is quite capable of convincing this Court to the contrary, so adept is she at play acting. I have come here today because, if the children were returned to the care of my daughter, it would not, in my opinion, be anything but detrimental to their well being". He sighed. "I am not proud at having had to come here. No man can be proud when he produces a rotten apple. I do hope I have helped a little, at least with the truth as I see it".

The Judge was clearly moved by his long and painful statement.

"Thank you, Mr. Johnston-Bloice. I appreciate very much your coming here today to assist the Court. I do not know whether Mr. Proctor or Mr. Lanthenby wish to ask you any questions? If not, you may go, or wait until the end of the hearing.

Mr. Lanthenby stood and said "No questions, your Honour". Mr. Proctor just nodded and sat down. He was speechless.

"If you don't mind, I would rather go; I find this whole matter very disturbing".

Of course".

Johnston-Bloice left the Court without looking left or right.

There was a few moments complete silence. Proctor had a word with Barbara, advising her that it seemed useless to proceed. With eyes blazing she told him to get on with it.

Proctor winced and was thrown off balance. The man who had just left the courtroom represented about a third of his firm's fee income for the year. He wished that he had known his feelings on the matter before. If he had he would never have accepted instructions from his daughter. He certainly did not want to lose Johnston-Bloice as a client.

David went back into the box. Very half heartedly Proctor queried David's version of events.

The Judge then retired for a cup of tea. Johnston-Bloice's appearance had certainly helped to reinforce his views in this case. He returned to the Courtroom to give his judgement. There will be no need for the Welfare Officer to give evidence.

"After hearing all the evidence and having seen the parties concerned together with the Welfare Officer's Report I reject the application for custody to be transferred. I am satisfied that the children must remain with the father until they are of age.

This is not part of my findings but I did feel that the grandfather's wish to see the children was sincere, and perhaps Mr. Markham you will ensure that a relationship of some kind is re-established". David nodded.

Barbara ran from the Court, yanking at her hair to free it. She could be heard down the corridor shouting.

"SUNK BY MY OWN BLOODY FATHER!"

David said his goodbyes, kissed Elizabeth and raced off to the other Court where his case of Andrews was still going on.

*****

Elizabeth felt vindicated once again. How many more times, she wondered, was her private life going to be aired in public? She travelled back to Scarborough alone.

The house was quiet, Elizabeth found Carol reading in her room. She looked up as Elizabeth entered, her eyes emanating a mixture of fear and worry.

Elizabeth took her in her arms. "I hope you meant it when you said you wanted to stay with us because that's what the Judge has decided". Carol looked up at her smiling and gave her a hug.

"Thank goodness for that, now I hope Mummy will stop being so silly".

"Would you like to hear what happened? If you prefer not to I will quite understand".

"Yes, I would, please; I want to get it straight in my mind".

Elizabeth took her through the day's events skipping particularly painful comments made - giving really a broad outline, to save poor Carol's already battered emotions.

When she came to the part where her grandfather had come to Court, Carol's mouth opened wide, and she gasped in amazement. When Elizabeth had finished Carol quietly went over to the window and stood looking out to sea. Elizabeth did not wish to interrupt her thoughts, and sat on the bed waiting patiently. After a few minutes Carol turned around.

"I would like to see grandfather again, if possible. Would you and Daddy mind?"

"Of course not, either I or Daddy will 'phone him within the next few days to make arrangements. Come on, let's go and tell the others. We don't have to go into details, at least not for the moment".

Robert and John were painting in the kitchen under the close direction of Maggie wearing aprons to protect their clothes. Nicholas, who was now seventeen months old was toddling everywhere and needed constant supervision. Maggie grabbed him and sat down with him on her lap. The three monsters really were a handful, she thought.

Pip was practising the piano. She had made great strides with her exams. Her piano teacher was so impressed with her natural talent that she felt that she would shortly need more expert tuition. If her enthusiasm continued at the same level, her teacher thought she might well be good enough to become a professional pianist one day, if she wanted to.

Pip never seemed to wish to do anything else these days in her spare time except play her piano. She would practise her scales and set pieces for two hours a day and longer at the weekends.

Elizabeth hated to interrupt her, but gently slid her arm round her slim waist, kissing the top of her head. For a moment they clung together in their own precious moment of love. Elizabeth told her about the Judges' Order.

"Oh good Mummy, I'm so glad, I do love Carol and Robert, but do you love me and John the best?"

Elizabeth thought what a tortured question, but there was no ducking out. "I love you all, yes, I suppose I love you and John the best, but you know that all love is different. You grow to love other children in the family, and as each day passes, you love them a little more, until they become part of you, whereas you always love your own children automatically from birth. With adopted children you can choose whether to love them or not, so that's why they are special".

"I love you, Mummy".

"And I love you too. Now, let's play a duet that will raise the roof and shake the others".

The strains of a polonaise drifted through the house, bringing the children running into the room to see who was playing, and they all ended up clapping to the music. Elizabeth hugged them all and despatched them either to bed or to finish their homework, depending on age and seniority.

PART TWO

FOUR YEARS LATER
1976

CHAPTER FORTY SIX

Update

David stood looking out of his office window. The snow was falling steadily drifts were forming against the shop windows, even though they had all been cleared the day before. It had been snowing off and on for six weeks. The nation was feeling the grip of the long freezing spell. It was now February 1976, and a great deal had happened in the last five years.

Britain had voted to join the EEC in January 1972. 1973 brought the property crash. Edward Heath introduced VAT, which effectively meant that businesses throughout the country were to act as unpaid tax collectors. He further introduced the three days week, which was considered by some to be his downfall. The miners went on strike; Heath lost his nerve and went to the country. He lost. In David's view, Heath's lack of personal convictions in his own policies lost him his job, and the country voted Wilson back into power.

In 1974 B.P. announced the first oil find in the North Sea.

Capital Transfer Tax was also introduced in 1974, the nurses got a 58% pay rise and inflation soared to 26%. 1975 saw a record number of bankruptcies.

Yes, the country had certainly been through some

turbulent times, and they were not out of the wood yet thought David.

Elizabeth's new office had been opened in 1972 within a year after they had first discussed it. She struggled through the property crash of 1973 but survived.

Elizabeth couldn't have chosen a worse time to open another office, but on the other hand, it was felt, if she could make a go of it in a recession, when the market picked up it was bound to be successful and she had been proved right. The Building Societies had lent far too much money, many to first time purchasers, way over the normal three times annual salary multiple and a lot of them simply were unable to keep up the repayments when their mortgage repayments suddenly shot up. There were a great many repossessions by the Building Societies. The money markets always seemed to swing in a pendulum. If only the lenders would hold back money when it was plentiful, to counteract the downward swings which always happened with alarming regularity thought David.

Christine had given birth to a little girl in August 1971. David had accommodated all her wishes. The small terraced house had been bought in her sole name.

The secret Deed of Trust was drawn up to secure the financial arrangements for her and the child. David had managed to leave out the question of private education. Christine had changed her name to Barker, and the child was christened Lucinda er. David saw them once or twice a week. It was sometimes difficult, but Elizabeth being in another office helped. Christine had recently been making overtures, wanting to have another child. David was busy heading her off.

Since his first mistake, he had always taken precautions. Barbara had sunk without trace since the Court case. She had cut herself off completely. Although it wasn't good for the children, after all she was their mother, at least her total absence allowed them to settle down into a normal family routine. David was pleased the children had re-established a relationship with her parents. On some occasions they had come to the house for afternoon tea and had seen all the children together, or Carol and Robert had gone to London to see them for the day. They had been picked up from the train by the chauffeur. Maggie always accompanied them on these visits.

Christopher was not working as hard lately. He was sixty-eight and planned to retire at seventy in two year's time, when he would be able to spend more time on the farm. His enthusiasm for the farm had been fuelled by Patricia. Their relationship had deepened, and they spent a great deal of time together, although they both still preferred to live separately.

David's new secretary, Clare Dickens, was quite short in stature about five feet three inches with brown curly hair she was married with no children, and apparently she had no desire to have any. She was the ideal secretary. Wearing sensible smart clothes and was dedicated to her job. David watched from the window as she slithered in the snow trying to get to the office. He shivered. The office was always cold first thing in the morning until the heating got going. As soon as she came into his room David asked her for a cup of coffee.

He was due in the Magistrates Court at 10 o'clock; his client had been caught driving under the influence of alcohol. David felt he could run a good defence on a technicality. From the information before him he did not feel that the Police had carried out the statutory procedures correctly. It was a game really. As soon as the lawyers found a loophole in the law, the law was amended to close it.

He remembered one incident when four young men were stopped by a traffic policeman. The driver wound down his window, and the policeman stuck his head inside the car to see if he could smell drink. One of the young men sitting in the back leant forward and with great presence of mind kissed the policeman full on the lips. The policeman could not believe what had just happened.

He withdrew hastily out of range and explained shakily that, if they thought he was going to charge them, only for them all to say in front of his colleagues and the Court that one of them had kissed him, they must be joking. He told them to clear off. David chuckled at the thought.

*****

Elizabeth was pleased with the way the office was developing. When you open a new office it takes quite a while for the public to realise your existence but at last clients were being recommended locally. She had done her fair share of touting around the building societies, banks and estate agents. This way of attracting business was frowned upon by the Law Society, but everybody did it.

How else were you supposed to speed up your volume of business she wondered? The Law Society could hardly prevent you from taking people to lunch, which usually resulted in a rapport being struck between them and as a result business followed; thus paying for the lunch and more. Some solicitors gave back handers, so much per case, but this was definitely considered to be unfairly attracting business and anyway Elizabeth did approve of it?

Her filing cabinet was getting quite full with new matters, and Trevor the assistant solicitor from the other office, was spending more of his time with her. She had taken on more Court work, but not too much because she couldn't afford the time away from the office.

The 'phone rang, Sally trilled down the line, "its Karl Burger to see you".

"Oh yes, Sally tell him to take a seat in reception I will be with him in a minute. I sent Trevor to file an urgent Petition at the Court. He should be back shortly, I won't be long".

Karl was buying a squash club and sports complex, and she wanted to have a look at it. She grabbed her briefcase, stuffed the file inside, pulled on her boots and snuggled into her fur coat.

Karl stood up as she entered the reception area, extending his hand and smiling broadly. "Good morning, Mrs. Markham, I'm sorry to drag you out in this weather but it's got to be done". He spoke with a thick accent. He was Dutch and he originated from The Hague. He had been a top squash international and still played as county level. His six foot frame was athletic and his muscles well tuned. His light brown hair was receding from his square face, with prominent bone structure, dancing blue eyes and an easy smile. He already had one business in England but this investment was dear to his heart.

Elizabeth replied "Oh that's all right. I'm glad you're driving. Let's go."

She explained to Karl as they drove that she wanted to walk the boundaries as shown on the contract plan. It looked as if he was getting less land, than the plan indicated. Also, the water supply came over a neighbouring farmer's land and there appeared to be no deed of easement. Without a legal right the farmer could cut off the supply, which Karl would not be able to do anything about, so that the property would be rendered valueless. The vendor's solicitors kept assuring her that it was in order, but without legal documents to prove it she was not convinced. However, as it was her job to see that it was put right, she intended to do just that. As long as the client understood the problem, that was all that mattered.

Karl pulled on his sheepskin coat and helped Elizabeth from the car. The wind whipped at her plan and it nearly blew away, as she tried to get her bearings. There were eight acres of land in all. They trudged through the snow to the corner of the field she was concerned about. Once there, it was quite clear the boundary line differed from the plan. A large corner of the field had been cut off amounting to a loss of about half an acre. Elizabeth felt that their efforts had been worthwhile.

She could now speak to the vendor's solicitors with renewed confidence. Karl had to take her arm as they stumbled back. The snow had drifted quite deep in places.

He showed her around the club, which had recently been built; unfortunately, the owner had run out of funds and gone bankrupt, and the official receiver was selling it. Karl felt sure that with the right publicity and his name, the punters would come in.

He at least did not have to rely on the club for his own income. His other investments saw to that. The gymnasium was well equipped, and there was a superb indoor swimming pool, complete with jacuzzi.

Elizabeth was impressed, and said so.

Karl took her by the elbow and steered her into the bar. "I hope if the deal goes through you will be one of my first members?" He looked deep into her eyes "After all, you told me you played squash before".

Elizabeth laughed. "You must be joking, that was ten years ago".

Never mind, I will teach you".

Driving back in his car, Elizabeth asked, "Supposing I get these problems sorted out shortly, when do you want to exchange and complete?"

"As soon as possible, but you must give me a little notice so that I can arrange for the bank to transfer the money from my account in Holland, now, how about me buying you some lunch?"

"I'm awfully sorry, but I have such a pile of work to do, I must say no, perhaps some other time. Lunch for me today will be a sandwich whilst I'm working".

As she sat in her office munching her dreary sandwiches, she wished she had taken him up on his invitation.

She opened her handbag and took out a letter from Jean Brown's mother. She, at last, had responded to Elizabeth's overtures. Ever since Jean's death, Elizabeth had written to her, updating her on Nicholas's progress.

Up until this letter there had been no response, and she had begun to feel her efforts were wasted. Then, suddenly this morning, a letter had arrived, asking to see Nicholas. Elizabeth was delighted, if not more than a little apprehensive at the thought of meeting Mrs Brown again. She replied immediately suggesting that she would take Nicholas down to see his grandmother one Saturday.

He had grown into a lovely boy. He was six years old and attending school. They had formally adopted him in 1973 after long discussions and much heart searching. He looked the spitting image of his father and, not surprisingly, was big for his age. Luckily, he did not seem to have inherited his father's temper being quiet and gentle.

Since Pip was obviously very musical, they were hoping to get her into the Guildhall School of Music. Patricia, being an accomplished pianist herself, was a great help to Pip whenever Elizabeth was away.

Carol was now fifteen and working hard for her mock o'levels. She wanted to go on to get her 'A' levels and then try and get into medical school to become a doctor.

Robert and John were nine years old and were in their second year at prep school.

They were weekly boarders from choice, which meant, she hoped, that they did not feel entirely shunned from home life as David had felt. David had hated the long absences from home which boarding school necessitated. She felt weekly boarding was a compromise.

Yes, they were all growing up. Elizabeth stood up and slapped her buttocks, "Mmm" she thought," perhaps I could benefit from some exercise".

It was a long journey to Surrey so Elizabeth decided to spend the night at her club in Sloane Street and continue the journey in the morning.

Nicholas was interested in seeing his Granny for the first time and asked lots of questions on the long train ride, most of which Elizabeth found she couldn't answer. He had already been told that both his parents were dead and that he had been adopted because he was special and they had known his mother. Elizabeth dreaded the day when he found out the truth. It could easily unbalance him. Carol and Pip had been sworn to secrecy, not that they were aware of all the details, but what they did know was still an emotional burden on them. Elizabeth felt that as he grew into adolescence, and she dropped the occasional hint about his father not being a very nice man, by the time he knew the truth he would have a certain picture in his mind, and the shock, when it finally came, would be slightly cushioned.

Surrey was certainly a very pretty county. They took a taxi from the station, arriving in time for lunch.

The taxi took them to a small thatched cottage, complete

with picket fence and Venetian well.

The door opened, and Mrs. Brown came out to greet them, pulling on her coat as she closed the door against the wind. She appeared much happier than last time but seemed nervous of the meeting, as indeed they all were. She bent down to shake Nicholas's hand, her eyes brimming with tears.

"Come on in, you must both be tired" she said standing up again and shaking hands with Elizabeth.

"It is very good of you to come".

"Not at all. You know I have always wanted you two to meet. What a lovely house and garden, it must be a picture in the summer".

Mrs. Brown preened herself, "Yes, it is nice. That border over there is full of hollyhocks, peonies, orange and red poppies, lupins and Michaelmas daisies - a real blaze of colour. The clematis runs right along the side of the house. Yellow roses cover the archway. Yes, it is a picture, even if I do say it myself. It was all planted by my husband when he was alive".

"Is the well still in use?"

"Yes, it is much better than mains, I won't go on it. Mind you, we used to draw the water by hand pump, now I have an electric mono pump, very efficient" she said proudly.

The wind howled round the corner of the house. "I don't know what we are doing chatting out here. It's freezing. Let's go inside".

She showed Elizabeth around the small cottage. The beamed ceilings were very low. A log blazed in the inglenook fireplace Nicholas immediately went directly to the fire and sat on the floor warming himself. The furniture was chintzy and oak. All of it seemed to be getting a bit worn. Upstairs there were two comfortable double bedrooms.

They all sat down to a lunch of stew, with carrots and

dumplings, which was very welcome. Rice pudding with jam to follow, Nicholas golloped it down.

After lunch they sat talking, and Mrs. Brown explained that, after her husband's death, she suffered from reactive depression and, with Jean dying shortly afterwards, she had sunk very low. But she had had time to think over the years and now she was feeling much better. She went on to say that she would like to see Nicholas whenever possible, and maybe when he was older he could come and stay with her for the odd week during the school holidays.

Mrs Brown then settled down to talk to Nicholas while Elizabeth read a magazine. Elizabeth felt they seemed to be getting on very well. Nicholas was busy telling her about his brothers and sisters and his toys.

The afternoon passed quickly, and they said their goodbyes after tea. Elizabeth wanted to get Nicholas to bed, he looked very tired. They both promised to write to each other.

CHAPTER FORTY SEVEN

The Web Tightens

Christine was fed up. Things were not going at all as planned. The agreement with David had been useful in the beginning but by now she had hoped it would have become a thing of the past and by now she should be Mrs Markham II. But David had remained resolute. Yes, he had kept his side of the bargain but, it was clear to her now that he had still no intention of leaving Elizabeth. She constantly congratulated herself on having had the brilliant idea of the Deed of Trust. The only snag was that it included a break clause, saying that if she reneged on the agreement not to tell Elizabeth, the Deed of Trust would come to an end, and she would be thrown back on her weak legal rights. She knew that she was far better off with the Trust Deed than relying on the law.

Although the house was in her sole name, it was now too small and poky for her. She felt that she should be in Elizabeth's place, enjoying a grander life style. Also she had recently felt that David's interest in her had been waning. He was very good with Lucinda, who was now four and a half, and who adored him.

Her cigarettes were on the table, dam, she would have to get up. Lighting one she resumed her prostrate position and pondered. She could not work out where she had gone wrong. She hadn't left herself go, her figure was still good. Her sexual appetite was as insatiable as ever. The trouble was that David did not always want sex when he called and she was getting frustrated.

She heard David's key turning in the latch. She unwound herself from the settee, running across the room she flung her arms around his neck and kissed him, without uttering a word.

David extricated himself and pleaded for a drink. Apparently Elizabeth was out for the evening, so he was a free agent.

"Can we go out? I'm so fed up with staying in."

"No, we can't. I'm simply not prepared to risk being seen".

"This is ridiculous, David, I can't live like a nun forever".

"It's your choice, my girl, you made up the rules. Now I suppose you want to change them. Well you can't. Anyway, Lucinda should be starting school soon, and your payments stop then. Have you been looking for a job?"

"No, I haven't, you know I want another child. I wanted to talk to you about schools. Where will Lucinda go?"

"The local state school, I suppose".

"Why should she go to a state school when all your other children, including Nicholas, go to private ones?" "Because it wasn't part of the agreement, and I don't trust you".

"You bloody bastard".

"If you're going to be rude, I'm leaving".

David got up to go. She melted into his arms and started to seduce him. He could never resist her. Anyway, she knew that he had nothing better to do.

He rolled onto his back. "I'll tell you what I will do. I will set up a Trust to pay for her school fees until she is eighteen. However she will have to go to the schools I dictate. I will have no argument over that".

She whooped with joy.

"David, you are wonderful. I do love you. You just lie there, and I'll fix dinner. Chicken pie and veg. nothing fancy, I didn't know you were coming", she called as she ran downstairs.

David thought more money. Never mind, she's right I do have a duty and anyway, I love Lucinda. God knows what will happen when she reaches eighteen. Christine definitely has got to pull her weight and get a job. He knew in his own mind that he wanted to extricate himself from the whole affair. But he also knew, that, he would continue to keep up the pretence and go to any lengths to protect Elizabeth.

Christine called him for dinner. Afterwards he went home as soon as he could decently get away.

The following day the weather was abating, and a thaw had set in. David had a long affidavit to dictate that morning, and he hoped his client would not be in floods of tears. He felt so helpless when clients cried. He was just about to collect her from reception when Christine popped her head round the door. He became more irritated than perhaps was necessary.

"What do you want?" he demanded "I'm very busy".

Christine looked hurt. "I wanted to see you for a few minutes".

"Well, you will have to wait until I have finished with my next client, which will probably be in an hour's time".

"All right, I will do some shopping and come back".

David wondered what on earth she wanted, but did not have time to dwell on the matter as his client was waiting.

Thankfully, this particular lady had finally decided the marriage was over and was emotionally very together. There were none of the expected tears, just a sensible business-like attitude which was a great relief.

He found Christine chatting in the typing room with the girls. He addressed her formally.

"All right, Christine, I can see you now, please come this way".

Once seated, Christine held forth "You know you mentioned about me getting a job. Well, I have already been trying without much success. You see, I only really like working for you. Can't I come back here?"

David was really taken aback. He felt the walls coming in and his cage getting smaller. Trapped!

"That is a ridiculous idea. I haven't got a vacancy. I can't possibly ask Clare to leave. Anyway, I'm very happy with her. No, you will have to think again".

Christine had that "I'm going to be difficult" look on her face. "David, I don't want to threaten but I can only be pushed so far.

I want a job and I want to work here. At least that way I get to see you every day", she spoke through gritted teeth.

David was sweating. He wished everyone would leave him alone to get on with his work. Defeat swept over him.

"All right, for Christ's sake, you can work for Ian the articled clerk, he needs a secretary. Not quite one of your calibre, but it seems I have no choice".

Christine beamed with delight. "Well, I can only work from nine to four because of Lucinda, and I hope not to have too much time off during the school holidays, just like Elizabeth" she said sarcastically. "I'll expect a top whack salary and I'll start on Monday. I knew you would see sense in the end". She blew him a kiss and left.

David sat there seething, not trusting himself to move.

CHAPTER FORTY EIGHT

Patricia in Trouble

The 'E' type Jaguar nosed through the gates of Tulham Manor. Christopher was waiting at the door to take delivery of his new car. Recently he had felt that he was getting a bit staid and had thought that a new sports car would give him some of his old zest back. The salesman made sure he was happy with the controls before driving off in his colleague's car. Christopher remained sitting in the car. Gosh, the dashboard seemed nothing but a mass of dials and knobs. My, this made him feel like a young blood again. He slipped the car into gear and released the handbrake. Her response was very sharp, and she lunged forward with a jerk.

He was due to pick Patricia up, but, on the way, he intended to call in to have a word with his farm manager Arthur Young about next year's crops. He particularly wanted to discuss subsidies with him. There was a representative from the ministry coming the following week to advise on the most lucrative crops to grow.

Most of his farming friends, like him, did not need subsidies to survive, but as the subsidies were handed out by the government with no strings, or very few attached, he saw no reason why the estate should not have the benefit.

The Ministry never investigated your financial means, and there was never any question of repaying the hand-out, so why not take it.

Most members of parliament on both sides of the House, he believed, either owned or had an interest in a farm, so they had more than the welfare of the country at heart when they sanctioned yet more subsidies for farmers. Of course after the war when the country needed to be self sufficient it made sense to give help to farmers who grew those crops which were essential but not as financially viable as other crops. The result of these free hand-outs was a very strong farming lobby. He felt the government should stop all these payments and make the farmers stand on their own feet like any other business in the country. The stranglehold grip they appeared to have on various governments over the years was a disgrace, but why should he stick his neck out, no-one wanted to listen, so he joined them.

He pulled up outside Arthur's office, who greeted him warmly at the door.

Arthur as usual was well prepared with all the paperwork neatly set out for his approval. The farm accounts for the past year appeared to be not too bad.

In the past year they had felled quite a few trees which had now been replaced with saplings and the sale of the wood had increased the profit margin.

Arthur wanted the farm to become more involved with contract work. They had the equipment Christopher in principle had no objection to the idea of expansion as long as Arthur could cope with it.

Christopher left Arthur drafting a list of farmers he would contact asking to quote for their contract work.

He pulled up outside Patricia's house exactly on time at twelve noon. They had planned to go shopping in the afternoon and to a concert in the evening. In a month's time he was opening his garden to the public for one day in aid of the NSPCC. The annual event was tiring, but brought him enormous pleasure. He could always rely on a group of stalwart supporters, regular women, who organised the various stalls and afternoon teas. This year Patricia had offered to help, and he planned to go through the details with her during the course of the day.

A police car was parked outside her house. As Christopher locked his car door, he wondered what on earth it was doing there. He quietly went round the back way, entering the house by the kitchen. Sitting at the dining room table with two policemen beside her she appeared to be in a dreadful state.

"What on earth's the matter?" Christopher asked. His face froze waiting for her reply.

Patricia was visibly relieved to see him and said in a strangled voice.

"I have just been burgled. I popped out to the shops, I was only gone half an hour and when I got back the kitchen window had been forced. All the silver and practically every small movable ornament or anything of value has been taken. They were very quick and efficient they must have known what to take".

One of the policemen stood up. "Mrs. Fraser, one of the fingerprint boys will be here shortly."

"Sir, I suggest nothing is touched until they have finished. We will then require a list from you, madam, of all items which have been stolen. I would also like you to give careful thought to anyone who has had access to the house recently, and who is not known to you. Also, keep an eye out for anyone acting suspiciously in the area. You never know, you may be able to give us a lead. Were the contents insured?"

"Yes, they were but most of the items taken are irreplaceable".

"Perhaps, madam, when you call, you can let us have details of the policy, just for the record. I'm sure you understand. Right, we will be on our way now your friend has arrived".

Patricia said miserably "You hardly ever catch this kind of burglar, do you?"

"We'll do our best, madam". They stood up put their hats on and left.

Patricia sat slumped on the settee. Christopher, perching on the arm, pulled her to him confidingly "I'm sure they will catch them, or him. Why don't you come and spend a few days at my house?"

She looked up at him. "No, I can't, I have to stay here".

"Now think about it, we can't do anything until the team from the forensic department have finished. Then we can tidy up, and you can make a list of items missing. I will get one of my trusted employees to come and stay here and guard the house twenty-four hours a day until you come back.

"I assume one of the spare beds is made up?" She nodded.

"Well then, no more discussion required. Ah! There's the bell. You sit there I'll get it".

They made themselves scarce and went for a walk in the garden whilst the three policemen took various samples and imprints of fingerprints they wanted. Christopher and Patricia then had to have their own fingerprints taken to exclude them from the enquiries. When the police had gone, Patricia tearfully started to make a list. The more she thought about it, the more she cried. She was hardly coherent, mumbling to herself. Christopher removed the pen and pad and said, "I think this can be done at some other time, you are in no fit state to do it now".

Harry, his employee has just arrived. Patricia greeted him and started fussing. Christopher took her by the hand and guided her to his car.

She hadn't known about the new car, it was meant to be a surprise. He settled her in the passenger seat and returned to show Harry round the house and give final instructions.

As they drove away, she found herself laughing and crying at the same time. "The most important thing is that you are all right. After all they are only possessions. Now buck up and dry those eyes, and I'll take you out to lunch at the golf club. I can then show off my car and my girlfriend at the same time," he laughed.

Patricia was tickled pink to be given full rein in the Manor's kitchen. Mrs. Lynch had gone home after leaving the food prepared in the fridge.

Christopher sat at the kitchen table, content to watch her lay the tray for afternoon tea. She found a rib of beef in the fridge for Sunday, there was a cold chicken pie waiting to be cooked and a homemade pork pie. Patricia smiled, as he held the pie at arm's length appreciating the decoration of the water crust pastry.

"It's one of my favourites" admitted Christopher. "Mrs. Lynch makes them for me once in a while they really are perfection to me".

"There's only one way to find out. Shall we have a small slice with our tea?"

"Yes of course, good idea. After tea I will show you to your room". He put his hand to his mouth.

"I completely forgot, you do not have a chaperone in the house."

Patricia giggled like a schoolgirl. "Oh, my Christopher you do make me laugh. It's a very kind thought, but I feel completely safe with you".

"Are you sure? What about your reputation?"

"I think I can handle that".

After tea he showed her to a bedroom three doors away from his. It was on the corner of the house and enjoyed two different views of the garden. It was also next door to a bathroom. The windows and four poster bed were swathed in drapes of rich velvet in a deep burgundy. The carpet was cream, with an Indian rug in front of the fireplace.

"I have always liked this room", Patricia smiled as she sat on the chaise longue at the foot of the bed.

Her face became sad again. Christopher went and sat beside her, and took her hand in his. "Come on, you have done very well. I will do my best to see that the culprits are found. Why don't you take a nap and later on perhaps you can have another attempt at making that list. You will find some writing paper in the desk over by the window".

She offered no resistance. Christopher quietly closed the door.

He went to his own room and fell asleep reading the Law Journal. When he woke up, he went downstairs to find Patricia preparing the dinner. She handed him a list of items which had been stolen.

Christopher glanced quickly through them.

"I would like to take a photostat of this before you hand it to the police, if you have no objection."

"Of course, I'm not expecting any results. I have more or less resigned myself to saying goodbye for good to my treasured possessions", she said with a deep sigh.

"Over dinner I will run through the details of the open house charity day with you".

She sat back in her chair, folding her napkin and placing it on the table. "Well that was a very nice meal, even if I say it myself Mr Christopher".

Christopher stood up and removing her chair for her, as a gentleman should. He took her hand and gently guided her to the settee. "How many times have I asked you to drop the Mr?"

"Oh" she said laughing "It's just habit, I will try and remember".

He moved closer and, placing his arm around her shoulders, he gently kisses her. She responded warmly, still holding her close, he whispered "I think it is time you and I got married. I get very lonely, and I'm not getting any younger. What do you say?"

Patricia blushed crimson "Now, Christopher, look what you have done". She placed her hands on her burning cheeks. "People like you don't marry the likes of me. No, it won't do at all, what will the local folk think? I am very flattered, but I must say no".

Christopher looked upset. "You surely must realise by now that I don't think like that. Over and over again I have praised your many excellent qualities. You are here with me now. I really can't see the difference."

"Well, I can assure you there is". She bent and kissed his forehead.

"You know I'm very fond of you, but I still must say no. I will just put the crocks in the dishwasher".

Christopher called after her, "Please think about it". Her reply was a grunt.

CHAPTER FORTY NINE

The Devil puts out his hand

Elizabeth had completed the purchase of the squash club on behalf of Karl Burger some months before. His appointment first thing that morning had been to sign documents for a further advance.

There was something about him that Elizabeth found very attractive. His presence seemed to fill her office. He exuded enormous amounts of nervous energy. Having at last been persuaded to join the club, she had agreed a little reluctantly to play a game of squash after work that evening.

At lunchtime she had dashed out and bought some sports gear. Although he could have kitted her out, she didn't want to arrive completely unprepared, which would look too amateurish. She had phoned David and told him she was working late and not to wait for her. She quietly wondered why she had lied and not told him precisely where she was going.

She managed to find a space in the car park which was pretty full; she became aware that she felt as excited as a young girl on her first date.

Elizabeth was puzzled by her own behaviour. Her nerve nearly left her when she saw Karl striding across the car park to greet her it was all she could do to resist jumping back into the car and driving off. She gulped.

There was no going back now.

He was smiling broadly and greeted her warmly, relieving her of her bag. "I'm so glad you came and didn't cry off at the last minute". She thought, if only you knew!

"I have booked us a court for eight o'clock. Here is the changing room" he said in that thick accent she found so sexy. What had come over her?

Surveying herself in the mirror she decided that she looked very sporty, even if her knees felt a bit wobbly.

Karl was in the bar chatting to the members. As she approached he came forward to greet her, and introduced her to the group of people with whom he had been talking. She found herself smiling and nodding politely. He placed his hand on her elbow and guided her protectively towards the court.

"If, as I suspect, you are not very fit, I think it sensible if we take things easy, I want to see what sort of strokes you have." Elizabeth turned to see a group of people watching from the gallery. Oh no, she thought, how embarrassing, hopefully they would soon get bored and move away.

She started to enjoy herself; the running and stretching were doing her good. Karl hardly moved, he didn't have to, it wasn't difficult for him to anticipate her every shot. As they played, he made gentle observations on the positioning of her body in relation to her strokes. After twenty minutes she found herself bathed in sweat.

Picking up the ball he took her by the elbow and guided her to the door. "I think you have had enough for one day. Go and take a shower, and I will meet you in the bar".

Elizabeth was amazed how submissive she felt in his presence. The cold shower made her tingle all over. Slowly dressing, she dried her hair and re-applied her make-up.

Karl was busy serving as she entered the bar. She made herself comfortable on one of the settees, feeling very relaxed.

Karl extricated himself and came over. "I have one or two things to do; I will then be free to join you for something to eat". He handed her the menu "You choose, and I will be back to take your order in a moment. I hope you don't mind waiting".

"No, of course not," she heard herself saying. What was she doing? She should have said "I must be going" and left.

He was back after about half an hour. The food was ready and they went into the small dining room to eat. They took a long time over their meal, with Karl being constantly interrupted by his staff with queries that only he could deal with.

Their conversation ranged over wide and varied subjects. She was surprised to find that they had so much to talk about. Eventually, the bar area started to empty. Elizabeth looked at her watch. She couldn't believe it, ten forty-five "My goodness, how time flies," she exclaimed. She stood up, "I really must be going".

Karl put his hand on her arm, "Please wait, the Club closes shortly and we will be alone. Please have a coffee with me before you go, it won't be long before the last stragglers go".

Elizabeth felt panicky, knowing she must go now. Her instincts told her how foolish it would be for her to stay she would only be inviting trouble. The wrong words seemed to come out of her mouth, "Oh, all right then, but it must be quick. I do have to go to work tomorrow".

Karl waved a cheery goodbye to the last member of staff and locked the door. He visibly relaxed as he came to join her, bringing the coffee with him.

"I'm glad you agreed to join me for a nightcap. This is always the loneliest part of the day for me". He looked sad. "I haven't told you about my wife, have I?"

"No," Elizabeth said uncomfortably.

"It's all right, I won't go into details. It's just that she died last year of cancer, and it's the night-times which are the worst".

Elizabeth asked tentatively, "Did you love her very much?"

"Yes, I did, but life must go on".

Elizabeth suddenly grasped her shoulder and exclaimed in pain.

"What's the matter?"

"It's my shoulder. It feels as if it's on fire".

Karl smiled, "It's only the muscle". He came round and sat beside her, "Turn round".

He placed his hand on both shoulders and started to massage, intensifying the pressure on the bad shoulder. After a few minutes it felt better.

"That feels much better, thank you".

"It is only the muscle in spasm. Very painful, but if you play on a regular basis you shouldn't have any problems".

His hands moved to the neck area, and the pressure reduced to stroking. She moved her head imperceptibly nearer to him. He gently placed a kiss on the top of her head, then on the nape of her neck.

She turned, "I must be going. I have a husband and children at home waiting".

"I know I'm sorry! It's just that I feel so close to you".

"Yes, I really don't know what has come over me". She stood up. Her whole body was tingling. He put his arms round her waist and pulled her towards him, "Just one kiss?"

She did not resist; she couldn't.

The kiss was a long one. It started gently, and became more passionate when his tongue entered her mouth. Although she wanted to surrender to him completely she knew that she mustn't allow it. She pushed him away. He stood there, transfixed, and stunned by his emotions. Then he walked slowly over to the bar, distancing himself from her.

"You are right, and I apologise. I hope you will come again. I didn't mean this to happen". He kicked the keys across the floor. "Please go. I don't trust myself to come near you again tonight".

Elizabeth ran to the car. Once inside, she sobbed over the steering wheel utterly confused by her emotions. David, what on earth was she to tell him?

She need not have worried. When she arrived home, there was a note on the hall table saying he had had to go away for the night on business. A warned case had suddenly come on for trial in London, and he would be staying at the Club.

CHAPTER FIFTY

The Law Society

It had been yet another long tiring day. Elizabeth leaned back in her chair, staring out of the window. She wanted to leave on time today. Last night, the children had had to do without her. Two nights in a row was too much. She simply must not disappoint them again. Four thirty, only half an hour to go. The telephone on her desk rang.

"Mrs. Markham, the Law Society are on the 'phone".

"Put them through".

"Mrs. Markham?" the imperious voice boomed. "Geoffrey Bone from the Law Society here, we are sending an auditor first thing in the morning to look at the accounts. I have tried to contact Mr. Christopher Markham whom, I understand, is the senior partner and also your husband, but they were both unavailable. Can you please tell me, are the accounts and ledger cards kept at the Scarborough office?"

"Yes, they are".

"Very well, we will send him there. Oh, by the way, his name is Mr. Slade. Good day to you, Mrs. Markham".

The telephone went dead.

Elizabeth was stunned. What on earth did the Law Society want? She knew very little of their investigatory procedures.

What she did know was that they only sent in the auditors if they thought there was something wrong with the books. She felt they were in order. She knew that the bookkeeper had not recently raised any queries with them. She was puzzled, and knew that she must contact Christopher at once. She picked up the telephone.

"Sally, try and get Mr. Christopher on the line. If he's not in the office try him at home". She found herself pacing up and down her office, racking her brains for an explanation. When her telephone rang, she jumped.

"Hello, my dear, how are you?" The relaxed voice of Christopher sounded down the line.

"I'm not sure. I've just had the Law Society on the 'phone. They are sending in an accountant, a Mr Slade first thing tomorrow to look at the books. The man who rang from the Law Society was Geoffrey Bone. He told me he had tried to contact both you and David without success and had then rung me. What on earth does it mean? Do we have any problems that you know of?"

Christopher groaned. "The Law Society is our governing body, and they will investigate if they have received a complaint".

"I know but can you think of a reason for them coming?"

"No, Elizabeth, I can't. We shall just have to wait and see. I will leave a note on David's desk. He's not back yet. No point in worrying. I will speak with you tomorrow my dear".

Elizabeth locked up and went home deep in thought.

Maggie was now well ensconced in the family. She got on well with Mrs. Fraser, and the children adored her. Although she was now twenty-one years old, she showed no signs of any interest in the opposite sex. Thank goodness.

Pip, now twelve, sometimes ate with them and sometimes with the younger three. When Robert and John were away during the week, Pip preferred to eat with Nicholas to keep him company.

Today, Elizabeth was home in time to join Pip and Nicholas for tea. It appeared that after all they didn't seem to know at what time she had returned the previous evening. Only Daddy had been missing at breakfast.

The telephone rang. It was David. "I'm sorry darling, the case is very heavy, and I have got to find out more information for the barrister so I might as well stay another night".

Elizabeth's heart sank; she really did want to see him.

Nevertheless, she managed to say "ok darling, I understand. I thought you might like to know that the Law Society telephoned the office just before closing today". She then told him about her conversations with Geoffrey Bone and his father. For a moment the line went silent, and she thought they had been cut off. David was obviously as shocked as she was.

"Well, I don't know what the hell they want. I should be back tomorrow. Any other problems?"

"Isn't that enough? No, none that won't keep! Goodbye, hope to see you tomorrow". She replaced the receiver feeling very irritated.

Carol was petulant over dinner. One way and another Elizabeth had had enough. "What on earth's the matter with you?".

"I hate eating alone. Where were you last night? I heard you come in at eleven thirty".

Elizabeth tried very hard to sound casual. "Oh, I worked late, went to see some clients who insisted on giving me dinner. Daddy wasn't here, so I stayed. Talked too much, I'm afraid". It was a rather large white lie but, after all, Karl was a client.

Carol was undeterred. "But you didn't know Daddy was

staying away for the night. He left for London after he spoke to you. I heard him speaking on the 'phone to Maggie. How did you know, did he 'phone you again?"

"No, I guessed it might happen, as the case had already been in the warned list for two weeks".

What does that mean exactly?"

Elizabeth was pleased to get off the subject of her activities last night. "Well, they can't afford to have well paid judges sitting around doing nothing, so to make sure that they always have a case to try, they put cases waiting for trial in what is called the 'warned list'. Then, if the case the judge is trying runs short or, in 'not guilty' cases the plea is changed to 'guilty,' the anticipated time for the trial to take will be cut short.

The solicitors involved in the next few cases have already been given warning by the clerk of the list, so they are on alert to have to drop everything or maybe one or two days' notice and go to Court. You can then find yourself waiting for ages in the Court corridors for the case in front to finish. Sometimes the Judge guesses that his time will be used for the rest of the day and you will be released to go, but only after considerable time has been lost. That is why, my dear, crime doesn't pay for the criminal or the solicitors. It's the barristers who make the money".

"Do you still love Daddy?"

"Yes, of course I do. What a question".

"I just wondered".

"Now, tell me about your work, any problems?"

The rest of the evening passed placidly, and Elizabeth took the opportunity of getting an early night.

*****

Dick Slade was heavily built and looked like a prop forward. Good looking, about thirty-five, mousey brown hair, short with a side parting, dark brown, unwavering eyes. He did not look like an accountant at all.

Christopher was ready for him when he arrived at nine sharp and ushered him into his office.

Slade was soft spoken. His manner was only just pleasant and he gave nothing away. All he asked was to be shown the books. Christopher had arranged for him to use a small office, the door of which opened on to the main hall, thus enabling him to observe the office in action, if he wanted.

Christopher was anxious to show him that they had nothing to hide.

Elizabeth was very curious about it all and at the first opportunity came over to Scarborough to see what she could make of him. The answer was nothing. He was civil, but kept himself to himself, asking for files as and when he needed them. David's convivial banter cut no ice with him either.

He was in the office for two weeks; he then left as silently as he arrived, only telling them he was going to write his report.

On Saturday evening Christopher joined them for dinner; they all sat round the dinner table discussing his visit and were all equally mystified at his sudden appearance and the reason for it.

*****

Christopher was tired. He'd been working very hard in the evenings making sure the garden was in perfect shape for the open day on Saturday. Elizabeth had been roped in to do the teas. Pip was going to help Mrs. Fraser on the cake stall.

Saturday arrived, and they were all at the house first thing, setting everything out in the garden. The weather looked as if it would hold, the sun was shining and the forecast was good. They were still going through a long dry spell.

Carol was delighted with the responsibility of setting up the 'bring and buy' stall. She had spent some time pricing up all the items donated.

At one o'clock the gates were officially opened. David was on the gate with Christopher and the boys, taking the entrance fee and directing the parking. Without direction, people tended to park anywhere. Much to Christopher's delight the cars kept coming.

By six o'clock the place was nearly empty. They had a record number of visitors, probably owing to the weather. All the stalls were sold out. The helpers were dismantling the tables and chairs and all the money was given to Elizabeth to count. The final total was nearly six hundred pounds - a record. Christopher shouted out.

"This calls for a celebration. I will open a couple of bottles of champagne. Come on, David, you can help me".

They left by eight o'clock and Christopher was once again alone.

Patricia had returned home after her short stay with him. Very independent was Patricia, thought Christopher. She had made no further reference to getting married, so he left the subject alone.

Christopher was not happy with the lack of progress being made by the police in finding the burglars he therefore decided to make his own enquiries about the people Patricia had mentioned on her list, which he had left with the police, after taking a photocopy. The window cleaners had been the last outsiders to visit the property before it had been burgled. It sounded rather corny, but one of the team of two men was new, the usual one was ill. Patricia had assured him that she had used the same firm for years and never experienced any problems before.

Christopher had also decided to employ a firm of enquiry agents. Their report had been illuminating. The movements of the man in question since the burglary were very suspicious. Christopher had not said anything to Patricia at this stage, in case of building up false hopes. One of his old clients was a police informer, and he had enlisted his help as well. It seemed that this suspect had been trying to sell some goods to fences. After a description of two of them, Christopher had felt it was time to close in.

He decided to take the police into his confidence. Initially, they were a little surprised at him bothering to become involved in a matter which, strictly speaking, was not his concern. They were embarrassed that his disclosures far exceeded their own efforts. Although they had interviewed the suspect, they had seen no reason to question him further. They tried to extract from Christopher his source of information but he had politely declined, nevertheless the police decided to plan a raid, a search warrant was obtained and as expected, after a thorough search of the house and yard the stolen goods were found buried under the floorboards of an outbuilding.

Patricia's face was a picture of delight when she saw the hoard at the police station. All the items, except three, were there. Christopher was still trying to get these back through his own contact. He would probably have to pay for them, but Patricia would not know that.

The police had heralded him as a hero, and the Chief Superintendent had recommended him for a Police Award.

His reward had been the look on Patricia's face, which had made it all worthwhile.

CHAPTER FIFTY ONE

An unexpected visit from Trevor

Having woken up early Elizabeth was lying in David's arms. She snuggled up closer. It seemed ages since they had been able to claim a few precious moments to themselves. There were endless things to discuss. She told him about joining the squash club, omitting any reference to Karl. The main worry at the moment was the wretched Law Society investigation.

David yawned and stretched. "They have got the power to close us down, but for the life of me I can't think what the problem is. If they don't contact us shortly, I will contact them. I'm not being treated like this for much longer. Anyway, come here, I want to kiss you. I do love you". He put his finger under her chin and looked deep into her eyes. Starting with her nose he kissed her face all over, at first little pecks and then with more passion. He came up for air. "Oh, by the way, I think I might join your squash club, do me good to get some exercise, give you a thrashing any day". He pulled her to him, squeezing her bottom. "Who played you the other evening?"

Elizabeth whispered "Karl Burger, the owner".

"Oh, yes, madam, and what does he look like?"

"Ordinary actually, he's Dutch. Not my type," she lied.

She looked at David's face. He was thinking of other things, thank goodness.

Karl always behaved impeccably when she visited the club, and made no further advances. He had introduced her to other women members with whom she had started to play. Afterwards, she would have a bite to eat and then leave the club about nine thirty. Her figure definitely felt more taut, this exercise, it was obviously doing her good.

She remembered she was in bed with David, her husband and playfully pulled the sheet over their heads.

They were disturbed by angry shrieks and yells coming from the landing, and Nicholas came haring through the door, flinging himself on Elizabeth for protection. She groaned at the weight of his body. Robert and John were in hot pursuit. They stood panting by the bed.

"Mummy" demanded John "Don't stick up for him he's being a perfect little beast".

"John, please stop shouting," commanded Elizabeth "And who said I was sticking up for him? I haven't the faintest idea what's going on. Perhaps you would have the good grace to tell me".

John puffed his chest up and took a deep breath. "You know the fort that Robert and I built out of Lego; well he's just ridden his bike right through the middle. It took us hours to get it right".

It was all too much for David.

"Daddy, stop laughing," shouted Robert. "I can see you shaking under the sheets. We want to know what he is going to do about it before we throttle him".

Elizabeth turned to the frightened Nicholas. "Well, what have you got to say?"

Nicholas pointed at John "He took my comic and wouldn't give it back, and Robert tied my shoe laces together, and I can't undo them".

"I would have given you your stupid comic back when I had read it".

"And I would have undone the laces if you'd asked me. I only did it because you are a perfect pest".

David sat up. He was laughing so much he couldn't breathe under the sheets. He raised his hand. "Enough is enough. Now, all three of you will apologise like young gentlemen to each other. Go on". They all reluctantly mumbled "Sorry" without much conviction.

"After breakfast, all of you will rebuild the Lego".

Nicholas started to cry. "I don't want to, because they will hit me".

"No they won't, I will be there to see fair play. Now, off you go, and stop fighting for goodness sake". He ushered them out of the bedroom, closing the door meaningfully.

"No peace for the wicked, we'd better get up". He stretched and went into the bathroom.

Elizabeth snuggled down under the bedclothes, muttering, "Just a few more delicious moments". There was a tap at the door.

"Come in".

Carol came in. I must say, thought Elizabeth, she was growing into a pretty teenager. "Hello darling, how are you? Did you hear the racket the boys have just been making? They are so naughty".

"Yes I did, but I decided to keep out of it. Elizabeth, can I ask you something?"

"Yes, of course, what's the problem?"

Carol flushed pink and started examining her nails.

"Oh, I see, is it a boyfriend?" she asked gently but inquisitorially. Carol nodded. "Well, what's his name?"

"Graham Fielding. I was wondering whether he could take me out to the pictures this evening. My homework is up to date and I feel like a change". Her voice was carefully modulated, trying not give anything away. Intact emotions are very important to a teenager.

"Can you tell me a bit about him? I'm sorry to pry, but you are still very young!"

Carol's voice took on a slightly bored tone. "His father is an accountant and is a partner in Fielding and Fletcher. You know their office is in the High Street. Graham is the same age as me and goes to the same school as Robert and John. What else do you want to know?" she asked lamely.

"Nothing, that seems fine to me, run along and make your arrangements". Carol's face was transformed by a lovely smile. She came round and kissed Elizabeth on the cheek.

"Thanks". She ran out of the room beside herself with joy.

David came in rubbing his hair with a towel.

"What was that all about?"

She told him.

"Oh good, that will cheer her up. Come on, get up, lazy".

David had just finished dressing when the 'phone rang. He picked it up. "It's Trevor here, Mr. Markham" said the hesitant voice "I wonder, could I possibly come and see you both this morning?"

David thought, Oh God, another day off ruined, but replied "Of course, what time?"

"Is eleven all right?"

"Fine, see you then".

David put the 'phone down and wandered in to see Elizabeth, who was lazing in her usual bubble bath "Who was that?" she asked.

"It was Trevor, and he wants to come and see us both at eleven, so you had better put your skates on. I will take Pip to her piano lesson at ten thirty. I can hear practising. I must say, she really is very assiduous".

Elizabeth had the coffee ready when Trevor arrived on the dot of eleven.

He looked nervous as she ushered him into the study.

"David should be here shortly, he has just taken Pip to her piano lesson. Ah, here he comes now".

"I'm sorry to interrupt your Saturday", he said as David arrived.

"Hello Trevor, what's the problem?" David closed the study door.

A sort of desperate look came over Trevor. "I'm afraid I have something awful to tell you". David and Elizabeth exchanged glances, but said nothing. "I'm afraid the investigation by the Law Society is to do with me".

David's eyes nearly popped out of his head, his concentration immediately became sharper and his eyes narrowed. "What do you mean?" Having second thoughts he then raised his hand to stop Trevor answering.

"Please don't say another word. I must call my father. He is, after all, the senior partner, and this matter is too serious to be treated lightly. He is entitled to hear anything you have to say first hand. I will go and 'phone him. If he is at home he will be able to get here within fifteen minutes".

David left the room. Elizabeth excused herself to get another cup for Christopher, leaving Trevor on his own. She caught up with David in the kitchen. "Father is on his way. He is not very pleased".

"What on earth do you think Trevor is going to tell us?"

"Your guess is as good as mine, but I bloody well aim to find out".

Christopher arrived, looking concerned and exuding an air that he was definitely in no mood to be messed about with.

The study was a bit compressed with four of them seated in it but Elizabeth did not feel like suggesting a move to the more relaxed atmosphere of the drawing room.

If there was a bad atmosphere about to be created, she wanted it contained in the study and not allowed to percolate throughout the house.

"Well, Trevor, what have you got to tell us now we are all assembled?" asked Christopher.

"I have made a fool of myself, and it seems, caused trouble to you". No one spoke. Trevor went on "As you know, I have been signing on the Client Account for some time. It's allowed under the Law Society Rules because I have been qualified for more than three years". He went on hesitantly. "As you know, a few months ago I bought a new car. My mother was lending me the money, and, as it didn't arrive in time, I borrowed it from the Client Account".

You did what?" shouted David. Christopher raised his hand. "Please David, let him finish. I want to hear what he has to say".

Trevor was squirming on the edge of his seat. "I thought the money would arrive any day.

You see my mother lives in Australia, and she had to sell some stock in order to help me.

The money arrived eventually. Unfortunately, three months had elapsed before I repaid the Client Account. I realise now that I should have borrowed from my bank, but I kept hoping the money would arrive any day. Anyway, it would be unlikely the bank would have lent it to me. I have no security".

"How did you write up the chits for the book-keeper?" Christopher demanded.

"I transferred some money from a client who had money in her Client Account onto a false ledger card. I then paid the money out as a deposit on a purchase".

Elizabeth's brain was working like an ice cutting machine, trying to remember details of how this could possibly have occurred without being picked up before.

"This is very serious, Trevor, you could go to prison. Is there anything else?" She asked.

"I am afraid there is".

"Oh no!" groaned David.

Trevor took a deep breath. He was by now perspiring profusely.

"A few months ago I made a conveyancing cock-up. I forgot to apply for the money from the Building Society in time to complete a purchase, so I borrowed the funds from another client whose money we had just received.

I thought it would only be for a few days and no harm would be done, but then the building society withdrew their offer as they had received a bad credit search.

The clients had obviously given false information on their application form. It took seven weeks to persuade another society, to lend. Luckily, there was a delay on the other purchase. I should have returned the money to the building society but I couldn't as I didn't have it. The building society consequently charged the clients interest. They were furious with me and as I could offer no explanation I paid the interest back to them out of my own pocket.

The firm's accountants must have picked up the mess on the ledger cards in their half yearly audit and reported the breaches to the Law Society which, as you know better than me, they are obliged to do. In case it's criminal, it seems that they decided not to tell you either. I have been worried sick ever since the Law Society arrived".

Christopher spoke first. "The fact that you have been worried, young man, does not concern me in the least. What do you think we have been going through, not knowing?"

Trevor hung his head in shame. Christopher stood up in order to remove any informality from the meeting.

"What you have just told us this morning is the most disgraceful story I have ever heard in my whole career. Stealing the money for your car is one thing. Make no mistake, it is theft.

That money in Client Account belongs to individual clients; you can't touch a penny of it without their prior approval. The mess over the purchase could have been sorted out if you had come to us. It goes without saying that you are instantly dismissed. I propose the following:-

I will call the police straight away and you will wait here until they arrive. On Monday morning first thing we will go to the Law Society, and you will repeat what you have just told us to them. I will then find out from them if there is anything you have failed to tell us. You are a very stupid young man to throw your career away over a car. The Law Society will undoubtedly strike you off the register unless you can convince them otherwise. David, would you please 'phone the police?"

Trevor started to weep; he was full of remorse and self pity. Christopher went to the door "I cannot stomach this behaviour either. For God's sake man, pull yourself together. We will leave you alone".

The partners all left without further comment.

Sinking into an armchair in the drawing room David exclaimed, "I need a drink, anyone like to join me?" Elizabeth went over to the drinks cupboard. "I blame myself, if I hadn't opened the other office, there would be no need for him to sign cheques".

David crashed his hand on the coffee table. "It will be all round the town through the local Law Society. Yet another stigma this firm will have to live down.

I am sick of it. I work all hours, for what? To continually have mud thrown at me about things which are not my fault".

Christopher upset put his hand to his chest. "David, calm down and stop shouting. It is most unseemly".

"I'm sorry father". He marched over and poured himself another scotch.

A squad car duly arrived. David took the officer to one side and explained what had just happened. "We felt you should be aware of the situation, if only to bring him up with a jerk. I cannot find out what the Law Society has discovered until Monday. He tells me that all the money has been replaced but that does not alter the theft angle as far as I am concerned".

The Officer went through into the study and spoke to Trevor. "I think you had better come to the station with me and make a statement".

He went back into the hall "Mr. Markham I shall also be requiring a statement from all of you in due course".

"I would rather wait until I have had a look at the books myself and then contact my accountants who, no doubt, will be able to help us all with some further detailed information".

"Yes, of course". The policeman turned to Trevor "Now sir, please follow me".

*****

Christopher was at the railway station on time for the six thirty to London. Trevor appeared from behind a newspaper, white and shaking. They hardly exchanged a word on the journey. Christopher buried himself in the Times, not having the inclination to engage in any form of chit chat. They took a taxi to the Law Society's Hall in Chancery Lane. Once

Christopher had made himself known, they were shown into a conference room and left for some thirty minutes.

At last a man appeared who introduced himself as Geoffrey Bone he was flanked by two other men. They did not apologise for keeping Christopher waiting and sat down opposite him at the table, their expressions giving nothing away.

Christopher launched into an explanation of his appearance this morning, telling then all about the sudden revelations of Trevor to him and his partners on Saturday. He now understood why Mr Bone had sent in an auditor at a moment's notice. Christopher concluded that he felt Trevor should explain himself to Mr. Bone personally. Also, he wanted to know from Mr. Bone whether there was any other reason for the accountant's inspection.

All eyes riveted on Trevor as he entered the room. He remained standing and related the events in much the same way as before, sometimes stumbling on his words.

When he had finally finished, Bone said rather wearily "Is that all?" He looked at Trevor unsmiling, eyebrows raised quizzically.

Trevor replied in a whisper "Yes, sir".

Bone said "Mr. Potts would you please go and wait outside whilst I speak with your principal". As the door closed he turned to Christopher. "Since you ask, Mr. Markham, yes, there are two further transgressions of a somewhat minor nature, I must say but, nonetheless, they are breaches of the Rules. I don't think they concern Potts, just not a tight enough rein on the accounts. It's a matter of issuing cheques on the Client Account before they have been cleared with the bank".

"Do you mean accident claims, where I pay the money out to the client as soon as I receive it from the insurance company, for instance?"

"Yes, I do".

"But we have always done that. If not, we get slated by the clients for holding on to their money longer than we should".

"Yes, but you should allow at least four days for the cheque to clear. You have issued the cheque to the client in some cases, and the credit has not hit your account until the following day".

"It usually takes three days for the client to present the cheque and for his bank to send it to mine, by which time the account is in credit".

"It does not matter, it is a breach. Kindly make sure it stops" he snapped. Christopher was fuming. The man is power mad he thought.

"Now, the situation with Trevor Potts is very serious indeed. I am glad you had the good sense to contact the police, saves us a job. We will, require statements from you all; we may then need to interview you separately, if we are not satisfied".

Christopher felt suffocated by the atmosphere. "I wonder if I can leave Potts to you. I have of course dismissed him. I feel I've heard enough and would like to get back to my office".

"I don't see why not". Bone's tone was slightly patronising "I'm glad you came up, we were about to contact you anyway".

Christopher nodded politely and left, not trusting himself to utter another word. He breathed a sigh of relief as he boarded the train. At least they all knew now what the problem had been. He hoped David had managed to make contact with the accountants.

*****

David thundered at Gillespie "That's no answer. We have been using your firm for years, and you didn't have the courtesy to 'phone one of us or call into the office. You knew it was Potts and nothing to do with us, you should have warned us".

Gillespie cringed. He hated trouble. "I'm only going by the rules".

"Bugger the rules. What you are really saying is you thought we were involved".

"I'm not saying that at all".

"Yes you are, otherwise you would have contacted me immediately you suspected anything, out of loyalty if nothing else.

God man, that's what I pay you for. Have you drawn up a report, or have you just crept to the Law Society?"

"No, I haven't prepared a report yet".

"Well, get on and bloody well do it, that you do owe me. It goes without saying that it will be the last report you do for my firm. Once you have completed it, I will have it checked by my new accountants. Yes, I have already instructed a firm who will be in contact with you. I've also put them fully in the picture".

Gillespie looked shattered.

David weakened "Look, I know you had to report it, but you also have a duty to me. You must have known that if there was anything wrong, you should have told us at once. Anyway, as the mutual trust between us is now gone, it's best if we part. I hope you can prepare the report within the next few days. Both the police and the Law Society are waiting for it".

Picking up his briefcase he closed the door behind him without saying another word. The accountant's reply, if any, was lost to the air.

David was still fuming over the Potts affair when he

arrived home.

It would be so nice to be left alone to get on with his work without these extraneous distractions.

That evening he had a flaming row with Elizabeth. The Potts affair had unnerved them all. The result of Trevor's untimely departure meant the office was once again in disarray. They all had to take on more work and deal with all the clients who wanted to speak to Trevor.

The row had been so bad that they had slept in separate bedrooms.

CHAPTER FIFTY TWO

Elizabeth Falters

Having Christine around in the office had not been the disaster David had expected. As she worked for Ian he hardly saw her during working hours.

He hated rowing with Elizabeth and consequently felt thoroughly out of sorts. He knew he wanted to see Christine that evening. He thought twice about it, but found himself reaching for the phone and asking Christine to come to his office. She practically leaped through the door.

"Hi, how are you?" she smiled "I've been missing you. When are you coming round?"

"Tonight! I will spend the night with you, if it's all right. I have had a blazing row with Elizabeth and need some soothing company".

Jolly good, she thought, but said "Oh dear, yes, of course, silly, I'll pop out shortly and get something special for dinner".

David felt slightly crazy at the moment and decided that if he was going to do something stupid, he might as well do it with Christine.

Elizabeth was also depressed. Every time they had a row the saga of Jean Brown seemed to get brought up.

It was an accident and she had been found 'not guilty' but the way David sometimes behaved anyone would think she had been found guilty.

She worked late, and then drove straight to the squash club feeling that a good game of squash would release some of her tension. She only hoped she could find a partner.

When she arrived, Karl was serving behind the bar he waved cheerily to her. She changed and wandered into the bar area.

"I don't suppose you feel like giving me a game. I can't find a partner, and I need to hit something", she said miserably.

"Oh dear, you do seem in a bad way. If you wait five minutes, I will be with you".

She went onto an empty court and started knocking up. Her annoyance centred on the ball. When Karl arrived, she was sweating and panting.

"My, you are in a temper. Keep it up and try and beat me".

"You must be joking". She played for all she was worth and ended up missing a shot and sitting on the floor laughing.

"I think you have had enough. You had better go and take a shower".

"My shoulder is hurting again".

"If you like, I will give you a massage. Don't look like that, I often massage female members. Take a shower, and leave your bra and panties on.

I will see you in the massage room in fifteen minutes".

He disappeared, leaving her once again left footed. However the thought of a massage cheered her up.

As soon as he placed his hands on her legs, she knew it was not such a good idea. He tried to discourage her from talking and to concentrate on trying to relax.

She in her turn tried to think anti-thoughts about him,

without success. The tension gradually eased from her body. The massage of her back and shoulder felt so good. He was standing beside her and asked her to turn over. As she did so she looked up at him. Her arms stretched out for him and she pulled him down kissing him full on the lips. He did not demur. Burying his head in her neck, his lips caressed her.

"I don't think this is the time or the place, someone might come in" she whispered in his ear.

Relax the Club is pretty quiet tonight. But, I agree, one must be careful". He went on kissing her, right down her back and decided he would lose control if this went on." I think we should continue this later at my house" he muttered, nibbling her flesh with his lips. Slapping her bottom playfully, he laughed "Get dressed, and I will go and see whether I can get off a bit early".

"May I use the telephone? I must 'phone home and tell them I will be delayed. Luckily the children are staying with my mother tonight, but I know Maggie will worry".

He pulled her to him "Why don't you tell them you won't be back tonight?"

She gulped. "Ok". As she dressed she thought, what would David say? She need not have worried. Maggie had informed her that he also had telephoned to say that he would be staying away for the night.

*****

Karl's bungalow was near the Club. She felt decadent as she drove her car into the drive behind him. He made them coffee, and they sat and talked and talked. "I'm not sure I should be here".

"Why can't you be honest with yourself, you are here because you want to be. On the other hand I do not intend to be your solace whenever you fall out with your husband".

"I am certainly very confused".

He bent and kissed her. "Does this help?" He lifted her and carried her into the bedroom. As he undressed her, he kissed and pinched her with his lips all over. She was on fire. His love making did not disappoint her. She fell asleep, in bed, in his arms, refusing to think of the consequences of her actions.

She kissed him before she left for work. He was still in bed. "I don't want you to feel used. I really wanted last night to happen. It's just that I am not sure that there can be any future in our relationship".

He rolled over. "I understand I knew you were happily married. I will have to accept whatever happens. I just can't resist you. You only have to crook your finger and I will be there. If I meet someone else, ok but for the moment, I only have eyes for you".

She laughed in spite of herself. "All right, see you soon". She scuttled off to her car.

Funnily enough, she did not feel in the least bit guilty and couldn't understand why. David telephoned her as soon as she arrived in the office.

"I'm sorry I didn't come home last night" he said.

"Oh, didn't you," she replied "I wouldn't know, neither did I". You could hear the silence.

"Will I see you tonight?" he asked.

"Yes, I suppose so, bye". She replaced the receiver.

Check mate.

*****

In fact, they both arrived home late from the office. He tried to communicate with her in a desultory sort of way. They ate their meal in comparative silence, with one or two stilted exchanges. Although they slept in the same bed that night, there was the largest possible chasm left down the middle of the bed. David rose early and left for work, leaving her to deal with the children with the help of Maggie. Coldness between them had definitely entered their marriage.

CHAPTER FIFTY THREE

Jonas has Fish Stolen

Jonas was experiencing a great deal of unrest amongst his employees. The Cod War had finally ended. On the 1st June Britain, Iceland and Oslo has signed a peace treaty, thus ending the third Cod War, which had been going on since August 1958 when Iceland declared fishing limits on Britain. This year it had all come to a head. On 7th of January, an Icelandic gunboat had rammed HMS Andromeda. On the 19th of the same month the British government withdrew protection for the fishing fleet. Diplomatic relations between the two countries were broken off. The government then had a change of heart and on the 19th of February despatched four gunboats to support the fleet. After this last minute show of strength, the government surrendered to Iceland's demands. The Hull fishing industry, as it was known, was virtually finished. Not surprisingly, the men felt the government had badly let them down. Generations of men had fished those waters for centuries, and now with the stroke of a pen by some civil servant who probably knew nothing about the fishing industry at grass roots level; it had all been taken away from them.

    Luckily, it had not directly affected the Scarborough

fleet as they fished around English waters.

Some of the Hull fishermen were prepared to travel the forty miles to work in Scarborough but the two factions did not get on very well, and the Hull men were not accepted. The positive effect on the Scarborough fleet was a larger demand for fish.

Recently there had been two fairly substantial thefts of fish from the warehouses, which made the men suspicious of each other. Security had been tightened. It was felt by most of the men that it had to be an inside job. The men were also demanding a wage increase. Not unnaturally they felt that with the growing demand for fish from their fleet, the bosses were making more profit so why shouldn't the men benefit as well? Unfortunately, it was not as simple as that. Dealing with a larger demand meant the overheads had gone up dramatically. Anyway feelings were running pretty high. Two meetings had been held but had ended in disarray.

Michael was quite adamant that the firm could not stand the demands of the men. He and his father had recently invested fairly substantially in new equipment and had replaced three coble boats. He felt that all the men knew they were assured of a job with their firm for the foreseeable future, and for that they should be grateful; particularly since there was a great deal of unemployment in the area at the time.

Michael had engaged a firm of private detectives to shadow certain men about whom he had his own suspicions.

The police were also quietly involved in the investigation, but Michael wanted to keep these private thoughts to himself for the time being.

Jonas was sitting back in his chair in the office, drinking his coffee from a large mug, when Michael came in. He slumped down in the chair, nodding to his father.

"I don't like it, da, there's some more fish missing this morning. Not a great deal, just a couple of boxes but some clever bugger is moving in and out as he pleases, and taking the piss out of us. The blighter takes the best fish too. We can't afford to go on losing money at this rate".

Jonas ran his hand through his thick hair, "Aye, I know lad, but we've got two men watching all the time. Christ you would think that they would notice alien movements. Not a word, what waste of bloody money!"

Michael held out two notes. "I received these this morning. They are both roughly the same. If we don't give in to the men's demands, my life's at risk".

Jonas took them and read them quickly. "You are to hand these straight to the police, son, don't mess about. You don't know fingerprints and such like. Well I can't sit about any longer. There's a new freezer unit being fitted today in Talon Street shop. I best make sure everything is going smoothly, see you".

He walked out, leaving Michael ruminating.

What a mess, thought Michael.

He didn't take the threats on his life seriously, some silly fool getting carried away probably. He decided to have another meeting with the accountants to see if a salary increase was at all possible and if so, how much?

Up till now they had always maintained that the firm could not afford it, yet he knew they were possibly running in profit, at least before all the thieving started. It would certainly put up the insurance premiums. In fact, they might even find it difficult to get cover.

He walked to his car and bent down to unlock the door. As he did so he noticed two men coming around the corner from the sheds. They stopped, surprised to see him. Then, realising it was too late to retreat and pretending not to notice him, they walked to their pale blue Volvo and drove away. They were two of the men Michael had his eye on. He mused. "They were certainly surprised to see me". He then noted the registration number of the car as he followed them out of the yard. Both of these men were comparative newcomers to the firm. It struck him that whenever there was trouble they had always been in the vicinity. He also had a feeling that they were at the bottom of the recent wage demand. But, so far he could not prove a thing.

CHAPTER FIFTY FOUR

Michael and Elizabeth in Danger

Maggie was having the weekend off, so Elizabeth had taken the children over to spend the day with her mother. The children loved Grannies cooking and she also spoilt them. They found in her someone to tell their problems to, she was a jolly good listener. Also Robert and John got lots of valuable tips from her as to how to get the upper hand on their chums at school.

Elizabeth just liked being at her old home. She hadn't told Hilda about any of her recent problems with David, but suspected that her mother would instinctively know that something was up. Hilda would refrain from asking any questions, because she knew that Elizabeth would tell her when she was ready if she wanted her to know. Elizabeth hoped that she too would keep a loving relationship with her children when they grew up and would give them in her turn the unqualified love she always received from her mother.

The children were all in the kitchen, chattering and helping Hilda.

Elizabeth sank further into the comfortable cushions of the settee, and was dozing off when Michael came into the room.

"Hello Elizabeth, didn't know the tribe would be here, any more coffee in that pot? What are you up to, you lazy thing, lying there?"

"Taking a snooze, dear brother, whilst the going was good, and you can shut up. Here's your coffee, sir" she yawned. "Anyway, how are the problems at work, any progress? Have the police come up with anything?"

"Nought, there are two blokes I have got my eye on. I saw them the other day looking very suspicious. Trouble is I don't have any evidence." He thought for a moment.

"I say, fancy coming flying with me? I have got my own plane now".

"Isn't that a bit extravagant?"

"Yes, I suppose so, but remember I don't have a wife and family to keep. I bought a Cessna one fifty, she's beautiful. I have named her Daisy".

"How much did she cost?"

"Fifteen thousand pounds actually, not bad, she is quite old, about ten years, but she goes like a dream. I had her thoroughly checked by a mechanic mate of mine, in addition to the air worthy certificate she already carries. The airport parking fees are quite high, pushes up the running costs, so I have decided to rent it out by the hour to help pay the bills".

"My, you do surprise me. It seems only yesterday you were learning to fly!"

"I passed my PPL. but that only qualifies me for fair weather flying in daylight. I wanted a night rating and IMC. and to get that I had to do a further five hours training. I have just completed the extra training".

"What's that?" Elizabeth pointed to a large book on the coffee table.

"Instrumental Meteorological Condition it encompasses many aspects of altitudes. Much too complicated for you to worry your pretty head about" he laughed.

"Don't you patronise me, young brother". She aimed a cushion at his head and nearly hit an ornament.

"Stop it," he raised his arms protectively. "Mother will be cross with us if we go and break anything. Are you coming or not? If so, we had better go and chat up mum, and see whether she will baby sit this afternoon. Then we really must fly! Ha Ha".

"You are incorrigible, come on," she said rising. "Sounds fun!"

Hilda came up trumps, and they sped off to Teeside airport. Elizabeth was quite excited at the prospect of flying with her brother. They parked and walked to the conning tower to get clearance for their flight. Roger, the senior air traffic controller, happened to be on duty. He was pleased to see Michael and cordially shook hands with Elizabeth.

Elizabeth looked at the view from the Tower and asked one or two polite questions. Roger told her that because of length of the runway, they were restricted on the size of the aircraft using the airport. They handled a number of short haul flights, which covered parts of Europe as well. The maximum number of passengers per flight was limited to forty.

Roger talked as he escorted them part of the way to the plane, as he was going that way. It was parked quite a distance from the main buildings.

Michael walked round the plane carefully, making the routine checks necessary before any flight. These are mandatory for any aircraft. By the time they took off, it had started to drizzle, but as they climbed, the weather improved. The winds were reasonably strong, but not sufficient to be a problem.

Michael had already decided on a flight path, overland to Scarborough and the docks. Elizabeth was fascinated.

This was her first flight in a light aircraft. The view below was superb. It was very noisy and she had to shout if she removed the head muffs through which she could also communicate.

"Could you show me where you saw Jack Big and the cove he holed up in?" Elizabeth asked "Perhaps we can also see the cliff delta and the bay he pulled into for his provisions. He certainly was a rugged and dangerous man, and yet Nicholas seems such a normal little boy".

"After all this time it is still very much on your mind, isn't it, poor girl. Never mind, I think Nicholas is super, you are doing a grand job of bringing him up. Jean should be very grateful to you. Not many people would have made the long term magnanimous gesture like you and David."

"Now look below to the right. There is Robin Hood's Bay, and you will see a cluster of rocks. It was there that Jack lived those few weeks. We are now coming to the shelf delta. I must go there one day. To the right is where Jack pulled in for his provisions. If we turn inland we should find the grocers shop. Poor old chap got quite a shock when he found out whom he'd had in his shop".

As Michael made his turn towards Scarborough and the docks, he looked down idly and noticed a small farm and cluster of outbuildings immediately below. He did a double take. It couldn't be, yes it was that pale blue Volvo which he had seen in the yard the other day. He looked at his instruments. They were flying at two and half thousand feet.

He turned to Elizabeth. "Look, it may be nothing but I want to take her down to look at that farm and cars below. Keep your eyes on them". He pushed the control column forward, and Daisy nosed down.

"Get my camera and field glasses from my case". There was such a marked urgency in his voice that Elizabeth did as she was told, then re-seated herself and put her seat belt on.

"I want to take some pictures; can you hold her steady for me"?

"Me!" Elizabeth squeaked. "Don't be silly, I can't fly".

"Look, take the controls. Here, right now, hold the column on that course." He pointed to the instruments. "If you need to correct the position, move the control column very carefully down".

Elizabeth started to perspire, but hung on to the column with her eyes glued to the instrument panel.

Michael was beside himself "My god, it is the Volvo, I can see the number plate. There are four men, they seem deep in conversation. Now they're opening the barn doors. A lorry's coming out.

They're putting a board over the name on the lorry. A small white van is arriving. It's them, bloody hell, the van is full of our boxes of fish which are being loaded into the lorry. Can you take her down a little lower?"

"What?" Elizabeth shouted.

"Just push the control column forward until you're at between seven and eight hundred feet. That's very low, so keep her steady. I must write down the number of the van. Just keep circling at precisely that angle. Good girl, you are doing very well".

Elizabeth was both frightened and cross with Michael for putting her in this position. I will give him hell when we land, she thought. "I don't feel very well" was all she managed to say.

"Christ, they have seen us. They are all looking up, gesticulating and making rude signs. I think we have seen enough, ok I will take over".

Elizabeth gratefully let go of the controls. She looked down, wiping her clammy hands, on her handkerchief.

"Michael, look out, there are two men with rifles, and

they are firing at us. For goodness sake, let's get out of here".

Michael saw that the men on the ground were now running after them, two of them stopping every now and then to take aim. He heard several cracks.

"Bloody hell, I was trained to fly one of the smallest aircraft in the world, not fight a war". He pulled the control column back and the plane started to climb. He pressed the transmitter button.

"Teeside airport, this is Golf Alpha X-ray".

"Golf Alpha X-ray, go ahead".

"Teeside Golf Alpha X-ray, would you alert the police at Scarborough. Possible thieves sighted at small farm six miles north of Brent. Lorry registration K575 KTS, white van 993 EST, Volvo Blue K245 TEN carrying possible stolen fish from Prince Fish Merchants, ask police to investigate. Warn them that two of the four men are definitely armed. We have been shot at, repeat, we have been shot at".

"Roger, Golf Alpha X-ray. Are you OK?"

"Confirm O.K. Teeside, I hope".

Michael and Elizabeth let out sighs of relief.

"I think we'd better turn back and forget the docks today". Suddenly the engine spluttered and stopped. Michael jerked "My god, the engine has failed," he shouted.

Elizabeth went rigid in her seat. "You must have learnt what to do in an emergency. Don't panic, and think".

"The plane will simply drop from the sky without the correct manipulation. I must trim for glide by pushing the control column forward by trimming the weight of the plane it should maintain speed at seventy knots. So far so good, now let's think to restart engine check fuel tap on, ok throttle mixture control, correct". He bent forward over the controls, sweat pouring from his face. He continued to tell himself what to do by speaking out aloud as if the manual was in front of him, primer pump locked, both magnetos on, turn the key".

Michael held his breath, nothing happened, the engine was not responding. The plane continued to glide. He hit the transmitter button.

"May-day, May-day, Teeside Approach, this is Golf Alpha X-ray".

"Golf Alpha X-ray, Teeside Approach, what's happened? Go ahead".

"Engine failed, looking for a field to land in".

"Roger, we'll try and follow you, good luck".

"Right, Lizzy, if I am right we have about two minute's air time left. Look there's a suitable field over there. I have to bank her and take her around; I must then try and judge her speed to land. Blast, I don't know whether I can do it. It looks easy enough in the manual.

I never thought I'd actually have to do it".

Elizabeth decided that this was no time for her to lose her nerve. They were either going to make it alive, or not. "You're doing great just tell me what to do".

"It's ok I'd rather do it if you don't mind. Fuel off, mixture turned to lean, mags off. Pull your belt tight, shoes off, hang on to anything. I am going to open the door ajar in case we get stuck. You do the same your side. Final flap setting 40, turn master switch off to electrics, here we go. Bugger the wind!"

The wind played with the light aircraft's wings, making it very unsteady. The ground came close the plane bounced a couple of times, and then landed. Michael thought they had made it safely as he tried to bring the plane to a halt but then wind had other ideas.

A sudden gust picked up the tail and tipped the plane neatly nose down into a ditch.

"Blast, come on, let's get out," Michael shouted. There was no response from Elizabeth who had somehow managed to bang her head when the plane tipped forward. Michael leaned over and undid her belt, and saw that she was unconscious. He climbed out of the aircraft and ran to the other side. It was impossible to move her.

She was a dead weight, especially in that position. Fuel was pouring out onto the grass. "Explosion! My God, come on, wake up Lizzy, please." He tugged and pulled, at last she started to moan. "That's my girl, come on push with your legs.

I've got to get you out of this plane, it's about to go up in flames". Elizabeth's subconscious responded. She pushed and pushed, Michael pulled, and they both fell out of the plane onto the grass.

"Can you move?" he shouted.

"Yes, I think so". Half dragging her, they staggered a safe distance away. They heard the ambulance sirens in the distance. Thank goodness, he thought, and passed out.

Michael sat up in the ambulance "I'm sorry about that. I feel fine now. No need to trouble the hospital".

The ambulance man, who was sitting between them, a man in his middle thirties with dark wavy hair and medium build, spoke with authority "You may be suffering from shock, so it will be all for the best if you let the doctor look at you".

Elizabeth was lying prostrate but conscious.

"How are you, old girl?" Michael asked.

Elizabeth was holding her head which was throbbing. She had a bump on her forehead the size of an egg. There was also a nasty cut on which the ambulance man had placed a cold compress. "Oh, I shall be all right. Apart from the bang on the head I think I twisted my ankle, it certainly hurts."

"You did very well to bring that plane down in the

circumstances. I'm very proud of you".

Michael turned to the policeman who was travelling with them "Have you any information on the thieves?"

"No sir, I have only just come on duty. As soon as you finish at the hospital and as long as the medics agree, I would like you to come to the station. The Inspector wants to see you. It seems you have had quite an eventful afternoon".

"You could say that. I do hope they caught the blighters".

Elizabeth received four stitches to the gash in her forehead. Michael found it difficult to understand how she managed to bang her head when she had been strapped in. He decided that she had probably been struck by an object hurled through the air as the plane had upended itself. Her ankle was bandaged, and she was advised not to put too much weight on it for the next few days. After the results of the x-ray were cleared with the doctor, they were allowed to leave and the police drove them to the police station.

Inspector Bluitt was waiting for them. Michael could not contain his curiosity any longer. "Have you managed to trace any of the vehicles and the men?"

"Yes, indeed we have, sir, owing to your vigilance and a smart piece of detective work of course. The number plates helped.

They didn't have time to change them, especially as you had identified the premises from which they were operating. We have all the men in custody. It seems that one of them has a bit of a grudge against your family. He is so full of hatred that it all came tumbling out".

"But I don't understand. I didn't think I had any positive enemies".

"No sir, none of us do. Apparently this man is called Wayne Big, joined your firm under an assumed name, I believe he is some relation to a man called Jack Big. I understand there was a lot of trouble back in 1970 with your family and Jack Big?"

Michael looked at Elizabeth, and they both nodded. "It would seem he was planted in your firm by a rival firm of fish merchants to do the maximum damage. Hence the wage demands and strike threats stirred up by these men. This is apart from the thefts which have been occurring. Wayne Big went one step further and wanted to settle an old score with your family on behalf of his cousin".

Michael stood up and wandered across the office. "I thought this trouble was something to do with that man, but I couldn't figure out what. What's happened to my plane, does anyone know why the engine failed? It has just had a complete overhaul".

"The engineers and investigation team are going over it now, and no doubt they will have a word with you direct. They did 'phone in to say the fuel pipe had been partially cut. Just enough for the fuel to drip out".

"That must be sabotage and attempted murder. They could have killed both of us".

"That we believe, sir is what they intended".

"But I don't understand. There was fuel seeping out after we had crashed. Surely the tank should have been empty".

"Yes sir, that was apparently from the reserve supply which, as you know, is held in the tank below the pipe line. There wasn't that much fuel left, just enough to start a fire though. You have both had a lucky escape, and if I may say so sir, not a bad bit of flying especially as I understand you've only recently passed your flying exams. Now, if you both feel up to it, I would like statements from you". Michael took Elizabeth's hand and winked at her. "We're ok aren't we Lizzy, but I must get you home soon you do look very pale".

Elizabeth smiled "Come on, let's get on with it then I

must 'phone mother and the children. I only went out with you for a bit of fun!" They all laughed.

*****

Elizabeth had to be driven to work for the next week because of her ankle, which seemed to be taking its time to heal. With Trevor now departed, they had advertised for another solicitor but, as yet, the vacancy was unfilled.

Ian, the articled clerk, was doing his best, but he was limited in experience and had to be watched at all times. Christopher and David were working flat out to keep the practice under control.

They had been informed that Trevor had been struck off the register by the Law Society and was awaiting a trial date, which they would have to attend. The Law Society seemed satisfied with the statements they had made and hopefully there would be no disciplinary hearing.

Patricia had, at last, given in to Christopher and agreed to marry him. As they were both widowed, the wedding was to take place in the village church.

There would then be a small reception at Tulham Manor for the family and a few close friends. Once Patricia had said yes, Christopher felt that there was little point in delaying at his age, and a date had been fixed for four weeks time. Patricia had put her house on the market and was clearly as happy as a lark.

Christopher, too, looked very happy. What with the Trevor episode, he'd needed cheering up.

They had all enjoyed being regaled with details of the horrendous flight with Michael. It was good to laugh about it now, as it was all over bar the trial. It had all happened so quickly. Jonas and Hilda were utterly amazed at Michael for taking Elizabeth on such a dangerous mission.

Although Michael naturally pleaded that he could not possibly have known what would happen, Jonas would have none of it.

"You fancy yourself as a bit of a private detective. Look how you went after Jack Big all those years ago. You had something in your mind when you went up in that blasted plane of yours. I'll be bound. Nearly killed my favourite daughter! Still, I suppose you did a good job".

Hilda put down her knitting and looked over her glasses. "Go on Jonas, you're right proud of him, and you know it. You haven't stopped jawing about your brave son ever since it happened. Why don't you tell him? Too stubborn that's you".

Jonas had just grunted and gone out to his greenhouse. It was a very hot summer and the plants needed constant care. He had to admit, he was proud of Michael, he was certain that there were not many people who could have acquitted themselves better in the circumstances.

CHAPTER FIFTY FIVE

The Effect on the Children

Carol was feeling thoroughly disconsolate. She had had a long chat with Pip who felt the same. It was quite obvious to them that their parents were not happy. A stilted atmosphere was pervading the house. David and Elizabeth were both often absent from home, not only throughout the day but most evenings as well. The girls had also noticed that both of them stayed away for the odd night, independent of each other with growing frequency. When they were at home they were barely civil to each other. The girls were feeling the strain but were helpless to do anything about it. The boys were noticing it too and had recently become more mischievous and disobedient. Maggie sometimes found her inner resources stretched to the limit, trying to keep control. Carol had heard her crying in her room on several occasions when the boys had been particularly beastly.

They both began to feel partly to blame for the tension between their parents. Sometimes they wished they had opted to go to boarding school.

At least this would have meant they were not involved on a daily basis and as such would not be asked to take sides.

The parental attitude showed its instability by the

varying of moods. They would either snap unfairly at the children or, because of their guilt or perhaps to get at each other, their approach would be treacly and sweet, but without any sincerity.

Carol had given up asking questions, and tried to ignore the situation by spending more and more time in her room or going for long walks.

Elizabeth was concerned that the low in their marriage was affecting the children. She loved them so much, but she was so tired with the work and responsibility of everything that she felt powerless to do anything about it.

She was not exactly sure of the precise moment when she realised that David was having an affair with Christine. The jigsaw was slowly forming in her mind with pieces from the past which she had previously blanked off and refused to accept.

David was feeling really middle aged. Nothing seemed to be going right recently. His workload had increased to such an extent that he no longer got any enjoyment from it. It was one hard slog from morning to night with seemingly no relief.

Christine was getting on his nerves and had been for some time. Her demands for material things were becoming obsessive. She never seemed satisfied. Her attitude was becoming more belligerent. At least Lucinda was enjoying school, which was some small mercy.

He was deeply concerned about the estrangement between him and Elizabeth.

There had been no specific row, just a gradual growing apart. They were perfectly civil towards each other, which did not necessarily help. A screaming match might have cleared the air. Elizabeth was making a separate life for herself. Her latest idea was to learn to fly. He thought that she would have had enough after the dangerous episode with Michael. Unfortunately, it seemed only to fuel her appetite for more. Where had he been on the day in question? With Christine, of course, he could only blame himself.

At lunch time he was interviewing yet another solicitor to replace Trevor. His C.V. was good, and as long as it looked as if they would get on, David had more or less decided to offer him the job. He couldn't go on like this, and his father was looking worn out.

His 'phone rang. "It's Christine. Can you spare me a few minutes before lunchtime?"

"I have an appointment, but if you're quick, come in".

She came round the desk and sat on his knee confidingly.

"For goodness sake, please get off, be careful!"

"It's ok; I have locked your door. If anyone comes, I'll simply say it was an accident".

She kissed him. It was no use, he still couldn't resist her. His hands found her breast beneath her silk blouse. He pulled away with effort.

"No, what do you want I really do have an appointment".

"I just thought you would like to know I am pregnant".

David's jaw dropped. "I don't believe it. I have always taken precautions, and anyway, I thought you were on the pill".

"These things happen, darling". She slid off his knee and left his office without another word.

David buried his head in his hands. What on earth was he going to do now?

CHAPTER FIFTY SIX

Tulham Manor

It was Saturday, and the whole family, including Patricia, were going over to Tulham Manor for the day in order to complete the final wedding arrangements. Elizabeth and David had declared a truce for the day and had sworn to each other not to have a cross word throughout the whole day. They picked Patricia up on the way, and somehow they all managed to squeeze into the Volvo Estate.

It had been a hot dry summer, and today was no exception. They all fanned themselves as they drove along. The children were planning the barbecue they would have at granddads.

David turned right at the top of the hill towards the village. Elizabeth pointed, "Look at the smoke billowing David; it looks as if it's coming from the Manor".

"My God, you're right, I had better step on it. Hold tight, everyone".

As they drew nearer they could see it wasn't coming from the main house but from the barns storing the hay and grain. Three fire engines were already there.

David pulled up outside the house.

"Now everyone, straight into the house. I don't want to

have to worry about the children. If it gets too bad, I may have to evacuate the house. I am going to find father".

He ran off in the direction of the barns. The fire had spread very quickly. The long dry summer would have created perfect conditions for a fire. Also the barns were made of wood. David saw his father running across the yard, shouting to the firemen to douse the surrounding farm buildings to stop the fire spreading.

David caught up with him. "How did this happen?"

"I don't know, but I can't find Arthur. He's got some sick sheep in one of the barns, and I hope the silly bugger has not tried to go in there, it's an inferno and a certain death trap, I must confess, I've been worried about this happening. We should have had some rain by now". He ran off in the direction of the sheds with his hand on his chest. David followed.

"Look father, don't strain yourself. Show me which shed and I will try and find him". His father was doubled up, gasping for air. He pointed in the direction of the far shed which was well alight. David ran over.

A fireman blocked his path "You can't go any further sir, it's too dangerous".

"I think our farm manager is in there. We must do something".

"What!" The fireman in control seemed to ignore him. He called to another fireman "Jack, fetch an ambulance and get some equipment, there's a man inside they think. I'm going in to take a look. Watch this bloke he's trying to be a dead hero".

A colleague joined him, and they entered the barn together. Two more firemen blasted the powerful jets on the building, trying to dampen the flames and give cover. The building was already starting to collapse. An ambulance screamed into the yard. Two ambulancemen ran with a stretcher and stood waiting for instructions at a safe distance. One of the fireman appeared at the barn entrance, dragging with him two unwilling sheep. He shouted "I haven't found him yet. There's a lot of sheep in there, best get a vet". He straightened his mask and went back inside. Within a minute he ran out again.

"I need some help, we've found the bloke pinned under a beam. Another beam is pinning down, Ian; it fell on him in front of my eyes. Reverse that tractor, and we'll try and pull the beam off with a rope, and watch that bloody water, don't drown us".

David had leapt on to the tractor and reversed as far as he could into the building. He had removed his jacket and soaked his clothes with water. He tied his handkerchief round his mouth, the fumes and the heat were terrible but the handkerchief helped a little.

They secured the rope and David put the tractor into gear. It strained forward and at one moment he thought the rope would break, but eventually the beam moved. The paramedics ran forward handing the stretcher to the firemen who ran back inside. They stumbled out of the barn, carrying Arthur prostrate and unmoving. A doctor ran forward. He had seen the fire from the road and had come to see if he could help.

The stretcher was laid on the grass, and the doctor knelt to examine Arthur. He gave him a pain killing injection, at the same time shaking his head. He turned "He is unconscious and is in a very bad way. I will accompany him in the ambulance to the special burns unit". Horror struck David as he watched Arthur being placed inside the ambulance. He could see that Arthur's body was extensively burned. He was covered in blood, and his raw flesh had matted with his clothes. David felt sick. He was glad his father was far enough away not to be able to see the state Arthur was in.

The firemen were calling for another stretcher. The one called Ian had been hardly clear of the building when the roof collapsed. He was dragged from the burning embers and placed in the ambulance. As the door closed, David could see the doctor erecting saline drips. A police car stood by to escort the ambulance to the hospital to give it a clear path; at last it sped away.

More firemen had arrived to relieve the first shift, who were now exhausted. Another ambulance was taking several of the firemen to hospital suffering with burns and asphyxiation. A vet was tending the few sheep they had managed to save. Some had to be put down. It took several hours to bring the fire under control.

Some of the panes of glass in the house facing the fire had cracked from the intense heat, and most of the others were very warm. Every scrap of David's clothing or what was left of it was completely ruined.

The children had been glued to one of the furthest windows, away from any danger, watching. Elizabeth and Patricia had made endless cups of tea and sandwiches for the men.

A whole courtyard of barns had been burnt to the ground. Christopher was in shock and could only mutter about Arthur. David decided not to tell him how seriously Arthur was injured. The whole disaster was bound to knock Christopher for six.

Christopher sat quietly in the drawing room preferring to be on his own. It wasn't the money or the buildings, it was the shock of the whole thing and he was desperately worried about his farm manager. He had noticed that David had not told him anything about Arthur, which he considered a bad omen. The doctor came and took a look at him and gave him a sedative, giving Patricia strict instructions that he was to stay in bed for the time being.

David, too, was also suffering from exhaustion. He was tired anyway, and today's exertions had completely drained him. Elizabeth was very attentive and insisted that he also went to bed. Neither man demurred happy to give in to the mothering. They both fell into a deep sleep in their respective bedrooms.

Elizabeth decided that there was little else she could do. The children were disturbed enough with today's events, and the best thing for them was to take them home to their own environment. The men could be safely left to Patricia.

Mrs. Lynch had just arrived and was standing her ground. The running of this house was still down to her, and she wasn't going to leave whilst Mr. Christopher was ill in bed. Oh dear, thought Elizabeth, not a good omen for the future. I'm off.

She knew that she had made the right decision. The day's events had certainly tired the children as well as disturbing them. They all seemed to want to be quiet. The boys went to bed straightaway, and the girls went into their lounge and sat watching the television, quietly chatting.

Elizabeth felt quite exhausted herself, her ankle was still playing up. She poured herself a stiff drink and lay peacefully on the drawing room sofa. Bored with her own company, she picked up the 'phone and called Karl. His thick guttural accent came on the 'phone. She briefly told him about what had happened.

"I want to see you so much. Can't I come over if David's away?" He begged.

"I want to see you too, but it's pretty dangerous. Carol is very vigilant and always asks too many prying questions" she paused, running her hand through her hair "oh, I don't care.

You can come over now. I'll tell the children you are a client on urgent business. I'll have to give you a false name".

"All right, it should take me about fifteen minutes. By the way, what's my name?"

"Mr. Jones and try not to speak too much. Your accent is such a giveaway".

Was she excited by the deception, or was it she simply wanted to see Karl? She ran upstairs and changed, combed her hair and re-applied her make-up. Ultra casually, she walked into the children's lounge.

"Pip, you must go to bed darling, and Carol, you must not be too late. By the way, I've got a client calling to see me shortly who has urgent problems. It may take a while, so I will say goodnight now".

"How boring," yawned Carol "I don't want to meet him".

"Darling, you won't have to, goodnight". She kissed them both and returned to the drawing room, armed with pad and pen from the study for the look of the thing.

She heard Karl's car draw up and opened the front door to greet him. They moved fairly swiftly into the drawing room and closed the door.

He was clearly nervous, but kissed her on the cheek, and she squeezed his arm indicating to him to sit opposite her on the twin settee. When they had settled themselves with their respective drinks, she told him all about the gruelling events of the day.

He was deeply shocked and understood why she felt like some company this evening.

Elizabeth was pleased he had come, but was very nervous, being acutely aware of the children's presence across the hall. "Talk about playing with dynamite" she said.

"Is it not possible for you to come out with me for a breath of fresh air or a drink? We needn't be very long. I must say, I feel also very uncomfortable sitting here".

Elizabeth thought for a moment. "Right, I will tell Carol that you are leaving, and that I am popping back to the office for some files to work on tomorrow."

"Anything to get out of here", he shifted uncomfortably. As she stood up, the 'phone rang. David had woken up.

"Hello darling, I am sorry about collapsing like that. I feel better now, shall I come home?"

"Have you and Christopher had something to eat?"

"Yes, we have been well looked after, Patricia and Mrs. Lynch seem to be vying with each other".

"Well, I think you should stay the night as its late and return tomorrow. Why not bring both of them to lunch tomorrow".

"Have you had a restful evening?"

Elizabeth felt the colour rising in her cheeks. Better to tell a white lie. "Well actually, I've had to see a client urgently. He's gone now, and I was going to pop into the office to get the relevant files. I would like to look at them tomorrow sometime. Mondays are always such a rush. Anyway I feel restive after today's events".

The tone of David's voice indicated that he had lost interest in the conversation. "You work too hard, but you won't listen to me; see you tomorrow".

Elizabeth replaced the receiver and expelled air by way of releasing tension. She felt so guilty. Anyway, hadn't he been doing the same to her for years, with Christine? Hadn't she been to hell and back as she watched him wrestling with two lives?

She had hoped that his affair would peter out without any actual confrontation, and then he need never know she knew. She feared however that the day of reckoning was drawing nearer when both sides would have to put their cards on the table.

He hadn't asked her for a divorce yet, but as relations between them had become strained recently she expected him to do so at any time. Yes, it was about time she considered herself, she thought.

She told Carol about her movements and conversation with David and they left in separate cars. She picked up the files, and they drove in convoy to a remote part of the cliffs.

Karl slid in beside her and, putting his arms round her, kissed her long and tenderly. She leant against him, enjoying the protection of his being. They decided to go for a walk and strolled hand in hand along the cliffs. It was a balmy evening, with a gentle warm breeze coming off the sea. They talked as they walked but her ankle started to hurt so they sat down looking out to sea. Lying back she allowed Karl to massage her ankle and cuddle and kiss her until, drawing breath, she felt that these precious moments must come to an end, and she must return home. Karl did not argue. He knew when he was beat.

*****

Whilst she prepared the family lunch the next day with the help of Maggie, David, Christopher and Patricia arrived mid morning.

Luckily, David, being the same size as his father, had been able to borrow some of his clothes. The adults were in a sober mood, however, the children had found the fire stimulating and exciting, not being able to understand the enormity of its consequences. They wanted to talk about it so David had to give them a warning look to stop them. They then lapsed into silence.

After lunch, David and Christopher went to the hospital to see Arthur Young. The news was very bad. Apart from extensive first degree burns and various broken bones, the heavy beam had broken his back, and the prognosis was bleak.

The surgeons told the distraught Mrs. Young that if he lived he would probably be a paraplegic, adding that they were not entirely sure because her husband was still in a deep state of shock. There was little hope of him being moved from intensive care as he was still on the danger list. Mrs. Young was trying to be brave but was beside herself with grief.

Christopher was very upset and hardly touched his tea. In order to try and take his mind off it, they went in to the drawing room to make the wedding arrangements. Christopher tried to make polite noises, but was clearly distracted with his own thoughts. After a short while, he excused himself, borrowed Elizabeth's car and drove himself home, just wanting to be alone. Patricia understood and asked David to take her home.

The silence in the car was broken by Patricia "Perhaps we should cancel the wedding as Arthur is so dangerously ill".

"I don't think it would help. Father has been like a cat with nine tails since you said 'yes' to his proposal".

"Yes, but quite apart from the damage to the farm buildings the accident to Arthur really has upset him greatly. I'm very worried about him".

"I must confess I agree" David said absently "I'll ring him later today and if necessary drive over to see him; although Mrs. Lynch is still there I gather she won't go home at the moment".

"That's right" replied Patricia through gritted teeth. David was lost in his own thoughts and failed to notice this subtle dig.

CHAPTER FIFTY SEVEN

Christopher Succumbs

David had decided to take the day off. He drove over to see his father at first light. It had been another airless night and he was glad of the refreshing breeze as he drove along. Something was troubling him but he couldn't put his finger on it. At the back of his mind he had some notion that the fire might start up again, as it was still very hot and the timbers had not cooled down.

He passed a milk float and gave it a cheery wave as he started to make his descent into the village. He had some vague idea of cooking himself breakfast whilst waiting for his father to get up. He parked outside the back door and let himself in with his key. Finding a bottle of water in the fridge he drank a glass and then went to check on the barns.

The charred timbers partly burnt and broken hung from the roof forming grotesque shapes, a sickening reminder of the devastating fire. He decided to give the fire brigade a ring he wanted them to check everything again.

As he walked back to the house he glanced up to his Fathers bedroom window, the curtains were tightly closed. He put the kettle on and found the morning papers on the doormat. It was now eight o'clock he made the tea and decided to surprise his father. As there was no reply to his gentle knock he opened the door and went in. Putting the tray on the table he drew the curtains.

"Come on Dad, wake up, I've come over to see you". As he looked down at his sleeping father the stillness of his body made his heart jerk. "Father, he took hold of his wrist, it was cold. David buckled to the floor. "Oh no father, don't leave me". Tears gushed down his cheeks and the lump in his throat threatened to choke him. Forcing himself to look at his father, he couldn't help but notice how peaceful he looked; all the worry lines seemed to have disappeared. His other hand was resting on something. David lifted it and picked it up; it was his mother's nightdress case. Both his parents had now gone, just gone, there were no goodbyes. Overcome with grief he fled from the room. David's mind was in a turmoil he'd had a funny feeling, which is why he had driven over so early, but he hadn't expected this.

Finding the number in the pad, he telephoned the doctor, who said he would come straight away. He then telephoned Elizabeth. She was very upset and said she would tell Patricia and bring her over.

The Doctor arrived ten minutes later. He swiftly climbed the stairs; David left him alone to carry out his examination.

He reappeared at the top of the stairs just as Elizabeth arrived with Patricia who was red eyed from crying, her hands were shaking with shock.

I am afraid he suffered a massive coronary embolism. He died straight away. I only saw him a few days ago, so there will be no need for a post-mortem. He had been having chest pains recently. I don't suppose he told you".

David and Elizabeth both shook their heads.

"No, I thought not. I just think that the fire on Saturday and the serious injuries suffered by poor Arthur Young was just too much further strain on his heart. Here is the death certificate. If you need me for anything else just call me. Please accept my deepest sympathy. He was a lovely man who will be sorely missed." David closed the front door and with leaden feet went back upstairs. He wanted a few minutes alone with his father before he was finally taken away. He sat down on the bed.

His father's and mother's life flashed before his eyes. He must have been sitting there for some time, when he was brought back to reality by Elizabeth gently knocking on the door. He knew that he must pull himself together. Kissing his father on the forehead he left the room, holding Elizabeth's hand.

The funeral took place in the local church a week later.

The church was packed to capacity, with many mourners waiting in the churchyard. Christopher, who passionately loved classical music, had requested that Bach's Toccata and Fugue in D Minor be played at his funeral. The tears ran down David's face as the final notes of his father's favourite piece of music finished. The choir sang "Abide with me". An old friend paid tribute.

He told the congregation that he had first met Christopher whilst on active service during the war. He had served under him on his last ship in the mid-Atlantic. They had remained friends ever since. He said he was a humble man who helped his fellow men without wanting any recognition himself, and had helped many charities and local people who could not afford the services of a lawyer. He was a man with a sense of good fun who always enjoyed a good joke, a very good friend to have. He would be sorely missed by all those who were lucky enough to have known him.

David took the reading, Corinthian Chapter 12. His voice rang out clearly for all to hear.

"Though I speak with the tongues of men and of angels and have not charity. I am become as sounding brass, Or a tinkling cymbal..."

The Vicar said a few personal words. David was one of the pallbearers who helped to carry the coffin. The others were three lawyers and two local farming friends.

Part of the strains of the Dead March in Saul by Handel filled the church as the coffin was carried into the churchyard.

He was laid to rest in the family vault next to Anne Marie, his beloved wife. The Vicar led the graveside prayers.

"The Lord is my shepherd I shall not want, He maketh me to lie down in green pastures..."

The mourners and the Vicar withdrew, leaving the family a few private moments of prayer at the graveside. Slowly, David linked arms with Elizabeth and Patricia, and led them away.

Only a few intimate friends and family had been invited back to Tulham Manor. David found it difficult to be polite and was relieved when the door closed on the last guest.

Patricia was devastated and was unable to pull herself together. She had completely lost heart. Being of retirement age she handed in her notice at work, took her house off the market and shut herself away like a hermit, transfixed by grief.

Elizabeth went to see her. She settled in one of the comfortable arm chairs and faced Patricia. "Now my dear, I know it all came as a great shock but I hate to see you so sad. You know that you are a member of the family and are welcome to come and see us at any time. The children miss you terribly."

Patricia's eyes welled with tears. "I just thought I would be able to see out my days with a dear companion.

I knew I could never take the place of Anne-Marie in his heart, and would not wish to, but we still had a very loving and deep relationship. I suppose I should be grateful. Don't worry about me, I will be all right."

She blew her nose. Elizabeth sat forward. "Also if you feel like doing something, I will be pleased if you worked for a few hours a week. After all you are still fit and healthy and perhaps it would take you mind off things. Anyway you can let me know." She got up to leave giving Patricia a big hug before she left.

CHAPTER FIFTY EIGHT

Confrontation Time

David and Elizabeth sat discussing their future. Tulham Manor was held in trust for David, then to be passed on to his eldest son. Elizabeth felt very unnerved. She did not want to sell "Charlene", thus relinquishing her rights to joint ownership, because she would never own Tulham Manor no matter what happened. With their marriage in such a shaky state, she felt that now was the time to have it out with David.

Four weeks after the funeral she approached David, who was sitting in the drawing room after dinner.

"Don't you think, David, it is high time we had a frank and open discussion about the future, or non future, of our marriage?"

David put down his paper and gulped. Oh not now, he thought, but then there was never a time that was a good time to discuss marriage problems.

She spoke direct and unwavering, years of controlled emotion being released to the surface.

"You have been having an affair with Christine for five years. Lucinda is your child. How do I know?

It doesn't matter, the point is, I do. Because I loved you so much, I lamely hoped the relationship would die a natural death, and we could get on with our marriage. I thought we had something special between us, and for a while I think we did". She stumbled, but regained her composure.

"But over the years we have become distant from each other. Oh yes, we are civil and polite, going through the motions. Well that's not good enough for me; it is a shallow empty relationship. I don't know why you stayed and haven't asked for a divorce before. Money, I suppose. Well, I have met someone who is special to me, Karl Burger. I am not sure of my feelings for him. All I do know is that he is kind and considerate and very fond of me. With the impending move to Tulham Manor I must sort out the property. I am not prepared to sell this house and divide the equity".

David sat forward in his chair and undid his top button, releasing the tension from his tie which was threatening to choke him. "You knew all these years and haven't said a thing. What a swine I have been. I wanted at all costs to protect your feelings. That's why I agreed to the bloody Trust document".

"Yes, I know about that".

"You knew! I give up, why on earth didn't you say?"

"Pride, I suppose. I was waiting for you to do the honourable thing and tell me yourself. Why do you think I opened the other office? I wanted to get out of the way. I couldn't stand to see you everyday, thinking up lies to tell me in order for you to escape to her. Then to add insult to injury you get her to work in the office again, it was unbearable. I thought my heart would be torn in two.

Sometimes the lump in my chest prevented me from eating for days. I don't suppose you have noticed, but I have lost weight; but then, why should you notice. You are not interested in me as a person anymore".

"You have got it all wrong. I need a drink. Can I get you

one?" She shook her head. He rose and went to the decanter, pouring himself a large scotch. "I can't blame you for that. I too was hoping that the relationship would end, but she always had the threat of telling you, and I didn't want to hurt you".

"David, I think you are being incredibly naive if you think someone who loves you, or rather loved you, deeply, cannot tell when your emotions are elsewhere".

"If only she hadn't got pregnant! I love you Elizabeth, and I want more than anything in the world for us to return to the loving relationship we once had. I don't love Christine, never have, lust would be the correct word".

"Well, if you thought like that you should have taken me into your confidence years ago. After all, I am your wife" she shouted. As the tears welled up in her eyes she ran sobbing from the room. He followed in hot pursuit.

He caught her on the stairs and put his arms round her "Come here, please" he whispered. He kissed her, and she returned his kisses. They became more passionate. She drew away, crumbling, on the stairs.

"It's too late, David. For goodness sake, can't you see that? I am going away with Karl. After we agree the division on this house, I intend to invest in another squash club and go into partnership with him. I refuse to discuss it anymore. I am emotionally exhausted. I will sleep in the spare room". She ran upstairs, sobbing.

David slunk back to the drawing room and poured himself another scotch. This is exactly what he had been trying to avoid. What a disaster. He could not believe it. She really had known all these years and not said anything. The strain on her must have been enormous. She had really loved him, he did not deserve it and now he had thrown it away. One thing was for sure, he wasn't going on with Christine.

Elizabeth had not got up by the time David left for work.

The children had been subdued, responding automatically to the atmosphere. He thought that they had obviously heard some of the row, if not all of it.

The desperate situation was that adults caught up in this kind of emotional turmoil were so involved with their own feelings that they were completely unable to reach out to help their children, even when they were clearly suffering.

David went first to the office and dictated replies to his morning post, leaving the rest for the new assistant solicitor to deal with.

He got in his car and drove straight over to Christine, who had been away from work for the last few days with a cold, or so she said.

She was probably sulking because he had not paid her any attention for some time, especially since his father's death. Apart from his lack of feeling for her, he had too much to do.

He walked in and surprised her. She was lounging on the settee, looking perfectly healthy to him.

"I thought you had a cold?"

"I have".

"Anyway, I haven't come here to enquire after your health. I want to talk to you".

She sat up, putting down the book she was reading.

"I realise that I haven't been paying you much attention for some time, but that's because our relationship really has run its course".

"What do you mean, what about the baby?" she yelled.

"I was coming to that. I didn't tell you when you told me about the baby, but I've had a private detective watching your movements over the past year. You know very well that you have been having, and are still having, an affair with another man". She stood up. He raised his hand.

"Don't, try and interrupt me. There is no point in your trying to deny it. I have dates, photographs, dinners out, the lot. In fact, I understand that you met him before you threw yourself at me. I don't believe for one second that the child you are carrying is mine. I have always wondered about Lucinda, she bears no resemblance to me at all".

"Since when did you get the courage to behave so masterfully?" she jeered.

"You are quite right, I deserve that comment. I have been gutless, I know, but that's because I was trying to protect Elizabeth". Christine looked to heaven and put on one of her bored looks.

"But, since she has known all about us and Lucinda, apparently for years, much to my distress, there is no problem anymore".

"She had the guts to tell you, did she? I wondered how much longer she could hold out. I've got to hand it to her, she's done pretty well".

It slowly dawned on David at last.

"You told her, you bitch!" She looked down. For the first time she was unsure of herself, realising that she had blown it. She spluttered "I didn't exactly tell her I just left certain documents and things lying around so she could not fail to miss them. Oh David, I wanted her so much to divorce you so that I could marry you".

"I bet you did, you disgust me. Well, you got your way; she is going to divorce me".

Christine came forward smiling "At last, now you can marry me".

"That's where your plan goes wrong. I never want to see you again, let alone consider marriage. The thought alone is utterly repellent to me. You are dismissed as from now. Don't bother to come to the office ever again.

I will send you your money in the post, plus some extra to cover dismissal. Your boyfriend can look after you and Lucinda and the new baby. How you both must have been laughing at me. Naturally, the Deed of Trust is, now at an end, since you broke its conditions. In fact, you can go to hell. My god, I feel so much better". He got up to go.

"She screamed after him "I'll sue you and ruin you", but she was talking to an empty room. David had gone.

Elizabeth called Karl and asked him to meet her for lunch in the office. She felt simply terrible. The household was in a tumult again. She had to get away. What should she do, take the children with her, or leave them with David?

Karl listened patiently and agreed to go along with anything she decided. He was returning to Holland to raise finance for the second club and wanted Elizabeth to go with him. She knew she needed to get away from the immediate tension which threatened to engulf her. She would discuss the mechanics of her leaving with David, and she would follow him in a couple of days. It would also be necessary to get a locum to cover the office. She took his hand. "Thank you for being so patient with me, and being around just when I need you." She spent the night with him at his house, and he left for the airport first thing.

David was not at all happy when she discussed the details with him on the 'phone. She kept the call brief and to the point. She would tell the children that she was going on a short holiday, and Maggie would look after them. In reality the children were so distressed she had called Patricia and gone to see her. She had explained what was necessary and asked her to help Maggie whilst she was away. Patricia said, "Of course I will help you. I must say I had noticed things had not been as they should be for some time.

The children will be naturally very upset; I will go to

them immediately. You go off and sort yourself out and give me a ring."

Elizabeth said, "Thanks for being a brick", and left. Luckily, a locum had materialised from an agency at short notice, so she was free to go. She wanted to get away without a face to face confrontation with David. She just could not cope anymore.

That morning she had gone home after David had left for work and the children were at school.

She packed in such a hurry that she hadn't the least idea whether or not she had even packed the correct clothes for the trip. She cared even less.

Her mind was racing as she waited at the airport for her plane to be called. All the things David and she had gone through together were now over. It had all been for nothing. She tortured herself as to whether she should have confronted him before, but it was too late now.

Perhaps she had always been afraid of the consequences of bringing it all to a head. The final rejection, she sighed. Her flight came up on the board. She picked up her vanity case and books and followed the other passengers as directed.

She settled herself in her seat, looking miserably out of the window. It was dark. She hated flying at night. Hopefully Karl would be there to meet her plane.

Once airborne, she picked up her book but was unable to concentrate. She swopped it for a magazine and idly flipped the pages.

The stewardess leant across the man she was sitting next to, "Madam, a glass of champagne for you, compliments of the gentleman back there". Elizabeth turned and looked over the seats.

David sat there, smiling weakly in a desperate sort of way. He signalled for her to join him, but the man next to her realised they wanted to sit together and offered David his seat, and he would take his in exchange.

David politely helped him to move his hand luggage and then slid into the seat beside Elizabeth.

"David, what are you doing here?" she asked in amazement, the colour rising in her cheeks.

"Chasing you, of course, you don't think I'm going to give up that easily, do you? I love you, and I always will, and I intend to win you back. I agree I have been a bloody stupid fool and deserve anything you care to throw at me, physically or verbally".

"Oh David!" she laughed in spite of herself.

"I have finally finished with Christine; I should have done it years ago. You and I are both equally guilty of not being open enough with each other. If you had spoken up earlier, I would have had the courage to get rid of her.

Anyway, I have had a private detective following her for the past year, and she has definitely been having an affair, probably even before our affair, as far as I know. She is pregnant, and it's not mine. I doubt if Lucinda is either, poor child. At least she doesn't bear my name".

He took her hand in his. She tried to pull away. "No, I intend to woo you as if we were starting all over again. I don't know whether I will win and beat Karl, but I'm going to give it a good try". He winked at the stewardess, who was all ears at this romance on the plane.

She couldn't fully hear the conversation which irritatingly was muffled by the drone of the engines. As already arranged with David she presented Elizabeth with an enormous bunch of flowers.

The other passengers loved it, and all applauded. Elizabeth blushed pink!

David clapped his hands in glee. "That is just for openers.

You wait and see, my girl. I have got a lot of loving to make up for! He raised his glass "May the best man win this lady's hand". Several passengers in the vicinity raised their glasses also.

Tears of joy slowly trickled down Elizabeth's face.

---THE END---

Sequel coming soon...

Made in the USA
Columbia, SC
18 October 2017